Redemption
Song

Laura Wilkinson

Published by Accent Press Ltd 2016

ISBN 9781783758692

Copyright © Laura Wilkinson 2016

Acknowledgements

As seems to be the way with me, there's a long list of people to thank. The contributions of these lovely folk have made *Redemption Song* a stronger book. You have my heartfelt gratitude. Any errors, and distortions of fact, are all my own.

In no particular order:

Phil and Julia Cook of Portslade Baptist Church for welcoming a non-believer into their church and home, and for answering questions that, at times, must have seemed very stupid indeed. Grace and generosity under fire.

Jo Canon, author and doctor, and Ian Williams, graphic novelist and GP, for answering all things medical.

Nick Ellis for information and help with bat questions. If you'd like to know more about these fascinating creatures: www.bats.org.uk.

Paul Bacon for advice on legal matters, court procedure and sentencing. I have taken some liberties with police procedure and court sentencing to serve the plot. I hope you'll be forgiving!

Fred Davies, aka the BigFella, for carpentry expertise.

The unnamed undercover copper for police procedure and a snippet of information that solved a whopping great plot hole.

My patient, and sensitive, beta readers: Katy O'Dowd, Julie-

Ann Griffiths, SR, Norma Murray and Elizabeth Donnelly. You are superstars.

The entire team at Accent Press who work so hard for their authors. Enormous gratitude. Special mention to MD Hazel Cushion for her vision and energy, and to my editor, Greg Rees, who has faith in me even when I don't and who believed in this story from the outset.

Sarah Rayner, bestselling author of *One Moment, One Morning*, and Araminta Hall, author of Richard & Judy Book Club choice, *Everything and Nothing*, for taking the time to read the manuscript and offering such generous quotes.

Big thanks also to the very many more friends and colleagues from real life, Twitter, Facebook, Pinterest and Instagram (we'd be here all day) who encourage and support me along each journey that it is the madness and joy of creating a novel. I'd be bonkers without you, assuming I'm not already.

And finally, my three lovely lads: the BigFella, Ginger1 and Ginger2. You don't much care about the bookish stuff, but there's so much love in your hearts, and that's what counts.

P.S. This is a work of imagination. Coed Mawr is a fictional seaside town. It is inspired by the beautiful landscape of North Wales and in particular the resort town of Llandudno for which I have held a lifelong love. As a little girl, my grandparents often took me and my sister there during the long summer holidays. In Llandudno you will find a pier, though no art nouveau ballroom; you will find a cable car linking the two Ormes (the Great and Little) but you will not find tall trees on the cliff top shielding the town from the mountains; you will not find Devil's Rise, nor Mr Roberts, Joe, Rain or Saffron. Like all the characters, they live only in this novel.

Forgive, and you will be forgiven.
Luke 6:37

Prologue

The couple stagger to the front door. Before he lifts the latch, he looks at her and says, 'We're good, aren't we?'

'We're good,' the girl replies, after a brief pause.

Outside, on the gravel driveway, a battered Peugeot purrs. It is out of place in front of this grand house, with its columns and porch. The girl leans towards the driver's side window and notices, for the first time, how old her rescuer looks. Not old, like the people she meets every day, but middle-aged. Flecks of grey in his hair glitter in the dull, dead-of-night light; his jowls sag. He is tired – and no wonder – but he is still a handsome man. She notices the way women react around him, all fluttering smiles and sparkling eyes; she sees the way he responds, all compliments and charm. Lately he seems happier in the company of relative strangers rather than those closest to him, but she could be imagining this. After all, she's not around so much now.

'Hiya. Thanks a billion. You didn't have to.'

'Yes, I did. Get in the back. Boys in the front tonight.' He smiles.

The car pulls away before she's finished clicking her seatbelt on. He's in a hurry to get home and it's quite a long drive, certainly for this time of night.

'So, the big match tomorrow?'

'Yeah.'

'Any of chance of winning? After a night like this? Not what you'd call the best preparation, eh?' The older man laughs and the younger one joins in. There is mutual affection and respect between them. The girl feels sad and yet very, very lucky.

'Who knows,' the boy says.

'You're young and it'll be good practice for the other big day this year.'

The boy reaches behind him and squeezes the girl's hand.

They twist and turn through deserted country lanes and she studies the backs of the men's heads, their outline and form. They are prime specimens, both of them. There is nothing to see out of the window, only the dense foliage of hedgerows, and the sky has clouded over; there are no stars in sight. They are travelling fast, in the middle of the road, and she is rocked from side to side. Her eyes feel heavy, and her head begins to loll, her neck no longer able to support its weight.

She is on the brink of sleep when a cry disturbs her.

'Brake!'

She hears the screech of tyres, feels the tilt of the car. And she is turning, rolling, bouncing off the interior of the saloon, the roof is coming towards her. She hears a cry – it is hers. There is a crunch. Then, nothing.

Silence.

No. Not quite. The hiss of the engine. She is crawling out of the smashed window, on her hands and knees. Her palms are covered in blood but she cannot feel any pain. Her engagement ring is no longer on her finger. She can't feel anything. The car is upside down, bonnet crumpled against a stone wall. A sheep lies dead at the side of the road, its small head at an impossible angle.

She hears moaning and crawls to inspect the front of the car. Both men remain strapped in their seats. The airbags haven't opened. The car is old, hasn't had a full service in years.

She begins to shake. It seems impossible, but she is alive.

Alive.

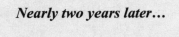

Nearly two years later…

Chapter One

Saffron pushed the accelerator pedal to the floor, head resting on the wheel, and turned the key for the umpteenth time. Zilch. Nada. Absolutely nothing. Not even the horrible screech of an engine trying and failing to catch. After slapping the wheel five times, she wrenched the key from the ignition and leapt out of the Standard, slamming the door behind her and kicking the wing on the driver's side – hard – before banging her fists on the bonnet. Her foot throbbed; even Doc Martens couldn't protect her toes from the force of her assault. Thank God these old bangers were built like tanks. The last car she'd driven, a modern one, was so flimsy she'd feared it might fly away in a high wind. It had reminded her of her father's model cars; the motorised ones he took racing with the other geeks, a hobby lovingly mocked by Saffron and her mother.

A seagull shrieked overhead and Saffron jumped.

Damn those birds. Another disadvantage of living here. Shit! Mum. She'll be worried.

She pulled her phone from her duffel coat pocket, hoping to find a local garage online as well as making the all-important call to let her mum know what had happened. No connection, of course. Nothing worked in this poxy place.

I only came here to be around for Mum.

'Bugger, bugger, bugger,' she yelled, hitting the bonnet over and over, voice thick with rage and frustration. Tears threatened. Fear of denting the car – it was a classic after all – and exhaustion, stopped her pummelling. She folded over the bonnet, rested her brow on the metal. The air was sharp; the engine had cooled already, the metal soothing against her dewy skin. Her throat contracted and her chest heaved with sobs. Lame. But she couldn't stop. Once upon a time, she wouldn't have described herself as a quitter or a fraud. But so much overwhelmed her these days and the truth, often mercurial, seemed more elusive than ever.

How was she to get home now? The day was closing in and the roads were icy, despite the so-called thaw promised on the news, and this road – if you could call it that, it was little more than a dirt track – was well shaded, particularly in the dip where the stone bridge crossed the river before the steep incline of the hill. Only a fool would attempt Devil's Rise in slippery conditions; only Saffron. There'd be no passing traffic. Locals steered clear in this weather, and there were no tourists at this time of year. The coast road was their route of choice, regardless. She thumped the bonnet a final time.

'You're not going to get it started that way.'

She jerked upright. Had she imagined a voice? A male voice? No. The silhouette of a tall figure loomed in front of a beaten-up Land Rover. How come she'd not heard its approach? They weren't smooth machines, not a like a Mercedes or a Porsche. She wiped away the remains of her tears, determined not to appear a useless cry baby. He walked towards her, raking fingers through brown hair. The sides were closely cropped – a number two, Saffron guessed – with a strip of weightier hair across the top. She noticed his torn jeans and donkey jacket. He looked a bit rough.

'It's not going to start any other way.' She scowled, kicking herself for sounding so belligerent. This man was her only hope of getting out of there. Her salvation – or damnation. He might as easily be Satan himself.

You just can't keep your big mouth shut, can you? Be nice.

Composing herself, she forced a smile. 'I've tried

everything.'

'You want me to take a look?' She noticed a pack of cigarettes poking out of his jacket pocket; heavy tar, judging by the gravelly voice. In hospital, she'd seen enough throats and lungs wrecked by smoking to know. A bad boy. Man; he looked at least thirty. He didn't sound like a local.

She shrugged.

'Open her up, then.' He stroked the Standard's bonnet, as you might a cat or dog; like something loved.

Saffron bent in and groped around for a lever. She couldn't find one; she hadn't got a clue how to open the damn thing. She understood the complexities of the human body: the skeleton, muscles, lymphatic and nervous systems. But an old car? No way. Head wedged beneath the steering wheel, hand groping about, she considered how she must look: backside in the air, pretending to know what she was doing.

'You won't open it from there.'

For the second time in minutes she jerked up, banging her head against the wheel in the process. Ouch. This bloke was turning out to be an almighty pain in the arse.

'That must've hurt.'

She stepped aside, longing to rub her throbbing skull, but refusing to acknowledge her pain. He was smiling, enjoying her discomfort. A base impulse to thump him flashed, but repairing people was more her style than damaging them. So instead, she looked him in the eye, straight-faced, and admitted that she didn't know how to access the engine.

'So you've not tried everything,' he said, stressing the 'everything', looking at her directly, grinning, daring her to return his smile. 'There's no internal lever.'

'Seems not.' She held his gaze but didn't smile, and as she stared she noticed that his eyes were different colours: one light brown, one green.

3

Heterochromia iridum. How rare.

'Like David Bowie,' he said, raising an index finger to eye level.

'What?'

'The singer. Brilliant. Big way before our time.'

It was only as he moved to the front of the car, slipped his hand under the bonnet, above the grill, and the bonnet clicked open that she remembered Bowie reportedly had eyes of different colours. She thought about telling him she understood but chose to remain silent. She didn't have to justify herself to a stranger, even if he did have nice hair and interesting eyes.

He'd not wanted to stop. But how could he not? It was cold, getting dark, and she was obviously in trouble. There might not have been another passing vehicle for hours, if at all.

Joe prodded a couple of cylinders and unscrewed the lid of the oil tank. At least, what he thought was the oil tank. He tried to hide his relief when it turned out he was right. He lifted the dipstick and inspected it: the level was good, that much he knew. Truth was, he knew little else about mechanics. He was a practical man – good with his hands; as well as being a skilled carpenter; he knew his way round a boiler, some basic electrics, and was useful with a paintbrush. But much as he enjoyed looking at and driving cars, the internal workings baffled him.

'Engine's flooded,' he guessed, sounding more confident than he felt. 'You'd never get her up the hill anyway. Not in these conditions.' He smiled at the girl, again, despite himself. She was a strange one, standing there, hands on her hips, for all the world trying to look as if breaking down in the middle of nowhere as light was fading from a late-winter's sky was no big deal.

Though she wasn't Joe's type – too lanky, lean bordering on skinny, dark hair with skin so pale you could

4

make out the light blue veins mapped on her forehead – she was intriguing. Not that Joe had a type. No woman, that was his current preference, but once he'd seen her, swinging those long legs at the unfortunate car's tyre, he'd been unable to drive by. He was a little spellbound, and when she'd looked at him, with those ice blue, furious eyes, well … She'd stirred something in him he'd not felt in a long time. Something more disconcerting than straightforward lust.

How old was she? She looked young. Twenty, maybe twenty-one, he reckoned.

Don't be a lech, Joe. She's angry, vulnerable. Probably got an ASBO hidden under those stripy tights. If they still have them.

A small voice inside his head muttered that the law had been altered.

'Can I have a smoke?' she said, pointing to the packet of Marlboros poking from his jacket pocket.

'They kill you. Anyway, they're not mine.' He hadn't intended to sound as forceful as he did, but he hated smoking.

The law has changed. Behaviour Orders or something now.

'You're not my dad,' she laughed.

'I'm certainly not.' She was a stroppy one.

'Where you headed? Coed Mawr?' he said, more kindly this time. It was the only place she could be going – only locals knew of the short cut – though judging by her accent she wasn't from round these parts. Surely not a tourist in February? She sounded like a Londoner. Was this another reason why he felt drawn to her: she reminded him of home?

'Only one place this hill leads to,' she said. 'You going there?'

He closed the bonnet. 'As you said, road only leads one place. Luckily for you.' He sighed; he'd banked on being

5

able to get the car started. That was stupid of him. He had no option but to take her with him.

Her voice raised an octave and she sounded as if she might cry. 'You mean you can't get this thing started?'

'Not today. And that's no way to refer to a beaut like this.' He patted the Standard and wondered what a woman like this wanted with a classic car. It was exquisite.

'But I can't leave it here. My mum'll kill me.'

Ah, that made sense; it wasn't hers. Of course it wasn't. Her anger was a way of disguising fear: she'd knackered her mum's prized possession. Joe wanted to laugh.

'We'll roll it to the side here; it'll be safe and I'll come back with a rope tomorrow.'

Her brow furrowed.

'Tow her to a garage, if she won't start,' he explained.

'You sure there's nothing we can do? It's just ... it'll be such a pain ... And how come you're so sure you can make it in that?' She pointed at the Land Rover.

Joe pointed at the deep treads on the wheels. 'This motor's built for all weathers.'

'Seems like I have no choice.' She stepped forward and slipped on the black ice. Lurching, Joe caught her by the arm, preventing her from hitting the ground. He held her until he was sure she was steady. She felt so fragile beneath his grip, like a wisp of air. With a temper like a hurricane, he imagined.

This close, he caught her aroma: patchouli. Normally, he hated that scent; it took him right back to his expensive, and loathed, private school where kids in the sixth form pretended to slum it by growing their hair and wearing handmade shirts from Peru, the powerful smell of the oil unable to hide the stink of money and privilege. But on her, it smelled good; warm and heady; in direct contrast to the chilly, distant young woman before him.

Once she was upright, she held out an outstretched hand. 'Guess we should introduce ourselves.'

He hesitated. 'Joe. Joe Jones. People call me JJ.' He reached for her hand, but he was too late. She'd withdrawn it.

She waved instead. 'Saffron. Saffron de Lacy. People call me Saffron.'

How did a young woman in a backend seaside town in Wales get a name like that? Joe wondered. Saffron. The name conjured vibrant colour, exotic spices, joy. This woman conjured graveyards, bloodless corpses, and angst with her heavy eyeliner, dark hair, and translucent skin.

'Nice to meet you, Saffron.' He rolled his arm and gave a deep bow. She almost smiled, and mentally he licked his finger and swiped the air. Point Joe.

After rolling the Standard into the layby before the bridge over the river, Joe hopped in the Land Rover, turned on the engine and then the heating while Saffron gathered her things. He wanted to make the journey as comfortable as possible and see if he could inject a little colour into those ashen cheeks.

To Saffron's dismay, Joe's motor couldn't get up the hill either. It slipped and slid and made no progress upwards. At least it didn't conk out in the process, but it did mean that they'd have to take the long way round to Coed Mawr, and that meant twenty-five minutes with him as opposed to ten. She tried the radio but couldn't find a clear station and there was no sign of any CDs. She had no idea what they'd talk about. Her head was swimming with how she'd explain to Mum, who would be sick with worry by the time they got back. Perhaps she'd get a phone signal once they hit the main road. She gripped the handle above the window tightly, leant her head against her arm, and gazed at the heavy grey sky. She hoped Joe would take the hint and keep quiet. She couldn't call him JJ; what kind of a name was that? It made him sound like a cheesy teen idol, or a rapper.

'Looks like snow,' he said.

So he couldn't take a hint.

'Ur-huh.' She continued to stare out of the window.

'Weather report got it all wrong today. A thaw they said.'

'Ur-huh.'

'Bet it's pretty here when it snows.'

'I wouldn't know,' she said, tilting her head in his direction. Obviously, he wasn't going to shut up, and the effects of a good upbringing were hard to shake off; she couldn't be so rude as to ignore him completely. He'd been kind, tried to help, given her a ride home. Without him, she'd have been screwed.

'How's that?'

Saffron explained that it was her first winter here, it had been unusually mild so hadn't snowed, yet, and it was, more than likely, her last winter here. So, no, she didn't know whether it looked pretty all covered in white, but neither did she much care. She wasn't planning to stick around for long. This was a gap before she went back to repeat her foundation year at one of the London teaching hospitals, Barts, King's, UCL, she didn't much care which; they were all good. Whichever one would have her in truth. Competition was fierce and she was no longer an ideal candidate.

'So you're a doctor? You don't look old enough.'

'I'm twenty-five this summer.' After a pause, her indignation settled, she continued, 'And I'm not a doctor, not yet. Right now, I'm not sure that I ever will be.' She wondered why she was confessing; she'd certainly not meant to. It had slipped out. She'd not even told her mum she wasn't certain she would return to medicine; they didn't talk like they used to. There was so much, and nothing, to say.

'Didn't think it was possible to take a break like that. Medical training's pretty intense.'

'They sure as hell don't make it easy. Anyway, how come you know so much about the medical profession?'

'I don't.' He laughed. 'Ignore me.'

She felt sick at the thought of going back. She'd need to put in extra work – catch up, and she wasn't sure she was up to it any more; she hadn't stepped inside a hospital for over six months. Her mind had been all over the place, what with the move and everything. She'd knuckle down soon; she had no choice. She couldn't stay here for ever.

He must have sensed her unease because he said, 'You'll be fine. No one likes staying behind. But for what it's worth, I think it's better to get a bit of life experience. It'll make you a better doctor, more empathetic. Experience a world outside of hospitals and pain and sickness. Same with teaching and any intense profession. There's a danger of becoming very insular. If that makes sense.'

'It does.' She turned away from the window. 'You sound like you know.'

'Yup. I messed up my A levels first time round. Everyone else went off to uni; I stayed behind. Resented it for a while, but when I went to college, I appreciated it more, studied hard.'

'What did you study?'

He laughed, dismissive. 'Nothing useful.'

Saffron was surprised. He looked like a labourer; someone who'd have left school as soon as possible. His knuckles were calloused and his fingernails were a bit grimy.

You're a terrible snob, Saffron de Lacy. He's probably got a higher IQ than you.

And as she looked – really looked – at him, she decided that he was better than interesting-looking. She was about to push him on what he did study but before she got the chance, he pulled into the main road into Upper Coed Mawr, turned to her, and asked, 'Where to, exactly?'

The honk of a horn; a screeching of brakes.

'Keep your eyes on the road!' she yelled.

'It's OK. Only a boy racer at the lights,' Joe said, obviously startled by her reaction. 'You OK?'

Composing herself, she reassured him she was.

'So, where to now?' he asked.

Oh hell. She'd forgotten to call Rain. She'd be livid when Saffron pitched up, relieved but furious.

'Drop me anywhere. Everywhere is close.' She needed time to gather her thoughts. Mum would be cross twice over: no phone call, and she wouldn't want to think of her beloved car abandoned at the river's edge overnight. She'd not wanted Saffron to take the car, but after some serious emotional blackmail Saffron had got her own way. Now, she wished she hadn't. The bus would have been so simple, but she avoided being a passenger as much as possible.

He was insistent. 'I'll get the car tomorrow, come what may. Let me explain to your mother.'

'I'm not five. Bit old for that, aren't I?'

'Sorry. You're right.'

She shrugged and pointed in the direction of home. Correction: where she lived temporarily. This would never be home.

It had never been easy – introducing people to her mum, and though Saffron knew she was far too old to feel awkward, she couldn't help it. She hated it. She hated her mum. She loved her mum. But if Joe did come in, Rain would curb her anger.

'Well, if you don't mind?' she smiled at him and he returned her smile, nodding.

'I won't stay. In and out.'

'Here,' she said, pointing, before bending to grab her overstuffed bag from where it lay at her feet.

'The vicarage?' His surprise was evident.

'Yeah. 'Cept, you don't really call it that. That's

Church of England. We're Baptists. I mean, Mum is. It's called a manse.' Saffron swung open the door and jumped down. 'Come on then, if you're coming.'

Chapter Two

The huge sign outside the church building proclaimed, *Jesus Christ, Our Lord and Saviour*. The church was plain, little more than a house, other than the large round window at its centre and the arched wooden door. To the left was another building – the church hall with a frayed banner draped across the front – and to the right, a house of pale brick, almost yellow, with a square bay window. Like the church, the house was shabby. Neglected, but still beautiful. The paintwork was in need of attention, some of the frames looked rotten, and the chimney stack was cracked. Mid-late Victorian, Joe thought, built about the same time as the church and most of the grander properties in the lower town.

Chapel, the Welsh call them chapels.

Saffron ignored the front door, with its coloured glass and brass knocker, and slouched down a narrow pathway running between the chapel and the house. Joe followed her through an unlocked wooden gate, after which the passage opened out into a garden, bare except for a small flower bed in front of the window, a thick yew in the centre of a frost-tipped lawn, and a gnarled wisteria at the far end.

At the back door, he waited patiently, saying nothing, while she scrabbled around in her bag for her keys. After several unsuccessful attempts to locate them, swearing like no vicar's daughter ever should, she tipped the bag's contents onto the concrete. There was still no sign of the keys.

She pushed herself up. 'You must have them.'

It was an accusation, not a suggestion. But she was right. Joe recalled that he'd taken them – the bunch large enough for a gaoler – to lock the Standard. He raced back to the Land Rover, certain he'd thrown them into the space behind the handbrake; the space where he normally kept change for parking.

When he returned there was no sign of Saffron. He walked back to the street and noticed that the front door was ajar. After rapping the knocker, he gave the door a push. It swung open to reveal a wide hallway with a black and white tiled floor. He called out but remained on the doorstep.

Saffron appeared within seconds, waving him in. She'd removed her duffel coat and Joe noticed she wasn't entirely devoid of curves. Still way too skinny though. He waited while she closed the door behind him, feeling uncomfortable and regretting his offer to give an explanation to her mother. It was awfully dark in there. It smelt of damp and old wood. He noticed a barometer on the wall and tried to read it. She stomped past him – the clumpy boots clattering on the tiles – and led him past a telephone table and into a cosy kitchen-diner thick with steam. The only notable feature was a huge Yves Klein print over the fireplace, its modernity out of character with the rest of the room.

Whatever Joe had expected Saffron's mother to look like it was nothing like the woman who turned from the Aga to greet him. Shorter than Saffron by maybe four inches, she was all smiles, curves, and tumbling blonde curls. Although it was mid-February she was dressed in a floral skirt and bright orange V-neck jumper. The only similarity in style between mother and daughter was a pair of ugly leather boots poking out beneath the hem of Rain's skirt.

And she was young. Youngish. Mid-forties at the most, he guessed, or very well-preserved. She must have been a

14

very young mother, though presumably not a single one? Did vicar's wives do that sort of thing? Maybe she'd had Saffron before she met her husband? Did vicars marry single mums? Joe's head spun.

'This is my mother, Rain,' Saffron flicked a hand in Rain's general direction and back again to Joe. 'Rain, this is Joe Jones, though everyone calls him JJ. He rescued me. The car conked out on Devil's Rise.' Joe could have sworn she rolled her eyes as she said JJ.

'Lovely to meet you, JJ.' Rain reached forward and took Joe's hand in a firm grip, shaking a little too enthusiastically. As she rattled his arm and shoulder, he noticed a plain cross on a chain nestled between her breasts. 'Thank goodness you were around. Imagine what she'd have done if you weren't passing by!'

'Walk, I imagine,' he replied, fixing his eyes on hers to avoid glancing down at her cleavage.

Rain laughed and Saffron snorted.

'Well, yes. Never thought of that! How silly,' Rain said. 'Would you like a cup of tea? I've just filled the pot.'

Saffron pulled a face and Joe accepted Rain's invitation; Saffron wanted him to leave, so he'd stay. She wasn't the only one with a belligerent streak. And it wasn't every day he found himself in the company of attractive women. In fact, he couldn't remember the last time he'd been in the company of one woman, and there was no chance of getting close or anything else remotely dangerous. A vicar's wife and her daughter. Perfect. He'd enjoy a nice cup of tea and possibly even a slice of cake – he eyed the fruit cake sitting in the centre of the table – and then return home, never to see them again, if he could possibly help it.

They sat round the table and Saffron poured the tea while Joe gave a brief low-down of what happened on Devil's Rise. Rain cut a generous slab of cake and passed it to Joe. 'For you, Saff?'

Saffron shook her head.

Joe stroked the table's surface; it was warm and smooth. 'Oak's beautiful, isn't it?'

Rain nodded and said, 'Family heirloom. How come you recognise the wood?'

'I'm a carpenter.'

'Like Joseph!' She put her hand to her mouth and laughed. 'JJ, Joe … Joseph.'

Saffron stared at her hands resting on the table and picked at the skin around her nails; pink flooded her lily-white cheeks. Joe thought Rain was charming and pretty, though she didn't intrigue him. Her daughter did.

Aware of the silence and the women staring at him expectantly, he coughed and said, 'Sorry?'

'Where are you working?' Rain said for, he guessed, the second time.

'Over the valley, across the border, on a school. They're expanding. Bucking the trend, there's been a rise in the birth rate and they need more places for September. Apparently.'

'And you were coming up Devil's Rise because …' Rain's question trickled away. 'Sorry, that's so nosy of me.'

'I live here.'

'Where?' Rain asked.

Why the hell did I tell them? 'On the outskirts of town,' he said, hoping this would satisfy Rain.

'In Upper Coed Mawr?'

He moved his head, vague.

'But you're not from round here?' Rain smiled knowingly. 'Despite the surname.'

Great. She moves from one line of interrogation to another.

'Not originally.' He didn't want to say precisely where and hoped Rain would drop this particular line of questioning. He really shouldn't have come in.

Saffron was clearly more interested in her fingernails because she was now bent over her hands. With her hair obscuring her face, Joe studied the top of her head. She wasn't a brunette. Not naturally. There was a trace of fair roots. So she was her mother's daughter after all.

'Have you been here long? We've not seen you about; we're quite new here ourselves, but we thought we'd met just about everyone. It's a tightly knit place, after all.'

'I'm not about much. Always working,' he said.

'You should come to church. It's a good way to meet people. And there's little else to do on a Sunday. Unless you fancy one of the boozers. The Nag's Head's supposed to be the best. Not that I'm an expert!'

'Mum,' Saffron said.

Rain turned back to the Aga sharply, and Joe watched her blonde curls swinging across her back; she really did have very pretty hair. She grabbed a spatula and vigorously stirred a pan of something delicious-smelling. 'I'm not trying to convert JJ, Saff. Anyway, you're in my bad books for the absence of a phone call earlier.' Though she tried to make light of Saffron's embarrassment, Joe detected an undercurrent: irritation, guilt, he couldn't be sure which. Rain turned back and addressed Joe, 'Not much to ask, is it?'

'It was my fault. I kept your daughter talking.'

'Come to a coffee morning if you prefer. Every Saturday. Ten till eleven thirty. The WI provide the cakes and they're bloody gorgeous.' She returned to stirring the contents of the saucepan and Joe took his cue to leave.

He'd protected her, made excuses for her. Why would he do that? It was nice, but she was nothing to him. While Rain's back was turned, Saffron peered at Joe through her heavy fringe, sneakily, hoping he wouldn't notice. A slippery feeling in her lower belly startled her. It wasn't hunger, even though she'd not eaten since breakfast.

17

Saffron couldn't remember the last time she'd felt hungry, not really hungry.

'Right. Better go. Thanks for the tea and cake.' He slapped his palms on the table, and stood. 'If I take the car key now, I don't need to trouble you at some ungodly hour – sorry – in the morning.'

Despite turning her head a little when Joe stood, Saffron didn't have a clear view of her mother's face, but Rain sounded disappointed. 'It'd be no trouble. I'm up early most mornings. Don't find it so easy to sleep. And please don't apologise for swearing. I can eff and blind with the best of them!'

'He didn't swear,' Saffron said, standing up so quickly stars flashed in her peripheral vision.

Her mother turned to face her, shrugged and raised her eyebrows.

'It'd be easier if I didn't have to drop by,' Joe said. 'I have to go to work for a few hours first and I don't find it easy getting out of bed. I'll sort her out on the way home.'

'Of course you must take them.' Rain took Saffron's keys where they sat on the dresser on the far wall and battled with the bunch, struggling to remove the car key.

'I'll take good care of her, I promise,' he continued, as he pushed the key into the front pocket of his jeans.

Rain showed Joe to the door; Saffron lagged a few metres behind. 'Thanks again for rescuing my daughter. It's so lovely to meet you. Our door is always open.' She extended her hand and he took it, placing his left hand over their interlocked grip.

Saffron experienced a strange twinge at her core; a sensation so unfamiliar that she didn't recognise it at first. Lust, or jealousy? Or both?

'I'll leave the car out front and push the key through the door. Save bothering you,' he said.

'Do knock. I'm usually about and you could have another piece of cake for your trouble.' Her mother was forever shoving food at people.

He nodded, non-committal, and then he was gone.

Rain leant against the closed door. 'Well, he seems nice.'

Saffron turned and ran up the stairs without a word.

Chapter Three

Back in the kitchen, Rain put a lid on the pan of stew and wiped the kitchen counter, though it was already spotless. There had been no need to stir the stew, it had been simmering away perfectly well by itself; she'd needed an activity. Unused to the company of young men, she'd been nervous. How ridiculous.

Rain had rambled in JJ's presence, especially when she'd talked about meeting people and suggested he come to a coffee morning. He must think her an absolute nut-job. How she wished she'd kept her mouth shut. She glanced at the terracotta-tiled floor and decided it needed a good clean.

After she'd filled a bucket with soapy water, she grabbed the mop, dunked it in the water, wrung out the excess and swept away at imaginary grot on the floor until her lower back ached. It had been good to have male company other than seventy-year-old parishioners who wanted to talk endlessly about the finer details of the Easter Fayre and whether or not the WI should be allowed to run the bring and buy sale on the same day as the men's chess club.

And what a male. Tall, well-built, handsome. With the most gorgeous eyes imaginable. One brown and one green. How unusual. Just thinking like this brought on a rush of guilt so great that Rain thought she might cry. Instead, she plunged the mop into the bucket and without squeezing out the excess slapped it back onto the tiles. Water slushed everywhere, splashing the legs of the table, the leather of her boots. She snatched a cloth from the sink and dabbed at the puddles. It was no good; the kitchen looked as if it'd been flooded; only newspaper would absorb it now. An evening edition of the county's daily rag lay open on the table, a photograph of a middle-aged woman with hair like Saffron's climbing out of a limo in the middle of the page.

Rain wished Saffron wouldn't dye her hair; her natural colour was beautiful, and just like her father's. Stephen. The stabbing sensation across her skull began as she tried, and failed, to conjure the image of him as he was in her mind's eye. But all she could see was the shell of a man with a passing resemblance to the love of her life laid out on the mortuary slab.

When the doctor had first pulled back the sheet she'd blown out a puff of air, a breath she'd been holding on to for goodness knows how long, opened her eyes for a second, shook her head and said, 'No, that's not him. That's not my Stephen.' The other professional, the one standing next to her, had taken her hand and said, 'Are you sure, Mrs de Lacy? I know it's hard, but please do look.' She opened her eyes and stared at the body; she didn't take her eyes off it, even though she longed to, but she couldn't look at the face. There was something familiar about it. She could see it in the reflection of the glass window in front of her. Something about the cut of the jaw, the unusual tip of the nose.

She forced herself to focus on the body, not the reflection. Her eyes crawled along the exposed shoulder to the neck. There was a small scar, a white snail trail in the delicate groove behind the shoulder bone where it joined the neck. It held her attention. Stephen had spoken of a childhood accident. Playing Blind Man's Buff he'd walked into a tree. A broken branch, with a jagged edge, had speared him. 'There was so much blood,' he'd laughed. Children didn't play games like that any more, she'd thought. It was then she admitted the body before her was, after all, her husband. The doctor went to pull the sheet back over Stephen's face, but Rain had stopped him. She leant over and ran her index finger over the scar, surprised to find the body still warm. Later, much later, Saffron had explained that it takes hours for a body to go cold.

Mist descended and Rain gripped onto the kitchen table to prevent herself from falling. She closed her eyes and counted to twenty, aloud, just as the doctor had instructed her.

Then they cried out to the Lord in their trouble, and he delivered them from their distress. Psalm 107:6

Once she felt normal again, she took the newspaper and threw its pages across the floor, watching the water leech into the words and photographs, distorting them until they were no longer readable. Her mind flipped back to JJ and Saffron. Had she seen a smile flash between them as she'd turned to attend to the stew? Did Saff like this man? Like, like? Rain's stomach clenched. It wasn't possible. She crouched to the floor and scrunched a sopping sheet of newspaper in her hand and threw it into the bin behind her.

Don't be silly. He's not Saff's type.

He seemed nice, but ... But. There was something about him. She couldn't pinpoint it.

It's too soon, even for Saff. But it would be nice for her to get out a bit ... And if he came to church, or a coffee morning, Saff might come along too?

Much as Saffron rejected any notion of faith, Rain couldn't help but believe it could bring her daughter comfort, if only she would allow it.

Satisfied she'd cleared the excess water, Rain stood and stared at the floor. With the heat from the cooker and the natural process of evaporation soon you'd never know that the floor had even been wet, let alone flooded. Everything repairs, she thought, aware of the now-steady thump of her own heart. We must see more of the handsome carpenter; I need to inject some youth into the congregation and Saffron needs to make friends nearer her own age.

Rain decided she would make it her mission.

What are you playing at? You idiot.

Joe slammed the Land Rover door and revved the engine, skidding on black ice as he swung out onto the road, away from the chapel.

A pretty face and you're offering to help, getting involved. You should have dropped the girl outside and gone on your way. There'd have been a hundred and one other blokes, all led by their dicks, happy and willing to come to her rescue.

He flew back home, as fast as he could without speeding. He turned into the beech flanked lane that led to the cottage. He thought about the vicar. Minister, he corrected himself; or do Baptists call them pastors? Whatever, Rain's husband. What would he think, when he found out? Perhaps he wasn't interested in earthly matters, focusing on the soul instead? Saffron hadn't mentioned her father at all. Her pale, luminescent face appeared before him, the pupils of those blue, blue eyes dilating. He shifted in his seat.

Joe didn't notice the oncoming car until it was almost upon him, he was so wrapped up in his thoughts. Swerving, he slammed on the brakes and skidded onto the verge. The other vehicle didn't even slow down, let alone stop to check he was OK. Bastard. Joe knew it was a bloke. An idiot in a fancy car. What was it? A BMW? Difficult to be sure in the dark. He took a deep breath, restarted the engine, and pulled off the grass.

An oncoming car here was unusual, though; very unusual. It was a one-way dirt track and although there were three cottages in the terrace where he lived, the other two were uninhabited. Uninhabitable, the letting agent had said. Joe's cottage had only just passed the environmental health inspector's test, the young estate agent had told him, hence the cheap rent. Average rents in Wales sounded cheap to Joe, let alone the rent on this dump. Not that it was quite such a dump any more. In the months Joe had lived there, he'd transformed the dark, poky cottage into a home that suited his spartan needs, and when a fire roared in the hearth it was almost cosy.

So what was the man in the expensive car doing down here? Perhaps he'd taken a wrong turn, got himself lost. But Joe felt uneasy. The entrance to the lane was well obscured, even in winter when most of the trees were bare. There was no signpost. No one would drive into the lane without knowing what they were looking for. Joe locked the Landy, resolving to speak with the agency the next day, to establish if the other cottages were about to be occupied.

Inside, the air was as cold and damp as outside. Without removing his jacket, he lit a fire, wrapped a potato in tin foil and threw it into the smoking wood. He wasn't hungry after the brick-sized slice of fruit cake at the vicarage, or whatever they called it, but he would be in a couple of hours. He considered venturing into the shed at the bottom of the garden, working on some ideas. After all, part of the plan was to experiment, to see if he could create beautiful things from wood, stone, flint; to see if it might be considered art. But there was no heating in the shed and the light was poor. He cracked open a tin of lager, switched on the Xbox, and lay on the floor ready to play.

He'd explored *Assassin's Creed*, *Oblivion*, and most of the *Call of Duty* type combat games, but *Fable* was still his favourite game. He liked that he could be whoever he wanted to be in the game: an old crone, a blind man, a dashing knight, a sexy, Boudicca-inspired woman. At first, he'd had a character enact all sorts of monstrous deeds but the game dictated that bad deeds were reflected in a character's appearance, so his character grew horns, became hideously ugly, and Joe tired of acts of violence. The release they offered, the sense of wish-fulfilment and satisfaction, was all too brief, and utterly pointless. Currently, he was a rotund, kindly knight who went about helping beautiful damsels in distress.

Joe drifted around the game looking for someone to save, but he couldn't focus. Having formed a plan of sorts regarding the mysterious car driver, his mind whirled with the dilemma of the girl, Saffron, and her nice, if cloying, mother. Joe wondered if Saffron's anger hid something. Something bigger than the teenage-like angst he'd mistaken it for initially. At twenty-four she was too old for that, regardless.

The Standard would have to be towed back; he'd made a promise and he never broke promises. But once the car was back with its owner, job done. If he was unlucky enough to bump into either of them, he would be polite but brief. He'd go about his normal routine and hope not to see either mother or daughter again. How long had they been in the town? Did Rain say six months? He'd not seen them in all that time. What could change?

Saffron ate more at supper than she had done in a single sitting since they'd moved to Coed Mawr. Her body craved sustenance; she longed to feel full, bursting, but that evening, even when she was so stuffed she feared she might vomit, the sense of longing didn't retreat.

In the study she tried to focus on her student copy of the *British Medical Journal*. She was interested in an article about ground-breaking new drugs to halt the progress of Alzheimer's, but after reading and rereading the same paragraph without absorbing any of it, she threw it aside and admitted defeat. What did it matter? She might never set foot in a hospital again, at least not as a doctor. She turned off the desk lamp, plunging the room into near darkness, and padded across the room to the window on the far side, opening it wide. Beyond the garden were fields, and more fields, as far as the eye could see in daylight. In the gloaming of a cloudy late-winter evening there was little to observe. It was black; blacker than Saffron thought possible. Light pollution was something she'd heard of, but not fully understood its effect, not until they were in Coed Mawr.

On clear nights the sky was rammed with stars; more than Saffron had ever seen. How did they all fit in up there? And how close did they seem? Unbelievably so. The first time she had looked at the night sky here was in late September when she and Rain had lain on the scrubby grass after drinking too much of a congregation member's home-made cider, given as a welcome gift. The blanket of stars overhead seemed so, so close she thought she might reach up and grab one, kiss it, and return it to the heavens. In their drunken state they had pretended to do precisely that. Perhaps they'd kissed Ben's star, or Dad's, Rain had said. Saffron had hoped she'd found her dad's.

A sharp breeze jolted her from her memories, sweeping over the exposed flesh of her neck and clavicle, and up towards her earlobes. A strand of hair brushed across her cheek, like a caress. Goosebumps prickled and despite the chill an urge to feel more gripped her acutely. She peeled off her thick black jumper and tore at the long-sleeved T-shirt underneath. Gasping with the shock of the cold, she pushed down her pelmet skirt and thick tights in one swift movement and stepped out of them, before unhooking her bra. Naked except for her cotton knickers, she stood at the window and, breathing deeply, allowed the air to assault her flesh and lungs. A thousand needle tips stabbed her. Her skin tightened so hard it hurt; arrows of pain skewered her ribs. She enjoyed the pain. She lifted her arms upwards and outwards until they were level with her shoulders, tilted her head back and closed her eyes. She imagined herself crucified, lanced with wounds, blood running over the pure white landscape of her flesh. She saw her corpse being embalmed with fragrant oils, strong male hands sweeping up and over the waxy undulation of her body. Her gaze drifted up the embalmer's arms to his chest, stubble-dusted chin, and eyes of hazel and green. She gasped. Joe. She opened her eyes.

A sudden movement across the window startled her further. She gripped the ledge. What kind of bird would venture so close to the window? Only birds of prey, owls and the like, would be out at this time of night. She leaned forward and studied the sky. The creature fluttered past. A bat? It moved like a bat, not a gull or other sea bird. In winter? Aware of her vulnerable state she closed the window. What the hell had come over her? Standing, almost-naked, at the window. What if one of those creepy farmer types was out and about, leering, hiding behind some bush? What if Joe had seen her? This thought wasn't as disagreeable as she felt it should be. Shivering, she dressed and left the study, abandoning her studies for yet another evening.

Snow fell throughout the night and Joe rose to discover that the extraordinarily beautiful pattern of ice on the bedroom window became considerably less beautiful when he realised it was on the inside of the pane.

He jogged downstairs to the kitchen and leant against the range while a pot of water boiled on the stove. He rubbed his bleary eyes, still not fully awake. It had been a strange night. If he dreamed at all, Joe's dreams were claustrophobic and dark; he'd wake with a jolt – usually at three or three thirty – overwhelmed with a sense of walls closing in on him. He'd feel trapped. A dragging sensation in his gut hinted at a crumbling of self. Much of the time he didn't know who he was any more. What he wanted. Closure? Escape? Revenge?

But that night he'd dreamed of burnt orange skies, bodies slick with perspiration, and the scent of sugar cane in the air. Through all this exoticism wafted the tall, shadowy figure of a pale young woman with sad blue eyes and a crucifix at her throat. The dream had been so vivid that when he awoke – shortly after seven – for a while he couldn't believe that it wasn't high summer, that he wasn't waking up in the Caribbean, the deep South, or a condo in Florida.

After coffee and toast he ventured out into the snow. The drift was so high at the front door he'd been unable to open it; in the back garden the snow reached to his knees. The Land Rover was unrecognisable as a vehicle, instead resembling a small hillock. After digging a path with a shovel resting against the side wall, he swept away snow from the roof, bonnet, and windows. His arms were soaked. The snow was easy enough to clear; it was light, like icing sugar, but the air was bitter and Joe suspected there would be a freeze later. Ice on top of snow was bad news. If he was to rescue Rain's Standard from Devil's Rise he'd have to get a move on.

He raced inside and changed his jumper, threw on a waterproof jacket, and grabbed a woollen beanie; his ears were freezing.

The Land Rover started with ease and Joe was glad that he'd attached the snow chains the day before. Being prepared, being ready for the worst case scenario, was Joe's forte. It had been a hard lesson.

He took the lane carefully and was relieved to find that once he was in the relative shelter of the upper town the drifts weren't quite so high. There was no one about; the place was deserted, and virgin snow lay on every path and road. All the shops were closed, shutters down, though by now it was almost nine. Steering right after the post office towards the track to Devil's Rise, Joe wondered if this was a fool's errand.

At the top of the Rise, he turned off the engine and climbed out of the Landy. The snow came to his knees, seeped through the denim of his jeans. He peered down the slope. Though it was impossible to be sure, the snow looked thicker than ever further down the hill. He would have to take the long way round, then either drag the Standard up or tow her back along the main road. It would take hours and he'd been due at the school – he glanced at his watch – over half an hour ago. He pulled out his phone and went to call the site foreman. No signal.

Great. Still, Joe reasoned, he wouldn't be the only tradesman who'd find it difficult to get on site today, let alone on time. He turned around and chugged back to the upper town.

At the crossroads he saw a man, maybe seventy years old, wading through the street, a large dog in his arms. The man looked exhausted, red-cheeked and sweating in spite of the sub-zero temperature. Joe stopped, yanked his hat further down over his face and wound down his window.

'You all right?'

The man turned. 'Popped out for some milk, I did. The wife likes it on her cornflakes. Shop's shut. Never been shut before. Thought I'd take the dog. Stupid idea. Poor beast is buried,' he replied with a strong Welsh accent.

The dog lifted sad brown eyes to Joe, as if to justify its indolence.

'Hop in. I'll drive you home.'

'There's lovely, boyo. Bless you.'

Even in the cold air the dog's aroma was pungent, filling the cabin instantly. Joe felt slightly nauseous, but it was a short journey, as the man had said, so he kept the windows closed.

'Right here. Next to the chapel.' He pointed to a terrace after the manse.

After the man had clambered down Joe hefted the dog, a Labrador, into his arms.

'Where you off to then?' the man said.

Head bent down low, Joe explained his mission.

'You don't want to be doing that, you don't, long way

round or short. It's not called Devil's Rise for nothing.' He looked back at his house. 'Ah, bless the little lady. She's cleared my path, just like she said she would. She's a good 'un, that one.'

Joe watched the man staggering down his path, the dog like a wet blanket in his arms. He kept one eye on the house next to the chapel; the house that was actually next to the chapel; the man's was next door but one. Joe rolled the Land Rover forward a little. He watched the pathway; clumps of snow flew through the air. He wound down the window. The sound of scraping, metal on concrete assaulted his ears. As he looked the top half of a figure emerged from behind the white mound. An unmistakable figure, regardless of the hood: Saffron. How kind of her to clear the neighbour's drive; it wasn't as if he was infirm, he looked pretty fit.

Without thinking Joe turned off the engine and jumped out. She was so thin, like the bare branches of the birch in the cottage garden. Clearing snow was back-breaking work. He ploughed over, but to his astonishment she didn't seem relieved at his offer of help. Instead she said, 'We might be stuck for days. It's not unusual for this dump to get cut off, or so the locals claim. Mum's been fretting about you. Worried you might try and get the car.'

'I was heading to the main road. Figure the ploughs and gritters will have made it safe.'

'It'll be days before they get here. The council didn't order enough salt; cutbacks and that.' She pushed back her hood to reveal her face, framed in a woollen bobble hat, locks of dark hair falling down the front of the duffel coat, twirling round the wooden toggles. She looked beautiful. A thought shimmied across his mind: wouldn't mind getting trapped with you.

'You always so angry?'

She glared at him.

What's come over you, Joe? Your good sense frozen?

31

Thought you were going to keep your distance. Shut up.

He waited for the bollocking, but it never came. To his astonishment, she dropped her gaze to the ground and bit her lip.

'Sorry. I'm not angry with you. Why don't you come in and have a drink. Listen to the news. See what they say about the roads. I don't think it's safe and you might be able to talk some sense into Mum.' She waved her arm in a circular motion. 'Rain. She's determined to go to work, but there's no point.'

'Radio's working in my car today. I really must be off.'

'No one'll be working.'

Despite the robust heating in the Land Rover, he could no longer feel his toes or finger tips. A mug of coffee or tea would be most welcome. He hesitated, searching for another excuse, and then she smiled at him, and it felt so good he found himself nodding.

'I don't bite, despite appearances,' she said, still smiling. 'And Mum will be so pleased to see you again.'

That's what I'm worried about. I cannot get involved with her, the chapel, you. No one. I should never have agreed to come in.

He watched Saffron walking away, shoulders hunched; the tall girl's affliction.

Too late to refuse now.

He was stamping the snow off his boots when he heard Rain's voice drifting down the hall. The door swung open. 'JJ! You have an uncanny knack of turning up at just the right moment!' She continued to talk, something about the car, clearing round the chapel, though he couldn't be sure because he wasn't listening. Rain stood before him in a cassock and a dog collar, the gold cross luminous against the dark fabric. She pulled on a pair of neon pink Hunter wellington boots. Saffron was indeed a minister's daughter, but it was her mother who was the minister, not her father. Joe hoped he concealed his surprise.

She gestured at her gown. 'Special occasion. You won't often see me in these. Go through. I need to have a word with our neighbour.' And out Rain went.

Chapter Four

Saffron was standing at the sink, holding the kettle, when Joe walked into the kitchen.

'Coffee?' she said, turning to face him.

She saw him clock the cafetière on the counter and without really understanding how, she knew he was an instant coffee man. He hesitated. Taking a jar from the cupboard to her right, she added, 'I hate the real stuff too. Makes me gag. Rain loves it, but then she grew up with a couple of hippies. Everything real and natural and all that.'

A broad smile broke over his rugged features, soft crinkles forming at the corners of his eyes. His teeth shone white against his skin.

'Instant's great. Can't be doing with the faff of real.'

Had she misjudged his taste? 'It's no bother,' she said.

'I hate real coffee,' he shrugged.

'Take a seat.' She pointed to the table.

Judging by his accent and the way he spoke, he was pretty posh, but he worked as a carpenter and liked instant coffee. It didn't fit somehow. She focused on making the drinks, afraid that her thawing towards him was obvious. Yes, he was a good-looking bloke: tall, nice build, interesting face, but she was meant to stay away from men a while longer if she wasn't to look like a heartless cow.

He looks younger this morning, fresher. Clean-shaven, and bright-eyed. He'd been working yesterday, he was probably tired. That might explain the roughness.

Fresher than she'd thought last night or not, he'd definitely had a shock. She saw it in his eyes as soon as he walked into the room. Rain, the minister. It got most

35

people. Ever since she was tiny, if she had to reveal that she was a minister's daughter – and she avoided this as much as was humanly possible – people assumed she meant her father. Wrong. Dad was an architect. Had been an architect. The familiar choking sensation at the back of her throat rose, her hands shook and granules of coffee fell from the teaspoon and scattered onto the counter top.

Not here. Not now. Please.

Joe saw her hands trembling. He'd been studying them to stop himself staring at her face – her lovely face – and the gentle curve of her body, clear through the thin black jumper she wore today.

A minister's daughter.

Joe's head swam. Was this a turn-on or a turn-off? Was she as pure as this suggested? Or was he being ridiculous? Minister's daughters were probably no different to any other young woman. Same desires, same needs. He'd never encountered one before, that was all, but when he saw the shaking hand, the smooth white skin, he sensed her vulnerability again, felt the tug, and he knew he must stay away from her.

But he couldn't leave. She was making him a drink; he'd promised to rescue her mother's car, and it looked highly unlikely that he was going to be able to do it today thanks to the snow. It was impossible.

He hadn't meant to look up at her face, but he did, and when he saw a tear rolling down her cheek, he grabbed the box of tissues from the table and lunged over, handing her a tissue without saying a word.

After she'd dabbed at her eyes, he didn't know what to do. Stand there like an idiot, watching, intrusive and cloying, or return to his seat and appear like an insensitive bastard? He shrugged and offered the tissues again. She shook her head and mumbled, 'Thank you,' and then looked right at him.

Before his gaze, more tears pooled, spilling over lashes thick with mascara. A brown-black droplet streaked down her face. He wanted to reach over and wipe away the teardrop with the pad of his thumb. Instead, he lifted the box of tissues yet again, but he lost purchase and it dropped to the floor. Simultaneously, they crouched to retrieve it, hands outstretched. Their fingers touched and their eyes met. He felt light-headed.

Saffron snatched back her arm as if she'd received an electric shock. She stood up, pulling down the stretchy fabric of her skirt. Joe grabbed the box, stood, coughed, and, unsure what else to do, offered another tissue.

'I'm fine,' she snapped, reaching towards a cupboard. 'Fine.'

'I always cry when I'm fine too.'

She laughed then. Not a belly laugh, but a laugh all the same. Covering her mouth and nose with the flat of her hand, she composed herself, and reached into the cupboard. She placed two mugs on the counter and sprinkled in coffee, straight from the jar. 'Sugar?' She held up a bowl.

'Please.'

'One or two?'

'What? Shakes or teaspoons?'

'I was thinking about my dad. He died, in an accident.'

'That's harsh.' It explained her anger. It was one of the stages of grief. He remembered it well. He stepped forward and went to touch her. 'I know what you're …' She stared at him, blue eyes red with rage. He froze, hand hovering in the air a few centimetres above her shoulder.

'With my boyfriend. Fiancé. My fiancé was in the same car.'

'I'm so sorry.'

'Why? You didn't know them. People say the stupidest things. I don't understand why they don't just keep their mouths shut. People die every minute, every second, of every day. Big deal.' She slammed the mug onto the table. Coffee slopped over the rim.

'You're right. Stupid. It's because people don't know what else to say. I didn't know what else to say.' He took a sip of coffee, though it was far too hot. He felt a blister forming on the inside of his mouth. She stared at him, unapologetic. 'Mind you, if you're going to be a doctor you might consider working on your bedside manner. That kind of pragmatism might upset some relatives.'

She burst out laughing and he wanted to take in every new detail of her face when it was flushed with happiness, but Rain breezed into the room and Saffron turned back to the kettle. She offered her mum a drink, her tone lighter.

'No thanks, darling. I need to visit Mrs Davies over at Bryn Coch, before the infant dedication. She's got no one.' Rain grinned expectantly at Joe and he had a nasty feeling he knew what she'd meant earlier by his turning up at the right time.

'Left at the next junction, please. This snow is crazy, isn't it?'

Rain had cornered JJ into driving her to the farm and she felt bad about it, but not bad enough to let him off the hook when he'd offered up a flimsy excuse. Mrs Davies was expecting her, needed her. She was an old lady – ninety-seven, she'd told Rain.

'Not as bad here as in town, just like you said,' JJ muttered.

'The weather systems round here are peculiar. Always have been. I grew up not too far from here,' she explained.

'You'd never know from your accent.'

'Oh, I left more than twenty years ago. There wasn't much here for young people back then.'

'Is there now?'

She laughed. 'It's such a shame. It really is so very beautiful.'

He nodded. 'I must try and get to work after this. How long did you say you'd be?'

She wondered why he stared straight ahead, resolute. The road was empty; they'd not seen another car on the three-mile journey.

He's cross with me, though he's trying not to show it, Rain thought. Why's he so desperate to get to work? Most people relish the excuse for a day off.

'Not long. I've got to get back for the dedication. Are you freelance?'

'Sorry?'

'As a carpenter. Are you self-employed?'

'Sort of.'

'Where do you work?'

JJ pointed. 'Is that it? Massive place for an old dear all on her own.'

The Davies farm was big, though nothing had been farmed there for decades. 'She still keeps chickens, but nothing else. She'll always offer me a basket. Do you like an egg in the morning? You're welcome to them. Saff barely eats and I worry about cholesterol.' Rain felt it was the least she could do for his trouble. She felt bad for virtually forcing him to take her; she knew how well she administered guilt-trips.

'I'll be as quick as I can,' Rain said as she slammed the Landy door.

'Will you have an Ovaltine, *cariad*?' Mrs Davies said.

Rain shook her head. It was a strange drink to offer at this time of day; Stephen had been partial to the odd mug last thing at night, until his sleeping habits went all skew-whiff.

Rain remembered the first time she'd found him on the sofa. A heavy sleeper from childhood, she rarely woke. But that night it had been uncommonly hot and Rain woke shortly after four with a raging thirst. Half asleep, she'd

39

staggered out of bed, unaware of the empty space next to her. She was on her way back upstairs when she'd heard the faint murmur of voices. The television was on in the front room. Stephen lay sprawled on his side along the sofa. The dawn light sneaked through a chink in the curtain illuminating his face. He looked innocent and young, and Rain had been filled with such longing she'd wanted to wake him and tell him how lucky she felt: the luckiest woman alive. She didn't, naturally. Stephen needed his sleep and without a solid eight hours he was irritable and bear-headed. And while she didn't know it at the time, that summer marked the beginning of months waking to find the other half of their bed cold and unused.

Yes, Ovaltine reminded her of Stephen.

'Ever so kind of you, Mrs Davies, but I really mustn't stay and you need to be careful with this milk. Make it last.' Rain gestured to the carton, which sat on the table with the loaf she'd also brought. 'If you need anything else, you must ask. They're saying the snow will clear tomorrow, but who knows!'

'Indeed. Always getting it wrong, here. It's the mountains, you know,' Mrs Davies said.

People had always blamed the mountain range. Rain wondered how a bunch of hills could foil the technologies of modern weather forecasting, but said nothing.

On the doorstep, Mrs Davies squinted into the sky. 'There's more snow in those clouds, you mark my words. Hope you've got that roof sorted out.' The old woman peered at the Land Rover. 'That your lift, then?'

Rain nodded. What else could it be? But Mrs Davies's comment about the chapel roof gave her an idea. The roof was in a terrible state of repair and the last lot of workmen had done more harm than good, according to the company who'd tendered for the contract last month. If more snow did fall, the weight of it could bring the whole thing down. A sheet of heavy tarpaulin kept out most of the rain – a couple of buckets caught the excess – but snow was weighty, and a freeze could signal disaster. She must get back to the builders, get it all sorted, a more accurate price. It was stupid of her to ignore it, hoping the problem might disappear. It had seemed so expensive. It would near enough empty the church funds. A telephone call, that's all it would take and work could begin. That's what the builder had said. 'Could get started immediately,' he'd said. Church members had approved the quote. Rain said goodbye to Mrs Davies and made her way to the car.

'It's warmer in here than in Mrs Davies's kitchen,' she said, slamming the door and sliding along the seat till she sat next to JJ. 'God knows how she doesn't feel the cold. She looks like a little bird but I reckon she's as tough as old boots.'

JJ laughed. 'Born in the days before central heating. Right, belt on. I need to get going.'

He's so cautious, won't move till I'm strapped in. 'To work?' Rain asked.

'Yes.'

'Where's that?'

'Other side of the valley, across the border.' He tipped his head at the seat belt again.

She clicked it in. 'Cheshire?'

He nodded, revved the engine and rolled forward.

She coughed. 'There's a problem with the chapel roof,' she said.

'Oh yeah.'

'The beams. They're rotten.'

'Oh yeah.' The car tipped and rolled towards the main road from the farm.

'I just wondered, with you being a carpenter, and being freelance ...'

'I'm not really freelance ... I'm on a big job at the moment. A school. And they're short of labour. Not really a job for one person.'

41

It was more information about his work than he'd offered when Rain had asked earlier, and she'd only been trying to make conversation, really. He didn't want to do the roof, that much was obvious, and Rain wasn't going to push it. Despite what JJ said about a labour shortage and the legacy of the last group of craftsmen, Rain knew there were plenty of carpenters desperate for a contract to repair the roof. Unemployment was rife in these parts. She would make that call as soon as she got home. What a contrary man he was. One minute all chummy and nice, the next distant to the point of almost being rude.

He fancies Saff, that's it. Nice when she's about, but when he's stuck with her mother, different story. Ha. Welcome to middle age, Rain.

Her pride was hurt. Crazy. Stupid. And true. It wasn't as if she was in the market, even. She was grieving.

Rain had always known this moment would come: the painful realisation she was no longer the most desirable. Youth trumped all. She had prepared for it years ago, when Saffron was approaching sixteen, her awkward beauty starting to bud at last. With her blonde curls and curves, Rain had demanded more male attention – Saffron's male school friends flirted outrageously – and Saff was too much like her father to be considered conventionally pretty, but her appeal was there, for those who chose to really look. But sixteen-year-old boys see only the obvious, heads full of Mrs Robinson fantasies. Saff's friends had often commented that Rain looked more like a sister than a mother, and at thirty-eight she had been much younger than most of the other mums.

It's a wonder she didn't hate me back then.

Saffron hadn't seemed bothered. If anything she appeared to take pride in her sexy, young mum. She was so in love with Ben.

'How things can change in eight years.'

'Sorry?' JJ said.

Rain jolted. 'What?'

JJ looked confused. 'What changes in eight years?'

Bugger. I'm at it again.

'I said something?' She stared at JJ's profile as he navigated the icy road.

He turned to look at her and then back to the road, nodding.

She smiled. *He must think me mad.* 'I do that sometimes. Talk my thoughts.'

He lifted his chin and she felt the need to explain. 'It's because of God.'

He raised his chin again.

'When I speak with Him I talk, out loud.'

'And you were talking to him just now?'

She laughed. 'Heavens, no. I just forget myself sometimes.'

'It's all right. Here we are.'

He sounded relieved to be back at the chapel. She was about to invite him in again, then realised he'd left the engine running.

Perhaps he doesn't fancy Saff, after all. Perhaps he does want to try and get to work. Why was I so suspicious?

Rain thanked him for the lift and clambered out, determined to back off. The roof would be repaired without his help; Saff would make some friends eventually. She needed more time, that's all.

Chapter Five

There was little sign of life at the school when Joe got there, though the snow wasn't as deep as back in Coed Mawr. There were neither workmen at the new build nor children in the Edwardian building which adjoined it. A quick once-over, peering through windows, revealed a handful of children with three adults in the hall making what looked like snowflakes.

A child spotted Joe, smiled, and waved at him. Alerted to his presence, the rest of the children waved and a teacher pushed himself from a crouched position on the mat and came to the window.

'Foreman's in the hut,' he said loudly, emphasising each syllable and pointing over Joe's right shoulder, as if Joe were five too.

'Cheers.' Joe waved goodbye to the staring children who yelled 'Bye!' in unison, and he turned towards the prefab cabin which sat on the far side of the playground. As he trudged over he wondered why the teachers hadn't taken the kids outside for a snowball fight or to build a snowman. It would be so much more fun than cutting out snowflakes; they'd probably done plenty of that at Christmas.

Derek was cradling a mug, a tabloid newspaper open on the small table before him, when Joe pulled open the door of the makeshift site office. A halogen heater glowed in the corner.

'Am I the only one in?' Joe said, as he closed the door. Derek wasn't the sort of bloke who bothered with niceties like hello and how are you. A straightforward

Liverpudlian, he didn't waste time spouting things he didn't really mean and expected others to behave likewise.

'So far.'

There was a pause. Joe moved to the kettle and grabbed one of the less grimy mugs. 'No one else'll bother. Hardly worth the effort now,' Derek continued.

Joe checked his watch. It was almost noon. 'I'll be off then,' he said, replacing the mug on the tray.

'Might as well.'

'Thaw's due.'

'So they say. Stay and have a brew, why don't you?'

Joe hesitated. Derek turned over a page and began to read. Derek was comfortable with silence and Joe was thirsty. He'd not had a drink since breakfast. He grabbed the mug again.

He'd almost finished his tea and was gazing out of the window at the lawn of snow when Derek closed the newspaper. 'Don't know how you can drink it like that, with the bag left in. Would set my teeth on edge,' he said. It was the most personal thing Derek had shared in months. Joe shrugged and drained the mug.

'I'll be off then. See you tomorrow,' Joe said.

He moved towards the door and had taken hold of the handle when Derek said, 'You drive a Land Rover, yeah?'

Joe nodded, wondering where this was leading.

'I need you on another job. Not too far from here, maybe an hour's drive. I quoted a while back so you'll need to price it up again. A church roof. Start as soon as they've accepted.'

'How come you're so sure they will?'

'You're cheap, and churches don't have much dosh do they now, soft lad.'

Joe knew exactly what was coming next. 'Where exactly?'

'Taff country. A seaside town. Woman vicar, sounded all right.'

'Why me?'

''Cos you're here. Any problems with that?'

What could Joe say? He had no contract, no rights. He didn't even get a wage slip in his weekly envelope. Being paid cash in hand like this was one of the major appeals of the job. Untraceable.

'It's not easy to admit this but I'm not that great with heights.' It was a feeble excuse, and they both knew it.

Derek grunted. 'You're here, so I'm giving you the job. Start as soon as you can.'

Joe hesitated. He was fed up of all the driving and he needed to work. Coed Mawr wasn't the only town with boarded up shops, abandoned caravan parks and teenagers congregated in bus shelters, cans of cheap lager at their feet.

'Look, kidda, I like you. It's why I'm giving you a chance. I can't keep you here. You're a liability.'

Joe had no idea what Derek was talking about. A liability? He worked hard; he was punctual, he was precise. No one could find fault with his workmanship.

Derek continued. 'There was a bloke here, the other day, after you'd gone. Asked after you – at least I think it was you, said he was looking for a mate, another southerner.'

'What did he drive? A BMW?' Joe replied, as casually as he could muster. The letting agent had known nothing of anyone visiting a cottage in the terrace when Joe had enquired. 'Did you say anything?' The words caught in Joe's throat.

'Did I hell as like. Thought he was from the tax, VAT or something. You're not the only one I pay off the books. Don't like people creeping round my business. You're not claiming benefits are you, soft lad?'

Joe shook his head, his eyes fixed on Derek's. He needed to be believed. And he needed to find out more about this BMW. He'd have to put in a call to Simon. 'I appreciate you keeping quiet.'

'None of my business. Now, here's the address. I'll send a couple of lads over to help as soon as you're sorted. No scallies. And a scaffolder. Collect your wages from the landlord of the Loggerheads on the bypass at the end of each week.' He handed over a scrap of paper. Joe glanced at it. The handwriting was virtually illegible but it didn't matter. He knew the address already.

The shop front of Wynne's was in-keeping with the air of faded grandeur throughout the arcade. The rows of canopied retail outlets, with their Corinthian columns, curved glass windows, and heavy chandeliers, must have been impressive in Lower Coed Mawr's heyday, but now they appeared tawdry, in need of a lick of paint and a good scrub.

Saffron pressed her face against the glass and peered beyond the mannequins for signs of life within. There were none. One of the orange-skinned dummies had lost a hand; it lay at its feet, minus a finger. She checked her phone. Eight thirty-one. The woman from the employment agency had said eight thirty, sharp. 'Mrs Evans is a stickler for punctuality.' Though clearly not window-dressing, Saffron thought, breathing onto her hands. It was still cold, even though the thaw had arrived just as the forecasters had predicted.

What a freaky place it was. Only two days ago they had been knee-deep in snow. All that remained were mounds of filthy ice at irregular intervals on the pavements. Frozen sculptures for dogs to piss against.

Saffron was grateful for the job. It was local, within walking distance of the manse. OK, so it was only part-time, but there'd be opportunities to extend the hours, according to the agency. She shuddered thinking of her debts.

'There's people queuing up for opportunities like this.

Don't come round every day,' the agency woman had said when Saffron had pulled a face at the prospect of shop work. 'It can't be worse than the soap factory.' This was true. Nine miles from Coed Mawr, the factory was a long bus ride. And it reeked in there. The work was mindless and repetitive, leaving too much time for thought. At first, Saffron had relished the solitary nature of her role – checking the conveyor belt for irregular shaped bars – and noise levels meant that even when a passing colleague did try to make conversation, Saffron could feign deafness. But hours and hours with nothing to occupy her other than her memories paled, and she had become sloppy; chipped, lumpy blocks were slipping past. A foreman of some description had reprimanded her. 'It's just not good enough. We have high standards. A reputation to maintain,' he'd barked and she knew that if she didn't get another job soon she'd be fired.

Wynne's flooded with light and Saffron blinked, the glare hurting her eyes after the murky gloaming of the arcade. It was the first shop to show any sign of occupancy. She rapped on the glass door and watched a rotund, middle-aged woman trot across the shop floor, her strides clipped by an ill-fitting, brown pencil skirt. Saffron diagnosed joint problems – knees and hips – in a decade or two. The legacy of carrying all that excess weight. She hoped the skirt, mustard-coloured shirt, and brown neck scarf wasn't a uniform.

'Good morning. You must be Saffron!' the wasp trilled. She sounded shockingly cheerful for such an unprepossessing morning.

'Hi. Mrs Evans?' Warm, dry air slapped Saffron's cheeks as she passed through the entrance.

'That's me. Come this way. I'll show you the staff room, your locker, and where you can get tea and coffee and the odd custard cream, if you're very, very lucky. It's a pound a week and most of us pay monthly. You can sign up once your trial period is over.'

Saffron loped across the shop floor, brushing past tightly packed rails of cheap blouses, skirts, and jeans, and a wall of footwear. Her nose fizzed with the smell of plastic. On the far wall, between rows of frilly knickers and bras in varying pastel shades, was a door. Mrs Evans produced a large key from her pocket and held it aloft with relish.

In the soulless room reserved for staff, Saffron threw off her coat and crammed it into the locker Mrs Evans held open for her. The older woman stood back and studied her. Given that her hair was held back in a low ponytail, she had removed her nose stud, though not the rings in her ears, and wore no make-up, Saffron wondered what Mrs Evans found so distasteful about her appearance, for it was obvious that she did.

'Now, dear,' she began, 'is that the longest skirt you have, because company policy states that hems much reach below the knee? Not just above the knee, not on the knee, *below* the knee. I'm not sure about the earrings ...' She paused before continuing, 'Tights must be flesh-coloured, and it wouldn't hurt to wear a little make-up, spot of lipstick. Looks like you've made an effort.'

'I'm sorry,' Saffron said. There was no way she would wear flesh-coloured tights. 'Trousers?' she asked, hopefully. *Please, God.*

Mrs Evans paused. 'Well, they're not banned, but no one else does ...'

What is this, the dark ages?

Her expression must have betrayed her for Mrs Evans added, 'But if it makes you feel more comfortable ...' She smiled, 'We have some smashing pairs on offer at the moment. Grab a bargain, why don't you!'

The morning passed without a single customer. Saffron learnt how to operate the till; Mrs Evans ran through the instructions three, maybe four, times. She swept the floor, polished the mirror in the solitary changing room and rearranged the footwear 'department', as her boss liked to call the wall. 'Boots to the bottom with sale tickets out, spring slippers and wellies in the middle,' Mrs Evans instructed. 'To draw the eye. It might not seem as important as the work you're used to,' the older woman rolled her eyes, 'it *isn't* as important as your profession, of course, but it matters to us.'

It was an odd establishment. Mostly clothes, women's, men's, and children's wear, it also sported toys, random cosmetics, batteries and other household items, and, somewhat optimistically, Saffron thought, a selection of sun creams, buckets and spades, fishing nets and crabbing wire. Did people really come here to holiday in the summer months? The horseshoe bay was lovely, nestled between the two rocks jutting out to sea and cradled from behind by the mountains. Clearly, the town had once been beautiful and thriving. But now? Her mum had likened it to herself: a rose long since bloomed, petals curled and browning.

When Saffron returned from lunch Mrs Evans was at the till talking to an overweight young woman. Without seeing her face, or knowing anything else about her, Saffron warmed to her, didn't write her off immediately as she had done most people here. The girl's hair was a badly dyed red; she wore thick black tights, red Converse trainers, and a green parka with a fishtail. She was the coolest person Saffron had seen in months, apart from Joe. Someone who looked like they were from the same planet as Saffron. She approached the counter.

'Mrs Evans tells me you've nabbed my job, you bitch,' the girl said, spinning to face Saffron.

'Sorry?'

'Now, now, Ceri,' Mrs Evans said, turning to address Saffron. 'You ignore her, dear. Thinks she's being funny.

Saffron, meet Ceri, my goddaughter. Ceri, Saffron.'

'Hi.' Saffron waved and looked into Ceri's face. A broad smile swept across it, revealing crooked teeth and the gleam of a tongue stud.

'All right.' Ceri tipped her head in a facsimile of a greeting. 'Take no notice of her.' She nodded at Mrs Evans. 'I did mean it. I've wanted to work here for years. Been my lifelong ambition.' Ceri raised her eyebrows as she spoke, a glint in her eyes.

'Mine too. Guess I got lucky,' Saffron replied.

The doorbell tinkled and Mrs Evans scurried away to 'serve her customer'.

'Harass the poor bitch, more like,' Ceri said.

They looked at each other and smiled.

Chapter Six

Joe checked his watch. It was well past lunchtime and he was still lounging around the cottage. He couldn't put off returning to the chapel any longer. When he'd towed the Standard back to Rain's that morning, it had been a relief to find both chapel and manse empty. He'd left the Standard in the manse car park next to the hall and pushed the key through the front door. The Labrador-owning neighbour had said Rain would be back to lead the afternoon prayer meeting at two thirty. Joe wondered where she'd gone without wheels. He needed to see the roof from the inside as soon as possible; Derek was keen for him to start work. He'd taken a brief look around already, the chapel door was open, but he'd felt like an intruder, poking around without permission.

Stiff with cold and from lying in the same position on the living room floor for hours, he switched off the Xbox, stood, rolled his shoulders and neck. Upstairs he searched for a hat – the chapel was icebox-cold. His beanie wasn't on the chair where he'd slung yesterday's clothes. Where the hell was it?

He checked amongst the neat piles of boxer shorts and socks on the shelves of the rickety wardrobe. Nothing. He was about to give up when, just in case, he checked the deep bottom drawer of the chest of drawers, where he'd thrown a random assortment of items after he'd first moved in. Useless items, but things he'd been unable to leave behind. He scraped through cards, biros and instruction manuals to softer items below. He caught his fingers on something hard and sharp. Unable to stop himself he pulled out the photo frame and turned it over.

A young woman: brown wavy hair, one brown eye, one green, fine-boned and golden-skinned. She held an arm over her forehead, shading her eyes from the glare of a Spanish sun. Her gaze made his heart stop. She was from a world so very far removed from this one in Coed Mawr that he'd managed to forget, most of the time. She was sunshine, this was winter. He stared.

'Allow yourself to feel the pain. Let go of the rage.' The therapist's words came back to him. To hell with that. He threw the picture back in the drawer, slammed it shut and raced downstairs. If he was cold in the chapel, so be it.

If Rain was surprised by Joe's U-turn regarding the repair of the chapel roof she didn't show it. Joe thought about explaining himself, but figured it might make things look worse so he didn't bother.

She led him up a wooden staircase – also in a bad state of repair – to the balcony, from which he would inspect the rafters, before returning to a gang of parishioners who hovered at the back of the chapel. Daylight snuck through the gaps in the roof, casting shafts of light on the organ pipes.

Below, Rain conducted the prayer meeting – the heating in the church hall was broken, though it couldn't have been colder than here in the chapel. He noticed how casually dressed Rain was, no sign of the cassock she'd worn for the visit to the farm. Joe couldn't make out what was being said, though it wasn't as quiet and reverential as he'd expected it to be.

He'd finished his preparatory inspection before the meeting finished. For a thorough and accurate quote he would need to get onto the roof, remove some of the slates. There was every chance the purlins might need replacing; wood under the eaves would almost certainly be rotten. If it was as bad as Joe suspected, he would need the help of an apprentice as well as a labourer. Jesus. No chance of working solo. Derek had been right. He considered inflating the costs. Perhaps they'd make do with a patch-up and the work would be over in days.

Not wanting to interrupt the meeting, Joe sat on the organ stool, his back to the keyboard and stared at the stained glass window. He felt like he did as a kid, back at boarding school, bored rigid during endless Sunday services. Weekends were always the loneliest. Some boys went home, though never the cruel ones he'd wanted rid of. Boys like Freddy.

Why don't you go back to where you belong? To your nice little bourgeois existence.

Joe hadn't known what bourgeois meant but he knew it was an insult.

Despite his aversion to places of worship, Joe admitted the chapel window was a thing of beauty. An abstract design, simple yet bold, it was different to the elaborate portraits of Christ and the saints in his school chapel, meek, awed, and yes, also beautiful. The colours swirled before him; orange dominant. The image of Saffron's bowed head at the kitchen table flashed in his mind, the tangerine roots at her scalp contrasting with her dark mane. He recalled her unflinching gaze when she'd told him about her fiancé in the kitchen of the manse. There was nothing meek about that look and the thought made him smile. He closed his eyes and the smell of stone, dark wood, and musty dampness enveloped him. The unmistakable scent of an old church. Not that he was overly familiar with churches of late, but he could recall the last time he'd been in one all too well.

Block it out, block it out.

He gripped the edge of the seat and focused his mind on the group below, straining to make out their words, sentences, meanings. He wondered if Saffron ever attended groups like this; came to church on Sundays. She must have been forced to as a child. If so, how did she reconcile her developing scientific knowledge with faith, if she had any? Did she share any of her mother's conviction, even a fragment? Joe doubted it, though he knew faith and reason were not mutually exclusive.

Leaning forward, he could hear the conversation. A sharp voice, frayed at the edges. 'I saw your daughter in town the other day. Saffron? Unusual name, isn't it? Won't find it in any Bible I'm familiar with!' There was a chuckle, the kind used to mask rancour and criticism should anyone challenge the actual comment. 'But then Rain is not exactly what you'd call common either, is it? Are you from a church family, Reverend?'

Another laugh. Joe recognised it as Rain's. 'Heavens above, no! A pair of old hippies, that's my mum and dad.' More laughter. But only Rain's.

'And what do they make of their daughter becoming a minister?' An old lady's voice.

'Well, I can't, in all honesty, say they approved. But it was OK; it was such a long time ago. I heard the call of God as a teenager, and I was strong-willed. They couldn't stop me. Live and let live, that was their motto,' Rain said. 'And mine.'

'Strong-willed,' another voice, male this time. 'Runs in the family, does it?'

'Do you ever visit your family, Minister? You grew up round these parts, I believe.' The old lady again.

'They passed a long time ago,' Rain said. Shifting gear, she continued. 'Now, before we wrap up … I received this yesterday.' She held aloft some kind of leaflet.

'Posted all round town, they were. I got one too.'

'And me.'

'And me.'

Rain again. 'Well, what do we think? It sounds like a very worthwhile cause to me. I've been thinking that we could play a role? Help raise awareness and maybe even funds.'

'But is it appropriate for a church to be involved in a campaign to save a place of frivolity, of dancing and drinking, and heaven knows what else?' the old boy said.

'Judging by the photos it was a beautiful place. And our Lord doesn't rule out fun,' Rain said.

A woman spoke. 'I danced there in my youth. Every Saturday night. Oh, it was magical, it was. The coloured lights, the mirrors and, oh, the windows ... Beautiful, it was, beautiful. On summer nights, when the windows were open, you could hear the sound of the waves, the sea birds, smell the salt in the air.'

Joe realised they were talking about the decrepit ballroom at the tip of the pier. Crumbling and neglected, it was all boarded-up and clearly hadn't been used in decades. It looked pathetic, though Joe could see that it must have been exquisite in its heyday.

'The flooring often rose. You had to watch your step, for fear of tripping over loose tiles. No way to impress the fellas, that!' said another woman, laughing as she remembered.

'Stupid place to build a ballroom, with all that wood. Bound to be trouble so close to water.' A male voice.

Rain broke their remembrances. 'The thing is, if redeveloped correctly – and from the research I've done, this is key, it could serve all kinds of purposes. It could help reinvigorate the town, attract visitors again. Do we, as God's foot soldiers, really want it to become a "leisure complex"? That is a euphemism for those awful gambling machines. The ballroom should be a ballroom once more.'

There were grunts of approval and Rain continued. 'And getting involved might be another way to lure,' she coughed theatrically, '*ahem*, entice, the younger generation to the church.'

Joe suppressed the urge to laugh.

Another voice. Male. 'Surely the youngsters won't be

interested in a dancehall. They're into rages and all sorts.'

'Ah, well, raves have had their day, Mr Roberts. And the space won't just be used for dances. It can hold art, exhibitions, gigs.'

'Gigs?'

'Concerts, Mr Roberts. Music concerts.'

'The youth of this town don't want concerts, Reverend!'

'How can we know, Mr Roberts? They never have a chance to go and see bands here. The space can accommodate whatever the townsfolk want it to, like an arts centre. I really do feel it could attract more visitors. And more visitors means a stronger economy. More work. What have we to lose? If I'm not mistaken, everyone here backs the restoration campaign. Let's get more involved.'

There followed vociferous noises of agreement, until the cantankerous Mr Roberts piped up again. 'And how do you propose to reach the youngsters, Reverend? Your daughter seems entirely uninterested in the activities of the church.'

Rain spoke and Joe marvelled at her control. If it had been him talking to the group he'd have wanted to thump the old git. 'You're aware I've set up a Facebook page for the church? We could use that for starters. Then posters, more school talks. I'll give it more thought.'

She's quite a woman, the Rev. Joe didn't think there'd be too many rural ministers who used social media to spread God's word. At least not in Wales.

'I'm not sure our Lord would approve of such methods, Reverend. The internet is bursting with evidence of all kinds of human misery and depravity,' Mr Roberts blustered.

And you'd know, wouldn't you? Joe longed to yell.

'And all kinds of human goodness and decency. Let's give it a go, shall we? Gosh, is that the time? Time to wrap up, folks. Till next we meet,' Rain said, clapping her hands together, with what sounded like forced cheerfulness.

Joe waited. He listened as church members lifted themselves off chairs, the groans and sighs fading to shuffling feet and the heavy clip of walking sticks on stone. Only then did he come down the stairs. He studied Rain's profile as she stacked plastic chairs. Her cheeks were flushed, despite the cold, her lips pressed together, folded in on themselves, as if she were biting down on them. There was a heaviness in her demeanour he'd not seen before. She jumped when he approached, as if she had forgotten he was in the chapel.

'Your flock disapprove of your methods, huh?'

Rain shrugged. 'That obvious? Some disapprove of me, which pisses me off even more. Flock? In many ways they're more like a pack.'

Unable to help himself, he laughed. 'You get that much?'

'More than you'd think. Funniest thing is that it's caught me unawares. I anticipated resistance, expected it really,' another shrug, 'when we first arrived. But there was none. Or so it seemed.'

'They let you get comfortable ...'

'On their best behaviour.' She smiled, as if remembering her duty to be kind, understanding. 'It's like family. We are a family. The church, I mean. And we're more critical of those we love than anyone else. As well as most forgiving, of course.'

'Are you critical of them?' He didn't follow her argument. Not really. He understood it was possible to acknowledge loved ones aren't perfect, when love is real, true. But to be more critical of them than others? No. He had been blind to the faults of those he'd loved.

Rain didn't answer. Instead, she tipped her head to the roof and said, 'So, bad as I fear?' She clapped her hands together and pulled them to her chest. Joe knew how to read people. When she was uncomfortable; when she wanted to close a subject down, she clapped.

'Difficult to say for sure.'

'You sound like a builder. And here was me thinking you were different! Can you repair it?'

Joe stroked his chin between thumb and index finger in a caricature of the rogue trader. 'It'll cost you.'

Rain laughed. 'We have money.'

'There could be a few months' work here. Once I've measured the building I'll quantity survey the materials and work out precise costs. Might be heftier than the first estimate you were given.'

'The Lord will provide. When can you start?'

'Soon as you OK the new price.' He smiled. It wouldn't be so bad. He liked Rain and no one visited the town in winter. He could keep a low profile. Of that much he was sure.

Chapter Seven

The house had felt different as soon as Saffron had stepped into the hall, and she'd seen the Standard parked outside, so it wasn't a surprise to discover Joe sitting at the kitchen table. Spread across the table was the debris of a late afternoon tea.

'Saffron! You're back early.' Rain leapt to her feet, gesturing towards the kettle. 'Tea?'

'Sure.' Saffron knew her mother was making an effort to be extra-specially nice; she'd used her full name. Unlike most children, Saffron didn't feel she was being reprimanded when addressed this way. She didn't like the abbreviation. Rain had always maintained that Saffron was a mouthful and when challenged by a six-year-old Saffron – she was a precocious girl, unlike her brother – Rain confessed the name had been chosen by Saffron's father. 'I liked Naomi, or Martha,' she'd said.

Saffron and her mother had argued, after Joe gave Rain a lift to the farm. 'It was SO obvious he didn't want to!' Saffron had said. She'd accused her mother of flirting, of forgetting she was a widow of less than two years, of not loving her father enough. 'No wonder Matthew went away.' Cruel, ugly words. False words; Matthew left before the accident. Their venom poisoned Saffron as much as Rain.

They'd not spoken since. Not properly. Saffron ached to talk about it. She hadn't meant any of it. She hated herself more than her mother. But what would be the point in trying to explain? Rain wasn't ready to hear the truth. She'd stop Saffron as soon as she said sorry; she'd hug her and tell her to shush now; they loved each other; they forgave; that was all that mattered.

But it wasn't.

'I should be off,' Joe said, getting to his feet.

'JJ's been looking at the roof, measuring up. And he brought the car back. I need to find a decent garage,' Rain said. She touched her forehead as if she'd forgotten something.

He checked his watch, though there was a large clock in front of him, on the strip of what remained of the dividing wall between the kitchen and dining area before the rooms were knocked into one. 'Only meant to stay for a quick cuppa.'

'You don't need to explain yourselves to me.' Saffron checked herself; she wanted to be nice. 'Please don't go on my account. I'll make a drink and leave you in peace.' She wandered through and took the kettle out of an astonished Rain's hands. 'You want another?' she said.

It was strange. She felt better than she'd felt in weeks. Happy, almost. Even allowing for the fact that she hadn't made up with Rain, which she was determined to do, starting now.

The afternoon in the shop had passed quickly and it had made Saffron aware of how much the factory had been pulling her down. Taking the job was another form of punishment, she saw that now, and while she wasn't going easy on herself, not by a long shot, she'd been unable to bear that particular torment any longer.

Ceri had hung round longer than Mrs Evans would have liked judging by the number of times she asked if Ceri shouldn't be off. 'What for? Not like I've got a job or nothing,' Ceri had laughed. Saffron enjoyed having her around. She hadn't realised how much she'd missed people of her own age. They'd talked clothes – how bloody awful those in the store were, music – they'd discovered a mutual love of McBusted; a guilty, slightly uncool pleasure – and men they fancied. 'McFly and Busted in the same band – what's not to like!' Ceri had shrieked, pogoing between menswear and ladies shoes to a song leeching from the lousy speakers. Saffron ensured the discussion about men stayed within the realms of fantasy – which film stars, musicians and models they fancied. 'I'd do so-and-so,' Ceri would say, at random intervals, curling her mouth into a leer.

The kettle clicked off.

'So ... how was it?' Rain said, hesitant. Turning to Joe, she added, 'Saffron started a new job today.'

'OK,' Saffron shrugged.

'Just OK?' Rain looked eager, greedy for information, scanning Saffron's face for signs, assuming she would be as unforthcoming as usual.

Saffron wanted to please, as a way of making up, and provided the detail her mother craved. 'I met a girl. She invited me to the Y Castell this evening.'

'That place! What would a couple of young women want in a dive like that? It's full of old men. Isn't The Nag's Head the best place? Or the wine bar? And I think you just said "The The Castle",' Rain said.

Ignoring the comment about her Welsh, Saffron smiled. 'How would you know, Mum? Anyway, that's why Ceri likes it. Says the wine bar is full of "pretentious twats".' She formed quotations marks in the air.

'Who is this Ceri?'

'I really do have to go,' Joe said, moving towards the door, sweeping his hand over the top of his thick brown hair, tracing the kinks.

I bet it looks good long too.

Rain bounded over. 'Thank you SO much for the car, roof, conversation ... everything really.'

There was an awkward pause. How would her mother say goodbye? Her natural impulse would be to kiss him on both cheeks, continental-style. She used to do that with even the most casual acquaintances, other than the majority of her congregation with whom she maintained a degree of formality. But Joe was about to become an employee, of sorts, and that would be plain weird.

Don't kiss him.

Joe spared Rain embarrassment. He held out his hand, and afterwards offered it to Saffron. His skin was rough, a worker's hand, warm, and his grip was steady and confident. Neither too hard, like those men who tried to prove their masculinity by breaking bones with a handshake, nor too limp, which Saffron found fey and off-putting, clichéd though she knew this to be.

'I guess we'll be seeing a lot more of you,' Saffron said.

'I'll be gone before you return from work most days. At least till the evenings grow lighter,' he replied.

Saffron wanted to say: the job's only part-time, I'm around in the mornings. At least until Easter when, according to Mrs Evans, the tourists arrive and business picks up. But she remained silent, lest her disappointment reveal itself.

Convinced he hadn't imagined it, Joe couldn't work out why Saffron was so much warmer towards him. He'd been sure she thought him a prize idiot. Her grip had been firm, but her hand was extremely cold and my God, her fingers were knitting-needle bony. Allegra liked to knit. She was in a craft circle, and it was full of young women, all like her, with shiny hair and toffee-hued skin. They knitted and sewed and made all kinds of crazy, useless things, like dining chair cushions and lavender bags. 'Meeting the granny yoof,' he'd joked.

Joe couldn't imagine Saffron knitting. Not in a million years. He could imagine her doing little domestic and prosaic. She'd held the kettle like a surgical instrument, though he struggled to see her in scrubs, too much colour.

What colour were they these days, green or blue? She'd been wearing black. The shapeless duffel coat again, which she'd not removed before he left.

Inside the cottage, Joe prepared supper. A simple dish of pasta with pesto, he shovelled it into his mouth straight from the saucepan, famished. He'd not bothered with lunch, too engrossed in a game. After supper, he slumped on the flea-bitten sofa he'd dragged from the shed and flicked idly through the free channels. Nothing on except lousy reality shows, full of people he would either despise or pity should he meet them. He picked up his book – a history of World War II – and stared at the pages, but he couldn't concentrate. He knew most of it anyway. He needed to find a new topic. At least till the spring when it might be warm enough to work in the shed. And come spring, the bats would be out again.

Might be nice to join the local bat conservation group ...

No chance. Way too risky.

The saucepan sat on the rug before him. He turned off the television, rolled onto his back, cradled his head in his hands and stared at the cobwebs stretched from beam to beam on the ceiling. No sign of the spider. He, or she, would be waiting, unseen and patient; confident that, trap complete, it was only a matter of time before unsuspecting prey arrived. Joe watched and waited. He was patient too.

Without a fire, and the heat of the food diminishing in his belly, he began to feel cold. He thought about the warmth of the kitchen at the manse, Saffron's smooth, cold fingers. He remembered the photograph of her brother on the kitchen dresser – what was his name again, something Biblical? He looked tall, hair the colour of sand, a solid build, though this might have been an illusion; each arm was stretched round the malnourished form of an African child. Had he inherited his build from their father? Rain was all rolling curves, like the soft hills of the South

Downs, but no way could she be described as heavy. Saffron was tall and slender, elegant, like a poplar. The brother was a missionary, in Burkina Faso, Rain had said with pride. Did Saffron resent her angelic younger brother? The one who did the right thing, followed the way of the Lord, spread his word, or whatever the saying was.

Stop it, you idiot, he said aloud, pushing himself off the sofa. Clean up, do something, stop brooding.

Clearing up took minutes and he was still cold. A walk, he would go for a walk. It was a clear night, the moon was bright, there'd be no need for a torch.

Joe had been a night-walker since childhood. Since the age of eight when the urge to escape the confines of the dormitory was so forceful he couldn't have resisted it if he'd tried. Not that he did try. He'd hated that school, and had sworn if he ever had children of his own no way would he send them away. No matter what. Those places were suffocating and cruel. Churning out future leaders, of the country, of business; emotionally retarded bullies or buffoons, perpetuating an anachronistic, unfair system. Freddy. An image of Freddy at ten years old sprang unbidden, wearing his pretend-serious, pretend grown-up face. *You gave me your homework for me to copy. I will not lie for you. It wouldn't be right, would it?*

Then another image: Freddy all grown up, in wig and gown, sneering, hectoring, lying, spitting at him beneath his breath. *You've only yourself to blame. She was always too good for you, too beautiful, too clever. Justice? This is justice. What did you expect?* He'd hated Freddy; he'd loved him.

Joe stopped, and took a deep breath. He was at the top of the hill, a mountain really. He loved the countryside here. Dramatic and wild, it stirred something inside him. The Celts, that's what I'll read about next, he decided. Warrior kings and queens, and tribes of painted savages.

Fair-skinned redheads.

Shortly after ten he found himself overlooking Coed Mawr; the lower town cradled in the deep crescent of the bay, lights sprinkled before the sea. The straight line of the illuminated pier. He weaved his way down the hillside and through the back streets. At a junction he stopped. Wasn't Y Castell round this corner? He shouldn't pass by the pub; it was inviting trouble. But it was the shortest way and it wasn't as if he intended to go in, sit at the bar and offer to buy her a drink.

He turned his head towards the window as he walked past, but the glass was frosted and grimy, impossible to see through. He shook his head, acknowledging his foolishness, disappointed all the same.

Before he reached the corner, he heard a choking sound, a retching. A drunk was throwing up in the gutter. But there was no sign of anyone. He heard a groaning. He stopped and looked to his right. In an alleyway, he saw a hunched figure. A shadow, female he guessed, stroked the other person's back. The form was familiar. Plumes of smoke swirled from the alley.

'Bloody hell, you weren't kidding when you said you were a lightweight. You need some training, you do. Stick your fingers right down. Only way you'll be sick.'

Female. Welsh. Hadn't Saffron said she was meeting a local girl?

'Saffron?' he said, hesitant, taking a step towards the alley entrance, hands raised in surrender. He didn't want to alarm them. Two women, one virtually incapacitated, in a dark alley at night.

'Wait a moment, lovely.' The Welsh girl's voice again.

'Know her, do you?' The girl stepped from the passageway onto the street, took a drag on her cigarette, flicked it to the ground and stamped on it.

He nodded. 'Her mother. And her. Yes.'

The girl tipped her chin, as if she wasn't sure whether

she believed him or not. One hand resting on her hip, she tapped a foot on the pavement. He wanted to laugh. What unlikely friends they made. A doctor-in-training and a Welsh Vicky Pollard. Saffron de Lacy was full of surprises.

'I rescued her, and her mum's car, from the bottom of Devil's Rise.' He thought mentioning the Standard might prove the veracity of his claim.

'Joe?' Saffron's willowy figure emerged. She appeared elastic, without structure. A rag doll. She dragged a hand across her mouth. 'You got a bottle of water on you?'

'I can get one.' He sprinted into the pub. It was almost empty – an old man sat at the bar staring at a pint of mild; a couple of men, boys really, fiddled with cues beside the pool table. He was served immediately.

Outside, Saffron leant against the wall which bordered the pub's front 'garden': a couple of plastic chairs and a pot containing some kind of shrub. Cigarette butts littered the paving slabs. She took a gulp from the bottle, swilled it round her mouth, turned her back to Joe and the girl and spat it out.

'You think she's a lady at first,' the girl said. 'I'm Ceri. Nice to meet you.'

'Joe.'

'I know; I heard.'

'Everyone calls him JJ,' Saffron said, facing them again, the bottle half empty. She didn't sound drunk. 'Thanks for this; you're a life saver.'

'Except you,' Ceri said to Saffron. 'Very nice to meet you. Mind if I call you Joe an' all?' Ceri offered her hand. 'Walk us home? I could do with a hand.' She jerked her head towards Saffron.

'I'm OK. Really. I'm not that drunk. I've not even been sick.' She looked at Ceri. 'Not for want of trying.'

She turned back to Joe. 'It's the best way to avoid a hangover. Get it out of your system, drink plenty of water, paracetamol before bed.'

'On an empty stomach?' Ceri shrieked.

'Paracetamol does not rot your stomach. It's a myth.'

'I'll walk with you anyway. I'm going that way,' Joe said, stuffing his hands in his jacket pockets to indicate he didn't intend to prop Saffron up, make physical contact in any way.

Ceri dominated the conversation as they walked. She was a right motor-mouth, but Joe understood why Saffron liked her. Earthy, funny, and sharp, she was good company. Ceri's house, or more correctly her mother's house – her parents had divorced when she was thirteen, she'd told them, her dad lived on the other side of town – was nearer than the manse. A squat terrace of three-up-three-downs.

'This is me then,' Ceri said, before throwing her arms round Saffron in an expansive hug. 'Been a great night. Let's do it again soon, yeah?' Ceri stood in front of Joe. 'I'd like to give you a hug an' all, but that would be a bit forward, wouldn't it?'

As he laughed, he heard Saffron blew air through her nose, a small huff of surprise. 'It would, but perhaps you do things differently here,' he said, taking her warm hand and placing a kiss on it.

Ceri touched the spot with her fingers and said, 'I'm never going to wash now.' Then she disappeared through the front door, leaving Joe alone with Saffron.

Chapter Eight

It was the first time Saffron had been alone with Joe since the unfortunate incident at the manse. The whole episode had been embarrassing – crying like that, for God's sake – and to make matters worse, she'd been rude to him. So presumptuous; telling him about Ben, stressing that he'd been her fiancé, as if Joe had made a pass at her, which he hadn't. He'd only been trying to offer comfort.

'I'm OK from here. Thank you. Thank you so much.'

'Your place is on my way. I have to go right past,' he replied, shrugging.

They walked in silence. Saffron's mind raced with possible topics of conversation, each discarded within nanoseconds as boring. Although she hadn't been anywhere near as drunk as Ceri thought, she didn't feel great. Her tolerance levels were low and she really shouldn't have had a second white wine. Certainly not a large one. It would have been so much more sensible to have a soft drink, or at least just a small glass. But it felt so good to be out and about, she'd forgotten herself.

'Do you prefer to be called JJ?' she said, at last.

'Not really. I don't mind either.'

'That's unusual. Most people are precise about their name, aren't they? I hate being called Saff or, worse, Saffy. Only Mum gets away with it.'

'What about your brother?'

'Matthew? Oh, yeah, he calls me Saff too. We don't speak much. Wi-Fi connections aren't great in Burkina Faso. So Mum told you all about him?' They turned into the road that led to the manse.

'I like that you call me Joe,' he said abruptly.

'I'll carry on then,' she said, after a pause. She saw the silhouette of the cross on the chapel roof against the midnight blue sky; she was almost home. But Saffron wasn't ready to face her mother's questions about her evening, the eager-for-good-news glint in her eyes. Rain so wanted Saffron to be happy – and Saffron wanted her mother to be happy, to be well – but it wasn't that simple. And Saffron wasn't ready to say goodbye to Joe; she still hadn't apologised. She searched for the right words.

'Here we are then,' he said, stopping. The chapel car park light clicked on and they both jumped.

'Are you tired?' Saffron said.

His eyes flickered from side to side; she'd confused him.

'I'm going to carry on. Clear my head,' she explained, hoping he'd walk with her.

'By yourself?'

'Why not? It's not like I'm in any danger of being mugged!'

'True.'

'Right. See you then.' She turned away. *Bugger it.*

'Which way are you headed?' he said.

Turning to face him again, breath held, she pointed at random, towards the sea she thought, hoping it was in the direction of his home. She had no idea where he lived. He said nothing, merely nodded, and on they walked.

She recalled him saying that the manse was on his way home. So, this direction was out of his way. She smiled to herself.

Questions rocketed, exploding in her mind like a firework display: how old was he, did he have family, how long had he lived here, where did he go to school, was he, as she suspected, from London too? But she didn't know how to begin; she was so out of practice. She had forgotten the art of conversation, the delicate art of socialising, getting to know people. People of the opposite sex. She'd been a skilled flirt, once upon a time. Before Ben. During Ben, she admitted.

At medical school, she'd flirted outrageously with her classmates, and when they went out on to the wards she'd seduced patients too: men and women alike, and mostly the elderly patients. Those old and wise enough not to misinterpret her words and smiles, actions intended to raise spirits, remind them they were as valued and desirable and important as they'd always been; to remind them that their crumbling bodies and minds were not all that they were, that they were so much more than a condition or an illness; that they were people, first and foremost. Care for the Elderly wasn't a popular area of medicine – the ambitious students wanted to be surgeons – but Saffron had known early on that it was where she wanted to be. She liked older people. Preferred them to younger people most of the time.

'I'm sorry I was rude,' she blurted.

'Were you? When?'

'You know I was.' Why did she sound so clumsy, so gauche?

'Forget it,' he said.

They weaved their way downwards into the lower town. She smelt the salt on the breeze; felt the sticky grasp of the sea; they weren't far. 'I don't believe in forgetting. It's an excuse for repeat offences.'

He laughed. 'You sound like a policeman.'

'Really?' She tucked a lock of hair behind her ear and looked at the ground.

'Though you've too many piercings for a copper.'

She touched the silver hoops running up the curve of her ear. 'I've too many for a doctor. I might have to take some of them out again soon. Mrs Evans, the manager at Wynne's, didn't look like she approved. Only put them in to see if the holes hadn't closed up altogether.'

'When did you have it done?' he asked, glancing her way as they walked, his eyes warm. She liked the flat cap he wore. Old-fashioned and idiosyncratic, it accentuated his youth.

'At thirteen. Mum went mental. It's amazing though, that the holes haven't closed up. I mean, the body has this incredible capacity to heal …'

They'd reached the promenade with its line of trees and ornate lamp posts. The bay spread out before them: the sea dark and slick, like an oil spill. The tide was in and it was high, little of the beach remained uncovered by water. They stopped before the ornate railings at the edge of the promenade, underneath a lamp. The railing paint was chipped and the corners rusty. To their left was the pier, the crumbling ballroom at its tip stretching towards the ocean, like a lover awaiting a sailor's return. Joe removed his cap, folded it into a pocket, and turned up the collar of his jacket, battening himself in against the sea breeze. It wasn't done for effect, she could see that. He lacked artifice, seemed unaware of his beauty, or not to care, and she liked this. Ben had been vain. At first, she'd admired the way he cared for his hair, his skin. He owned more products than she did. Ben fussed and primped; the focus of his attentions commonly his hair, with which he was never satisfied. It was wavy, like Joe's, but rather than letting it do its own thing or cutting it short, Ben was forever cajoling it into the latest must-have style.

'You should finish your training. You said you might not …' His voice trailed away, as if he thought he'd said too much.

Surprised he'd remembered such detail about her life, she gripped the railings and stared at the horizon. The iodine tang of seaweed on the air assaulted her stomach. Cold seeped through the metal and into her bones. Could she go back to London? She couldn't stay here.

He found his voice again. 'It's none of my business.

But we need doctors. People who actually do things, rather than pretending to do things, or bullying others into doing things.' Saffron wondered who he was thinking of. 'The ability to care for people, repair them, is a real skill, a vocation. I don't know you, but something tells me you'll be a good doctor.' He laughed and rubbed his fingers across his brow, shaking his bowed head, 'Jesus, I sound like a right creep ...' He lifted his head and turned from the sea.

She looked at him, his face illuminated by the lamp, one of many dotted along the promenade. They were less than an arm's reach apart. She could see the stubble on his upper lip and chin; she longed to stroke it, to discover if it felt soft, or rough like sandpaper. She longed to touch him, the pull within her as unstoppable as the tide.

She moved towards him, then stood on tiptoes, cupped her palms over the curve of his shoulders, and pressed her mouth against his, eyes tight shut, frightened to discover what his might reveal. Like lovers in aspic, frozen in a moment of passion, neither moved.

His lips felt warm and soft, inviting, but he did not respond. She held him fast; he had not pushed her away. Tears stung beneath her eyelids. She remained glued to him. After long seconds, she felt his hands over hers, prizing them off him. She pulled away and opened her eyes.

To say he was taken aback was an understatement. And not only by the kiss. He'd been surprised when she wanted him to walk with her – she'd not said as much, but he'd understood her meaning. Why did he succumb? Because he'd fancied her from the minute he saw her kicking the car on Devil's Rise. Who wouldn't? She was gorgeous. The stroppy, kick-ass attitude fooled no one, not least him. But he'd meant to stay away, to resist her. All women. He had too much to sort out.

She was lovely. That was a problem. Now this?

I need to be careful. Keep still. Do not move. Oh God, she smells good. Stop. It. Right. Now.

It was a herculean act of restraint, one he congratulated himself on later, peeling her off him. It would have been so easy to respond, to kiss her back, explore her luscious mouth, rake his fingers through her hair, but she was vulnerable, grieving; she'd been drinking. He couldn't bear to see the look of regret on her face next time they met. That would be horrible. She'd think he kissed her out of pity. This was classic rebound behaviour.

But the expression on her face, now – it was unbearable. Her ordinarily pale eyes dark and wide, her lips trembling.

'I smell of alcohol?' she said, clasping a hand over her mouth.

He shook his head, unable to find words.

Would I have cared if you did? Probably not. We're not squeamish like women, not fussy. But then you're probably not squeamish either, are you?

There was nothing sanitised about medicine, caring for the sick, festering, and dying. Not a profession for the faint-hearted. All that pus and shit. A messy business, not one he was sure he could stomach. Seeing people reduced to a mass of flesh and blood and bone. In pain, raw and exposed. It must be exhausting.

'Bugger, bugger, bugger.' She stared at the ground and clasped her hands about her head. 'Sorry, I thought … I don't know what I thought …'

He longed to take her by the hands, fold her in an embrace and tell her how beautiful she was. Instead, he coughed and said, 'You might regret it. Your fiancé …'

'Ben. His name was Ben.' She straightened up, buried her hands in the pockets of her duffel coat. A gusty breeze from the sea whipped her hair across her cheeks, bringing with it a change in the atmosphere once more. 'Let's go back. It's getting late and Rain will worry.'

There she goes again – the child within the woman.

The walk back to the manse was brisk, without the easy conversation of the outward journey. She was brittle, as was he, and Joe was glad when they reached the chapel.

'Here you go,' he said with forced cheerfulness.

'Thank you,' Saffron said.

'For what?'

'Walking me home. Not ... you know ...' she shrugged.

'No problem.'

She turned and walked up the path to the side gate, dragging her feet, the recalcitrant, insecure girl again. He wanted to shout after her: 'It's not you; it's me. It's complicated.' But he knew it would sound crass and empty, like an excuse. He took his cap from his pocket, jammed it down over his head, and turned towards home, his guts heavy, like concrete.

Chapter Nine

The engine juddered into life. To feel the bone-rattling motion was such a comfort to Rain she didn't put the Standard in gear and move off immediately; she sat there, seat belt on, and allowed the smell, sound, and sensation of the car to cloak her. She loved its noisiness. Not for her the gentle purr of modern engines, the sulphurous whiff of a catalytic converter, a dashboard shouting at her with its array of red and orange lights. She stroked the leather encasing the simple dials. How fantastic that the young mechanic had been able to fix her so easily.

She saw her neighbour wandering down the road in the mirror – he was giving the Labrador its morning walk – and determined not to get into yet another conversation about the car, she flicked on the indicator, slipped the car into gear, and pulled away from the kerb. She needed to get a move on anyway, she reminded herself, feeling mean. He waved and she lifted her left hand in response but kept on moving.

The hospital was half an hour's drive away though she wished it was further. It was silly really, this reluctance to go today. She liked Mair Shawcroft; she missed her lively charm at church meetings, her perfume – Lily of the Valley – and her bright white trainers, incongruous with her favoured outfit of elasticated-waist trousers, floral blouse, and a single string of pearls. 'Ever so comfy they are, *bach*,' she'd said of her footwear. Mair's hips were giving up on her and she'd had a replacement on her right side, and Rain wanted to check in on her. She knew Mair would be disappointed if she didn't, though she would never say as much. Mair had never been critical of Rain, unlike some of her flock who seemed only too happy to point out her shortcomings. Or was that Rain imagining things? It was possible. She was over-sensitive. The previous minister, a man, and a local, had been extremely popular.

But JJ had noticed it too.

Why was she so keen to stay in Coed Mawr this morning? JJ was to start work on the roof now that scaffolding shrouded the chapel. Perhaps that was why she didn't want to leave. It would have been nice to greet him on his first proper day, offer him a cup of coffee. Though perhaps it was better she wasn't there. His presence unsettled her. There, she'd admitted it. She waited at the traffic lights, tapping her fingers on the steering wheel.

He seemed like a nice enough man. He is nice, she corrected herself. So what is it? He's handsome, he's polite, well-spoken, thoughtful, obviously well-educated, more than you might think for the average tradesman, she guessed. He'd understood the Latin inscription on the plaque in the church hall. Now that had surprised her. An image of him standing in the chapel, head tipped to the roof, flashed into her mind: his broad back, square shoulders, low-slung jeans only thinly disguising a shapely bottom.

A horn honked and Rain jumped. The lights were green and the driver behind was agitated. Flustered, she crunched the gears, waved an apology to the driver, who was now flashing his headlights at her, and kangaroo-jumped forward before stalling.

For heaven's sake, what on earth was wrong with her? She tried again. Accelerator slammed to the floor, she turned the key. Another screech but the engine didn't catch.

You bloody fool, Rain. You've flooded the old girl's engine.

Another hoot on a horn. Then another. A different one. A queue was forming behind her.

Breathe, breathe. One, two, three, four ...

The man behind honked again and again. She glanced in her mirror. Mistake. He was red-faced and scowling, hammering the palm of his hand against his steering wheel. He was rabid.

Sweat gathered on Rain's brow, under her arms. There was no point trying the engine, it needed time.

The sounds ganged up on her.

Six, seven, eight, nine ...

She rested her head on the wheel. *Eleven, twelve, thirteen ...*

She heard the slamming of a car door and jerked upright. Oh no. He was coming over. Her chest tightened, her heart went into overdrive. Thump, thump, thump, thump, thump. She was going to explode, definitely explode. What a mess of the car she would make. Like a raspberry jelly explosion, with bone-coloured bits of wafer. Hysteria built, her vision began to blur. The man was banging on the window.

Don't look, don't look.

It's a panic attack, a panic attack. You are not dying. You are not dying.

Fourteen, fifteen, sixteen ...

She turned her head and looked at the man. He was shouting, she thought, though she couldn't hear the words. His mouth opened and closed but no sound came. He reminded her of a fairground puppet from her childhood. They frightened her even then, monstrous, ugly things with their permanent smiles, livid red lips, and startled eyes.

Another bang, on the passenger window this time. She turned. A woman. Back to the man. He was still talking. But he didn't look angry this time.

'Are. You. OK? Can you open the door?' he mouthed.

81

Yes, yes, those were the words. He wasn't shouting at her; he wanted to help.

But Rain couldn't move. Instead she gripped the wheel harder.

'Mrs de Lacy. Reverend? Are you OK?' The woman mouthed. 'I'm going to call the manse. Is your daughter at home?'

How does she know my name? Who is she? I don't know her. I know every member of my congregation. Every single one.

The car began to spin, the nausea built, and the darkness gathered. The woman shrank and shrank, sucked away into the black hole. And then: nothing.

When Rain opened her eyes, she saw only the sky, grey and blinding in its fuzziness. Then, a face peering down at her. 'Hello. Mrs de Lacy? You're back. You fainted. Thank goodness for this old car, huh? No central locking.'

It was a paramedic.

'Panic attack. I get them from time to time. I'm OK now.' She went to push herself up, but the medic held her down, gently.

'Give yourself a moment or two.'

'It's freezing down here. My bum's numb.' She managed a smile and he laughed.

Rain drank a mug of strong tea at a café and called the hospital.

'No need to worry, Reverend,' the nurse said, 'Miss Shawcroft won't mind one jot. You drop in whenever you can. No need to worry about visiting hours.'

It hadn't been easy getting rid of the paramedics. What fusspots they were. It was only after she'd pointed at the sky and said, 'I've someone far more powerful than you looking after me,' they'd decided it was all right to leave her. She'd been joking about the big man upstairs.

She ordered another drink, added two heaped spoonfuls of sugar, and stirred. *Miss* Shawcroft. Rain had forgotten that Mair had never married. 'Never met the right man,' she'd said. 'Courted by plenty,' she'd added with a wink, 'but none were quite right.' Rain had asked if she'd ever been tempted to settle for Mr Nearly-Right, to which Mair had replied, 'I'd rather be on my own than with someone who wasn't absolutely in love with me and with whom I wasn't absolutely in love with back. What would be the point?'

Rain found her relatively newly single state hardest to bear when she was out and about. All those empty spaces, nasty little gaps and potholes she fell down on the less than vigilant days – reaching for a hand to hold when strolling down the high street or along the beach, turning to ask for an opinion in a queue, sitting in a café sipping a latte, aware of the pitying, questioning eyes: Is she waiting for someone? Stepping into a pub or a restaurant of an evening was inconceivable – And at church. How had Mair spent a lifetime with all that space around her?

Men marry for someone to come home to; women marry for someone to step out with. She'd read it somewhere and realised, now, it was true.

Rain missed Stephen when she was home, of course she did, but not in the same way. Not the space in the bed – she'd been used to that being empty. No, she missed someone to collapse with onto the sofa. Someone to fold underpants for. Loneliness was a vast space within her. She felt like the castle in *The Sleeping Beauty*, full of creatures who had once lived and laughed, but who now slept, frozen and empty, like death. She waited for someone, something, to hack down the thorns and break the spell, bring her back to life. Only her faith prevented her falling from coma to true death.

Rain sipped at her tea, unable to taste or feel anything but the unpleasant coating of sugar on her teeth. She picked up her phone again.

Not due at Wynne's that day, Saffron was still schlepping about in her pyjamas, moping, when her phone rang. Tempted not to answer, she walked away at first but the ringtone was insistent – she'd chosen it deliberately – and she was compelled to pick up. She figured talking to Rain – anyone – might take her mind off the events of the night before. Nevertheless, she couldn't disguise the irritation in her tone.

'Everything all right, Saffy?'

'Why wouldn't it be?'

Had Rain seen Joe? He wouldn't have said anything, would he? '*Mrs de Lacy, your daughter made a pass at me last night. Could you tell her to keep her paws to herself please?*' Saffron shuddered at the thought.

'No reason, no reason. Probably me, projecting again!' Rain chirped.

Saffron sensed her mother's forced cheeriness. 'What's up, Mum?'

'I've had a bit of an episode ...'

'A bit?'

Saffron was dressed within minutes. She had intended to take a leisurely bath, to wash away her dirtiness, the lingering scent of alcohol and cigarette smoke in her hair, the shame clinging to her flesh, but despite Rain's reassurances that her panic attack had been minor, Saffron wanted to be with her as soon as possible.

Head down as she bolted up the path, Saffron didn't notice the Land Rover until it was too late. She lifted her head at the sound of a car door slamming and almost collided with Joe. Mumbling sorry, swiftly followed by hello, and fiddling with her hair to shield her eyes, she continued down the street. Dismayed to hear footsteps behind her, she stopped and half turned. What was he doing? Was he going to follow her into town?

'Everything OK?' he said.

Without looking at him, she answered that it was, and hoped that would be the end of their conversation, such as it was. She couldn't bear excuses or, worse, attempts to rake over things best forgotten. Conscious of her filthy hair, last night's clothes, and lack of make-up, she dipped her chin further into her coat, peeping at him surreptitiously through strands of hair she'd pulled over her face. She wished she looked her best rather than her worst, to remind him what he'd turned down. He wouldn't get another chance.

'See you later then,' he said, a faint colour discernible on his cheeks.

'Yeah,' she said. Not if I can avoid it, she thought, scuttling off.

But she couldn't rid her mind of the image of his face, those extraordinary eyes contrite and pleading.

'Why don't you come in?' Rain asked. 'Mair won't mind, it'll be more fun than sitting here in the car park –'

'And you won't have to feel guilty if you're there for ages!' Saffron said it kindly, though she meant every word.

Rain smiled, reached over and touched Saffron's hand, which still rested on the gear stick though she'd switched off the engine. 'You've got me there! It'll get cold here too.'

'I can turn the engine on.'

'What a waste of petrol! Think of the environment.'

'I've a coat on.' Saffron looked at her mother, her eyes shining, still watery and a little glazed. It was the way she looked after an episode; it was the same expression people wore after bad news, when operations hadn't been as successful as hoped, when the drugs weren't working, when despite how hard the medical staff had worked there was little else to be done. Saffron wanted to hug her mum and tell her everything would be all right, eventually. But how could she do that when she didn't believe it herself? How could things ever be right again? The best they could hope for was OK.

'I hate hospitals too, Saff. Please.'

Rain gripped Saffron's hand harder, pressing her bones into the plastic handle.

'You've done it before, since … You do want to go back, don't you?'

Saffron sighed, there was no point arguing. She didn't have the energy; her mum was right. She wanted out of Coed Mawr and medicine was her route. She would go back, she would. She pushed aside thoughts of the damage she might inflict; her incompetence. It was the only route she could justify leaving Rain all alone for. She still worried about her mum so much. She could hardly move to London to work in a shop, even one a step up from Wynne's, Selfridges or Harrods for example, though any shop would be a step up from that pathetic excuse for a department store. And what else could she do with her MBBS and nothing else? Work for a multinational pharmaceutical company, pushing drugs? She'd rather slash her wrists and be done with it.

Rain gave one last push. 'And if you're with me, it means I can get away faster. Mair's lovely, but she can talk for England. You have to do it eventually.'

'Don't you mean Wales?' Saffron smiled and retrieved her hand from underneath her mother's grip; it was beginning to hurt. 'OK, but you might have to catch me if I faint.'

Anxiety swept over Rain's face. 'Is that likely? You've seemed so together, so strong, since …'

Saffron shook her head. 'Course not. I was joking.' Not that she could be sure. She hadn't been near a hospital since the hot day last July when she'd walked off the ward, sweating, limbs quivering, heart palpitating. The startled faces of her fellow Foundation Year One students as she threw off her badge and declared, 'I can't do this,' plagued her.

The image mingled with memories of the previous summer, when her world had been crushed as easily as the car against the wall. Concertinaed, trapping her in a role she'd planned to escape.

But Rain was correct, in part. To the outside world Saffron had done a brilliant job of holding it together, of being stoic and brave and just getting on with it all. Until, almost a year afterwards, she'd dropped out of her medical training, becoming angry and withdrawn. And then the meltdown, total collapse. Holding it together like that had acted like a pressure cooker on her emotions. The resulting explosion was messy. Unlike strangers, Rain had seen all this. She'd blocked her mind to it, though. Her mother was so very, very good at deception.

'Mum, I'm not going to pass out. I'm much more worried about you. Let's go.' She flung open the door and leapt out, her gut liquid with nerves. Dawdling would give her time to bottle out. It was important to get inside a hospital again. The first step towards going back. And it wasn't as if she was going in there as a doctor, pretending to be someone who could make everyone better. She was a visitor, nothing more.

She bent down and knocked on the window. Rain was fussing, still sitting in the passenger seat. 'Come on!' Saffron shouted.

Chapter Ten

As it transpired, Saffron didn't have to go on to a ward, and though she'd felt distinctly wobbly she'd made it through the main doors without hesitating. Miss Shawcroft, Mair as she insisted upon being called, was in the day room, sitting in a wheelchair, stuffing a knitted doll. She made them for the children, she said, though Saffron couldn't imagine any child wanting to cuddle up with the creature laid on Mair's expansive lap, one loose, under-stuffed leg dangling over Mair's knee. With large buttons for eyes and a stitched on scowl – surely meant as a smile – it was nightmarish.

Rain retrieved a box of chocolates from her bag. Saffron stared at the doll.

'Ugly old thing, isn't she?' Mair said.

'Don't be silly,' Rain said, offering the gift.

'I like her,' Saffron said.

Mair picked up the doll and shook it. 'She looks like she's had polio, though you're far too young to know what I'm talking about. Now, pull up those chairs, why don't you, *bach*? We'll stay here. Much nicer than the ward.'

Saffron wasn't sure that it was. Mediocre watercolours, of country scenes and coastal ways, hung at odd angles on magnolia walls. The walls were marked and grubby, in desperate need of a fresh coat of paint, and the only decoration other than the awful prints was a bunch of fabric flowers in a chipped vase on the windowsill. The stink of disinfectant underpinned by piss and blood and pain lurked, the unmistakable scent of a hospital and one Saffron barely used to notice.

89

'I know what polio is,' Saffron said.

'Course you do, *bach*. You're a doctor. Though I'll bet you've not seen a kiddie with it?'

'I'm not a doctor yet.'

'But you will be,' Rain added.

Mair shuffled in her seat. 'Why did you leave?'

Rain leant over and touched Mair's arm. 'You remember what I told you?'

Mair blinked, shook her head, as if disappointed with herself, and sighed.

Rain continued, 'Stephen, my husband, wasn't the only one …'

Mair stared at her, blank.

'… in the car.'

'Damn my bloody memory,' Mair said, holding Saffron in her gaze. She shook her head. 'Bugger old age.'

Saffron nodded. 'It can be a bitch at times, no mistaking. Medicine can't solve everything.'

'Saffron!' Rain squealed.

'Now, now, Reverend. If it's OK for me to swear then it's OK for Saffron.'

The old lady was barely recognisable as the pearl-wearing flower arranger Saffron had seen at meetings in the manse and hall with other church members. She leaned over to Saffron and whispered conspiratorially, 'Life's a struggle and full of disappointments. But you'd know all about that, wouldn't you?'

'Sure do.' Saffron smiled.

'It must be hard for you. Not believing and all. Your mam and me, see, we have our Lord, and he's a great comfort. I've not been too lonely, and I'm not afraid of death –'

'You're not there yet,' Rain said, tutting as if Mair were a child.

'For the Kingdom of Heaven awaits me and there I will find peace, I'll find the greatest love of all.' Mair tipped her face to the cracked ceiling and for a moment Saffron thought she might shout, 'Hallelujah'. She wondered what it might be like, waiting a lifetime for a kind of happiness, a promise of bliss. Especially when there were no guarantees. After all, no one had come back and said it – Heaven – was definitely there and just as described. No one had proved it, and proof was everything, for her. She envied her mother's faith at times.

'Mind you, if you find love down here, grab it with both hands,' Mair continued. 'Go for it full throttle, no holding back. Not that there's much talent round these parts.'

Rain choked on her milky tea.

Mair placed her hand over Saffron's, veins roping between swollen knuckles. Her grip was surprisingly firm. 'Nice-looking girl like you, you'll find another. I had offers, but I wasn't pretty like you.'

Saffron took in the older woman. The girl was still discernible beneath the mask of old age.

You might not have been pretty as a young woman, but you were handsome. Strong-featured, a direct, bold gaze. Oodles of sex appeal for those unafraid of it. A woman born into the wrong era. What a waste.

'She will find love again, though it's too soon right now,' Rain said.

Mair tutted. 'Nonsense.' She looked at Saffron and clenched her fists as she said, 'If it comes along, grab it.' She turned to Rain, wagging a finger, the other fist still tight, 'And you.'

It had rained while they were inside the hospital. They walked across the car park in silence, the only sound the slap of boots hitting puddles. The conversation raging inside Rain's head was loud and furious. Saffron loped ahead, her body shapeless in her duffel coat, thin legs accentuated by her heavy boots.

She looks like Minnie Mouse. And to think I was envious of those legs. So long and lean. They look like a goat's. Her kneecaps look swollen. I could snap her in two if I tried.

Rain wondered, momentarily, when was the last time she'd seen her daughter eat.

She ate like a pig the other night – when was it again? All girls eat like gerbils these days. So much pressure, all that Photoshopping and TV shows. Even actresses are thin as reeds. At least the pretty ones are.

Had it been like that when she was a girl? Rain couldn't remember. "Heroin chic" had been all the rage, but she was a mother at twenty-two and had only just completed her theology degree. No time, or money, for messing around with women's magazines and faddy diets, worrying if the latest fashions would fit. Stephen was still a student. It took years to qualify as an architect. It was a wonder they got by at all, let alone Stephen walking away with a first-class degree, as Rain had. Saffron had opened the car and climbed into the driver's seat. Rain reached for the door handle and noted her fleshy hands.

Most people lose weight when they're stressed. It seems to have the opposite effect on me.

She flung open the door.

And what was all that, agreeing with Mair Shawcroft? Another man. Indeed.

She flopped onto the seat, the leather sighing beneath her weight.

I can't imagine even looking at another man!

'Belt up,' Saffron ordered.

'Sorry?' Even to her own ears Rain sounded sharp. Had she been thinking aloud again?

'Fasten your seat belt?' Saff said.

'Why are you huffing?'

'I'm not.' Saffron rammed the key into the ignition and rattled it.

'Be careful! You'll break it!'

'It's always stiff, you know that.' She jiggled it around again, as if to deliberately incense Rain.

'Well, I'm just saying –'

Saffron yanked the key out of the ignition and turned to face Rain. 'Mum, what's wrong? And don't say "nothing".'

Permission granted – invited – Rain opened the sluice gate and out poured all those words and feelings that had been filling her head since Mair had casually told her she must grab any man that came her way.

'How can you possibly believe another man could catch my eye such a short time after your father's passing? I am grieving. Grieving.' She sounded out the last word, emphasising the 'ee' sound, like a teacher giving a phonics lesson, the catch in her voice betraying her. She sucked in air, noisily. 'I'm mourning the loss of the man I love with all my heart, love like I love Jesus, the best man, a man amongst boys, a man who worshipped me, who was good and kind and caring and provided for all of us without complaint, who put his own ambitions on hold so that I might pursue God's calling. Who converted for me. Me! Did I ever tell you that, Saffron? Your father wasn't a believer, not when we first met, but he loved me so much and I knew that he had it in him, that faith, that goodness, that hope, it was just that no one had tapped into it before. No one until me. And our Lord. Oh, he said he went into the church to follow me but he was following Jesus, it was Jesus who led him there, through me, because He sees what no one else can see, what's really, really, inside people. What's inside you, Saffron? You. That you can believe I would find another man attractive. Another man! Unbelievable! Can you so easily cast off Ben's love? Is this what this is all about? I cannot cast off your father so easily.'

Exhausted, she slumped back in the seat, reached over

to the belt and clicked it into the holder without another glance at Saffron, who at least had the good grace to remain silent.

Stunned, Saffron turned and stared at the misty windscreen, eyes burning. She saw nothing but droplets of rain trickling down the pane, gathering others on the way, growing larger, slowing, splintering off, tracing another path to the base of the glass.

Do not cry. Do not give her the satisfaction.

After a couple of seconds, she lifted the key and steered it carefully into place with trembling hands. The car started without fuss.

Saffron loved her father, more than she loved her mother, she'd often thought. He was generous in spirit in a way Rain clearly wanted to be but couldn't quite manage.

I wish it had been her.

Stephen was no saint. She wouldn't have recognised her father from Rain's description had she not known to whom Rain was referring. His lack of saintliness was what she loved about him most. Saffron loved the way he challenged the church, balancing faith with scientific theory, the way he respected her lack of faith. He was greedy – for alcohol, food, life. He gorged on life in all its messiness. He clashed with Matthew no end.

And he loved women. Saffron often thought her father's faith would have been so much stronger had Jesus been female. How Stephen loved women. All women. He teased and flirted outrageously with the old ladies of the Dulwich congregation. How they loved it, their waxy cheeks blooming with colour, returning them to the first flush of youth when their bodies were something to enjoy and be enjoyed rather than a source of discomfort, pain, and disappointment. He flirted with Saffron's friends, plain and pretty alike. He made them feel good about themselves. Not in a creepy way. He was never inappropriate, always charming.

He was useless at most practical matters, despite his brilliance as an architect. DIY was left to Rain to do or organise, and he drove as little as possible despite having a licence, much to Rain's annoyance. The ferrying to and from clubs and parties and events was left to her. He was self-absorbed and distracted much of the time. Late for dinner, forever forgetting parents' evenings, graduation ceremonies. Never helping with the washing-up. Saffron remembered the petty arguments.

No, Stephen was no saint, but Saffron knew she was loved and this was what mattered. Her heart stalled at the thought of him, at his absence.

Why did you die? Why? Why? It should have been me. I wish it had been me.

The grey of the road zoomed into view. Saffron saw the kerb. Too late.

Rain screamed.

The car jolted as it made contact with the pavement, ricocheted off the kerb, and veered into the middle of the road. Saffron pulled on the handbrake. The car came to an abrupt halt.

They sat there, for a second, stunned and breathless. Then they burst into tears, there, in the middle of the road, as oncoming traffic slowed, honked, and tooted at them.

Chapter Eleven

Joe was on the chapel roof when he heard the distinctive chug of the Standard. The damage to the roof was greater than he had thought. Most of it looked like the original, the one built around the mid-nineteenth century. Slates must have been replaced after storms and the small areas of the underlying structure that had received some maintenance were obvious, but the rest looked like the original. Joe was impressed by the craftsmanship. Nothing was built to last like this any more. Despite its simple, functional appearance, without fuss or frills, little in the way of decoration, the chapel had been built with care and love; he wondered how long it had taken. Monuments like St Paul's had taken hundreds of years; the chapel in his school, decades, with its intricate stonework, carvings, and icons. The gargoyles lurking under the eaves, watching the boys trooping in each Sunday morning and waiting to pounce, had terrified him when he'd first arrived. They gave him nightmares. It wasn't long before he realised the creatures to be frightened of were not those made of stone.

Think you're something, don't you? Idiot.

A kick in the shins, in the scrum during rugby. A jab with a sharp pencil at the back of the neck, a shove in the corridor, bathroom, dormitory. Small things in themselves. Together, less so.

He heard a door slam and glanced down, momentarily forgetting that he'd never quite got used to working at heights. He hadn't been lying entirely when he'd told Derek he wasn't keen on it. Dizzy and faintly nauseous, he gripped a scaffolding pole before composing himself. He needed to speak with Rain about the extent of the damage. It would be easier to replace the entire roof than to attempt patching up what remained.

Joe's stomach hadn't entirely recovered when he reached the ground. He took off his hat and wiped his brow, which was slick with perspiration. He noticed the Standard was parked on the road outside the chapel. Strange, usually Rain left it in the car park or outside the manse. He glanced at it again as he closed the chapel gate, turning left towards the manse.

Someone was sitting in the driver's seat, though the engine was silent. He bent forward, intrigued.

It was Saffron, hands on the wheel, arms locked, staring straight ahead, tears streaking her cheeks. Conscious of her trance-like state and not wanting to frighten her, he straightened up, ready to creep away, but she turned her head and looked directly at him – though he wasn't convinced, at first, that she actually saw him. He half-smiled, apologetic, as if he'd been caught, fingers in the biscuit jar, and mouthed, 'Hello.'

Without replying, she continued to stare at him and her tears gained momentum. Her shoulders began to shake and, unable to hold her breath any longer, she gasped, sudden and sharp, clutching at the air, her hands reaching to her face, covering her distress. He opened the door and reached for her shoulder. It trembled beneath his touch.

'I could use a drink. How about you?' he said. He was crouched down, legs apart for balance, and his muscles were beginning to ache. He'd rested there, in the car doorway, one hand on the door handle while she'd cried. He'd asked no questions – until now – and she'd offered no explanation.

She wiped her eyes with the heels of her hands, smudging her make-up, and lifted her head to address him. 'I need several. Jump in.'

'Is that a good idea?'

And she laughed, loud, chin tipped backwards, her mouth so wide he could see all of her teeth. They were perfect, no fillings, no crooked edges, just perfect. Laughing suited her and a surge of pleasure coursed through him. He pushed himself upright, his toes tingling with the beginnings of pins and needles. She clambered out, shrugged her hood up and locked the car. Without speaking they walked away from the chapel, down towards the lower town.

Outside Y Castell Joe paused. They'd been silent the entire way. Joe had lifted an arm occasionally to indicate direction and Saffron had nodded her approval, but they hadn't uttered one word. He noted that it felt comfortable; she wasn't someone who felt the need to fill space with mundane chatter, unlike Allegra. Joe had never been one for small talk.

'It'll be dead in there,' she said. 'Could we sit on the beach instead?'

'Sure. It's a bit early for a drink anyway.'

'Bollocks. We'll go to the offy. Bargain Booze is nearest the sea. It's always rammed with teenagers buying cheap cider and extra strong lager but the selection is sick.' She pulled a face as she said 'sick' and Joe realised she was not only aping the teens she spoke of but making a sly reference to the last time they'd stood outside of Y Castell.

So she has a sense of humour after all. She's mocking herself.

The tide was in so they sat on a promenade bench on the far right-hand side of the bay. As far away from the manse as possible, Joe noted. Saffron led the way, almost skipping along the prom, gaining speed as she went. It was the child in her surfacing again and it made him smile even though he was glad of the seat when she finally stopped. She unscrewed the cap of the wine, raised the bottle, and said, 'Cheers,' before drinking from it.

She passed it to Joe. He shuddered as he swallowed. The wine was tepid. He'd checked the fridge at Bargain Booze but the spotty teen in charge had forgotten to restock it. 'Bleugh. Tasted better lighter fluid,' he gasped as he offered her the bottle.

'What did you expect for £3.99?' But she smiled as she spoke. She'd insisted on paying her way and didn't have much cash; she'd scrabbled half the amount together from loose change at the bottom of her bag, which seemed to contain almost everything a woman could need aside from a purse. 'No point,' she'd said, shrugging, 'can't use my card anyhow. No money until my first wage packet from Wynne's.' Joe didn't own any plastic, not any more, not since he'd moved here.

'This,' he held the wine aloft, 'is almost undrinkable.'

'Are you used to the finer things in life? A delicate Sancerre, or a passable Pinot Grigio?' she said.

He pulled the corners of his mouth downwards. Had he given that much away already? 'Actually, I prefer beer.'

'Figures.'

So maybe she hasn't got me sussed after all.

'Suppose you're used to roughing it, being a student and all.' He took another swig; it didn't taste quite so bad this time and the alcohol running through his veins was taking the edge off the chill in the air. He'd offered his hat to Saffron and though she'd refused, he'd not put it back on, aware it didn't suit him as much as others he owned. He rubbed at the stubble on his chin, wishing he'd shaved.

Saffron took the bottle from him and drank, long and deep. Clouds drifted across the horizon revealing a scarlet sun, low in the sky, its reflection warming the pewter sea. Wet with wine, her lips gleamed as she pulled the bottle away from her mouth.

'Oh, I could use a cigarette right now,' she sighed, gazing over the water.

'No chance.'

She turned and raised her eyebrows.

'So it's true what they say about medics. Heard the rumours at college but was never sure if that's all they were: rumours. There was a medical school next to the university but I never mixed with the doctors,' he said, aware he'd revealed a whole host of detail without thinking. He couldn't explain why, but he trusted her.

'What's true?'

'Work hard, play hard. Doctors drink more than average, smoke more. Live dangerously. Suppose it's being surrounded by death.' He lifted the bottle to the light to see how much was left. Just under half. Christ, they'd necked it quickly. She'd be sick again if he wasn't careful.

'You're not going to believe me – after last night and now this – but I'm not much of a drinker.' She tried to suppress a smirk.

'You're not much of a doctor.' He could hardly believe he'd said that. What an idiot. Did he really want her to hate him?

She laughed again. Her face softened and glowed, and those blue eyes sparkled, and he wanted to make her laugh again and again. But he didn't know any jokes and wasn't often witty. That was a one-off, a fluke.

'Actually,' she said, wagging her finger at him, 'I went into a hospital today. First time in … aw, Gawd knows 'ow long,' she said in a fake cockney accent, voice slurring a little.

'You'll make a medicine woman yet.' He shifted closer. A waft of patchouli blended with the iron tang of the sea.

'You make me sound like a witch.' She slugged from the bottle and he'd meant to suggest she took it easy but she was too fast and he didn't want to sound boring.

He pointed at her hair. 'Why do you dye it?'

'I don't.' She shook her head, pouted, playful and flirtatious. 'I dye the roots to confuse people.'

'Must be a pain.'

'I like pain.'

The urge to kiss her was powerful. She was smart and sexy, and no matter how much he told himself she was messed-up and dangerous and nothing but trouble, he was drawn to her. Impossibly so. At first, he'd thought it was as simple as straightforward lust. It had been a while. She was good-looking and young and around. He'd not been near a woman, let alone touched one, since ... forever. And he'd not wanted to, till now. It had been easy to axe all thoughts of women and sex – OK, easy-ish – but no more. There was something about Saffron he found hard to resist, and it irked him.

She slid along the bench and leant forward. Their faces only centimetres apart. She was definitely drunk. 'I bet you like your women all natural. Blonde and tanned, small and curvy. Feminine. All woman.' His chest tightened at the mention of small women. But desire overrode the discomfort. He ached for a kiss, to be able to turn back the clock to the night before, when they'd leant against the railings a little further along the promenade, staring out to sea. When she'd pressed her lips against his. When he'd frozen, unable to respond.

He could smell the wine on her breath, sweet and warm. What an idiot he'd been. And now she was toying with him, taunting him. He knew it; she knew it. And it was almost fun. Almost. A blurred line between pleasure and pain.

'How did you guess?' he said, looking directly into her eyes.

'I'm psychic. I'm a witch, remember.'

They were so close, only the bottle between their thighs kept them apart. The air was thick with desire and temptation and dropped barriers.

It would be so easy. Lean forward, cup her chin and place your lips on hers.

He was stuck. Unable to move to her or away from her.
'Wicked witch? Or good?'

'Bad. Most definitely bad.'

He moved towards her face.

With only a hair's breadth between them, she leapt to
her feet, snatched the wine, and declared, 'To the beach!'
She raced to the gap in the railings, to the crumbling
concrete steps to the beach, stumbling and weaving. He
staggered after her. It was a bad idea to let her go near the
water, she was drunk, tipsy at best. The tide had retreated
but the water was perilously close. A gust of wind seared
his ears.

At the bottom of the shingle-covered steps he caught
her arm. She leaned away from him and they were trapped
in a rope-free tug-of-war. 'It's not safe,' he cried, the wind
whisking his words out to sea.

'Live dangerously, you said,' she laughed, her hair
swept across her cheeks, blown up off her forehead,
tendrils silhouetted against the horizon. Her forehead was
smooth and broad. Aristocratic. Like a princess.

And that was it. He propelled her, hard, towards him,
and kissed her salty, wine-sweet lips.

Live dangerously, he thought, waiting for the slap.

It never came.

Instead she folded into him as he did into her, even the
sound of the waves fading to nothing as he lost all sense of
time and place. Everything except this moment, right here,
right now, the taste and smell and feel of her.

Her lips parted and she kissed his top lip, his bottom lip,
slipping a hand round his neck, raking her fingers through
his thick hair. He wrapped an arm round her waist and
they pressed each other into their bones. A wooden toggle
on her coat jabbed into her hip bone. The wine bottle
thumped against her thigh.

He pulled away suddenly. Saffron longed to grab him

by the collar and heave him back, but she was disorientated, unsteady on the shingle and dizzy with wine and desire. She toppled. He caught her with both hands, steadying her, before releasing her. She rested against the wall and closed her eyes, trying to control her breathing. Too embarrassed to look at him. Why had he kissed her and then pushed her away? Did her breath stink? Was she a useless kisser? The silence that had felt so comfortable earlier was now unbearable.

'What did I do?' she said.

'I'm sorry,' he said.

She opened her eyes – a chink – and gazed at her feet. She could see his boots in her peripheral vision, round-toed, steel-capped no doubt, the hem of his jeans folding on the brown leather. He wore his jeans low on the hip, she recalled, remembering the shape of him from the back – the slim hips and shapely backside that even a pair of baggy jeans couldn't disguise. Disappointment strangled her; she could not speak.

'I shouldn't have done that. It's taking advantage. You've necked that wine, in a short space of time. Even if you're not actually pissed, your judgement isn't as it should be.' He paused, hoping for a response, she imagined. Well, she wasn't going to give him one. He was wrong.

He tried again. 'I'd be lying if I said I'd not be happy with a rebound kiss … whatever … I would. But in the end, I don't think you'd be happy. It would make you miserable.'

She looked at him, the clawing in her belly stealing throughout her body, scratching away at muscle, tendons, sinew, nerves. 'So you're doing this for me? How very gentlemanly. How very generous and selfless. How do you know I wouldn't be grateful for a pity shag? Sorry, kiss.' She saw him flinch and wanted to retract her vulgar, unkind words. But how could she? How could she explain that she liked him, *really* liked him? She'd been unfriendly almost every time they'd seen each other.

How could she explain that she wasn't grieving; at least not in the way everyone thought she was?

Chapter Twelve

Ben wasn't the love of Saffron's life. She had been infatuated, for a time, flattered, and she certainly loved him, but not in the way she should if she was to spend the rest of her life with him. She had never been *in* love with him and while they might have spent a long and superficially contented life together, she wasn't prepared to settle for that. Not at twenty-something, maybe not ever. This uncomfortable truth had revealed itself only weeks before the accident, when, with finals out of the way, wedding preparations had gathered pace and a distant event with a mirage-like quality was fast becoming a reality. It was early June, and the wedding was booked for late July, before Saffron was to begin her foundation year.

As a scientist and pragmatist, she knew Ben was a perfect mate. He was healthy and strong and intelligent; he radiated alpha-maleness. Good hunter, good provider, good father. His gene pool was faultless, aside for a lack of faith, Rain had said; only half-joking, Saffron suspected. All her friends were attracted to him and men admired him. Her parents, especially Rain, adored him. Both rational and level-headed, Ben and Saffron rarely raised their voices at each other, let alone argued. Theirs was a perfectly balanced, harmonious relationship.

Doubts first stole in during the choosing of the venue for the reception. Ben had suggested a room above a pub. It was cheap and convenient, and they were running out of time. But Rain had spoken with a friend from church, a congregation member with an enormous house on the common in Dulwich. This friend had offered her garden, and marquee, and when, under duress, Saffron and Ben had gone to take a look, the daughter was there with photographs of her own wedding reception held in the garden. It was decorated like a fairy glade and afterwards, as they wandered back to the station, Ben had mocked the overblown romanticism of the affair. 'Jesus, it looked like something a glamour model would have gone for! And that dress! Fuck! She looked like she'd stepped into a candyfloss factory explosion. And what a total knob-end in that top hat and tails!'

Saffron sniggered in agreement, but inside she'd been thinking about the joy in the woman's face when she'd shared the photographs, the love in her voice as she spoke of the day, her husband, the arguments they'd had over the colour of the flowers and which drinks to serve. Saffron couldn't imagine ever feeling the same way about her and Ben's day, feeling as much love for Ben as this woman did for her husband. She radiated it, even just looking at photos of the man. Saffron had thought the image of someone radiating love clichéd and unbelievable, but there it was. Saffron had turned to gaze at Ben. He was a prime specimen and Saffron observed him in much the same detached manner she would a jar in a science lab, or a body on an operating table.

Over the weeks, these feelings grew. She began to notice how friends behaved with boyfriends and lovers. How husbands and wives reacted to news of their loved ones, good and bad, in the hospital. She questioned if she had ever felt such depth of emotion for Ben, and concluded that she hadn't. They were a habit. At almost twenty-three? Anxiety gained purchase. She spoke with Rain, obliquely, about her concerns. 'Pre-wedding jitters, that's all, Saffy. We all get them,' her mother had said. But Saffron felt sure it wasn't and she could ignore it no longer.

They'd been invited to a party, out in the sticks –

somewhere in Kent – and the last train was the thirty-three minutes past eleven. During a visit home, Saffron had mentioned their dilemma. Stephen offered to collect them but Saffron was insistent. 'Dad, it's miles. It's a Saturday night. It might be late, and you'll have to drive us up to my place and then back here. We'll take Ben's car. I'll drive. No problem.'

'I don't mind, Saff. Do anything for my favourite daughter.'

'Your only daughter.'

She hadn't planned to speak with Ben that night, but there was a fight, in the garden, boyfriend and girlfriend, a couple she didn't know. They went for each other like a pair of wild cats. Screaming, shouting. Like most people Saffron left them to it and went inside for another orange juice. She was sick to death of the stuff but tap water was the only alternative. She searched for Ben who she'd not seen in a while. Sure he wasn't inside, she pulled on her cardigan and drifted out to the garden again. All was quiet.

The garden was huge, more like the grounds of a stately home than someone's house. She plodded across the lawn, her uncomfortable heels sinking into the spongy grass (why on earth had she worn heels? Had Ben insisted? He hated her boots) and walked through the arched doorway in the wall, past raised vegetable beds, and towards what she had been told was the pond. 'More like a lake,' Ben had whispered in her ear.

There was no one at the pond – lake. Ben had been right. But there was a summer house on the far side and a faint light flickered through the windows. Intrigued, Saffron crossed the wooden bridge which bisected the water at its narrowest point. There was someone in the summer house, she was sure. As she came near, she recognised the sounds of a couple making out and unable to walk away, spellbound, she sat on the damp grass and listened as their cries ricocheted through the air.

109

Afterwards, they said each other's name in breathless, tender huffs. It was the warring couple and their lovemaking was as intense and ardent as their fighting had been. The strength of feeling between the unknown lovers sent Saffron reeling. Crying, she pushed herself up and walked back to the house.

Ben found her in the kitchen where she was drinking a glass of punch. Nauseous but resolute, she said, 'We need to talk.' Noting the seriousness of her tone, he grabbed a bottle of wine from the upright fridge – there were dozens in there – and they headed out to the garden, finding a bench in a quiet spot by the vegetables.

Shaking, mouth dry, guts clenching and unclenching so hard she thought she might empty the contents of her stomach, Saffron cried her way through an explanation, an honest exploration of her feelings.

Ben listened quietly until she had finished, holding her hands in his, squeezing them from time to time, encouraging, reassuring. He was such a decent man.

His relief was palpable. 'I thought it was just me. That this was the way it was. I've nothing to measure it against. My mother and father are hardly role models.' His voice cracked.

'Mine are, I guess. But unless you've felt it yourself, it's still all academic, isn't it?' Saffron snuffled, wiping her nose on the sleeve of her cardigan.

'Do you think it exists? True love?'

'Who knows? But there has to be more, doesn't there? We're like an old married couple, or brother and sister, stuck in a rut. We're a habit and we're only twenty-three.' She smiled now. 'You scared?'

'You're joking! Think of all the women I can fuck! Scared shitless of telling people though. Mother will be so disappointed and Dad will be furious. The wanker.' His laughter became tears. It was the first time she'd ever seen him cry.

Her stomach tightened. 'I've no idea how to tell Mum and Dad. They'll be so upset. They'll miss you. You're like another son to them.'

They hugged each other. 'We'll stay friends, Saff.'

'Defo! No change there.'

They talked and talked. And in a strange way, Saffron enjoyed it. It was the first time they'd shared deep, heartfelt emotions. It was a heady cocktail of relief, fear of the unknown, and sadness at the pain and disappointment they would visit on others. She would miss him, of course. It was only when Ben went to refill her glass she realised how much they'd drunk. No way could either of them drive.

'Damn,' Saffron said. 'We'll have to sleep in the car, drive back in the morning.'

'We can't. I've a match first thing. It's past two, we won't be legal to drive until mid-morning at the earliest.'

'It's a Sunday league.'

'It's important. Last game of the season. We'll get a cab.'

'But that'll cost loads. I'm totally skint and we'll lose so much money what with cancelling everything,' she wailed, guilt surging through her again. Stephen and Rain had already forked out a considerable amount of money on the wedding, money which might be hard to recoup in full. And she owed them so much already. Everything. Medical school didn't come cheap.

Ben groaned. 'Fuck. Forgot about that. Another thing for Dad to be mad about, the tight bastard.'

'I'll call my dad. He offered.'

'You can't. Look at the time.'

'I'll call him at five thirty. They're always up with the birds. He'll be here before seven. There are no trains on a Sunday so we really have no choice. We'll have to collect the car on Monday. What a cock-up.'

'Rather you than me,' Ben shrugged. 'Might as well go

and grab a coffee as we're not going to get any sleep.'

Saffron didn't think she'd have slept regardless. She wouldn't relax until she had broken the news of the break-up to her parents. She would tell them as soon as Sunday service was done.

'So you called your dad and he came to fetch you because you'd had too much wine to drive?' They sat on the shingle, backs resting against the promenade wall. It was falling into place: her anger, her grief, her guilt.

'I texted him, right then. Of course, I didn't, like, expect him to answer. I thought he'd be asleep, pick up in the morning.' Tears swam in Saffron's eyes. Joe wanted to tell her to stop. She didn't have to explain. He got it. It was too painful, to say it, to listen to it. But she continued. 'He turned up sometime between three and four. He looked tired. And he'd never been keen on driving; Mum did most of it. They often joked it was a miracle he'd passed his test. It should have been me behind the wheel. He wasn't used to windy country roads, and he was going too fast. Something was bugging him, I felt sure.'

'Were you hurt?' Joe asked.

She didn't look at him; she continued to stare at the horizon. 'Ben was killed outright. Wouldn't have felt a thing, the doctor said, though how he could have known is a mystery. Not like anyone's come back and filled us in. I didn't say that to Mum, though I think she knew. Me?' She turned to Joe. 'A few cuts, some bruises, nothing. Now that was a kind of miracle. A sick, stupid joke. Mum couldn't explain how her precious God had taken the lives of two innocents, when the guilty one, me, the one who'd done wrong, walked away unharmed. What kind of a God is that? It's bollocks, all bollocks!' She spat the last sentence, eyes wide, red and bloodshot.

'You've been punished. You're suffering.'

She frowned.

'You're trapped. You've trapped yourself. You didn't tell anyone that you and Ben split. You've played the grieving almost-wife. You can't move on because you're supposed to have lost the love of your life. You feel guilty, responsible. And on top of that you are grieving the loss of your father and a man, Ben, for whom you felt love, whether you were *in* love with him or not. You must miss him.'

'I do.'

'It's an enormous loss. Stop with being so hard on yourself.' He took her hand, pushed his thumb gently down the grooves between the bones from knuckle to wrist, something his nanny used to do when he was a child. It was such a comfort to him then; it still was. He did it to himself even now, revealing the lost boy in need of love and comfort.

'What are these bones called?' he asked.

'Metacarpals – why?'

'They feel so delicate, so fragile. Yet they're incredibly strong. They work hard.'

'Like all of the body.' She stared at him and he longed to kiss her. She turned away and stared at the floor. She gasped, suddenly, began to shake. 'I prayed on the roadside. Before I made the call,' she said, her voice quiet, cracking.

Confused, he shook his head.

'I've not told you the worst of it.' Her chest heaved. 'Ben died instantly, but Dad didn't.'

She paused.

'Nothing can be worse than watching a loved one die,' he said.

'It can. After I climbed out of the car, I expected to see them doing the same. I was in shock. When they didn't, I returned to the upturned car. Ben was nearest and easiest to reach. I felt for a pulse. Nothing. He looked fine. There wasn't even much blood on him. It looked as if his neck

113

was broken.' She glanced at her hand and back at Joe. 'I held Dad's hand. There was a groan. That was when I realised he was alive. I told him everything would be OK, that I'd call for help and that he was to hold on in there. I didn't know if he could even hear me. As if he could do anything else. We say the stupidest things, under stress. I was screaming, not talking. It was a miracle the person on the other end of the phone understood me at all. It took ages for her – I think it was a her – to get all the details. I was hysterical. And while I waited for the ambulance, I prayed. I didn't do anything I'd been trained to do. I was useless. I prayed to a God I'd spent half my life denying existed. Arguing with Mum and Dad about their stupid beliefs. Perhaps that's why my prayers weren't answered.'

'You did the right thing. You called for help. Stop beating yourself up,' Joe said.

'But that's the point. I didn't. I didn't do the right thing; I didn't *do* anything. I sat there. Paralysed. Praying.' Her voice grew louder and louder. 'When the paramedics pitched up, he'd stopped breathing. For how long, I had no idea. I'd not checked his pulse, not given CPR. Basic stuff. Basic.

'The paramedics shocked him, got him breathing again, his heart pumping. They didn't know me, they whispered between themselves, medical terms. But I heard. I knew. Brain damage. "If he survives, who knows what the damage will be?" That was the implication. By then, I was in gear. But it was too late, way, way too late.

'At the hospital they took Dad to theatre. Internal bleeding, severe. They removed his spleen, a kidney. But it was the bleeding on the brain that got him. They did their best, they said. More than I'd done. I felt so ashamed. I *feel* so ashamed. There was barely a scratch on me.' She laughed at this point, bitterly. 'Just like in the movies. We can do so many amazing things. We have all these gizmos and knowledge and expertise. We can virtually rebuild people. But the first few minutes are crucial. Crucial. It's the first thing you learn. Nothing could save my dad, my lovely dad. He died before Mum even got to the hospital. I think she hates me for that.'

'What?'

'Being with him when he died. It should have been her.'

'I'm sure she doesn't.'

Saffron shivered. 'Whatever. She'd hate me if she knew the truth. I hate me.'

'She wouldn't and nor should you. We all make mistakes.'

The proprietor of the first guest house looked askance when Joe asked if they were serving afternoon tea, but the second was welcoming. A plump woman ushered them into the front room and sat them at a table in the bay window. 'Now there's a lovely view,' she said, arms folded across a generous bust. Saffron didn't know what she was talking about – it was almost dark. Fifteen minutes later the landlady presented them with china cups of milky coffee and a selection of cakes and buns from a wheeled trolley. The coffee was surprisingly delicious and Saffron returned to something almost approaching normal, though the beginnings of a headache pulsed at the base of her skull.

It had felt good to admit she hadn't loved Ben in the way she should have, while simultaneously acknowledging her grief at his death. One of her great fears about the breakup was that people would blame her, cast her in the role of scarlet woman. Before the party, in her darkest moments, she'd dreamt about Ben dying. She'd imagined how easy it would be that way; she was such an emotional coward. She'd not have to break his heart, she'd get shedloads of sympathy, and she'd be free. It was a win-win situation. What a bitch she was.

The reality was light years away from her fantasies and she was tormented by the thought she'd brought all this on herself, it was all her fault. Be careful what you wish for; it was something her dad used to say.

Dad. Sharing her darkest secret had been even more of a relief. All those clichés about burdens were true after all. Perhaps Joe was right, perhaps her inaction at the scene had had no impact. He might have only just stopped breathing. She'd been told that surgeons were advised against operating on friends and relatives. Perhaps no one would have blamed her. Joe didn't seem to hate her.

'You not having one?' he said, ramming another fondant fancy into his mouth. It was gone in a single bite.

She shook her head. 'Don't want to spoil supper.'

Joe leant forward conspiratorially and whispered. 'She went out and bought these specially. Wasn't expecting customers and we pitch up. It would be rude not to.' He popped a mini-muffin into his mouth. She took a cake and bit into it. It tasted good. 'You need to tell Rain. About Ben and you. Not the other thing,' Joe said.

'Why? It won't change anything and it will hurt her.'

'Because it's honest and you'll feel better. She'll understand where you're coming from.'

'And I can go out with you and she won't be mad?'

He sighed. 'That's not what I meant.'

She wished that it was.

'I shouldn't have kissed you. I could blame it on the wine but that would be pathetic,' he said after a pause.

'We're even. Forget it.' Why was she saying this? She didn't want to forget it; she didn't want him to forget it.

He drained his cup – it looked tiny in his hands – and stood up. 'Right. Let's get you back. Rain will worry.'

'I'll go back alone, thanks.'

'Let me pay the bill and we can walk back together. We're headed in the same direction – it would be crazy not to. And weird. We'd have to make an effort to take different routes and one involves a much harder climb.' He smiled. 'At least part of the way.'

'OK. But we part well before the manse.'

'Rain doesn't approve?'

'It's not that. She likes you. It's just ...'

'I get it.' He dug his hand into his front pocket and pulled out a twenty-pound note.

'I owe you,' she said, 'I feel like my conscience has been saved in some way. Thank you.'

'You owe me nothing.' And he turned and ambled towards the small reception. She noticed the beginnings of a tattoo poking out from the collar of his jumper as he tugged on his jacket and wondered what it might reveal.

Chapter Thirteen

Rain stared at the clouds, watching them scud across the pale blue expanse. It looked like a spring sky but the air was raw. She shivered and wrapped her cardigan across her chest, and tipped her head upwards once more. This time, she noticed the remains of the purlins bisecting the sky, interrupting her view, and shifted on the pew. Golly, no wonder people shuffled in their seats during a service, the wood was unforgiving, even for fleshy backsides. She pledged to get more armchairs for comfort's sake; her congregation was still elderly, despite her best efforts to attract younger people.

With the slates off and only part of the wooden skeleton remaining, the interior of the chapel looked very different. The place was so exposed, like a woman without her make-up. Light swept down the length of the aisle, flooded nooks and crannies, baring cracks and chips and dirt which had lurked unnoticed in the shadows for decades. The organ pipes were yellowed, like pub walls in the days before the smoking ban. The whole place needed a facelift, not just the roof.

Bit like me, thought Rain, as she pushed herself up. She felt so very, very heavy, so weary and listless, weighed down by something she sensed but couldn't identify. The feeling had grown since the visit to see Mair Shawcroft. She'd considered visiting her GP, but he would only mumble and nod and write out another prescription for diazepam. And she was through with that. The drug seemed to carve out her centre, so while superficially she appeared unaltered, she was fundamentally different –

hollow. And if she lost her core, she lost her connection to God and without this connection she was rootless, vulnerable to withering and a spiritual death.

She couldn't recall why she'd come into the chapel. Comfort? Reassurance? And if so, why? Her memory failed her at times. Perhaps she'd wanted only to see what it was like without its roof? JJ's apprentice, a boy called Tyson – wasn't that a dog's name? – a Scouser judging by his accent, had knocked on the manse door the previous evening to check there was no service or meeting planned the following day.

'The rest of the roof's coming off and it'll be brass monkeys in there,' he'd said, hands on hips, staring at her breasts before lifting his eyes to hers. It took considerable effort to hold his shamelessly appreciative gaze, to brazen it out.

When JJ had explained that his boss was sending over an apprentice to help with the contract, Rain had expected a teenager with limited social skills and low self-esteem. Instead, she'd been greeted by Tyson: almost twenty-one and confident bordering on cocky, with an air of the predator about him. Reassuring herself it was probably all front, she was nicer than ever, though she made an effort to be less flirtatious than usual, and thanked God her congregation had an average age of sixty-plus. They could admire his good looks – and JJ's – without any danger of the feelings being reciprocated, hearts being broken, and work suffering as a result. She knew, from Stephen's hilarious reports of the numerous office romances at the council offices where he'd worked as an architect, the detrimental effect on productivity of love affairs. She wanted the work on the chapel to be completed as soon as possible. All this testosterone was playing havoc with hers and Saffron's moods. She'd caught Tyson leering at Saffron, but she seemed to want to steer clear of him. Something else to thank God for.

Before she could take hold of the handle, the chapel door swung open. She stepped back quickly to avoid being hit by the door and gasped.

Another workman stood before her. 'Oh, I'm so sorry. Had no idea you were there, Reverend,' he said with a Welsh lilt, extending his hand.

Delighted by his good manners, Rain took his hand and shook it. 'You must be the new ... assistant. Nice to meet you.'

He laughed. 'No need to be so polite. I'm the labourer. Call a spade. I won't be offended.'

Rain took another step back to let him in. He took off his cap as he came into the chapel lobby, holding it with both hands in front of him. This small act of old-fashioned respect pleased Rain more than she could have imagined. She looked at him again. A shock of thick grey hair framed a lived-in face. 'Call me Rain. You are?'

'Eifion. Eifion Parry.'

He was of average height, maybe five feet nine, wiry. And old for a labourer, Rain thought. Weren't they usually strapping lads who'd left school without any GCSEs? He must have left school when the exams were still called O levels. He remained in front of her and Rain realised she was blocking his access. 'Sorry, sorry,' she said, stepping aside, waving him through, 'come in.'

'I need to get up,' he said pointing at the sky. 'Help Tyson from this side.'

'Rightie-ho. I'll leave you to it.' She walked past and turned again before she went through the open door. He was waiting for her to leave before making a move. 'Are you local?' she said.

He nodded.

'I'm glad. The last boy was hopeless. Forever late, not turning up. Drove JJ round the twist. Had too far to travel, he said.'

'That's what I heard,' Eifion replied politely. 'I believe

121

I have you to thank for the work. Very grateful, I am. Not much of it round here, as I'm sure you know. Especially at this time of year. Might be more if your pier campaign is successful.'

'Not at all. I'm sure you got the job on merit. All I said to JJ was perhaps the boss might be better off looking for someone nearby.'

'Well, it did the trick and I'm grateful.'

'And it's not *my* campaign. The church is one group of many wanting to restore the ballroom and not have it knocked down to build some ghastly gambling den full of tat! You should get involved.'

'To be honest, I can't believe the building's not listed.'

'Indeed.'

'I hear you grew up round here yourself.'

'Not far.'

'You'd never know from your accent.'

'University down south cured me of it.' She checked herself. 'Sorry, that sounded shockingly rude. It's a lovely accent. Warm, friendly. I honestly wish I'd not lost mine.'

'Better than a Brummie one, at least, eh?' He smiled; he was teasing, and she smiled back. 'I'd best get on,' he continued, 'otherwise I might find I get the sack too. Nice to meet you.'

'And you.' She pulled the door behind her and trotted down the path, keen to reach the warmth of the manse kitchen, smiling to herself all the way.

Tyson irritated Joe. He radiated a powerful energy, one which Joe identified as competitive. Tyson was a great carpenter, better than Joe really, even though he hadn't yet completed his NVQ3. But it wasn't that. Joe admired Tyson's skill, his attention to detail, his speed. And boy, was he fast. No, it wasn't that. It wasn't even the crude comments he made about Saffron – and Rain. Joe knew from the looks Saffron gave Tyson that she considered him an idiot. It wasn't even the way Tyson mocked Joe as older and slower when they clambered over the roof, Tyson virtually skipping over the wet slates, Joe on all fours creeping up the pitch. 'Come on, old man,' he said, every time. Thirty was hardly old, though Joe had to admit that at twenty-one he'd considered anyone over twenty-five ancient.

What bugged Joe was the way Tyson forced himself on to people. He didn't respect privacy or distance; he was a space invader. He imposed, took a hold and wouldn't let go. He was an energy drain. And this quality reminded Joe of Freddy, despite the obvious differences between the two men. There had always been something of the leech about Freddy; he'd suck you dry, if you let him.

You need to get a grip. Tyson is not Freddy. He is a force of nature, that's all. You're probably jealous, you stupid bastard.

Joe climbed the stairs to the bathroom, his boots thumping on the bare boards. He ached all over. Still young or not, his body rebelled against the rigours of the work on the chapel roof. How on earth Eifion managed it, Joe had no idea. He was middle-aged. Joe turned on the taps and waited for the brownish sludgy water to run clear.

He liked Eifion. He was polite, a hard worker, kept himself to himself. Joe knew almost nothing about him, except that he ran a rock shop on the pier during the summer months and struggled to find work during the winter. Rain spoke highly of Eifion, though Rain spoke highly of everyone. She was always kind, looking for the best in others. He could do with a bit more of that himself, minus the hopeless naivety Rain sometimes demonstrated.

Tyson has a certain charisma, just as Freddy had.

Probably still has, Joe corrected himself. You need charisma and charm to control people the way Freddy did, to persuade them, manipulate them.

Their schoolmasters had fallen under his spell, not

reprimanding him for the open top button of his shirt, the stunted length of his tie, the against-regulations belt. Joe smiled at the memory; he couldn't help himself. Like many others, he'd tried to ape Freddy's style, mimic his confident, almost-but-not-quite belligerent tone, but he'd failed, taking the rap from master after master. Freddy had been like the Artful Dodger, with a clean face and aristocratic bearing, breaking all the rules but lovable all the same.

Thinking of Freddy, like this, Joe's stomach muscles clenched. He held his hand under the tap; the water was very hot, and Joe allowed it to sear into his flesh. It was an attempt to take his mind off the rage building inside him. How cruel Freddy had been. The courage it had taken for a young Joe to report the relentless bullying ...

'Take a seat, boys,' the head commanded.

The leather was cold against Joe's bare thighs; the seat so deep his feet couldn't reach the floor; his legs dangled like a toddler's over the edge. Freddy was tall for his age, well-built, and his feet rested on the polished floor with ease.

'So ...' the head continued, 'What is to be done with you two chaps?' He smiled at Joe and then at Freddy, who returned the grin. Joe's mouth was set, his teeth clenched. He felt the need to urinate.

'We need to repair the damage, sir,' Freddy pronounced. 'I've been a bit of a rotter and I am truly very sorry.' He reached across and touched Joe's hand, which gripped the expansive armrest. 'I've been having a tricky time, sir, what with Grandpa passing on and my father's promotion and not seeing him so much.' He looked at Joe, who wondered why Freddy was talking like that, all funny, using words that you only read in books. But it was true: life must have been difficult for Freddy. Joe knew that grief did strange things to people.

'And what would you suggest, Freddy?' the head said. 'Perhaps some special time together, playing games, eh? How about here in my office for a time and then we'll move you outside. Build trust.' He glanced at the phone console on his desk – one of the lights on it was flashing. 'Pretty sure you two will become firm friends once you get to know each other properly.'

At the head's instruction they shook hands, and in the weeks that followed they played Connect Four, draughts and chess in the musty-smelling office, tennis and croquet outside.

Croquet was new to Joe, but he showed natural flair – or beginner's luck – and when it looked as if he might take the game for the second time, his stomach turned like a fairground ride. He fluffed the next shot, and the next.

'You're doing that deliberately!' Freddy said, leaning on his mallet.

'I'm not.' Joe felt his cheeks redden.

'Don't you want to win?'

Yes and no.

'Croquet's –' they said in unison.

'Not really my thing,' Freddy continued, smiling. 'You're good at it.'

'Thank you,' Joe whispered. 'It's not my favourite game. Bit sissy.'

They both laughed – really laughed, with each other rather than at each other. Abandoning the stupid game, they kicked stones around the gravel path and raced up on the field. And as the head had predicted, friendship followed.

Joe clenched his fist, pressing his nails into his palms. The skin on the back of his hands turned a livid red. He watched the bubbles frothing towards the taps before turning on the cold water. He peeled his work clothes off, and shook from his mind an image of Freddy on his knees,

125

begging for mercy. It was wishful thinking.

At the side of the tub lay two books about Welsh history. Recent purchases from the ramshackle bookshop on the main drag in Lower Coed Mawr. They had looked interesting enough, but he wasn't in the mood this evening. He clambered into the metal tub, with its chipped enamel, leaving the books on the floor.

Submerged in the warm, comforting water, Joe allowed his mind to drift. How was he to get back at Freddy? Despite Simon's digging, there was no sign of malpractice. Damn. He racked his brain but he was drawn back to events earlier in the day, back to Saffron.

He'd shown Tyson his haul from the bookshop and when he'd pulled out his booty, Tyson had scratched his head and declared that he'd never read a book in his life.

'What, *never*?' Joe had replied, astonished. 'Not, like, at school even?'

'Wasn't there much. Saggin' most of the time.'

After Tyson had explained that sagging was Scouse slang for playing truant, Joe had admitted a begrudging respect for Tyson's honesty. He'd wondered if Tyson *could* read, but didn't dare ask. As they'd been talking, Saffron appeared from the manse – on her way to the afternoon shift at Wynne's, Joe supposed.

'Bet she reads lots of books,' Tyson had said, tipping his head.

'How can you tell?'

Tyson had shrugged. 'Dunno. She looks clever. Her looks say: clever, beautiful bird. You know how sometimes you see a bird and she's fit and all that, but you just know she's thick? Well, she's, like, the opposite of that.'

Tyson mightn't read books but he isn't completely daft. Saffron is most definitely a bright woman.

Saffron. Beautiful, lovely Saffron.

He shook his head under the bath water, allowing it to

pour into his ears, blocking out the rest of the world. It had been wrong to kiss her. What had possessed him? But she'd tasted so good; she'd tasted so *right*. Their mouths had moulded together like a pair of shoes in a box. Perfect.

He raked his fingers through his hair, digging his nails into his scalp as he went, sending shivers down his spine. He longed to run his fingers through her hair, to lift it from the back of her neck, exposing the delicate skin, to kiss it, caress it. Move from the soft, hidden skin to her earlobes, cheeks, and eyelids.

He sat upright, flinging droplets of soapy water across the bathroom. Steam rose from his body – there was no central heating in the cottage and the electric fire on the wall had only one bar glowing orange. It gave out barely any heat at all.

Stop thinking about her. Stop it. Stop it now.

He pulled his knees to his chest and hugged his legs, the sharp air pricking at his wet skin. It occurred to him that he hadn't thought of Allegra all day. When was the last time he'd thought of her? Days ago.

Amazing. Incredible.

Goosebumps rose on his arms and he heaved himself out of the water, pulling at the threadbare towel draped over the rail. It only just wrapped round him. He longed for thick white towels made from Egyptian cotton.

He raced to the bedroom though it was no warmer than the bathroom. If anything it was colder. Roll on the summer. Late spring, even. Anything but these cruel temperatures. He threw the towel over his back, grabbed the other end with his free hand and swept it back and forth, the rough fabric tearing at his flesh.

Summer. The work on the chapel roof would definitely be over by then, even if they fell disastrously behind schedule, and once the job was done he would have no reason to stop by the church, the manse, see Saffron ever again. He stopped drying himself and allowed the cold air to snap at him.

What harm could a few dates do? He hadn't imagined her disappointment when he pulled away from her. He was sure of it. She liked him. He liked her. What harm could being friendly do?

He shivered, violently, and almost jumped into the clothes piled on the floor by the window. There were no socks. He crossed to the small dressing table and as he went to open the top drawer, he caught his shin on the bottom one which jutted out a fraction. He kicked it in frustration before sinking onto the bed to pull on the clean socks. He glared at the offending drawer as he rubbed his shin; the drawer that contained evidence of his other life. *Allegra, Freddy.*

As he stared an arrow lanced him. Pain seared, splintering his thoughts. He remembered his therapist's words: 'Allow yourself to feel the pain.' Joe allowed only rage when he thought of Allegra. What was happening? Was this a breakthrough? Confused and uncertain, still feeling a throb in his leg, he pushed himself from the bed and crawled over to the dresser. Instead of closing the bottom drawer, he yanked it open. The picture frame lay on top. He picked it up.

Turn it over, he whispered to himself.

We could be brother and sister.

He stared at Allegra, at her honey-coloured skin and wavy brown hair and eyes of different colours. Rage bore down upon him, pressing into him, drenching him with its blood-red stain. It tightened around his throat, choking him. It twisted in his belly and guts and punched at his chest and in his head till he felt he might explode. It was a sensation he knew well, too well perhaps.

But he never gave himself permission to give in to pain for fear it might dissipate his resolve, tear him in two, rendering him weaker. He held rage close, as comforter, protector, partner.

He felt the pain rising towards his throat.

I can't do this any longer.

He threw back his head and bayed at the ceiling. There, on his knees with the photograph resting on his thighs, he roared. Months and months and months of pain and loss burst from him in one long howl. Afterwards, he folded in upon himself, forming a curl of flesh, like a foetus. He fell sideways and lay on the hard floor, pressing the photograph into the tender flesh of his belly.

Joe came to with a jolt, shivering. Had he fallen asleep? His phone was buzzing, rattling on the chest of drawers. He clambered up, but he'd missed the call. There was no name, but he recognised the number – it was Simon's. Well, Simon could wait a while. He looked at the time; he couldn't have been asleep for long, but he felt as light and refreshed as if he'd had eight hours solid. Pain hadn't destroyed him; it had freed him, in some small way.

Chapter Fourteen

It was the brightest morning they'd had since the autumn, Saffron was sure. Definitely the sunniest she could remember. All winter Coed Mawr had been in permanent shadow, even when it wasn't raining or snowing.

She woke to a bedroom she barely recognised; one cast in a golden hue so syrupy that when she threw back the heavy duvet the nip in the air took her by surprise. She sat upright, retrieved the cover and lay down again, the heat in its folds warm and soothing. She rolled onto her side, the duvet under her chin, and stared at the pale curtains.

They'd come from her parents' bedroom in the neat Victorian terrace the de Lacys had occupied in leafy Dulwich. It was the largest room in the house with the widest windows. Saffron occupied the smallest bedroom in the Coed Mawr manse and these were the only curtains wide enough, such was the difference in size between the houses.

Dulwich had been cramped with four occupants. Though her father and mother had bought the house before property prices in the capital soared, it was expensive for a trainee architect and minister with children to support. Even after Saffron's father qualified they were unable to afford somewhere bigger. 'De Lacy Mansions is just perfect,' Rain used to say. Rain's stipend remained at pittance levels and as churchgoing decreased in popularity it only got smaller. But they were fortunate, they were told by Rain on numerous occasions, when, as teenagers, Saffron and Matthew moaned about their shabby home, their functional, battered cars, and the lacklustre camping holidays in France. 'We have our own home – thanks to your father. Many ministers live in church property all their working lives, and what happens when they retire, huh?' Rain had said. Saffron's dad had looked embarrassed.

He was hopeless with money. He earned a half-decent salary by the time Saffron went to secondary school, but the rows about their lack of money were hard to ignore. They didn't happen often – her mother was far too nice for that – but when they did they were ferocious, with Rain accusing Stephen of all sorts of unimaginable acts – gambling was one Saffron remembered vividly – and Stephen shouting back that it was his money and he would do what he 'sodding well liked with it' anyway. Saffron had cried herself to sleep that night.

Was her parents' marriage any rockier than most? She'd thought so at the time but when she'd confided in gob-on-legs Shannon, her best friend at school, it became apparent her home was an oasis of calm compared to what Shannon lived with. But relations between her parents had been increasingly strained over the past few years, Saffron admitted. There was often an atmosphere when she visited from her university digs and Rain carried an air of barely concealed desperation.

Saffron hadn't thought about her parents' marriage in ages – it hardly seemed to matter given what had happened. But now, staring at the textured-cotton, cream curtains which belonged in her parents' bedroom, that most intimate of places, waves of memory lapped over her. Why did Rain talk about Dad as if he were a saint? He wasn't, and Rain hadn't thought so either before he died. She still loved him, of that Saffron was certain, but Rain hadn't been blind to his foibles. Her mother understood the complexities of love and romance, Saffron thought.

Joe was right. She had to tell her mother the truth about her relationship with Ben.

According to the clock on the dressing table, it was eight o'clock. She could hear the rattle and clash of pans and plates below, even from here on the third floor. Rain had never mastered the art of emptying the dishwasher quietly. Saffron threw back the duvet and in a single leap pounced on the clothes slung on the nursing chair by the window. Once she had the first layer on, she peeped through the curtains. The sky was blue and studded with foamy clouds. She checked the street below – empty bar the Land Rover – before recovering her jumper from beneath a pile of dark clothes.

She'd been trying on the contents of her wardrobe the night before – a sort-out. Anything she no longer wore she would donate to a Nearly New Sale the WI were organising to raise funds for the pier ballroom fight. According to Rain, the campaign was gathering momentum. Locals wanted the ballroom back to its former Edwardian glory and a battle with the local council had begun in earnest. The council appeared to favour the cheaper option, and that meant destruction, not renovation.

Saffron stared at the black mound of clothes. She really ought to inject some colour into her wardrobe, but she'd grown so used to wearing black she wouldn't know where to start. And black was easy, practical – everything went with everything. She didn't have spare cash for new clobber anyway. The charity shops here were full of frumpy blouses and eighties jackets, all drenched in the distinctive, minty odour of mothballs. She pulled on her black skinny jeans and opened the bedroom door. The smell of toast wafted from the kitchen – Rain had burnt it again.

From the bathroom she padded down the first flight of stairs. The study door was ajar and she caught a glimpse of the fields beyond the garden, shadows from the clouds moving across the expanse of green changing its tone from forest dark to lawn bright. She stepped inside and opened the window wide, enjoying the prickle of the spring air now that she was bundled up. The countryside spread out before her, the distant hills looming, the tall trees which gave the town its name lined up against the horizon. The sun showed itself and cast a glow over the scene. It was spectacular.

I've never appreciated how beautiful it is. Is this why Mum believes? Is her faith rooted in the majesty of this landscape?

She leant forward, her arms resting on the windowsill and closed her eyes, enjoying the warmth of the weak sun on her cheeks. She imagined the distant roar of the sea; she could taste the salt in the air, hear the gulls and the faint hum of traffic from the back road. A clattering and gruff yell disturbed her. She opened her eyes and turned to the left, towards the sound. The back of the chapel was in her sightline. Two figures, silhouetted against the sky, stood on top of the roof. She caught her breath, almost overcome with dizziness on their behalf, before composing herself and craning further forward.

She recognised the figures as Joe and Tyson. Tyson moved nimbly across the pitch and retrieved whatever had been dropped, Saffron couldn't make out what. He then disappeared down the far slope.

She focused on Joe, who remained on the ridge, his back to her, bent double, hands gripping the remaining slates, steadying himself. He touched the peak of his cap with one hand, to ensure it didn't fall off, she imagined, and to her surprise pushed himself upright, and looked out over the horizon as she had done only minutes before. She held her breath; it looked so precarious. He wobbled; she gasped. He curled down, squatted on all fours, turned and sat gingerly, this time facing the manse. She leant back a fraction, into the safety of the window frame, unsure if he could see her as she could him. He remained in outline and she continued to stare, admiring the cut of his square shoulders, remembering his profile, also in shadow, as they'd walked across the mountains and back down into Coed Mawr, the night she'd been out drinking with Ceri. She'd watched him then too, surreptitiously. The long straight nose, the curve of his skull as it met his neck, the locks of hair swept across the top of his head contrasting with the cropped sides. She thought about those incredible eyes – one hazel, one green – mesmerising and unnerving, the way they'd darkened as he looked at her, as they sat on the bench on the tree-lined promenade, drunk on wine and things unspoken. A rippling in her belly. Lower than that. A stirring, a clenching, the pull of desire. No, it was more than that. More than physical longing. She liked him. He intrigued her; she trusted him without knowing why. He'd prised her open like a clam, with the slick, shiny knife of understanding, and she'd not seen it coming. Rather than shrivelling, retreating, she'd offered herself up to him. And it had been OK.

A breeze brushed her forehead, pulling clouds across the sky and she realised with a start Joe was no longer in shadow. She could make out his features and he was staring right back at her. She froze, transfixed. A clawing stole from within, radiating outwards, like heat from a flame, so powerful she thought it must be visible. Shaking, she waved – a pathetic effort to disguise her embarrassment at being caught out, exposed. She laughed at her folly and the sensation at her core dissipated. He waved back and she stepped away, closed the window, and padded downstairs, attributing the grasping in her belly to hunger, though it was like nothing she'd experienced before.

In the kitchen, Rain held the toaster upside down over the sink and shook it hard, convinced there was a piece of burnt toast or crumpet caught in the grill. It was the only possible explanation for the plumes of black smoke that had risen from the appliance when she had used it moments ago. She put the toaster down on the draining board, picked up a knife from the rack and jabbed at the mesh inside the toaster.

'Jesus, Mum, what are you doing?'

She span to face her daughter, brow furrowed.

Saffron raised her hands in supplication. 'Sorry. But really, Mum, you've not unplugged it. Have you any idea how dangerous that is?'

'It's not on.' She jabbed again at the appliance.

'But you've not even switched it off at the wall. Jesus, electricity, metal. Do I need to spell it out?'

'Quit that kind of swearing.' She replaced the toaster with a bang. 'Bugger it, I give up.' She turned again to face her daughter and smiled; she really would like Saffron to eat something and an argument was a sure-fire way of ensuring that she didn't. She'd leave the kitchen in a huff before Rain could tempt Saff with her pre-planned selection. She could use the grill.

Rain clapped her hands and began. 'Now, I know that you're not what you'd call a breakfast person, Saff, but today I'm convinced I might be able to tempt you.' She grinned and hoped she hadn't overdone it. Since the accident, her once easy-going, pliant daughter had become one of those obstinate, belligerent types, ready to pick a fight, determined to do the exact opposite of whatever Rain wanted, seemingly for the heck of it. Not all the time, but often enough to wrong-foot Rain, to bruise her. That role had always been Matthew's, and she found it impossible to predict when Saffron would be in lovely mode or beastly mode. She was quicksand, shifting, dangerous. Rain held her breath.

'I am a bit hungry this morning.' Saff smiled and Rain breathed out.

'Fantastic! So … I've quite a menu. Ready?'

Saffron nodded and Rain reeled off the selection. 'Full

English – or should we say Welsh?' A ridiculous giggle.

Get a grip, Rain de Lacy. Stop being so desperate to please. It drives her away.

'Welsh Rarebit. Croissants with freshly brewed coffee – milk and sugar. Crumpets – done under the grill,' she nodded towards the cooker next to the Aga, 'cereal – the usual, cornflakes, muesli, porridge ... Must be the sunshine!'

'What?'

'Brought out your appetite – this glorious morning, after all the rain last night.'

'A croissant would be nice – plain, not butter or jam – and a coffee. But I can make it. Let me make breakfast for us both. I never cook,' Saff said, moving towards her.

'You never eat!'

Saffron stopped.

You bloody fool, Rain.

'It's why you're so lovely and slim,' she drew the outline of a small, curvy frame in the air with flat hands. 'You look great in those jeans. I could do with taking a leaf out of your book.' She slapped her rear.

Saffron pulled the corners of her mouth downwards, half smile, half grimace, and looked, imploringly, at Rain. 'Too slim?'

Rain focused on remaining neutral, unsure whether to agree and risk spoiling what could be a wonderful start to the morning: breaking bread with her lovely daughter. 'You're beautiful.'

'And so are you.'

Rain stepped aside to allow Saff the simple pleasure of preparing the meal and moved over to the table, picked up the mock-up of the latest parish newsletter and began to proofread it, ready to lay it aside immediately should Saffron wish to talk.

'Here you are, madame. Continental breakfast á la de

Lacy.' Saffron placed the tray of coffee, croissants and condiments in front of Rain.

'How wonderful! Thank you, darling.'

Rain locked fingers and pulled her fist under her chin. 'For what we are about to receive may the Lord make us truly, madly, deeply grateful. Amen.'

Saffron giggled at Rain's small joke and joined her on 'Amen.' *Truly, Madly, Deeply* had been a favourite film of Rain's before the accident and she had often inserted it into grace, much to everyone's amusement and, after overuse, exasperation. Saff's laughter pleased Rain more than it should have.

'Shall I be Mum?' Rain said, reaching for the mugs.

'If the boot fits ...' *Toy Story* had been one of Saffron's favourite films as a child. Animated features remained a guilty pleasure.

'I hear the cinema is showing the new film by that Japanese fella – whatshisname? We could go together. I'll book tickets.' Rain ran with her advantage. Saff was amenable.

'Yeah, why not?'

'When would be good?'

Nail her while you can.

'Lemme get back to you on that.'

'OK,' Rain said, brightly, keeping the disappointment from her tone. 'Milk, sugar? You won't want it black. It's rather bitter, I'm afraid. They didn't have our usual so thought I'd try this. Never again!' Rain waited for the objection but it never came. She stirred in a heaped teaspoonful of sticky brown sugar and poured in the cream of the milk. She loved that a milkman – and it was a man – still did doorstep drops in Coed Mawr. It was so reassuring to find the bottle waiting each morning, even if the birds did take off the top.

She watched her daughter sipping the coffee, holding the mug with both hands, eyes cast downwards, and Rain wondered if it tasted thick and rich compared to her usual black, if the silkiness of the cream coated her mouth and teeth. She popped a croissant on a plate and pushed it in front of Saffron. Saffron looked up, her blue eyes wide. She opened her mouth to speak, but changed her mind and nodded her thanks instead.

Rain longed to ask if everything was OK but didn't want to break the mood and nodded silently instead. She took a croissant and tore it open, the interior stretched and yielded. Puffs of steam rose carrying the buttery scent into the air. She scooped up a large dollop of jam, dropped it into the pastry, and took a bite. Butter and jam oozed out, running down her fingers. She licked them clean rather than taking a tissue from the box Saff had thoughtfully placed on the table.

'Oh, that's good,' she moaned. 'Right this minute, who cares about calories?'

'Did you know, when you met Dad, that he was ... the one?' Saffron said, gazing intently at her mother. It was one of 'those' Saffron stares; a look that unsettled Rain in its intensity.

She laughed, a short, snappy kind of laugh, more a harrumph than a laugh. Where was this question leading? For she knew it was leading somewhere. Saffron didn't do idle chatter. Not often. 'Like love at first sight?' Rain said.

'If you like.'

'I think so. It was a funny time for me. I'd not long been reborn, less than a couple of years. I was totally, truly, madly, deeply in love with Jesus.' She checked herself. 'I still am. But it was the honeymoon period. Your dad chased me. More than I did him, at least.' She wished she hadn't demolished that croissant so quickly, she felt a little nauseous all of a sudden.

'But how did it feel?' Saffron stressed the 'feel'.

Rain laughed again. What was the matter with her? 'The usual. Butterflies in the stomach, weak knees. All those awful clichés. Though love seemed to increase my appetite rather than diminish it, more's the pity!'

'Quit with the fat thing, Mum. You're not. Though you might consider your cholesterol levels occasionally. Is it OK to talk about this?'

The queasiness increased. 'Yes, yes. Happy memories. Happy.' Rain lifted her mug to her mouth only to find it empty. 'But you know how it feels.'

'I'm not sure I do. Did.'

Rain looked at Saffron, waiting for more.

Saffron paused. 'Ignore me.'

What does she mean?

Rain remained silent.

Saffron picked up her croissant and took a large bite.

Conversation over then, thought Rain, relieved.

Chapter Fifteen

The key wouldn't open the door to the church hall. Rain couldn't understand it. Only days ago it was fine. She kicked and heaved against it to no avail; the door wouldn't budge. She checked her watch. There were twenty minutes before the prayer meeting was due to begin. She had to drag the chairs from the store cupboard herself – the members were far too decrepit to help – and turn on the recently fixed heating to take the chill off the air. She didn't want any of them to die of hypothermia. Congregation members were in short enough supply as it was without her inadvertently bumping some of them off. In one final, desperate attempt she launched herself, shoulder first, at the door. It always worked for the police in crime dramas. The door remained steadfast. Furious, she stomped to the chapel. JJ would be able to help, she felt sure.

But there was no reply when she hollered his name into the rafters. All of the slates had been removed and what looked like a thin tarpaulin covered the skeleton of the roof. Surely, he must hear her through that? She cupped her hands around her mouth and called again.

'He's not here. Gone to the wood merchants. Is there anything I can help you with, Reverend?' It was Eifion, all smiles, and she noticed that his teeth were straight and white. Quite a contrast with his swarthy complexion, gained after years of working outdoors in all weathers she presumed. 'I hope so! I've a prayer meeting in less than ten minutes and I can't get into the hall. The blasted door's stuck.'

'It'll be all the damp weather. Wood swells.'

'But it opened the other day. I don't understand it,' she said, exasperated, clapping her hands together.

Eifion turned towards the exit and said, 'Right then. Let's be having it.' He marched off with Rain in tow.

The prayer meeting members waited on the path while Eifion removed the entire lock mechanism. Rain had suggested they wait in the chapel, or the manse kitchen, though there weren't enough chairs for them all to sit, but they had ignored her pleas, content to watch the drama of the jammed door unfold. Their lives must be very dull indeed, she thought. She tipped her eyes to the sky and mouthed, 'Sorry. Bad morning.'

Eifion pushed open the door, lock barrel in hand, and the group applauded and traipsed in. 'Thank you so much,' Rain said. 'Without you, we'd have had to cancel the meeting and that would have been an absolute calamity for some of us.' She nodded towards Mary Campbell. Mary had no one, nothing, in her life bar the church.

Eifion smiled and she noticed that he did so with his eyes as well as his mouth. What a good, kind man he was. He pointed at the gaping hole in the door and said that he would ask JJ to pick up another barrel while he was out. 'I'll fit it as soon as I have it, so no need to fret about all sorts getting in.'

'I wonder what broke it?'

'Probably you, thumping the door and rattling the key. It's bent, you know.' He held the key aloft. 'Don't know your own strength.'

'Oh, I'm not strong, far from it,' she said, making her way through, conscious her members would be waiting in the cold, still standing.

'You're stronger than you think.'

'Hey, man, how you doing?' There was lots about Simon

Joe liked – really, really liked – but he didn't like the Americanised lingo and accent Simon affected whenever he was on the phone. He didn't speak like that in person, in court, or anywhere else, as far as Joe could tell. Simon was a Home Counties boy, Hertfordshire, and mostly he spoke as you would expect.

'OK. You?'

'Cool. Look, I'm calling because I figured you'd wanna know Allegra is looking for you. I mean, seriously looking for you. She's out and she's hired a private dick and all.'

'Seriously? No way.' Joe stopped dead and another pedestrian almost collided with him.

'Yup. She asked me outright if I could recommend anyone, given my line of work.'

'Jesus. She got parole?'

'Yeah, good behaviour.'

Joe remembered the strange car in the lane weeks ago, the man who'd been asking questions at the school building site and wondered if the PI had made progress. 'When'd she hire one? Why?'

'Seems to think she's got the power to lure you back. Crazy chick. She said she'd tried one guy, recommended by Freddy, but he was kinda useless.' Simon wheezed and paused to drag on a cigarette. A roll-up was almost permanently attached to his fingers, which were stained a dark brown as a result. So she was in touch with Freddy. That would please him, no doubt. But this could work for Joe, this delusion, this arrogance. Could he get to them both in one fell swoop?

'Thanks for letting me know. Keep me in the loop, yeah?' Joe replied, hoping the next man Allegra hired would draw a blank as the first clearly had.

'Sure thing, bro.'

'Simon, I like you, but I am not your bro. OK?'

'Sure. Sorry.'

Joe hung up and looked around the high street. Lower

Coed Mawr was almost deserted, no sign of anyone, let alone suspicious looking strangers. And perhaps this new guy wouldn't come up this way regardless. After all, Joe had left no trace. Still, he'd have to be careful. No more popping down here for lunch. And he needed to think; he still didn't have a plan. There were lots of fantasies, but nothing he could actually execute. Allegra's career was over; there was no scope for professional ignominy, not short-term, and she didn't have a boyfriend.

Her father. He's a shit, a duplicitous, amoral wanker.

Allegra was a daddy's girl. Perhaps that was Joe's route in – disgrace by association, with the added benefit of an emotional blow. The sound of a car backfiring made him jump. Thinking about Allegra and PIs made him nervous. He caught sight of the entrance to the shopping arcade in his peripheral vision.

Has Saffron started work yet? Get a grip. Grab a sandwich, get out of here.

He stepped towards the bakery on the corner of the arcade, kidding himself he was tempted by the smell of hot sausage rolls.

He was making his way back to the van when he saw Saffron. She was some distance away, but moving down the sweep of the main street. Her lope was unmistakable. He slowed his pace, lingering outside shops, peering in without seeing the wares on offer, more interested in what the reflection might reveal. She neared. He stared into a ramshackle charity shop.

'Hi. Fancy seeing you here,' he said, casually.

'Fancy.'

'You're early for work. Grabbing lunch first?'

'Er, no.' She stuffed her hands into the deep pockets of her duffel coat. It was warm for the time of year and he thought she must be hot. Her cheeks were flushed pink.

'Looking for something?' he said.

She furrowed her brow.

'Shopping,' he explained.

'I'm not much of a shopper. I was heading for the beach.' She looked past him and shrugged. 'Join me if you like.'

He almost dropped the paper bag he held in one hand. It contained a sandwich and a sausage roll. 'Got your eyes on my Coke, eh?' He lifted the condensation-drenched can in the other hand. She smiled and his heart soared.

On the beach they walked westwards, kicking pebbles and lumps of mangled seaweed as they went. 'I love being so close to the sea,' she said after a period without conversation. He liked that about her; she was comfortable with silence. 'It's liberating. I feel free, even though I know I'm not. I'm as trapped as the next person. But when I look at the skyline,' she pointed to the wispy clouds beyond, 'there's a sense of how big the world is, how infinite, how explorable.' She laughed at herself and he liked that about her too. The gentle breeze whipped her hair off her face, revealing her profile. Hers was a strong nose, long and straight. Noble. No upturned button nose like those on dolls or cartoon women.

'Why do you dye your hair?' he asked, focusing on the shingle.

She stopped, compelling him to do the same. 'You've asked before.'

'You didn't answer.'

'I fancied a change. Don't you like it?'

He didn't know how to respond. It wasn't that he didn't like it. 'So when did you dye it?' he asked instead.

'Before we came here.' She carried on walking.

'A new you?'

'If you like.'

'I'd like to see your natural colour.' Had he overstepped the mark? It was personal and almost flirtatious, and he'd said he wasn't going to go there. But he'd seen her face from the upstairs window of the manse, the way she'd looked at him. He'd felt her before he saw her. He'd almost fallen backwards from the force of her scrutiny and he'd sat down on the ridge so that he could be within her gaze for longer. God knows, he hated being on that roof for any longer than he needed to be, but he'd forced himself. Because of her. He'd not imagined that look, had he?

She stopped again and turned to face him. 'I can't go back to being the person I was before.'

He didn't know what to say. He knew exactly what she meant but he couldn't tell her that. It might lead to questions. Questions he wasn't sure he was ready to answer. Not yet. Maybe not ever. 'Are you hungry?' he said, holding up the bag. Grease had seeped through the paper, creating shiny, transparent patches.

'Doesn't exactly look appetising,' she said, screwing up her nose and looking considerably less noble than earlier. More cute and sexy and approachable.

'There's a sandwich too. Brown bread. Cheese and piccalilli.'

'The yellow stuff? Yuck.'

'Ever tried it?'

She shook her head.

'Then you must. It's surprisingly good, despite the radioactive shade.' He moved to the promenade wall, crouched, and placed the bag on the shingle. He smoothed pebbles and marine debris with his palms, creating a flat area on which they could sit. The exposed sand was ever so slightly damp.

'I'm really not all that hungry.'

'But it's lunchtime and you're thin. That part of the new you, too?' He parked himself on the spot.

'You're very personal, aren't you?' She stood above him, staring down at him, through him, and he began to regret starting this conversation. He went to reply but before he could apologise, she bent, took hold of the bakery bag and sat down. From her pocket she pulled out an anti-bacterial handwash and doused her hands. She offered him the bottle of gel. 'Old habits. Always carried these on the ward,' she shrugged. She handed him the sausage roll and picked open the plastic sandwich container, pulled out half and took a large bite. She didn't take her eyes from his as she began to chew.

It was clearly an effort and as she swallowed, he said, 'Not your favourite? Something to take the taste away?' He pulled the ring off the can, the hiss of escaping gas incongruent against the sound of the lapping waves, gulls, and the breeze gusting round his ears.

She took a large swig and shuddered as she swallowed. 'I'm not keen on fizzy drinks either.'

'What do you like? Apart from cheap wine and the occasional cigarette?'

'Neither of those things really. I don't know. I liked blackcurrant cordial as a child and snakebites as a student. And I used to love shepherd's pie and roast chicken.'

'I'd have had you down as a veggie.'

'What about you? I've told you all about me and I know almost nothing about you.'

It was bound to come to this. He could hardly have expected her not to ask questions. He wasn't prepared to lie. Not to her.

'I like meat, video games, history, bats, and art. Sculpture, mostly.' He pushed himself upright and took a drink from the can. 'Sand's wet.' She noticed he didn't wipe the rim as Ben would have done.

'Most blokes I know like video games. Let me guess, *Call of Duty, Grand Theft Auto*. Bats? That's weird.'

He laughed.

'History. That's interesting. Any particular period? And sculpture. Favourite artists?' She'd found history quite dull at school, though she'd got an A* like the other nine subjects she'd studied at GCSE. History was too much like a story for her liking and so it reminded her of the Biblical fables she heard over and over as a child. She'd been hopeless at art, though she'd enjoyed visiting exhibitions.

He brushed sand from the seat of his jeans. 'You know lots of blokes then? You must have done at medical school.'

'Actually, more women study medicine right now and don't change the subject. Which period?' She clambered up. It was obvious he wasn't going to sit down again and she supposed she should think about making a move. Wynne's called.

'The usual. The wars and all that.'

She raised her eyebrows in mock disapproval, though she was a touch disappointed. How predictable.

'But I've a new book on the Celts. Boudicca and all that. Looks great.'

Had he sensed her disappointment? He wanted to please, she thought. She hoped. 'You like strong women?'

'Yeah.' He extended the vowels as if unsure where she was leading him. 'Though not axe-wielding, murderous types.'

She laughed but inside a little part of her shrivelled. She wasn't strong, she was anything but.

'Look, this is fascinating, but I have to get back to work,' he said.

Why did he do this? Withdraw just when she thought they were getting somewhere? Perhaps he didn't like her. Perhaps he was being nice because he had to be, because he was working for her mother. But she'd seen the look he gave her from the roof. Had she really got it so wrong? 'Yup. Me too, I guess.'

As they returned to the high street, Joe asked if she'd spoken to her mum about Ben. Ashamed at her cowardice, she fudged her reply, and said that she'd not really had any time alone with Rain. 'Our house has a constant stream of visitors and she's out a lot.' She was about to expand on this when a familiar voice cut through her excuses.

'Hiya!'

Ceri waved from across the road and yelled, 'How you doing? Nice to see you, it's been ages.' She leaped into the road, stopping the traffic with an aggressive wave of her arm, as if it were the drivers who were in the wrong rather than her.

'I love the way she pronounces "you". Eifion, the labourer, does the same,' Joe said, waving back at Ceri.

'Me too,' Saffron whispered.

'Fancy seeing you here. You not hot in that coat, Saff? Flippin' boiling it is, today.' She fanned herself and Saffron wondered how Ceri fared in the summer when she assumed it genuinely did get warm. March wasn't even out and it snowed in April, occasionally, according to the locals. Barely stopping for breath, Ceri continued. 'I am SO glad I bumped into you. I've got a job – I know – incredible, isn't it? Looking after a couple of brats three days a week.'

Saffron wondered what kind of a parent might leave Ceri in charge of their children, lovely though she was.

'I know, I couldn't believe it. Offered it to me straight away. References and CRB check dependent, of course. I did a trial – took 'em down to the play park, whizzed 'em round on that wheel thing, pushed 'em on the swings, played tag, bought 'em an ice lolly. Bloody knackered I was but they liked me!'

Joe was laughing. 'I bet they did,' he said.

'I didn't take any shit from 'em either.' She beamed at Joe. 'Anyway, what I'm trying to say is let's go out for a celebration drink. All of us? My treat. Tonight.'

Saffron paused, wondering if Joe would agree.

'I'm not sure. You two probably want to catch up? Girl

149

talk and that?'

'Bollocks. We're not girly girls. Nice to have a man about.'

Saffron glanced at Joe. She didn't want to share him, but if it was the only way to see him again … And she wanted to see Ceri, very much.

'Maybe,' he said.

Ceri beamed. 'Great. Eight o'clock. Y Castell. Be there.' And off she skipped.

'OK. I have to run,' he said. 'Have this. You might get hungry later.' He passed Saffron the bakery bag.

'What about you?'

'I'll be fine.'

'See you later then.'

'Maybe.' He smiled and walked away.

She drifted towards the shop wondering why he wouldn't commit. She threw the bag in the bin by the entrance, flattened her windswept hair, and prepared for Mrs Evans.

Chapter Sixteen

'Right, get that down your neck.' Ceri plonked a pint of lager in front of Saffron.

'Not sure I can drink all that. A half would have been fine,' she said, eyes darting round the pub, settling on the door. He wouldn't come, she knew it. Might as well accept it and enjoy the night. Ceri was great company.

'Do your best. All I ask. Cheers.'

Saffron raised her glass, beer slopped over her fingers. 'Congratulations. Here's to a long and successful career in child-minding.'

Ceri spluttered, spraying lager over the table. 'Bollocks to that. I want the low-down on our man with wood before he arrives,' she said with a glint in her eye. 'What is going on with you two? I'm mad jealous, of course, but as a friend I have to say well done, he's bloody gorgeous, he is.'

'There's nothing going on.' She took another sip, the beer tasted bitter and harsh, the slight fizz shooting up her nose and into her brain. She shuddered.

'That's rubbish, that is. I see the way he looks at you. Have to be blind not to.' Ceri emptied almost half of her glass in one long gulp.

Unable to reply, Saffron stared at her drink, heat rising from her breast, creeping up her neck. So she hadn't imagined it, after all. Pleasure and guilt stole to the back of her throat. She tried to take another drink. The smell made her heady. She forced it down, allowing the rush to dizzy her mind further. She didn't deserve such happiness, did she?

The feeling of joy didn't last. Though she had expected it, Joe didn't show, and her disappointment was crushing. Friends of Ceri's turned up shortly after ten and though Saffron knew this was a perfect opportunity to make new connections, friends even, she used it as an excuse to bow out of the evening. Ceri was too drunk to make a concerted effort to persuade Saffron to stay, but wobbled to the door with her to say goodbye.

'Sure there's a perfectly good reason why he's not here,' Ceri slurred, an arm draped over Saffron's shoulders. 'Don't you fret. Love is in the air, I know it.'

'Thanks, Ceri. You're a pal.' They were both mistaken; Joe didn't like her. She suppressed an urge to cry.

'I meant to ask. Have you met my dad yet?' Ceri leant against the door frame, propping the door open. Saffron heard cries of protest from inside the pub. The night air was cold. 'He's working on the chapel. First job in ages. He's so grateful to your mother I think he might convert!' Ceri laughed.

'How bizarre. What a coincidence.'

'Not really. Small place. Everyone knows everyone, and their business. See you!' She fell back into the pub.

Everyone except for Joe, thought Saffron. No one seems to know much about him. Or me.

As Saffron turned the corner, tears pooling, a combination of the sharp breeze and childish disappointment, she caught the outline of a figure sitting on a garden wall up ahead. A figure she'd recognise anywhere.

'Joe?' Her voice quivered.

'Hope I didn't make you jump.' He stood.

'How long have you been there?' She moved towards him, swallowing back her tears, determined he should not notice.

'A while.'

She stood before him, his face half lit by the street

152

lamp.

'A long while. Walk with me?' He extended his hand.

She took it.

Weaving through the twisty back streets of pastel-coloured houses, they climbed the rise into Upper Coed Mawr in silence. There were no words to describe the feeling between them, no words Saffron could find. She focused instead on the sensation of his hand wrapped over hers and was glad she hadn't worn gloves. He felt hard and warm and tender; calluses on his fingers rubbing against her untarnished flesh. Every now and again, he would give her hand a small squeeze, one of reassurance, or encouragement, but for what Saffron didn't know, or care. She just liked him pressing himself into her finger bones.

A fox's cry jolted them from the magic of the walk, the floating up the hill. Joe turned to look over his shoulder and whispered, 'There he goes.' A dog fox slinked across the road, following the call of the female. Saffron gazed up at Joe, a tug in her belly, a weakening in her spine. Kiss me, kiss me, she longed to say. But he wasn't watching her, instead he looked beyond her and she wondered what he thought, what he felt, his inscrutable features giving nothing away.

Joe couldn't look at Saffron. He felt her gaze, like the sun on cold cheeks, but he didn't dare turn and lower his eyes in case they revealed too much. Instead, he allowed himself to be swallowed up by her scent – musky, heady, sexy, unmistakably her – to be consumed by her presence. Intoxicated and woozy, he closed his eyes.

'Look at me,' she urged.

And it was impossible to resist her demand.

He swept her ragged fringe from her forehead and ran his fingers from her temples to her chin. He bent forward and his mouth met hers in a kiss. A kiss like he'd never kissed anyone before. A first kiss. No, his first kiss was a let-down. Sixteen years old, at a party held at Freddy's parents' house while they holidayed in St Tropez. A girl: beautiful, heavily made-up, drunk, she'd tasted of vinegar and nuts. Saffron's touch promised passion, peace, danger, release. Contradictory, unpredictable, irresistible. He wanted it to last for ever.

She craved Joe like nothing and no one before. Was this what love felt like? Was this what people meant when they spoke of an almost unbearable ecstasy? Or was she confusing it with infatuation? And how did people tell the difference? She was falling from a cliff, out of control. Unstoppable.

No. She could not lose control.

She pulled away and embarrassment enveloped her. Was he able to sense her need, her fear? He hadn't let go of her hand. He rubbed his thumb between the metacarpal bones.

'Let me show you my home. Let me cook for you. Feed you,' he said at last.

'What, now?'

He laughed, quietly, and let go of her hand. Cold air brushed her palm, but like an amputee who claims to feel the missing limb, she imagined he was still there, like a glove, shielding her. 'Tomorrow. About eight. I need time to get the ingredients … Decide what to cook.'

'I don't know where you live.'

'I'll draw a map. Drop it through the letterbox tomorrow morning, before you go to work.'

'An address? A telephone number?'

'I've only a work phone. Don't use it for anything else.'

'You could make an exception?' Why didn't he want to give her his number?

'Not yet.'

She didn't ponder on his foibles. He'd asked her to

dinner – like a date – and she wanted to jump up and down, squealing, like a kid on their birthday.

Stay cool, Saffron, stay cool.

'You'll find my place. Don't tell anyone.'

'I won't.'

He kissed her again, chastely, on the cheek and said, 'I'll walk you to your door.'

Her mum was already in bed, reading her Bible, as she always did before she fell asleep. Saffron popped her head round the open door and offered to make camomile tea, knowing she would find it hard to sleep. Rain thanked her but declined.

Saffron lay in bed staring at the ceiling, replaying the scene on the rise over and over. The memory of the kiss awakening her body time and time again.

Rain put the phone down and tried to stem her anxiety. The member due to lead the midweek service later that day had come down with flu. He was younger than most of the congregation, though not by much, so she wasn't overly concerned about his health per se. No, she was more concerned about her workload that morning. She had home visits to attend, a flower arranging class to oversee, brasses to polish and now she had a service to think about and plan. Ordinarily, she might have been able to bring her planned Sunday service forward, but this week she'd been unusually tardy and hadn't given that service any thought yet.

The brass-polishing was the obvious thing to drop but Rain couldn't bear to see it so dulled. It reflected her love of Christ and she needed it to shine, shine, shine. Now more than ever, it seemed. Anxiety was an ever-present threat to the equilibrium of her day to day existence once again. She'd thought she had it under control but it had reared its ugly head. She blamed it on the state of the roof.

There was no roof. She felt as exposed as the chapel, her lid right off. She wished they'd hurry up but the weather had slowed progress on occasion, too wet and wild to be safe for the men to work.

You need to be ever-vigilant against anxiety's presence, she pondered, rummaging in the drawer of the kitchen table, sure there was a bottle of diazepam buried in amongst the bills, batteries, biros and other debris. Ah-ha, there it was! She squinted at the label, the print small and faded, and reached for her reading glasses. They were not on the table. Bottle clutched in her palm she raced to the living room. No sign. She pounded upstairs to check her bedside table. No sign. Her heart rate rose, a combination of rushing through the manse – it was large and she was unfit – and her anxiety gathering momentum.

Remain calm. Think.

She'd taken her Bible into the bathroom that morning. Sure enough, her glasses rested on the ledge behind the tub. She read the label. The prescription was over eighteen months old; it must have been one of her early ones. Why hadn't she finished the course? Did drugs have a sell-by date like food? Surely, they couldn't do any harm?

She threw a pill to the back of her throat and turned on the tap. As she drank she realised she could think about her message while she polished the brasses. If she took a notepad, she could jot down ideas if she deemed it necessary. Services were not over-planned or rehearsed. She liked to have a theme and a broad outline with three or four quotes ready to repeat. There had to be a degree of spontaneity, to allow the words of our Lord Jesus Christ to flow through her. She was his conduit. Drug swallowed, she turned off the tap. Her heart rate slowed. She wished she'd not panicked. How foolish to resort to the diazepam.

Thank you, Lord, for providing the solution. Forgive me my weakness.

Taking a deep breath, she made her way downstairs and

gathered her things for the home visits, noticing for the first time that Saffron still wasn't up. The coffee in the pot would be cold.

Joe, Tyson, and Eifion sat on the lush grass at the back of the chapel, sheltered from the wind, eating their lunch, slurping on wet sand-coloured tea made by the piano player who always arrived early to run through the hymns for the forthcoming service. Joe had been disappointed to discover that the beautiful organ with its ivory pipes hadn't been touched in decades. Instead, the congregation sang along to an electric keyboard set to piano mode, the lyrics displayed in large type on a roll-down screen suspended from the balcony. The chapel was a quirky mixture of old and new. An iMac sat on a table alongside the pulpit, wooden pews lined the space with modern easy chairs at the back for the infirm.

'How long do these things go on for?' Tyson said, between chews on a pasty. Usually, on Thursday afternoons, he disappeared into town, or Joe sent him to suppliers or on other work-related missions.

'An hour and a bit,' Joe replied, without looking. 'And shut your gob while you're eating. I don't want to hear you chomping or see the masticated remains of your lunch.'

'The what?' Tyson said, mouth full.

'Never mind.' Joe glanced at Eifion who smiled and lifted his eyebrows.

Clouds gathered in the sky, obscuring the weak sun. A downpour was forecast and the service was unlikely to finish much before four o'clock. Joe could feel damp seeping through his jeans. He stood. 'Take the rest of the afternoon off. You've worked like Trojans.' *Especially you, Eifion.*

'Nice one, la,' Tyson said, leaping to his feet, brushing his hands over his backside. 'I'll see yas in the morning.' He disappeared, leaving half a mug of tea on the grass.

157

'Lazy beggar,' Eifion said, bending to collect the mug. 'Bet he's always got a woman to clean up after him.'

'What about you?' Joe asked.

'Divorced.'

'Sorry to hear that.'

'Don't be. We had some good years, got a beautiful daughter. We just weren't designed to make the course. Not everyone is.' He finished his tea and picked up Joe's empty mug too. 'What about you? Anyone special?'

'Came close once. Not sure I'll ever go there again.'

'We all get our hearts broken at least once. We all recover and go round the block again. It's the human way.'

'Most. Not all.' Was Joe's heart mended? He couldn't be certain. Its strength hadn't been fully tested; he'd not seen her since that final terrible day. Joe wasn't sure why he was sharing this with a man he hardly knew. He trusted Eifion, unlike Tyson and almost everyone else he could think of. He was solid, honest. Dependable. Everything Freddy wasn't; everything Allegra wasn't.

'Look, are you sure there's nothing I can be getting on with? There's nothing for me to go home to,' Eifion said.

Joe tried to think. He needed to get to the supermarket to buy food, but there were hours before Saffron was due and he needed to keep himself occupied. All afternoon his mind had whirred; it had been hard to concentrate on anything other than Saffron de Lacy. He couldn't get her out of his head. Perhaps he was healed.

His thoughts were interrupted by the sound of singing – 'My Jesus, My Saviour' – heartfelt, totally unlike the singing in his school chapel where boys mumbled, voices flat, and the masters scowled at those not singing at all.

'Lovely, isn't it? Singing like they mean it,' Eifion said.

A single voice rose above the crowd, loud and passionate, and completely out of tune. Both men laughed. 'That'll be the minister,' Eifion said. 'Can't sing for toffee.

Was the talk of the town when she first arrived. Never heard anything like it, they said. And she's Welsh! By birth. Spent too long in England, some said.' He was laughing, but Joe detected affection.

People only tease those they're fond of.

'I like her,' Joe said.

The older man turned away, too late to disguise the blush creeping up his face.

'Go in. Watch the service,' said Joe.

'Long time since I attended chapel. Not sure they'd have me.'

'They'll have anyone. They're desperate.'

'Even you?'

Joe hadn't considered going in himself. He knew it would please Rain, but that could lead to more badgering to attend coffee mornings and the like. He should keep a low profile in the town, especially after the latest news from Simon. But Saffron would have had to attend service after service as a child. How must that have been for her?

Eifion spoke again. 'Might be an education.'

Another hymn caught Joe's attention. Sung in Welsh this time, the emotional punch all the more powerful for it.

'Ah, "Calon Lân",' sighed Eifion, his hand to his chest, 'gets me every time.'

'And the Rev can't join in, which helps,' Joe said.

Eifion smiled. 'I hear she's trying to learn, so enjoy it while you can.'

Joe's curiosity got the better of him. 'OK. You're on. But I might duck out without warning.'

Rain was addressing her audience when they slipped in. She offered a prayer, eyes scrunched, chin tipped to the roof. They lowered themselves into the wide chairs at the back and an elderly lady nodded and smiled. 'I'm Mary,' she said, more loudly than Joe thought polite.

Rain offered prayers for various members of the church

and their friends; she thanked God for the work on the chapel, for the wood the builders worked with, for their skill and perseverance. Joe wondered if she'd seen them enter, if she'd peeped while praying. Taller than most, he looked over the sea of grey and white hair and wondered how many came to the church later in life, as the spectre of death loomed ever closer. Rain continued her sermon. Without anything before her, no paper notes or prompt cards, she spoke of the wind of the Holy Spirit, the pure, clean, oxygen required for the spirit to cleanse, that in order for a fire to burn it needed air. She likened the removal of the roof to a cleansing for the church and all its members. Her testimony seemed to come from the heart; no monotonous reading from the Bible for her. She spoke casually and personally, a stream of consciousness.

Joe was admiring the craftsmanship of the pews when Rain's testimony caught his ear again. She asked for the members to offer a prayer for someone close to her, a non-believer.

'I ask that you pray that she may find peace. For she is troubled, dear friends. She cannot forgive and she will not open up her heart, but I feel her pain, Lord. Save her, love her, protect her. Show her the way forward.'

Joe knew Rain addressed her God but she could have been talking to him. She could have been speaking about him, but he could hardly teach Saffron about forgiveness.

The first bars of the next hymn rang out and the congregation stood. Some raised their arms, palms open, as they sang. Eifion leaned over and whispered, 'You ever wish you had that kind of faith?'

'Sometimes,' Joe mouthed back. The old lady on his left, Mary, rapped his arm and smiled broadly at him.

Christ, she's going to try and convert me if I don't get out of here fast.

He joined in the song – it was the only traditional hymn of the service and the only one he knew. As it finished

Mary leant over again. 'Me, oh, my, you have a wonderful voice, young man. A gift, aye, a gift,' she said in her Scots burr. Joe nudged Eifion and indicated that he needed to go. He slipped out, leaving Eifion to admire Rain.

Chapter Seventeen

Before she left work, Saffron snooped around the underwear section of Wynne's on the pretext that it needed tidying. Customers regularly pulled pairs of knickers out of the five-packs and it was quite a job folding them correctly so they slipped back into the plastic wallets neatly. Assuming the full five were still present, which often they weren't. It was a well-known shoplifting ploy: a single pair did not set off the alarm. Saffron admired the ingenuity.

Like everything else in the shop, the bras and pants selection was miserable and on the whole the quality was poor. Skimpily cut, thin fabric, trimmed with stiff, scratchy lace. There was a tiny range of more luxurious items but even with Saffron's staff discount (a measly ten per cent) they'd come to more than she could really afford. And it was kind of sluttish, to invest in pricey underwear on the eve of a date. It wasn't as if she was even sure it was a proper date. They weren't going out. She hadn't got a clue what to wear and she couldn't dress up too much in case Rain starting asking awkward questions. She'd been fretting about it from the moment she'd woken up.

'Now, this will provide the lift you need,' said Mrs Evans, bustling over, holding aloft a black bra with cups large enough to fit over Saffron's head. 'You've quite a pair for such a skinny thing. You'll need a slightly smaller size though.'

Appalled, Saffron replaced the briefs she was holding and mumbled she was browsing rather than looking seriously and she really must dash.

'It's important to feel nice inside as well, you know. Doesn't matter if no one can see. You know and that's what counts,' Mrs Evans trilled as Saffron went to collect her bag. Sod the underwear. It probably wasn't going to be like that anyway. Joe might only have been being friendly. All day she'd re-run the events of the night before, questioning, doubting that it had happened the way she remembered it.

The plain white envelope was jammed in the letterbox when she'd staggered downstairs around eleven that morning. Saffron wondered if Joe had waited until he'd seen Rain leave. If Rain had seen it, she would surely have asked questions. Saffron never received snail mail.

Later, she tucked the envelope, containing the all-important map, in the back pocket of her jeans. She touched it for reassurance before she left the house, on the pretext she was meeting Ceri for a quick drink. Rain tried to disguise her disappointment that Saffron wouldn't be spending the evening at home and Saffron felt guilty. She knew how lonely her mother was, despite her protestations to the contrary. She agreed to set an evening aside. 'We could go out on Saturday night. Try the pizzeria on the seafront. It looks OK and you can't go wrong with Italian. We could go for a drink afterwards. Wherever the fancy takes us!' she said. It was an expression of Rain's.

'That'd be lovely, Saff. I'll book a table. Can't wait.'

Joe's map was detailed and easy enough to follow but she'd never have found his place without it; it was tucked away on the edge of the town, down a dirt track that looked like a private road. As advised, she brought a torch and was glad of it. Once on the track, it was pitch black without it. Creepy. The silence of the countryside, the emptiness, spookier than any dodgy area of London. Saffron hummed as she walked, flinching at every crackle and rustle. After a while, the path opened out to reveal a shadowy row of tumbledown cottages. They could easily have been mistaken as derelict; the soft glow of a single light the only clue one of them was inhabited.

She rapped softly on the front door. The knock echoed about the enclave. Her heart roared, from nerves or excitement she couldn't tell. She squeaked, 'Hello,' when he opened the door.

Even in the gloom of his hallway she could see how different he looked in this, his home environment. Stripped of his work clothes, his hammer and saw, the pencil tucked behind his ear, sawdust sprinkled over his hair, he looked trendy, more urbane and edgy. Still beautiful; more so, perhaps. His feet were bare.

Neither of them moved, they simply looked and smiled, as if neither of them could believe the other stood before them. Joe recovered first, stepped aside and said, 'Come in.' She followed him down the narrow hall, the smell of burning wood mingling with the lemony scent of his aftershave.

A fire crackled in an open hearth, casting an orange glow over a room notable only for its austerity. There was nothing personal or comforting whatsoever, no pictures on the walls or magazines lying around. The only hint at personality a small collection of video games and DVDs, a low pile of books, large ones, definitely not novels. She imagined it was how a clean squat might look.

'I'm not used to visitors,' he said, gesturing towards a settee with a large dip in the middle, like a crater.

'Should I feel honoured?' She'd meant it as a joke, but it sounded spiky and critical.

'Do you?' He smiled and, grateful for his generosity, she smiled back. 'Take a seat, m'lady. I'll go check on the grub. Can I get you a drink?'

She remembered the bottle she had in her bag and pulled it out. 'White,' she said, shrugging. 'I didn't know which you preferred but I remembered you drank the lighter fluid we bought that day and figured … I should have brought beer. I remembered you like it, but you don't usually serve beer with supper,' she floundered. She knew almost nothing about him.

'I am partial to the rough stuff too.'

'Oh, no … this is OK. I think. It was pricey so I hope so … Oh, crap, that sounds awful.'

He was laughing. 'I know what you mean.' He took the wine. 'Please sit down. Make yourself at home.' He checked himself. 'Comfortable. If you can. Sorry about the state of the sofa.'

When he returned from the kitchen with two glasses – tumblers – she was sitting on a cushion on the floor, staring into the fire. She'd taken her boots off.

'That better than the sofa, huh? Sorry about the glasses.' He held aloft of bottle of red. 'Do you like red? It goes better with the food. Hope you're hungry.'

'Red is OK. Smells lovely. What is it?'

'Lamb stew, slow cooked.' He squatted opposite her and placed his glass on the beaten up coffee table. The heat from the fire seared into his back. He moved round, closer to her, but not too close. He wanted to see her, to admire her.

She looked beautiful, her pale face illuminated by the fire, the rest of her melting into the darkness of the room. There was an ethereal quality to her and he found it hard to imagine her suiting the orderly, clinical, well-lit environment of a hospital. He corked the wine and poured it to stop himself from staring.

'Should let it breathe, but I forgot to open it earlier.'

'I wouldn't be able to tell the difference anyhow. You know wine, then?'

'Not really,' he lied. Until recently, Joe had been up on the most fashionable wines, the best vintages, which vineyards produced the richest, fullest wines. By most people's standards he was a bit of an expert. It wasn't a passion of his, he did prefer beer, but once upon a time it had been important that he knew which wines to order in a restaurant, how to make an impression.

She raised her glass. 'Cheers.'

'Cheers.' He sipped at his drink. Not bad, not bad at all for a supermarket wine. He'd chosen carefully and well.

'I love a real fire. We had one at home, in London, but only on special occasions. Too much like hard work, Dad said. I loved the sound of him chopping wood in the garden. He let me have a go, once, with his little axe. I swung it so hard it bounced off the block and landed in my foot. Ruined my wellies. I still have the scar.' She peeled back her sock to show him and stroked the arch of her right foot as she spoke.

'Must have been painful.'

'Not really. It hurts more now. Every time I see it, I'm reminded of him and the stupid stuff we did together.'

'That must be hard. We can change the subject.'

'Actually, it's nice to be able to mention him without feeling like I might upset someone. Mum. Rain.' She took a gulp of wine.

'Is she mad at you, 'cos ... you know ...' He thought how hard it must be for Rain not to wonder ... if Saffron hadn't drunk too much that night, if Stephen hadn't driven out into the countryside, if he'd taken it more slowly, not been so tired. It must have been hard for her not to blame her daughter, just a little bit.

'God, I wish.' Saffron's response was emphatic. 'I wish she had been, was. You wouldn't believe how I've longed for her to shout and scream, to talk to me about it. To blame me. Anything. Allow me to talk about it. She closed me off then and she still does now. She rambles on about it being God's will and how we will all be reunited in the end, even though she knows I don't buy into all that, and

167

when she does talk of him, it's like he was some kind of saint. I thought for a while this would rock her beliefs. How could it not? But no, she takes comfort from it. It's like a blanket, it keeps her warm, but she covers her head with it, blinds herself with her blanket of religion. She's so good about everyone, so kind, so forgiving. I asked her to forgive me, once, and she said, "There's nothing to forgive." What horse shit! I should be punished.'

'Why? Haven't you been punished enough?' He fiddled with his glass, running his finger round and round the rim till it made a faint wheeze. 'What was he like, your father?'

'Human.' She looked at Joe, her eyes wild. 'Like, not a saint.' He smiled at her, encouraging. 'A risk-taker. Easily bored. Funny. Impulsive.'

'I like him already.'

She tugged at her foot and crossed her legs, into a lotus position. Joe noted her flexibility, how pliable, like rubber, she seemed. 'What about you? Family?'

'Nope. My parents were killed in a plane crash –'

'Oh my God, I'm so sorry. Here's me wittering on. I had no idea,' she said, an intensity in her tone he found unnerving. But he'd started now and he had to explain.

He shrugged. 'You didn't know. I was eleven, but I hardly knew them anyway. Packed me off to boarding school as soon as they could, spent most of my holidays there. He worked abroad. I was never sure doing what. I said the diplomatic service when asked, or the secret service if I was trying to impress. He was as far off from James Bond as you can imagine.'

'So how come a posh boarding school kid ends up as a carpenter? I didn't think they'd allow that sort of thing? You rebelled, right?'

He paused.

The moment to put her straight came and went, and shame trickled through him. He liked her. He'd revealed something of his true self, but in the end he'd chickened out of telling her the whole truth and he couldn't work out why. He wanted to, in a way. Perhaps it was the comment about Stephen, being a risk-taker. Perhaps it was talk of forgiveness.

'What about you? Why medicine?' He steered the conversation back to her.

'Why not? I was good at science, not much good at anything else.'

Now she wasn't being honest. He stared at her, waiting for the truth.

'I thought I could help people. I was fascinated, am fascinated, by our capacity to heal and repair, with and without help. The body is this incredible mystery. I liked puzzles as a kid.'

'You will go back, finish your training?'

'Yeah, I can't stay here for ever. But only when Mum no longer needs me around.'

The realisation she would go eventually saddened him. But that was crazy. He wouldn't be here for ever either; he'd have to move on, wouldn't he?

She continued. 'For ages I didn't think I'd be able to do it again. After failing my dad so spectacularly.'

He wanted to argue that she hadn't failed her dad, but thought better of it. She'd not accept it, he was sure. 'What about your mum? Will she stay here? It's a small town, her choices will be limited. She's still young enough.'

'I don't know. Her mission is to increase numbers, the church needs it. I feel bad about her, I do, but I can't ...' Saffron's feelings of guilt were almost palpable. Joe regretted even mentioning Rain.

'Of course you can't. Right, let's eat. I'm starving. You can wash your hands in the kitchen if you like. Not much in the way of home comforts here, but it is clean.'

She delved in her bag and brought out her hand wash gel. 'Always got this.'

'You must have been a girl guide.'

'No way. Far too much like the military.'

He stood and disappeared into the kitchen.

The stew smelt good. He hoped she'd like it. He'd remembered the stew on the Aga at the manse kitchen all those weeks ago and presumed she must like it. He filled the bowls – one bought that afternoon in the supermarket, along with another fork and spoon – and placed them on the newly acquired tray.

Saffron tried to finish the meal Joe had prepared for her but nerves prevented her. He asked if she didn't like it, claiming not to be offended if this was the case, and she did her best to reassure him. Conversation stalled occasionally. He wasn't like other men she'd known, who seemed happiest when talking about themselves. He seemed much more interested in asking her questions and while she was, on the whole, happy to oblige, as the evening drew to a close she felt she understood him little more than she did at the start. He revealed almost nothing about himself and she couldn't for the life of her read him. She considered herself quite perceptive but her powers failed her that evening.

Around eleven she began to make a move towards home. Tomorrow was a work day. She asked if she might use the bathroom before she went. Like the rooms in the cottage she'd seen – the living room, the kitchen, the hall – it was shabby but clean, and devoid of a personal touch other than a solitary toothbrush in a tumbler like the one they'd drunk wine out of. Above the sink was a cabinet with mirrored doors. She slid a door open slyly, wondering if she might find a packet of condoms. He'd not so much as laid a hand on her all night, though she'd caught him staring at her when he thought she wasn't looking. The cabinet contained nothing more than a can of shaving foam, a packet of disposable razors, and a box of aspirin.

Disappointed, she closed the door and ruffled her fingers through her hair. It was a bit flat on top and this accentuated her fair roots. She needed to re-dye it, or touch up her roots, but she'd resisted for reasons she couldn't pinpoint.

As she made her way across the narrow landing, she peeped into one of the bedrooms; there were only two. It looked like the one Joe used, though she couldn't be sure. She leant in further, her eyes adjusting to the gloom. It contained a double bed − made with hospital-like precision, the blanket pulled tight and smooth across the mattress, the corners folded like an envelope, top sheet folded crisply over the blanket − a small wardrobe, a chair and a dresser. Incongruous against the order and frugal nature of the room was an untidy pile of clothes by the near wall: jeans, jumpers, T-shirts. What was that, almost hidden, beneath? It looked like a picture frame.

Saffron knew it was wrong but she couldn't help it. She tiptoed in, crouched by the clothes and eased the frame out. A woman and a man. Arm in arm, smiling at the camera. It was difficult to be sure in only the overspill light from the landing but the girl could have been Joe's sister. The same wavy hair, straight white teeth. And her eyes − they were different colours too. The boy was blond and handsome, square-jawed, high cheekbones, he carried an air of certainty. Their embrace was casual, like one between friends rather than lovers. Why hadn't Joe mentioned a sister? Where was she now?

Aware she would raise suspicion if she didn't move back downstairs, she replaced the frame and crept out.

He insisted on walking her home and she was grateful despite initially saying she'd be fine. In the darkness he took hold of her hand and her heart rate increased. Would he kiss her goodbye? She hoped so. Her mind flitted between dreams of kissing him, feeling him against her,

171

and the image of the beautiful girl in the photograph. Perhaps he'd not mentioned her because it was too painful to do so? And if so, what had happened to her? And who was the boy? A friend from school? He'd not spoken of any friends in Coed Mawr, apart from Tyson and Eifion who weren't really friends but colleagues.

Close to the bottom of the lane, she stopped, not wanting to be drawn back into the light. 'Isn't the night amazing? I never fully appreciated it until I came here. True darkness. You can lose yourself in it. It hides so much.'

He didn't reply immediately, the only sound the rustling of birds in the undergrowth. They stood very still. 'It's another world. Kind of magical, mysterious.'

'Like under the sea.'

'Not really. That's what's incredible. Everything changes with the setting and rise of the sun. It's the same place, but entirely transformed. Alien.' He paused. His tone altered, as if embarrassed by the romanticism of his earlier comments. 'It is great for hiding in.' He turned to her, a grey, shadowy figure. 'I ran away from school. A lot. Always at night. I grew to understand this world, while my hunters didn't.'

'Were you never afraid? It's kind of scary.'

'At first. But I grew to love it, felt like it belonged to me. Or I belonged to it. This world empty of people.'

A creature swept overhead, disturbing the air. Saffron flinched.

'A brown long-eared,' Joe said, tipping his head.

'Bats,' she said, something falling into place. 'That's where your interest in bats comes from?'

'Yes,' he whispered. 'Though they're more social at dawn. Few are out this late. It's gleaning, feeding. There'll be more soon, as they come out of hibernation.'

She shuddered. Bats were creepy. Flappy rodents, smelly, if she remembered a trip to the bat house at a small zoo as a child correctly. 'They're a bit of a weird hobby.'

'I can think of weirder. They're misunderstood, like many creatures of the night, but especially so. They don't deserve their bad reputation.'

'Dracula has a lot to answer for,' she laughed, though she wondered if he felt the same way as the bats, misunderstood, if it was why he was holed up here, hidden in amongst the dense woodland.

A fox screamed in the distance. He pulled her towards him, the smallest tug on her hand, and she fell into him, into a kiss as deep and dark and all-consuming as the night. She pushed all thoughts of what he concealed from her busy head. All that mattered was him, right here, right now.

Chapter Eighteen

'Is this too mutton?'

Rain appeared in the doorway in a red dress which finished above her knees. Ready twenty minutes earlier, Saffron was sitting on the sofa half-watching a quiz show, fiddling with her phone, willing Joe to text her. The kiss in the lane had emboldened her and she'd pushed a piece of paper with her number on it into his hand, prepared before she'd left the manse, whispering, 'Call me.'

'You'll see me again?' he'd said.

Such doubt had surprised her. But days had passed and no call, no text. She'd scanned the chapel roof as she'd walked past on her way to work the day before, averting her eyes when Tyson looked over and smirked. She'd not dared look earlier, either.

'Well?' Rain said. 'That bad?'

'No. No. It's fabulous,' Saffron said, glancing over. 'You look fantastic. If I'm half as gorge as you at your age, I'll be very pleased.'

'But what about the knees? Baggy old lady knees?'

'You can hardly tell in tights!'

'So they are saggy.'

Saffron threw her phone on the sofa. 'No!' He wasn't going to call now. She looked again at her mum. Rain hadn't altered her make-up in years. It was more noticeable because she'd put more than usual on. As a teenager Saffron had copied her mother's look with disastrous results – their complexions were so different, the shape of their faces, everything.

You could do with updating your style. Or wearing less.

Or both. You're so pretty; you don't do yourself justice.

The thin pencil line of kohl underneath Rain's eyes gave her a slightly hard look and the blue on the inside of her eyelids was just plain dated. Saffron stepped towards Rain. She'd never be able to tell her though.

'You look nice too,' Rain said as they moved into the hallway.

Saffron huffed. 'I'm in my jeans and a jumper.' She sat on the bottom stair and laced up her boots.

'It's your face. You're wearing less make-up. Less eyeliner. Suits you. Brings out your eyes.'

'Thanks. Too much can be ageing.'

'At your age!'

'At any age.'

Why are you so dressed up? We're only going to the pizzeria on the front. And wasn't that dress Dad's favourite?

She'd not seen her mother in it for years.

Rain turned to the mirror in the coat stand and swept her index finger underneath each eye. 'Do you think I have too much on?' Her voice trembled.

'I wouldn't have said so … but now that you've wiped some off … Brings out your colour too.'

'It's too much?' Rain rubbed at her cheeks.

'It's fine. You're lovely. C'mon, we'll be late. Place might be packed, we'll lose our table.' She flung a jacket on and ushered Rain outside.

Eight fifteen on a Saturday night and the pizzeria was almost deserted. Rain felt over-dressed and super-conspicuous. They were sitting in the window seat at the waiter's insistence; it was the last place she wanted to sit but she'd felt so sorry for the restaurateur she'd been unable to refuse. She knew it would make the place look more inviting if there were customers visible from the outside.

176

It was a family-run pizzeria, with décor she'd seen Europe-wide: green, white and red tablecloths, raffia-covered wine bottles the shape of gourds doubling as candlesticks, and mediocre reproductions of Italian landmarks on the walls. It was pleasant and cosy, and she welcomed the familiarity of it.

Rain glanced over at the couple hunched at the back of the restaurant: middle-aged, not speaking to each other, sawing away at their pizzas with grim determination, a half-carafe of red wine between them. Her stomach roiled and she turned back to her daughter. There was an aura about Saff; she couldn't pinpoint what it was, but something was different. She wore the same clothes; same deliberately messy hair-do, though she'd noted that her roots needed retouching.

'Red, white or beer, Mum?'

Saffron's question made her jump. 'Oh! Erm, I'm not sure. What do you fancy?'

'Anything. You choose.'

This went on for some time, each refusing to make a decision. The tinny muzak playing in the background irritated, like a fly buzzing about her ear. She found it hard to concentrate.

If Stephen were here, he'd have ordered before he sat down, for everyone.

There was a repeat performance when it came to the food, each of them dithering over a menu that wasn't expansive, asking what the other was having, chopping and changing. Even the waiter, who was hardly rushed off his feet, grew impatient. In the end, Rain went for her default choice: gnocchi – to heck with her hips – and Saff hers: salad niçoise. The waiter shuffled off, the initial spring in his step gone.

'Is that all, Saffy? A salad? My treat.' Saffron gave her one of her looks and Rain backed off. She must stop nagging her about eating; Saff was healthy, sensible; she'd always been lean. Tonight was meant to be lovely, a chance for mother and daughter to spend some quality time together.

Saffron picked up her beer and swigged from the bottle. Rain twitched. She hated that and it wasn't as if Saff was a student now. Why couldn't she pour it into the glass provided?

'So, how was it at the shop today? Busy?' Rain said, sipping at the wine. It tasted like vinegar.

'The usual.' Saffron rapped her fingernails against her empty glass and stared out of the window. All Rain could see was Saffron's reflection. Could Saff see anything of the street?

'And what's usual? You don't really talk about the shop.' Her voice seemed to echo round the room.

'There's nothing that interesting to say. It's a job. It's OK.'

Saff seemed so distracted. 'Oh, I understand that it must seem ever so dull after all the excitement of medicine, the drama, the importance ...'

'It's not *Holby City*.' Saffron turned away from the window, back to her, and smiled. 'Look, Mum, the shop's fine ... I ...' Her smile faded away with her words.

The door swung open and a large group of maybe a dozen people trooped in, aged seven to seventy. The restaurant erupted into activity. Another waiter appeared from the bar as coats were collected, tables were joined together, cutlery and condiments transferred from one table to the next, menus distributed.

'How lovely!' Rain said above the commotion. She leant across their small round table and whispered, 'There'll be some atmosphere now.' The music grew louder to compete with the ebullient laughter and squeals of the family party. She watched the father of the youngest child hold a chair out for his wife, place a napkin on her lap and deposit a kiss on her cheek. Stephen did that for her in the early days. 'Big family.' She smiled at Saff who only shrugged and took another gulp of beer. Goodness, she'd almost finished the bottle.

'Steady, Saffy.'

'It's only a small one.'

Rain was drawn to the family again as they shouted out drinks orders. What was the celebration? Or maybe there wasn't one. Maybe they were just celebrating being together, all of them, one large extended happy family. Rain's guts twisted. How reduced her immediate family was now. Matthew was away and heaven knew when he'd be back. Her parents were long gone; Stephen's had emigrated to Australia years ago. She'd met them only once, at their wedding. Money was tight for the de Lacys senior after a bankruptcy so they'd not come back for a visit, not until the funeral, and though she and Stephen often spoke about making the trip out there, somehow it had never happened. Money wasn't plentiful in their house either, what with Stephen refusing to move from his post at the council to a better-paid position in a private firm. University colleagues of Stephen's had established their own practices and made a fortune during the gentrification of formerly undesirable areas of London. One had offered Stephen a job but he'd refused. 'Why should the private sector nab the cream of the crop? Don't public buildings deserve the same love and attention?' he'd shouted. Rain admired his socialist principles, but couldn't fend off twinges of envy whenever they visited friends' homes.

The waiter arrived with their food and, famished, Rain tucked in. Saffron pushed food around her plate, the eggs and tuna untouched. 'Gnocchi's surprisingly good. How's your salad?'

'Tuna's tinned.'

'Oh dear, and you don't eat eggs. I've often wondered why you're such a fan of niçoise. Shall we order something else? I'd hate for you to leave hungry.'

'It's fine.'

'Really, it's no bother, no bother at all.' Her voice rose higher and higher.

'Mum. I don't want anything else.' Saffron's comment landed during a lull in the lively conversation at the next table. It was loud and sharp. Silence bit. Then, a child's cry, the bars of the next song on the CD. Rain stabbed at her gnocchi, but she could no longer taste anything.

Saffron reached across the table and touched her arm. 'Sorry, Mum. I'm edgy. I need to tell you something and I don't know how or where to begin. I should have said something ages ago, but I couldn't find the words ...'

So, I was right. She's leaving.

The gnocchi felt like a ball of tissue paper in her throat.

Rain always knew Saffron wouldn't stay in Coed Mawr for ever. Of course she knew that. Saffron came with her because she was ill; she'd had a breakdown. She needed to be cared for, comforted, away from the constant reminders of the harsh blow life had dealt her. Dealt them both. When Saffron was healed, she would return to medicine and that meant leaving. Back to London. But it was too soon. For Rain. She wasn't ready to be left alone.

Trembling, Rain put down her fork and held her daughter's hand. 'The beginning. The beginning is always a good place to start. And you mustn't worry about me. I'll be fine. I'm never alone, not completely.'

'Mum, I'm not about to leave ...'

Relief surged over Rain. She listened as her daughter began to speak and then the trembling spread through her entire body.

She'd had no idea, no idea at all. Had she ever known her daughter? 'I thought we were the same. That we understood one another because of our loss. Often, I felt your loss was even greater. After all, you lost out on all the years of happiness I'd had, the years of love, experience,

180

and togetherness I shared with your father. I have so many memories to enjoy and treasure. You don't. I prayed for you.' She felt betrayed. It was irrational, she knew that, but nevertheless, all this time.

'We never spoke about it. We've never shared our feelings about it. You won't talk about how you feel. You just accept it. You won't let me talk about Dad. Not really. And I couldn't talk about Ben because everyone spoke like he was the love of my life, like they knew what I was going through when they had absolutely no fucking idea. I couldn't express the grief I felt, feel, because it wasn't what people wanted to see. It wasn't what you wanted to see. You wanted me to feel like you. But I can't. I was angry. I'm still angry. I feel guilty and confused and like the worst person on earth sometimes. Don't you ever get tired of it, Mum? Being so good. You don't blame me, you don't blame your God, you don't blame anyone. And it's like my grief for Dad has been relegated to second place, because, well, he was my father, not the "love of my life". I've been trapped in a lie.'

'Maybe there's no one to blame.' Rain's voice seemed to come from somewhere outside of herself.

'Maybe there isn't.' Saffron sounded exhausted. 'But don't you ever, even for a minute, feel angry? Feel so sad you can't even weep, get out of bed, listen to someone grumbling about some lame, inconsequential detail of their life?'

'There have been moments of anger, of course.' Rain rolled and unrolled the corner of the tablecloth. 'Are you saying you felt no love for Ben?' She could hear the hurt in her voice; she had loved Ben, like a son.

'Jesus Christ! Of course I did. But not love, love. Like a brother. No, not even that ...'

Ignoring the blasphemy, Rain said, 'How can you be sure? All love changes.' She looked at Saffron's creamy complexion, her plump lips, her smooth neck. She's so

181

young, younger even than her years. How can she understand what happens to love?

'I know, I just know.'

'Were you in love with someone else?'

'God, no!'

'So how can you be sure?'

'Because I am.'

Was that a flush she detected? Saffron turned away from her scrutiny, and after a pause, continued. 'How was it for you, with Dad?'

'Full of respect, companionship, understanding –'

'At first?' Saffron interrupted her.

Rain coughed. 'Well, he followed me, into church. He wasn't a believer then. He converted, for –'

'How it felt, not the facts. I know this story …'

Rain closed her eyes. How had it felt, all those years ago? Magical, dizzying, all-consuming. She smiled at the memory and Stephen appeared. She pictured herself, sitting in the pew, sneaking a peek between her praying hands, the back of his head visible in the pink glow between her fingers. How clever he was to sit in front of her. Most boys would have positioned themselves behind her, giving themselves the advantage, watcher not watched. But not Stephen. Always the maverick. She pulled her praying hands down from her eyes to her mouth and because she wanted to reach over and kiss that lovely neck but couldn't, she kissed the air trapped in her palms instead.

Her desire verged on debilitating; she could hardly function. She questioned if her feelings were unholy, unnatural, and her minister directed her to the Book of Songs in her Bible. She gorged on the verses with their lush vineyards, heavy scent, and lovers with legs like marble, and when she touched herself in the darkness of her room she felt closer to God.

Was it all about the physical? Yes and no. Yes, because

182

it was that which consumed her, which drove them into each other's arms. No, because there was talking and laughing and a sense of connection like nothing she had experienced before, not even that first, life-changing connection with God.

Emotion choking her, Rain tried to convey this to her daughter, who sat silent and attentive.

'How could you be sure it wasn't infatuation?' Saff said, blushing again.

'I couldn't. You can't, I don't believe. Perhaps it's about reciprocation ... true love travels both ways, infatuation doesn't always. Who knows! I've only ever loved your father ...' Rain stopped and stared at Saff, whose colour deepened.

How had she missed it?

Saffy's in love. With JJ.

The realisation winded her. She stabbed her fork at the gnocchi. She covered her mouth with her palm, took a sip of water, pretending the pasta was too hot.

It was so obvious there was no reason to doubt or question her instinct. The light within Saffron, the way she was around him. It could only be love.

Ha! What a foolish woman, you are. It was there, right from the start, when he came into the manse after rescuing her from Devil's Rise. She wasn't embarrassed about you – your role in the community (though that would be a first) – she was awkward because she didn't understand what was going on. Didn't understand her raging emotions.

JJ. A niggle of suspicion. She'd felt it before. Why? What was it about him she didn't entirely trust? She'd mistakenly thought he was attracted to her, hoped he was, even. The silly insecurity of a middle-aged widow. She longed to warn her daughter. Be careful. Love is joy; love is pain; love is inescapable. But Saffron was radiant. So happy. How could she not be happy for her?

'Do you think I'm a bad person, Mum? I grieve for Ben, just not in the way everyone thinks and not like I do Dad. I know it's my own fault, keeping it secret and that.'

'You sensed I needed you to feel the same as me.'

'Perhaps. Thank you.'

'For what?'

'For listening. For understanding. For being so *nice*.'

They laughed.

'Thought that drove you mad.'

'It does. C'mon, let's pay up. There's ice cream in the freezer. We can eat the lot, from the tub, when we get home.'

'You mean I can eat the lot.'

'That's going to change. A lot's going to change from now on.' Saff waved at the waiter who scurried over, and Rain wasn't sure if she felt happy or sad.

Rain held her open Bible to her face and inhaled. It smelt of the church and pear drops and a lifetime of comfort, but she was struggling to find solace. She wasn't angry with Saff; she felt afraid for her, and sad. All this time and she'd only just felt able to speak the truth.

What is it about me that makes it so difficult for Saffy to be honest? I've failed her in some way.

She wondered when, if, Saffron would tell her she was in love with JJ. Rain tried to be happy for her, but all she could feel was a deep, deep melancholy. Her daughter's heart was about to be tested and Rain suspected it wasn't as strong as it would need to be.

Chapter Nineteen

Joe hated Sundays. It was the longest day of the week without the distraction of work; the day he felt most alone. Whenever there was an opportunity to labour he took it. He suspected it was one of the reasons Derek liked him so much, though it wasn't appropriate on this job, obviously. But this Sunday was different; he had an option, if only he was brave enough to follow through. He'd woken early, tense and excited.

He lay in bed, staring at the ceiling, and held his phone between his thumb and index finger and flipped it over and over on the mattress. He pulled it towards his face and dragged up his contacts. Contacts! He had so few: Simon, Derek, Tyson, Eifion, Rain and, now, Saffron. His thumb hovered over her details. Was it too early to call? She'd been out the night before with her mother. Rain had announced their plans when she'd brought Joe a mug of coffee on Saturday morning, as was her habit if she was about. No matter how many times Joe said he was fine with instant, she insisted on making real and she always took time to make conversation, no matter how busy she was. Joe knew it wasn't all about being nice; she was trying to suss him out. He intrigued her and this made him nervous. She'd stopped inviting him to coffee mornings and the like weeks ago and realising that he would not come to her, she came out to him.

The phone screen went black. Decision made. He would not call Saffron yet. He clambered out of bed and ran a bath.

Shortly after ten thirty, when Rain would be inside the

chapel preparing to meet her congregation and Saffron would be alone in the manse, Joe called. She didn't pick up immediately and it occurred to him he might have misread her. Maybe she wasn't as keen as she'd appeared. Maybe she'd changed her mind, had time to reflect and decided he wasn't worth the bother after all. Maybe she'd spoken to Rain, told her about Ben, and Rain had persuaded her to play the grieving girlfriend until a decent amount of time had passed. However long that was supposed to be.

He was about to hang up, his throat tight, disappointment scratching the insides of his lungs, when a breathless voice stopped him.

'Hello?' She sounded as if she was walking; he could hear a whistling. Wind?

'Saffron? Where are you?'

'On top of the cliffs. It's amazing up here; the view of the bay, the town, is amazing, the mountains in the background are awesome.' She sounded full of joy.

'Will you wait for me?'

'What? You'll have to speak up. The reception up here's terrible.'

He bellowed into the phone, realising she might not have picked up instantly because she hadn't heard it. She wasn't playing hard to get. How could she? She couldn't have been sure it was him. He blocked his number to everyone.

'Yes, I'll wait for you,' she replied.

He was out of the cottage in seconds, carried by a lightness he'd almost forgotten was possible. He jumped into the Landy and roared down the lane.

His phone rang as he pulled into the visitor centre car park. Simon. He had to take it.

'Yeah.'

'Yo, man, how you doin'?'

186

'Good. Look Simon, I'm in a bit of rush.'

'On a Sunday? Yo. Sounds like the old days.'

'Cut to the chase, Si. Please.'

'Great news. The private dick's headed west. Jumped a train to Holyhead – I sure as hell nearly pissed myself when I saw that booking – and then a boat to Ireland. Dublin. Way off, man. Way off.'

Today is going to be a very good day indeed.

'Brilliant. Si, can we talk in more detail tomorrow evening?'

'Sure. Love to hear what you've got planned for those fuckers.'

'OK. Tomorrow.'

Joe had nothing planned, that was the truth of it. Vague ideas, but nothing more. His head was full of the here and now. Saffron.

'Joe?' Simon said.

'Thanks for this, Simon. I'm glad you called.'

Joe threw back his head and whooped. Thank God the car park was empty.

From the visitor centre he strode towards the cliff and the view over the sea, fighting against the wind as he went. It came from the south, warm, hinting at summer. He was glad it blew inland. Saffron might well have been blown over the edge. She was sitting on the grass, legs stretched out before her, looking at the turbines which spotted the horizon. He slid alongside her and she turned to greet him with a smile so welcoming the day got even better. He felt impossibly happy and leant over and kissed her on the cheek.

'Hi,' she said.

'Hi.' Nothing else needed saying. He rested on his arms, elbows straight, mimicking her, hands grazing hers on the damp ground and they gazed over the landscape without speaking.

A cable car groaned into action and rocked down the hillside to the bay.

'Ever ridden one?' he asked.

'Nope.'

'Want to?'

'Not particularly. Shall we go somewhere? Out of Coed Mawr. Exploring. I've been here over six months and I know little of the surrounding area.'

'It's a national park. Meant to be beautiful.' He'd not ventured far either.

'Only one way to find out.' She got to her feet and, wiping her palms over her backside, turned towards the car park. 'Race you to the Land Rover.' And with that, she was gone, pelting down the slope, arms and legs flailing, skipping more than running, long hair flying over her head. She was no athlete, so he watched for a few seconds, to give her a head start, and then he broke into a sprint, charging after her.

I'd run for miles to catch you. Miles and miles.

Without a map or any idea where they were heading, he followed the road which cut into mountains draped with wispy clouds. The road grew narrower and narrower, jagged rocks the colour of pewter spiked from the heather-dusted, coarse grass. As the Landy rolled slowly past, the odd grazing sheep lifted a head to regard the intruders, bemused and nonchalant. Such staring unnerved Joe somewhat. Those blank, yellow eyes.

After an hour, they stopped at a village deep in the heart of the mountains, popular with walkers and climbers judging by the shops lining the higgledy-piggledy streets. A noisy river bisected the centre and after buying pasties and drinks from a bakery they followed it until they reached a waterfall. They sat on a slate wall and devoured the pies, the crashing water making conversation almost impossible.

Joe watched Saffron as she drank from the can. Her

legs dangled over the wall, the dark water pooled below her. 'This OK?' he yelled. 'Not exactly romantic.'

She turned her head so that she faced him, her blue eyes unnerving, as well as transparent. 'I disagree. It's one of the most romantic places, ever.'

They leant forward, their mouths meeting in a kiss. Joe felt the caress of the splashing water from the falls brushing his cheek and though he didn't say so, he agreed with her.

'You going to finish that?' he asked, nodding at the half-eaten pasty sitting on the paper bag by her side.

'Yes. I'm ravenous,' she said, ramming it into her mouth.

From the village they drove further into the mountains until they reached an expanse of water. 'Is this Bala Lake?' Saffron said, 'I read about it somewhere. We could hire a boat. Might be fun?'

Joe shook his head. 'Can't be, we're too westerly.' Something about it looked man-made. 'Let's stop anyway. Sun's out.'

He pulled over and they jumped out. Saffron bounded over to a sign, while he collected his sunglasses.

'A reservoir,' she announced, as he approached. 'Says something about Liverpool City Council here. That's weird.'

'I wonder if it's the place Eifion was telling me about. They destroyed a village to build it. Moved everyone out and the water wasn't even to supply Wales. There was an outcry, protests. Led to an increase in support for Plaid Cymru.'

'What?'

'Welsh Nationalist Party. My pronunciation is probably horrible. It was one of many things which helped the move for devolution.'

'Wow. You certainly have some random conversations.

How come you got talking about this?'

'The pier really. And Tyson's a Liverpudlian.'

'You've lost me. The Tyson bit I get. The pier?' Her brows furrowed.

'Eifion has a shop on the pier. One of the developers fighting for the contract is English apparently. They want to pull the ballroom down. Insult to injury. If they win, that is.'

'I love piers. I remember the one at Brighton best. Never went as a kid, but when I was at med school we used to go down for the odd weekend. Just for the hell of it. They're so tacky, they're sick.' There it was again, that child-like joy, excitement.

He pointed ahead, to some kind of monument, and they followed the road which bordered the reservoir. The sun beat down, warm for early April.

'Do you remember the West Pier? Before it burnt down? Before it was nothing more than a skeleton?'

'Not really.' She stopped, closed her eyes and tilted her face at the sun.

So she isn't a child of the night, despite her Gothic style.

They strolled on, leisurely and comfortable. 'I took a tour of it, the West Pier. When it was dilapidated rather than ruined, when they were still arguing about whether to restore or develop. Though it had been badly treated, and ignored, and was covered in pigeon shit,' he screwed up his face at the memory, 'you could still see what it had been once. Its splendour. I loved it. I wanted to restore it, make it better.' He checked himself; he was about to reveal too much.

'It's hard to disguise what we are completely and the same is true of objects. I mean, I've seen people ravaged by disease and age, but you can still tell what someone might have been like in their youth, whether they were beautiful or not, before the cancer or dementia got to them.

Do you know what I mean? That was always an attraction with medicine. I could help make people better, get them back to what they really were, and not what they had become. Most of the time. And if not, I could care. Treat them with respect, dignity.'

He wasn't sure he agreed with everything she said. Some people were expert at hiding their true nature. 'Maybe.'

'We should get involved in the pier campaign. Mum's heavily into it now.'

'Maybe.' *No way, too public. Even if that PI has gone to Ireland.*

She stopped. 'I'm ashamed to admit this but I've never been on the pier at Coed Mawr.'

'So you don't love them that much,' he teased, reminding her of her earlier comment.

She kicked at the grass, head down. 'I've not really given Coed Mawr a chance. Always seen it as a prison, somewhere to escape from as soon as I can, even though I came to escape the memories.' She glanced up and smiled, ruefully, before returning to kicking the ground. 'And take care of Mum. Keep an eye on her.'

'Let's go back. Walk along the pier, buy some chips, sit on a bench and see if we can keep the scrounging gulls off our food. Or we can just wander along it for a bit, and I can take you out to dinner. Somewhere decent.'

'I'd love that. Chips on the pier. Forget the fancy restaurant.'

Caught behind a tractor and then stuck in a traffic jam, it took almost two hours to get back to Coed Mawr. Saffron was surprised by the number of cars on the road until she remembered the schools had broken up for Easter. Wynne's was selling chocolate eggs and Mrs Evans had instructed Saffron to be more vigilant now that the children were on holiday. 'There'll be hordes of them in here. And they'll as soon have them eggs as look at you. Same every year. Thieving beggars. I don't know why Mr Wynne insists on letting them in so many at a time. "Restrict the numbers," I say. "Other shops do it." But he won't listen. Silly old fool. Don't know why he made me manager if he won't let me implement ideas, I don't.'

The sun was way past its zenith when they stepped onto the pier; the sticky air cold, a reminder that winter was barely out. Most of the huts were closed, or closing, many were boarded up. Saffron looked down at the sea through the gaps between the boards, thrilled by imagining what would happen if they collapsed.

'I'm not sure the chip shop will be open. Do you want to turn round? We could go to the one in town,' Joe said.

'Let's carry on, I can wait.'

She was enjoying the walk, enjoying the little huts with their candy-striped façades. She tried to guess what they sold or offered from the names painted across the tops, those that were clear enough for her to read. There was tarot reading, hand-made jewellery, doughnuts. All the usual pier offerings. Gulls perched on the railings and watched them as they passed, hand in hand.

Just the other side of the amusement arcade in the middle of the pier, Saffron noticed a faded red and white striped stick perched on the top of one of the huts. It could have been a barber's pole, but she guessed it was Eifion's rock shop. As they neared, a head poked out of the saloon style doors.

'Well, hello there. Fancy seeing you here,' Eifion sang.

Instantly, Saffron and Joe released their hold, arms falling by their sides.

Another head appeared besides his: Ceri. 'Watcha! Buy a stick of rock, why don't you?' She waved a pink stick. 'Or a dummy if you prefer?' She brandished a transparent red rock dummy. Saffron had coveted them as a child, always refused by her parents. She stopped in front of the shop and laughed. 'No thanks. I value my teeth.'

'You and every other bugger round here. Dad blames the Americans and all those perfect gnashers.'

Joe addressed Eifion. 'Business slow? Might pick up during the holiday weekend itself?'

'Might do.' He circled the hut with his eyes. 'Need to spruce up this place before the summer season. Needs a new roof and counter, window frames are rotten too. But it all costs and the rent's gone up by you wouldn't believe. Lick of paint if nothing else.'

'How comes you two are out and about?' Ceri appeared beside them, leaving her dad to close the window and shutters.

Saffron and Joe went to talk at the same time. He waved an arm, indicating she should speak first. 'We bumped into each other on the prom. Both hungry, thought we'd get some chips.' The lie came easily and she knew had he spoken, he'd have lied too.

'You'll be lucky. Place has closed down. Surprised you eat chips, Saff,' Ceri said. 'I'm starving too. We could all go into town.'

Eifion appeared beside his daughter. 'Toppling like dominoes, they are. At this rate, might be the last shop standing this end of the pier. I wonder if it's that,' he pointed to the tumble-down ballroom at the far end, 'that puts people off. It needs to be renovated, it really does.'

Joe peaked a hand across his forehead and looked into the sky. A flock of starlings swarmed overhead. 'Let's take a look.'

Eifion was reticent. He wasn't sure the structure was entirely safe, he said, but Joe argued, convincingly, that if it was in serious danger of collapsing the whole pier would have been closed to the public. Ceri was keen to investigate, as was Saffron.

'Life doesn't get any more exciting than breaking and entering!' Ceri said, charging towards the tip of the pier.

Chapter Twenty

A few metres in front of the entrance to the ballroom a makeshift barrier decorated with frayed yellow tape stretched from one side of the pier to the other. Tacked above the double doors was a wooden board with hand-painted lettering: Danger. Do Not Enter. It had a bodged feel to it, as if cobbled together by amateurs. Joe wondered who was responsible for the site while the wrangling over restoration or a new building played out. From what he could see the interior of the ballroom was magnificent. Externally it reminded him of the Taj Mahal, with its domed roof, twisting spires, and arched windows. Much of the glass had been smashed or blown out of the windows but coloured fragments remained at the edges and it brought to mind a church. This was a temple too, once, a place to worship at the altar of pleasure.

Saffron was talking to Eifion about the pier's ownership. Joe hadn't been listening fully but this line of enquiry caught his attention. He refocused on the little gang who stood admiring the structure.

'A trust owns the pier,' Eifion explained. 'The dispute is over the exact nature of the work to be carried out. The council has the power to veto planning and so forth. There are many who want the ballroom to stay, to be made like new again. There's a minority who want to tear it down and have something new.'

'And that's what's delaying everything?' Saffron said.

'Yes. And in the meantime, the structure's getting more and more ruined. Getting harder and harder to make good.'

Joe was only half-listening again; he was considering if

it was safe to enter. He swung one leg, and then the other, over the barrier and stepped towards the open doorway. The frame felt solid enough. He leaned in. It was a shell, pretty much, but it wasn't the building itself he was interested in any more. He thought he saw movement in the far corner; he definitely heard something stirring. He made his way across what must have been the dance floor to the far left hand corner, stopping occasionally to wipe his fingers over tiny heaps of dust. Underneath the beams, the floor was splattered with pigeon waste. A dead chick lay decomposing beside an empty bottle of vodka, half a dozen cans of Special Brew, and a neat pile of cigarette butts. Whoever had been here was a heavy smoker. Joe wasn't the first intruder. Near the corner, Joe craned his neck and peered at where once there must have been a ceiling.

There, where the stud wall had crumbled. He was sure of it. Movement. He tiptoed closer, his eyes never leaving the rafters. He stopped again. Yes. He was right. It came again, a stirring, and just as he thought it was about to move …

'Oh my God, it's flipping disgusting in 'ere.'

Ceri.

He jumped and spun on his heels, finger pressed over his mouth.

Behind Ceri were Saffron and Eifion, treading gingerly across the dance floor, heads circling, eyes sweeping across the space, admiring. They stopped dead when they saw Joe, hushing them all.

Without speaking, Joe pointed to the eaves and they looked up, mystified, and, judging by the glaze in their eyes, anticipating something horrific.

Saffron looked back down at him first and mouthed, 'What?'

'A roost,' he whispered.

'Roost?' Ceri said, at full volume. 'I can't see no

chickens.'

The others turned and, in unison, said, 'Hush!'

'Bats. Pipistrelles,' Joe said. 'They might be out at sunset. Not sure if it's warm enough. Shall we wait and see?'

'You're kidding me, right? No way, am I staying here till it's dark. Place is spooky enough as it is. I'm out of here,' Ceri said, edging backwards.

Joe turned to Saffron, who stood by his side now, eyes fixed on the eaves. Next to her was Eifion, also fixed on the eaves.

'You've fantastic eyesight. Whatever made you think they might be here?' Eifion said.

'A hunch. I've been fascinated by bats ever since I was a boy.'

'All boys like Batman and that,' Ceri said.

'Maybe. But I was interested in the real animals, not the fantasy. I still am.'

A gust of wind rushed in; a can rattled across the floor with a tinny echo. Joe turned to find Ceri creeping back towards the group, mouthing, 'Sorry. Me and my big feet.'

'Hey, don't worry. Look, I think it's too cold for them anyway. They're probably still in torpor. If we stay our body heat will disturb them too. And you're right about the light. We should get out of here. Leave them in peace.'

From her pocket Saffron pulled out a small hand gel and offered it to Joe. 'You touched the floor,' she said.

'Bats are clean. Their droppings are only crushed insects.'

Saffron screwed up her nose and he took the gel. He wanted no excuses not to be able to hold her.

Back on the working section of the pier, Eifion indicated to Ceri they needed to make a move. 'What about chips?' she said, petulant.

Eifion glanced at Joe. It was momentary, but it was

enough for Joe's message to be clear: Leave me alone with her. 'I've all the ingredients to make shepherd's pie, your favourite, *cariad*. Mince'll turn if we don't make it tonight,' Eifion said. 'And you're back at your mam's tomorrow.' Ceri shrugged an agreement.

They walked to the end of the pier, stood underneath the old clock, and said their goodbyes. Joe knew Eifion would be discreet. Joe'd never said anything to the older man, but Joe knew he understood that Joe didn't want anyone thinking badly of Saffron and he didn't want Rain, or anyone else, poking around in his business.

Joe and Saffron remained still as Eifion and Ceri ambled away. Joe watched and saw how alike they were. The same lilting gait and solid frame; the way they held themselves. Family. Something he'd never had. The closest he'd got was Freddy and Allegra.

Ceri turned and, walking backwards, shouted, 'Have a good time, lovebirds! You might have fooled him,' she gestured at her father, 'but not me. Sharp as, I am.' And with that she turned her back on them and linked her arm in her father's.

Alarmed, Joe turned to Saffron, who shrugged and pressed her lips together. 'She guessed ages ago that I liked you.' She slipped her hand in his. It felt cool and comforting. 'It's OK. She's not as gobby as she first seems. I trust her implicitly. I think Mum'll be fine too.'

Joe smiled, but he wasn't convinced. Not at all.

Rain was nervous; she could feel it throughout her body.

She surveyed the hall. Was it really big enough to accommodate the Cub Scouts as well as the junior group of the Boys' Brigade? How she wished she hadn't offered the hall to the scout leader. It was a character flaw, this impulsiveness. She never used to be like this; Stephen was the impulsive one. She was measured and controlled, just like Saff.

She'd felt sorry for the man. That was it. When the leader, who wasn't even a regular at church – he'd been twice, maybe three times in the eight months she'd been here – had mentioned that the scout hut was out of use while essential repairs took place, she'd merrily said they could use the church hall. What she hadn't anticipated was a meeting time clash with the Boys' Brigade. Again, somewhat rashly she realised, she'd said she couldn't see it being a problem. The brigade was all about promoting habits of respect, obedience, and discipline, though she admitted now there was precious little evidence of such traits in the boys. Their behaviour was more animal than Christian. And as for the scouts, wouldn't they be worse? There was no ethos of promoting Christ's kingdom there. It was all about knots and running wild in the countryside. Given half a chance the boys would revert to savages.

The area was still tribal in tone. To Rain, there was a sense of the outpost settlement about Coed Mawr, a frontier town in the Wild West. Visitors from neighbouring towns were treated with suspicion. The Cub Scouts and the Boys' Brigade were rival gangs and trouble was surely brewing.

Trembling, Rain trotted outside and looked at the sky. Perhaps the scouts would be content to use the grassy area out front, or even the small one at the back? Now that the work on the chapel roof was almost complete, JJ had removed most of the tools and materials dumped there. It would be perfectly safe. Dark clouds hovered overhead, threatening. She withdrew to the hall and took a deep breath. It would have to do.

Goodness me, Rain. Whatever happened to your Christian charity? The boys will be charming, delightful. All will be well. And it might stay dry.

She began to put out chairs. The volunteer who ran the Boys' Brigade had twisted his ankle on a hike the group had undertaken some weeks ago and recent activities had consequently been more sedentary. Without clear instruction from him this week, she placed the chairs in a circle. He'd said they were going to do either a photography project or a cooking one. She couldn't imagine they'd want tables for photography, and for cooking ... well, they'd need to retreat to the kitchen. As for the scouts, she hadn't a clue. She wondered if she should divide the space in some way. A line of chairs perhaps, or a line of chalk on the floor?

Goodness, it's going to be chaos. The noise will be insane. And Dear God, if they do cooking, the mess afterwards ... Though cooking will keep them apart ... Bugger, I must remind them to clear up after themselves.

Her mind whirred.

'Hellooo?'

Rain jumped. She'd not heard the bell, or the door. Goodness, anyone might have come in. She turned to find Eifion creeping into the hall, looking apologetic.

'There was no answer, but I could hear the scraping of the chairs. The door was open ...' his voice trailed away and he stopped moving.

'Oh, please don't apologise. It's my fault. In cloud cuckoo land again.' She waved him in. 'How can I help you?'

He bit his lip. 'I'm here for the scouts. And the Boys' Brigade, as a matter of fact.'

'Oh. I had no idea.' What a surprising man he was. 'The Boys' Brigade too?' She was confused.

'I know Leigh, who runs it, and his ankle's got worse. They think it's a break now, not a sprain. And he told me about sharing the hall, how you very kindly said the Cubs could use the space too, and I thought it might be tricky, what with them all in here, so I suggested we bag them in together. Do a joint activity. It'll be good for the boys too. See how the other half lives, make new friends, develop skills of co-operation.' He smiled. 'Though that might be over ambitious with those little sods!' He screwed his face up. 'Sorry.'

'No need to apologise. I've been fretting about that.' She noticed the carrier bags in his hands for the first time. 'What are you going to do with them all?'

'Make rock,' he said, confidently. And then a little less confidently, 'if they behave themselves.'

'That is ambitious. Won't you need adult helpers? There's hot water involved if I'm not mistaken.'

'I've mates pitching up, but any extra is more than welcome. I'll need someone to supervise those out here. After we've sorted the pencils, string, and paper clips, I'll divide them into two mixed groups. One in the kitchen, one out here making posters advertising the rock. Fancy it?' he said.

'You know what, I do. But only if I can help in the kitchen. I'd love to see how it's made.' What a clever man he was. Promoting his business while doing some valuable community service. He was absolutely wasted as a labourer. 'Let's get some tables out and more chairs and then we'll get the kitchen ready.'

'It's not like the rock you'll find in shops. More like crystals. And it takes time for them to form, so the boys will have to wait. There'll be no instant results. The best things are worth waiting for, don't you think?'

'I do. I absolutely do.' She waved him on towards the kitchen, aware that her heart rate had returned to normal and she was looking forward to the next couple of hours.

Once tables and chairs were laid out, Rain led Eifion to the kitchen where they organised the pans, sugar, and food colourings. At Eifion's suggestion they measured out the sugar and put the requisite amount into cups ready for the boys to stir into the water.

'The trick is adding it slowly, watching and waiting for signs that no more can be dissolved,' Eifion said. He held up a bottle of cochineal. 'And I bet you a quid none of them will go for pink rock!'

'I'm not really a betting sort,' Rain replied. It was only a figure of speech; he probably hadn't meant it seriously. She regretted taking him so literally; she couldn't help it.

'Of course, you're not. I'm so sorry. Stupid of me.' His eyes were warm and honest, cradled in crumpled folds of weathered skin.

'My husband, Stephen, he liked a flutter, as he called it. Not that it was as harmless as the expression implies.' She felt herself tighten, surprised she'd said it aloud. She'd denied it to others for so long, when they were in Dulwich, but now it no longer mattered and it felt surprisingly good to say it aloud.

'The church doesn't approve?' Eifion said, though it was more of a statement than a question.

'Heavens, no. It was his one weakness, and even his faith couldn't stop him doing it. He won a few times, you see, and we had Saff's university education to pay for. He didn't lose a lot. He was careful like that. But he shouldn't have been doing it at all. That was the problem.'

'If it was his only weakness, I really shouldn't worry.'

Rain stared at Eifion, his image mingling with blurred images of Stephen. Her stomach clenched and unclenched. She felt so peculiar again. What did he mean?

'Are you all right, Reverend? You look a little pale,' Eifion said. He reached out a hand and placed it over Rain's. With the other he touched her shoulder. She looked down at her hand, as if it belonged to someone else. She was gripping the counter's edge. 'We're none of us perfect,' he continued.

She blinked. 'No, we're not.'

'Hi.'

Rain and Eifion jumped. His hand leapt from hers, as if guilty, though there was nothing to be embarrassed about.

It was Saff, peering into the kitchen through the large

hatch. 'Just came to let you know I'm off out. Don't wait up.'

'You've not long got in from work.' Rain said. 'You're out all the time these days.'

'Hardly.' Saffron turned to leave.

Rain turned to Eifion and smiled. 'With Ceri?' she asked, but Saff was nowhere to be seen; the sound of the slamming door punctuated her exit.

Chapter Twenty-one

The walk to Joe's cottage took twenty-five minutes. It had taken her less the first time, but this time Saffron was leisurely. Keen to see Joe, she'd been ready early. A quick wash and freshen up after work, a change of clothes and she was done. With little to distract her at the manse, other than her medical journals which she couldn't concentrate on anyhow, she'd decided to leave. She picked up the decorated chocolate eggs she'd bought from a boutique sweet shop she'd discovered in Upper Coed Mawr. It was the Easter display that had caught her attention, all that sunshine yellow.

She tried to enjoy the walk, take in the natural world around her, but couldn't. The image was seared on to her retina: Eifion was holding hands with her mother when she'd popped into the church hall to say goodbye.

For sure, they'd jumped apart, as if stung, when she'd spoken, but it was too late; she'd seen them. Eifion was single; Rain was single. It wasn't a crime, as such. But really? Less than two years since they'd laid her father to rest? After everything Rain had said about grief and time and respectable distance? Saffron felt sick. It was an affront. To her father, to her and to Rain's precious God. She'd wanted to scream: 'Get your hands off her!' but she knew it wasn't all Eifion. If anything, the fault lay with Rain. After all, Eifion had been divorced years, Ceri had said. But her mother? Her mother belonged to her father still. Surely? And Eifion wasn't a chapel-goer. How did that compute for her mother? She couldn't be with anyone who didn't believe.

Breathless and light-headed, Saffron stopped and bent double, her hands gripping her knees, the bag containing the eggs swung from her wrist, the plastic cutting into her skin. A smell she couldn't quite identify enveloped her. It wasn't unpleasant as such. It was a familiar countryside scent but right now it added to her sense of nausea. After minutes, she lifted her head and, after regaining her balance, walked on towards the lane.

It didn't add up. Rain talked about her dad as if he were a deity. If Rain had the power to award him a sainthood, Saffron was certain she would. But then, her mother was still a bit crazy. She tried to hide it from Saffron, but Saffron knew. She had eyes and ears.

She thought about Eifion. She didn't know the man, but he seemed all right. Nice. He was very nice, she admitted. And about the same age as her mum. But compared to her dad, her lovely, clever, remarkable dad, he was nothing. It wasn't possible, it wasn't.

Joe was waiting as she approached the cottage. Standing in the open doorway, one arm resting against the frame, he appeared relaxed. A broad smile, as welcome as the sunrise, swept across his face as she neared and she resisted the urge to run into his arms, push her face against his hard chest, relish the solid masculinity of him, inhale his scent. Instead she stopped and held the bag aloft. 'I brought some eggs,' she announced.

He folded his arms. 'Planning on staying for breakfast? You're full of surprises.'

'Chocolate eggs.' She stressed the 'chocolate', teasing him, but she felt heat rise on her cheeks. He did that to her: reduced her to a blushing, awkward girl, not the capable, cynical woman she'd considered herself once upon a time.

'Milk or plain?'

'Both. I didn't know what you like.' She moved closer.

'No white?' He still blocked the doorway.

Her heart sank. Who'd have thought it? A grown man liking white chocolate. 'That's for kids, isn't it?'

He laughed. 'Kidding. I like something darker. Rich, strong, slightly bitter, best taken in small bites.' His eyes bored into hers.

She stepped closer still. They were within touching distance. 'It's better for you. Anti-oxidants and all that.'

'I like the very best.'

'This is it.' She lifted her arms a touch, palms open.

He leant in and kissed her. She submitted to the moment, the bag of eggs swinging against their sides as they embraced.

Not all of the eggs were broken. Saffron wished she'd wrapped them more carefully, or taken the shopkeeper up on her offer to gift wrap them, but she was short of cash, as always. It didn't matter. Four were perfect and she'd bought too many to eat in one sitting. Joe said he'd put them in the fridge for next time.

Next time. Had two little words ever sounded sweeter? Saffron didn't think so.

After a supper of fresh mackerel cooked over an open fire in the ramshackle back garden, they sat on a bench, swathed in blankets, watching the flames, the night stealing up around them. They fed each other fragments of chocolate, licking the residue from each other's fingers.

He took her hand. 'Is this OK? Staying here, tucked away in this tatty old place.'

'You're thinking I'd rather be wined and dined in some posh gaff in town?' She pulled a face. Were there any posh places in Coed Mawr? 'Or some fancy place nearby?' She couldn't blame him. She was an urban girl, a Londoner, for whom the stay in this rural outpost was a temporary glitch. She'd made no secret of her disdain for the place when they'd first met. She cringed at the memory of her behaviour. But what of him? He wasn't from round here either, and how long was he planning to stay? For ever? Surely not? What drove him here? Work? 'This is perfect,' she said. And after a pause, 'I never thought I'd say this but I'm getting used to this place. I like it.'

He raised his eyebrows.

'I'd have hated anywhere, where I was in my ...' she pointed to her head. 'It was autumn, everything was dying, the town closed down for the winter. It was dark, cold. I was miserable –'

'No!'

She punched him gently on the shoulder. 'But everything seems so much better now.' Self-consciousness gripped her; she'd drive him away. 'Telling Mum about Ben and all that. I'd never have done that if you'd not encouraged me.'

Turning from the fire towards her, he said, 'You would. You're strong, Saffron. Stronger than most, stronger than you realise.'

She didn't think he'd looked more handsome than he did right here, right now. 'Time heals too, doesn't it?' she said. She thought of her mother and Eifion and her father.

'Does it? I'm not so sure.' He turned away from her, raked his fingers through his strip of thick hair, his mouth tight. She thought of the girl in the photograph, in a room she shouldn't have been in. That girl was the source of Joe's pain; she knew it. He was grieving; it was obvious. She couldn't believe she'd missed it till now. Too self-absorbed, she conceded.

'Joe, have you lost someone you love too?' It hurt to say it. Envy pricked, irrational and ugly, but unstoppable. There was another with a hold on Joe's affections.

He remained fixed on the fire, silent, hunched over, his forearms resting on his knees, the blanket a crumpled heap at his feet.

'I saw a picture, in your room, last time I was here. I shouldn't have been snooping, it was an awful thing to do, but it's too late. I saw it. The girl. The one who looks like you.' She reached over and placed her hand over his, relieved he'd didn't flinch or pull away. She would have deserved as much. 'Is she your sister? Did something happen to her, Joe?' she babbled, once started, unable to stop. 'Please, tell me. If you share, your pain will be lessened. I can't promise it will go away, but it will lessen.'

I can help you. Open yourself to me.

'Not my sister,' he said. 'No.'

He shook her hand away and Saffron felt the earth crumbling beneath her, ready to suck her in. She should never have started this.

'Far from it. And she's not dead. She's very much alive.'

Saffron was falling.

Joe's first thought when Saffron confessed to poking around in his bedroom was that it served him right; he should have chucked the picture away months ago, years ago. He waited for anger to control him. Anger at Saffron for being such a Pandora, rage at Allegra for maintaining a hold on him, a grip so fierce he couldn't get rid of a stupid holiday snapshot. He'd destroyed all the other mementoes, why not that one?

Because every fire needs to be stoked, you stupid, stupid bastard. You're not even sure what you feel for her.

He dropped his head onto his knees. To his surprise, he didn't feel angry, he felt strangely relieved.

'I'll go.' Saffron stood and tossed her blanket onto the bench next to him. 'I'm so, so sorry. It was a terrible thing to do, unforgiveable.' She started to move towards the back door.

You can't let her go. Say something. Anything.

'Don't go,' he stammered.

Tell her. Explain.

'What did you say?' He could hear the tremor in her voice, a rustle in the weeds beyond the lawn, the crackle of the wood in the fire.

'I said, don't go. Stay. Please.' He lifted his head a fraction and stared at the fire. A log was no longer recognisable as wood. Grey, dusty, and glowing orange at its end, it had transformed.

Nothing can withstand fire, not for long.

'She's a girlfriend? A wife?' Saffron said, almost a whisper, as if she was afraid to even say it.

He nodded.

'Where is she now?' Saffron remained standing.

'Far away.' But not far enough, not really. Was anywhere far enough?

'Do you still love her?'

He heard the pain in Saffron's voice and it was a rope round his neck, twisting, tighter and tighter. He looked at her.

'I hate her.'

Light from the fire caught the tears rolling down Saffron's cheeks, though her words were controlled; the shaking in her voice had stopped. His heart froze.

'To hate is to love. You can't have one without the other, Joe. They're two sides of the same coin.'

Turning away from the force of her gaze, he stared at the fire. Allegra: golden and dazzling, she drew you in with her promise of warmth and magic. He'd known there must be danger. Nothing that powerful came without it. But he'd assumed he could control it. How wrong he'd been. He remembered Allegra's golden limbs, her spellbinding smile, her veneer of mystery and sophistication, the promise of unforgettable nights. Everyone wanted her. And her eyes. So unusual. So like his. It had felt like a sign, a sign they were meant to be. And it was because of all this he ignored the warnings, the tiny scalds, blisters from getting too close, trusting too much.

'I don't love her. I didn't love her. It was infatuation,' he said.

'Can you be sure?'

'I didn't know her. Not really. And you can only love someone you know.'

'Mum says love travels both ways. That's how you tell the difference.'

In his peripheral vision, Joe watched her pulling the skin on her knuckles. She was such a fidget, whenever she was nervous, and he longed to leap up, take her hands and kiss those joints and her tears and tell her not worry, that all would be well, that he loved her, that he had some things to sort out and afterwards he'd tell her everything she needed to know. The truth about him. And then the decision would be hers. He couldn't be sure she would want him any more. He wouldn't blame her if she didn't.

'Rain's smart. She's right. Love travels both ways. And it sure as hell didn't with Allegra.'

'Allegra? It's a beautiful name. She's beautiful, judging by the picture,' Saffron said, sitting down again. She managed a half-smile, though an air of defeat surrounded her.

'Appearances can be deceptive.' He laughed at the cliché, lighter now Saffron sat beside him, wasn't going to run out on him. She wanted to believe him. He felt it.

'What happened? And why do you claim to hate her?'

He ached to be honest, he really did, but he was frightened. Frightened that if he told her his truth, he'd lose her.

'The usual. She left me for another. My pride was hurt more than anything.'

'So why the hatred?'

'It's a character flaw. I have an unnatural desire for revenge. Always have done. Very Old Testament.' He smiled. This much, everyone would agree was true.

'Remind me never to wrong you.' She smiled and he felt so relieved he wanted to punch the air. 'Mum says you shouldn't take revenge, you must leave room for God's wrath. It is his to repay, he will avenge.' She looked away, sadness washing over her. 'Perhaps that's why he took Dad and Ben. Though it doesn't add up for Mum. She'd done no wrong; she didn't deserve that.'

He took her hand. 'Too right. Makes no sense. And I can't believe God is such a bastard either.'

'Oh, I don't know. Some of those stories, Samson and Delilah ...' She was smiling again.

'Thought you took no notice of all that religious stuff?'

'When you grow up with something, it seeps in. You can't stop it. Like a slow bleed, it has an effect eventually.'

Past its zenith, the fire's heat was fading. Saffron shivered and Joe threw the blanket over her shoulders. He looked into her eyes. 'I don't love Allegra.'

Saffron pulled her mouth downwards, a sort of smile.

'Wait here,' he said, getting up from the bench.

He went upstairs to the bedroom, removed the back of the frame, pulled out the photograph and returned to the garden. Outside, he showed Saffron the picture and tossed it into the embers. They watched, silent, as the paper curled inwards, blackening at the edges, dissolving into weak flames and then, finally, nothing but ash.

'She's dead to me,' he said. 'Ashes to ashes.'

Maybe it's time to let go of vengeance too.

'You didn't have to burn it. I believe you anyway,' Saffron said, but something in her expression told him that while she wanted to believe him, she didn't. Not quite. She was far too smart for that.

'I like you, Saffron. I really do. Come here,' and he pulled her towards him and kissed her long and hard, as if, were he to let go, he might never see her again.

Chapter Twenty-two

Pushed up against the railings, Eifion studied his shop. He moved round the hut opposite and surveyed his own from the other side. Saffron could read nothing from his expression.

'You'd think he was inspecting Buckingham Palace,' Ceri whispered, leaning against the hut, one foot resting on a large tin of paint. Saffron held a bundle of brushes.

'This place used to be his pride and joy. Mam joked that he loved his rock more than he loved her. He said no way because he could lick her for ever and not feel sick. I wanted to vom when I heard that, I can tell you. Not what you want to hear when you're a kid. Your parents getting fresh with each other. Disgusting.' After a theatrical shudder, she hollered at her father, though he was no more than a few metres away. 'Will you get a move on! Saff's got to be in work for two o'clock and I've to collect the brats from playschool at three.'

No matter what she called them, Ceri adored the children in her care; she didn't fool Saffron, or anyone else for that matter. Ceri had found her calling. Some mornings Saffron met them in the park or on the beach and watched in wonder as Ceri struck a perfect balance between firm and fun.

'What went wrong?' Saffron asked.

'Visitors stopped coming, or not so many came anyway. And they stopped buying rock. I think he liked the chit-chat with the holidaymakers as much as anything. Took him to other places he said.'

'I meant between your mum and dad.'

'They started to make each other sick, I suppose.' She kicked the can and hoisted up her jeans which had fallen well below her hip line, exposing the top of her bottom. 'I've had enough of this, I'm making a start.'

Obviously sensing his daughter's impatience, Eifion crossed and instructed them to tape the dust sheets around the base of the hut so that the pier boards wouldn't get covered in paint. Once that was done, they were to sand down any areas of the woodwork where the existing paintwork had flaked. 'Preparation is everything, ladies. Get that right and the paint will glide on.'

'Sure thing, boss,' Saffron said, rolling up the sleeves of her old sweatshirt. The sun shone and she felt warm. She might even have to take off her outer layer.

'Are you sure I can't persuade you to wear some overalls, girls? You might start a trend?'

They shook their heads and set to work. Ceri gossiped, often speaking of people Saffron had never met. But she didn't mind. Ceri was entertaining and through her stories the history of the town and its people emerged. Everyone was connected in one way or another. Mair Shawcroft had dated Eifion's granddad, who was a bit of a lad back in the day, but when his childhood sweetheart fell pregnant he was forced to dump Mair and do the decent thing.

'Oh, poor Mair.' Saffron remembered the advice Mair had offered at the hospital: to grab love with both hands if it came your way. She wondered if Mair had regrets, if Mair had 'held back' as she'd said, because of her religion or the mores of the time. She'd continued to visit the old woman, once at the hospital and a couple of times as she recuperated at home, and while Mair had shared many stories from her life, she hadn't told Saffron about a man she'd loved marrying another.

While Saffron and Ceri talked, Eifion set up a worktable and began sawing wood, ready to repair the counter and shelving inside, the rotten window frame. He chipped in occasionally, often to correct his daughter when she got her facts wrong or over dramatized for effect. After hours of scraping and sanding, they were ready to begin the undercoat on the hut exterior.

'Cup of coffee first, I'd say. And some jam butties for my very lovely helpers. Not every day an old man's labourers are beautiful young women. I could get used to this!' Eifion said, rummaging in his bag before pulling out a flask, plastic beakers, and a large Tupperware box.

'Looks like I pitched up at the right time.'

Saffron turned.

Joe.

She ran a hand across her forehead, tucked a loose strand of hair behind her ear, and wished she'd worn more make-up. She looked best in a dusky half-light. There, in the sunlight, she felt as shabby as the pier itself. She thought of Allegra, golden in the Mediterranean sun of the photograph, and how she must compare. He'd said he no longer loved Allegra, but she'd known it wasn't the whole truth. She hoped that one day it might be.

Feigning a need for shade, she rested a hand across her forehead. 'Hi. Didn't expect you. Haven't you work to do?'

'Chapel's almost finished. Few bits of snagging here and there and it'll be good as new. Didn't Rain say?'

Rain hadn't but Saffron had known they must have been close to completion. She was ignorant about building work but even she could see that the roof was repaired. She didn't want to admit it, for it would mean Joe might move on. He went where the work took him, she supposed, and it was clear his home was temporary. It had been on her mind to ask him last time they got together, tentatively, she didn't want to scare him off, but with the revelation about Allegra it had dropped off her agenda.

'Coffee, then? A buttie?' Eifion offered the box, the sandwiches squashed and curled, jam leaching into the white bread like blood on swabs.

'Don't mind if I do. I'll work harder for you if the engine's stoked,' Joe said.

'You're working for him?' Ceri pointed from Joe to her dad.

Joe nodded. 'Sure am.'

'How comes you can afford to pay him and not me then, Dad?' She had her hands on her hips, mock-affronted.

Joe interrupted. 'It's a favour. From one mate to another. I'll get another job soon and you never know, someone here might be in need of repairs too.'

Saffron stared at the boards, a stupid grin fixed on her face. He was staying; he wasn't going, not yet. She determined to help find him more work in Coed Mawr. She'd ask customers in the shop; the sellers on the pier, the congregation, Mair and her cronies. Mair knew just about everyone in town, and their business. As did Ceri. She blocked all thoughts of what would happen when it was her turn to move on.

'Gonna look smashing, it is, when it's done. Shame I couldn't get it all tarted up for the Easter weekend, but there's the summer to come,' Eifion said, smiling and admiring his hut once more. He looked towards the end of the pier. 'And if they get the ballroom sorted ... well, who knows, it could be a major attraction. Just what the town needs.'

'Steady on, Dad!' Ceri rolled her eyes. 'Ever so fanciful he is sometimes.'

They settled on benches a little along the pier, Eifion and Joe on one, Saffron and Ceri on one opposite. The coffee tasted of plastic and metal and left a sour coating round Saffron's mouth but she didn't care. Eifion offered the sandwiches. Saffron shook her head.

'No wonder she's such a skinny bitch,' Ceri shouted across the width of the pier as she stuffed a sandwich, whole, into her mouth. Ceri never did anything at half-volume: speaking, eating, laughing. 'Hope you don't swear like that round those kiddies, Ceri,' Eifion said.

'Course I bloody don't!'

'She eats for me,' Joe said. He stared at Saffron and she felt herself blushing.

Saffron turned to Ceri. 'As a matter of fact, I've gained some weight recently. Can't you tell?'

Ceri smirked. 'I noticed. But you're still a rake, you cow!'

'It feels very odd, sitting opposite like this, shouting over at each other. People'll think we're mad. There's room for you here.' Joe tapped the seat next to him.

'There's an offer I can't refuse,' Ceri said, leaping up and over. She sat between her father and Joe. 'Come on, Saff.'

Self-conscious but unable to refuse, Saffron walked over. Somehow, sitting next to Joe like this was a public acknowledgement of what they were to each other, even if she didn't know precisely what that was herself. She wasn't sure if Joe was comfortable with this, or, indeed, if she was. Ceri knew, as Eifion did, after the evening on the pier when they'd crept into the ballroom.

But it was crazy to refuse. That would hardly allay suspicions; no one passing could possibly know. They were four people crushed together on a bench on the pier, taking a break from their labours. It wasn't as if there were notes hanging off the edge of the bench: *This man and woman, there's something between them. She doesn't fully understand what it is yet. She thinks she's in love with him, and he says he likes her. She knows he likes her. But there's something which stops them growing: the past, secrets, lies, she can't tell which. It sits between them, like a virus, and the moment they treat it, it mutates, changes shape, and is more impenetrable and resistant than ever.*

Saffron was acutely aware of Joe's thigh pressing

217

against her own, the warmth from his body flooding into her. His fingers brushed hers and she knew it was no accident. Without looking at him, she gazed out across the bay and smiled. The pastel-coloured buildings along the front shimmered in the sunshine, as sweet and tempting as a stick of rock.

Between visits Rain needed some fresh air. What was it about elderly people that meant they either sat in rooms so over-heated ordinary folk were in danger of spontaneously combusting, or were content to live out their golden years in environments that made Antarctica seem cosy? Mair Shawcroft fell into the former category and Rain was sweating, actually sweating, by the time she left Mair's sheltered accommodation. She'd deliberately worn layers so she might peel them off as required, but short of sitting on Mair's velour settee in her bra and knickers, after half an hour she had nothing else she could take off. The tea had been over-sugared too. She'd offered to make it, but Mair had insisted, hobbling to the kitchenette with her walking cane.

In the street, Rain leant against a wall, lightheaded and nauseous, and swept her hair up off her neck. It was so thick it was like wearing a scarf at times.

Forgive me, Father. Forgive me.

She'd been short with Mair when the old lady took out her photo album, keen to show Rain proof of her sporting prowess as a girl. You mustn't spend so much time looking back, Miss Shawcroft, she'd said. Live in the moment. Mindfulness they call it. Or look to the future. How about that? Rain had noticed how her voice got louder and louder, as if she were speaking with a child or someone with hearing difficulties. Mair had many problems but her hearing wasn't one of them.

But Mair Shawcroft didn't have much of a future, did she? She was very old. Rain acknowledged her comment had been directed at herself. But it wasn't as if she did look back that often. Hardly ever. And when she did, she couldn't recall the things she wanted to. It pained her to admit it but she could no longer remember how Stephen sounded, the precise timbre of his voice. The only recording she had – a perfunctory voicemail asking her to pick up some milk on her way home – disappeared when her last mobile had packed up. The salesman didn't know what to make of her outburst when he offered her a new phone with all the latest gizmos. She'd ranted about no one repairing anything any more and what on earth would happen when all the landfills were teeming with mobile phones. The meek won't inherit the earth, plastic will. Plastic and bloody Apple, she'd shouted. The young man had stood there, silent, the rash of acne across his cheeks growing redder and redder.

The familiar shaking began in her hands. But she had taken the last of the diazepam some weeks ago and knew that she must resist visiting the doctor. Things had been improving with Saffron, hadn't they, and the chapel roof was finished, and the summer was approaching. There was so much to look forward to. It was a glorious day.

She checked her watch. Plenty of time before she was due at Mr Harrington's. He wasn't a stickler for punctuality, thank heavens. Or cleanliness, Rain noted, dismayed at the prospect of having to sit in his stinking living room. She must get on to social services again. What on earth had happened to his home help? All the more reason to enjoy a break and some clean, fresh air first.

She headed towards the sea, determined to blow away the cobwebs, look at the day anew. It really was beautiful.

As she neared the promenade she caught a waft of sticky sweetness, doughnuts, and remembered the kiosk at the entrance to the pier.

My blood sugar must be low, that's why I'm so

irritable. I'll treat myself.

The pricing was such that it made no sense to buy only one, so Rain purchased ten doughnuts, pledging to eat one or two and take the rest to Mr Harrington's. The sound of the merry-go-round lured her onto the pier itself and she drifted along, surreptitiously munching on the doughnuts as she went.

She paused before the Punch and Judy kiosk, all boarded up, faded lettering across the top, and wondered what children made of it. They probably loved it. All that chasing and thumping and hitting and mayhem. Children, especially boys, loved violence. Slapstick violence. In Matthew's last email home, he'd sounded quite distressed. Villagers were afraid to visit the mission for fear of reprisals from extremists in the region. Some of the stories he'd heard were horrific. She longed for him to come home but knew that he wouldn't. Not yet. It was too soon, too many reminders. He'd lost his father and their last words were bitter and cruel. But hiding wouldn't solve anything, would it?

Isn't that what you've done?

Do not be afraid of what you are about to suffer. She remembered the words from Revelation.

She dropped the bag of doughnuts, some of which rolled out onto the wooden boards. Gulls squawked and swooped down, pecking and snatching at the cakes, the now empty bag. She recoiled, covered her face with her forearms, frightened by their screams, flapping, and hooked beaks.

'Oh, oh, oh!' She curled further into herself, the squall of the gulls intensified.

'Reverend? Are you all right?'

She unfurled, slowly, embarrassed, brushing away sugar from the corners of her mouth.

'Cheeky devils. They're pests, they are. Saw one snatch a lolly from a kiddie just the other day. Lucky he didn't lose his hand. What do sea birds want with sweeties, I ask you?' He turned sharply and snarled at a lone gull perched on the railings. 'Get away with you!'

'Thank you. They startled me, that's all. Made me jump.' She could hear the blood thumping at her temples, though she noticed it was slowing too. Eifion, he had that effect on her. So calming. So kind.

'And the greedy beggars have ruined your snack.'

She noticed his work clothes, the sawdust in his hair, and remembered his shop. And that Saffron had said she was helping him and Ceri that morning. Blast. Saffron would think she was spying on her, which wasn't the case at all. She'd clean forgotten. Saff was so secretive these days. Rain blamed JJ.

Eifion continued, ushering her forward. 'Come and join us for some coffee and biscuits. If you're very lucky there may even be a few butties left. We're just along here. Saffron and Ceri and Joe.'

'JJ?'

Eifion nodded. 'He prefers Joe. Probably too polite to tell you.'

She looked ahead and saw them, sitting on the bench, all scrunched up together, very cosy. As they approached, Rain expected Saff to leap up, but she didn't. JJ stood and offered Rain his seat, which made her feel ancient and less amiable rather than more so. She refused, politely. JJ remained standing.

'Surprised to see you here, Mum. Haven't you got visits or something?'

'Cup of coffee?' Eifion held the flask aloft.

Rain shook her head.

'She won't drink instant,' Saffron said.

'It's not that. Not that at all. I'm full of tea.'

'Jam buttie? Or perhaps I can tempt you to a bourbon?' Eifion smiled and offered the Tupperware box with one hand and a pack of biscuits with the other.

'Thank you, no. I'm fine.' She addressed her daughter. 'I felt like a breath of fresh air after Mair's place. You know what it's like.'

Saffron nodded. She'd complained about the heat herself the last time she'd visited Mair. Rain knew then that it wasn't just her; Saff was incredibly cold-blooded, and if she said it was warm, it must be tropical. She had no meat on her, that's why she felt the cold so much. Though as Rain studied her daughter, sitting on the bench on the pier, she noticed she'd gained weight. It was difficult to tell what was going on under all those baggy layers, but it showed in her face. There was a softness in her cheeks Rain hadn't seen in almost two years. Typical Saff to be so contrary. Most girls lose weight in the first flush of love, not gain it.

Rain looked at JJ. Could she detect if Saff's feelings were reciprocated? Not that Saff had actually told her anything about her feelings yet. He was impossible to read.

Feeling awkward and unsure what to do, Rain checked her watch. 'Well, must dash. Things to do, people to see.' She looked at the hut. 'And I can see you've got your work cut out.' She turned to Eifion. 'It's a lovely shop. Absolutely charming. There's something so cheerful about rock. Looks lovely, all laid out. I used to spend hours as a girl choosing sticks for friends and family as presents from holiday.'

'Certainly makes dentists cheerful,' he replied, laughing, though she could tell her comments had pleased him. He glowed with pride. 'You be all right getting off? Had a friend with a bird phobia once.'

'I'll be absolutely fine. But thank you. You're very thoughtful.'

She began to walk away, then turned back and spoke to JJ. 'You'll be wanting to be paid and then you can collect the rest of your tools from the chapel?'

'You don't pay me. It's not my company, I'm just a

hired hand. But yes, I'll collect my things if you need them out of the way. There are a few jobs left but they won't take long. Tyson should finish them this afternoon. I'll swing by later. There's the meeting,' JJ said.

Blast. She'd forgotten about the ballroom meeting. Was he meaning to come? To get involved?

'That would be good. Nice to get back to normal. No offence,' Rain said.

'None taken.'

She smiled at Eifion. 'Thank you for your help earlier. Much appreciated.' She walked towards the end of the pier, deciding to take a look at the shops before moseying down to Mr Harrington's.

Saffron was furious with her mother. She didn't buy that horseshit about needing some fresh air. Rain knew Saffron was helping Eifion and Ceri this morning; she'd only mentioned it over breakfast. What was she doing? Checking up on her? Possibly. But what was much more likely was that she was sniffing round Eifion. The work on the chapel was finished so he'd have no call to be up there again, not unless Rain had managed to rope him into running yet another Boys' Brigade session, or the ballroom campaign. Rain had wanted to see Eifion.

And she was verging on downright rude with Joe. Saffron could hardly believe it. Rain was nice to everyone. Everyone. What the hell was going on?

Chapter Twenty-three

The manse was empty when Saffron returned home after her shift at Wynne's, the silence punctuated only by the leaking tap in the downstairs bathroom. Saffron ground the tap round as far as she could and wondered if Joe knew anything about plumbing. There was a note from Rain on the kitchen table explaining that there was a ballroom campaign meeting in the hall and she would see Saff around eight thirty 'assuming you're home'. Saffron drifted to the cooker, lifted the lid of the pot sitting there and turned up her nose. Yet another stew.

She made a pot of tea and wandered upstairs to the study. Joe was busy that evening; he had to see his boss, pass on some invoices for materials, talk over the final work done on the roof, return with the final bill for Rain. She'd asked what he might do for work now the chapel contract was complete; if he would move away. 'Not if I can help it,' he'd said. 'I'll spend time working on some sculptures – the shed should be warm enough now.'

Prospectuses lay scattered across the desk. She preferred to read hard copies, flick through the pages. She couldn't make a decision without holding something real, substantial. 'How old fashioned, Saffy!' Rain had said. Saffron ran her fingertips across a glossy cover, reading the embossed lettering of the university hospital as if it were braille. She knew she must apply soon; her time in Coed Mawr was drawing to a close. Barts, Kings, UCL. They were all so very far away. What did Bangor, or Wrexham, have to offer? Were they an impossible commute from Coed Mawr? Her mind raced.

It would please Rain if she didn't return to London. Or would it? Her insides shrivelled. Perhaps her mother was healing faster than she thought. And that would be a good thing, wouldn't it?

Saffron felt bad about her uncharitable thoughts. Her mother deserved to have friends of her own age, male or female. Stretching over the desk to the shelf, ignoring the brochures, Saffron picked out a novel instead, blew the dust from its top, and lay on the small sofa staring at words on a page without absorbing any of them. Her eyes felt heavy.

Saffron jumped, disorientated. She must have fallen asleep. The air was fuzzy with sunlit dust motes. She checked the clock; it was only a little after seven; she'd not slept for long: fifteen minutes at most. Stretching, she pondered what to do.

I could go to the meeting, show my support. Mum would like it.

The welcome Saffron received was indeed warm. Rain leaped from her seat to grab another chair from the stack at the edge of the room. A dozen or so people, including Mrs Evans, Mair Shawcroft, and Mr Roberts, sat around trestles that had been pushed together to form a makeshift boardroom table. There were piles of paper and pens scattered around, a jug and water glasses, tea cups, and a plate of crumbs and a couple of broken Rich Tea biscuits. In front of Mr Roberts was the chapel iMac. After a cursory wave in her direction, he returned to his former position: nose almost pressed up against the screen, brows furrowed in an expression of absolute bewilderment. The others nodded and smiled in Saffron's direction.

Rain placed the chair next to Mair Shawcroft and Saffron sat down. 'Lovely to see you here, *cariad*. We could do with some fresh blood, new ideas. The tea dance was a roaring success and raised some cash —'

'Mum said.'

'It was full of old farts, of course,' Mair continued.

A couple of people tittered and Mr Roberts looked up from the screen. 'Now, I wouldn't say that ...'

Mair interrupted him. 'I would. It's all very well getting leaflets printed outlining our case, rallying support in the town, but who in hell – sorry, Rev – is going to deliver them?' She swept her gaze around the table.

Mr Roberts sighed. 'We're not all decrepit.' He stared at Saffron as he spoke.

Rain spoke. 'Indeed, we're not!'

A ripple of laughter.

'I'd happily deliver leaflets,' Saffron replied.

'Me too,' said Mrs Evans. 'I'll see if I can get Ceri and some of her mates on board. Eifion, too. He has a hut; it's in his interest.'

'That would be wonderful,' Rain piped up.

She'd love that, Saffron thought, having Eifion involved. 'How about some posters, for people to display in windows? Do you have enough money? A petition, to present to the voting councillors? After all, they hold the power,' she said. It would be fun to get involved, something to occupy her when she wasn't working or seeing Joe.

Her ideas sparked an animated discussion and Saffron's thoughts drifted. The voices became a distant burr and she jumped when the door slammed.

She turned around to see who'd entered. Joe. He looked as surprised to see her as she imagined she did to see him.

'Sorry for interrupting,' he said, his eyes fixed on Saffron.

What the hell? He'd said he had to go and see his boss, sort out invoices. Why did he lie? And why is he here?

'It's always good to have new members,' Mair said, smiling.

Rain chipped in then, inviting Joe to sit, asking if he'd

like a cup of tea.

'Thanks, but I can't stay. I came to let you know that the ballroom is a bat maternity roost. Thought it might be important for the campaign, what you present to the council.'

'Bats? What on earth have bats got to do with it?' Rain said, pushing a cup of tea at Joe, despite his polite refusal.

'They're protected, by law. Any work will have to be done sensitively, depending on the time of year.'

'And you can bet your bottom dollar that those bastards – sorry, Rev – who want to tear the ballroom down, wouldn't know sensitive if it came up and slapped them round the chops,' Mair said.

'Precisely,' Joe said.

Mair leaned over to Saffron and whispered, 'Clever as well as handsome, isn't he?' It was loud enough for everyone to hear and to her horror Saffron felt herself blushing. She dropped her gaze to her lap but not before she saw Joe flush in her peripheral vision. Fuck.

'Right, well, I'll … be off,' Joe said.

'Come again,' Mair said.

'I might just do that.'

After the door shut behind him, Saffron counted to thirty, before standing. 'Excuse me, I've just remembered something I have to do. Mum'll fill me in.' And with that, she walked as slowly as she could muster to the exit. As the door closed behind her, she broke into a run.

The Land Rover was parked on the road. So he'd waited, perhaps knowing she would follow. That was a good sign, at least. As she approached she began to feel foolish. What would she say? He wasn't answerable to her. She had no right to be cross with him. She should have stayed put. Her pace slowed, though she knew he must see her in the wing mirror.

'Climb in a moment.' He leant out of the window. 'Let me explain.'

'There's no need.' She coughed and tapped the toe of her boot on the pavement.

'There's every need. You think I lied.'

'I don't.'

'I'm off to Derek's now. But I've been back to the ballroom – I had my suspicions when we were there, but I needed to be sure, and now that I am, I needed to tell them. I remembered your mum mentioning the meeting. I had no idea you'd be there.'

'It's fine. You don't have to justify your actions to me.' It was strange, speaking to him like this: him in the Land Rover, her on the pavement, though they were separated by more than a vehicle door.

'You don't trust me.'

'I do. Go. It's getting late. You'll miss him.'

She watched him pull away, feeling uncertain and adrift. Unsure what to do – she couldn't go back to the meeting – she retreated to the manse study and stared at pages of the novel, without reading any of them.

In the kitchen, Rain was stirring the stew. The table had been wiped clean, placemats set, and a bottle of red wine rested in the centre with glasses either side of it.

'Take a seat. Pour yourself a glass. I'm so glad you waited. I hate eating alone.'

Saffron didn't like to say that she hadn't, so merely nodded and did as instructed, pouring her mother a glass too. Rain served a steaming bowl of stew and sat opposite. She clasped her hands and closed her eyes. 'For what we are about to receive, blah, blah.' She opened her eyes. 'He knows what I mean. No need to spell it out every time. Cheers! Here's to the new roof and a new ballroom.' She clinked her glass against Saffron's which still sat on the table.

Saffron stabbed at a lump of potato; overcooked, it disintegrated as she pushed the fork through the flesh. She wondered why Rain didn't mention her sudden exit. She must have known she'd gone after Joe. 'What about the kitchen, in the church hall? Hasn't there been talk of it being modernised?'

'It is only talk, Saffy.' Rain was cheerful. 'There's other, much more crucial, work that needs doing first. The damp in the hall for one. And there's no money left in the pot.'

'For sure.' Saffron stirred her fork round the vegetables. Fat gleamed on the surface of the gravy.

'Eat up, Saffy.'

'I'm not really hungry. Sorry.' She put down her fork and sipped at the wine.

'What a shame. It's your favourite.' Rain stretched over and squeezed Saffron's hand. Saffron waited. Would her mum mention the meeting on the pier, apologise for her rudeness?

'How long is the drive to Bangor, or Wrexham?' It came out in a rush, garbled.

'Goodness. I'm not sure.' Rain looked at the ceiling. 'Less than an hour to Bangor, traffic depending. Why?'

'Joe would know for sure.'

Rain blanched. Then, casually, she said, 'Would he? How?'

'He travels about a bit.'

'I had no idea.' Rain sounded sharp, all trace of her good humour gone.

The conversation was not going the way Saffron had hoped. She tried to steer it back to purpose. She wanted to sound out the notion of applying to repeat her Foundation Year One somewhere closer to Coed Mawr.

'You seem to know a lot about JJ?' Rain put down her cutlery, her forearms rested on the table, fingers linked, as if she was about to say grace again.

Saffron studied the grain of the wood. 'Not really.'

Tell her. What's the problem? She knows about Ben.

*It's almost two years. Just say it: I am seeing Joe. No. Big.
Deal.*

'You're in love with him.'

Saffron almost choked on a gulp of wine.

'Why have you kept it from me? I don't understand. All
those evenings when you said you were going out with
Ceri. You were lying. Why?' Rain continued.

'Because I knew you wouldn't like it. Look at you
now.' She ventured a glance at her mother. Rain's eyes
gleamed too brightly; she wore a fixed smile, one of pity,
and it irked. Her mum had no need to feel pity for her. She
was happy, happier than she'd ever been. Saffron was
enraged. How dare she?

'It's not that I don't like it, Saff. I'm frightened for you.
You're vulnerable. So easy to take advantage of.'

'As are you.'

'I'm not sure I know what you mean.'

'I think you do.' Saffron held Rain's gaze. They were
like children, engaged in a battle of wills. Who would
crumble first?

Saffron watched her mother's eyes grow redder, more
watery. Then, so suddenly it made Saffron jolt, Rain
clapped her hands, rolled her eyes and laughed. The
laughter was high-pitched and hollow. 'You think Eifion
likes me?'

'I'm sure he does. But that's not the issue, is it? He's a
free agent,' Saffron said, her voice shaking, betraying her.

'What are you saying?' Rain felt her lips trembling, her
mouth drying.

Saffron took a deep breath and answered in
dispassionate tones, relaying the facts, like a doctor might
discuss a patient's condition, though she refrained from
offering a treatment. Eifion was a nice man, a good man,
and he liked Rain. She was attractive, she was alone, and
she encouraged him. He would never have made his

231

feelings clear if there had been no encouragement. Saffron said she wasn't certain how she knew this, she just did. And the problem was, Rain wasn't really free, was she? She was a widow of less than two years; she was grieving her husband – Saffron's father – and it was embarrassing and wrong for her head to be turned by the first man to show interest, to treat her like a woman and not only a minister. It wasn't Rain's fault; she was all over the place, probably didn't realise how the signals she put out could so easily be misinterpreted. She probably didn't even realise what she was giving out. Grief can do that, distort things.

Rain marvelled at her daughter's inability to draw parallels between their circumstances. She recoiled from Saffron's underlying disapproval at her supposed encouragement of an admirer. It was disrespectful of Stephen's memory, she'd said. Rain felt the distant rumble of anxiety at her centre. Like a gust of wind, a tremor beneath her feet, like standing on the platform at Brixton staring at the tunnel as a tube train approached. She resisted the urge to fall onto the tracks and give in to her fear.

You are frightened and adrenaline is flooding your body. This is why you shake. It is OK.

Anxiety merged with wrath.

How dare Saffron? Jezebel. Bitch. Traitor.

Bile flooded her. 'You accuse me to excuse your own behaviour. And yours is worse. You act on base emotion; you're conducting some kind of a relationship with JJ, this man you barely know, know nothing about. Have you had sex with him?'

Saffron gasped.

No, then. Thank God. But she wants to; I can almost smell her desire.

'Is it not disrespectful to Ben? The years you shared together?' Rain spat.

'I didn't love him. Not like you loved Dad. It's different, different,' Saffron said, her voice raised, brittle, all pretence of control gone.

Rain's mind whirled. She could barely feel the shape and size of her grief. It was never still. It changed shape constantly, slipped from her fingers, springing into the air like the jelly-gloop Matthew had loved as a child. It had acquired dust and dirt as it had fallen onto carpets and soil but the heart of it eluded her still. She longed to tear it apart and discover its core but its molecular make-up wouldn't allow it. God offered her comfort, of course, but it wasn't enough.

It isn't enough.

The realisation winded her.

The train approached, zoomed past, blowing her hair from her face, almost blowing her off her feet. Tears spilled down her cheeks, a ball of concrete rose up her chest into her throat, strangling her.

'Your father was about to leave me.' It was a whisper, a rustle of dry leaves, like the talking bulrushes in the story of Midas and his ass's ears. It seemed to come from elsewhere, outside of herself.

'What?' Saffron whispered.

Rain opened her mouth to speak, to repeat it – to say aloud again that which she had not even acknowledged in the deepest, most secret part of herself for almost two years – but instead of words came a wail, a braying, a heaving of choking, sobbing, snot and tears and spit. She was aware of tissues appearing in her fingers, a glass of water materialising in front of her, but nothing else. When she did speak, after how long she had no idea, all she could say was, 'Dear God, dear, dear Lord, help me please.'

But it wasn't her faithful God who helped her, it was her daughter. After plying her with tissues and water – which she didn't drink but was grateful for it being there – Saff had steered Rain upstairs, laid her on her bed, removed her sandals and pulled the duvet over her. She'd drawn the curtains and pulled the door to, though she didn't close it. As she'd left, she'd said, 'I'm downstairs, Mum. Just call if you need me. Anything at all.'

Rain lay in the gloaming on her back and stared at the ceiling, her entire body wrung out, heavy, and desperate for oblivion. She resisted closing her eyes and focused instead on the glass lampshade, the veins of colour running through the bowl, dull without a lit bulb, but visible all the same. She knew that if she did shut her eyes, she would be lost to memories of Stephen in the days before the accident, the days after he'd told her he was leaving. She'd blotted them out so well, for so long. But they were like film and her brain, developing chemicals. The paper looked blank, but the images were all there, waiting to be revealed. They only had to be held under the liquid of her conscious mind.

Truth claimed her and she remembered him as he was, then, and not how she wanted to remember him, how he had once been. She remembered the Stephen who was never around, who couldn't look her in the eyes, let alone take her hand, kiss the back of it, and call her his angel, as he once had. She remembered the Stephen who returned in the middle of the night, if he returned at all, and slept on the sofa, leaving a trace of perfume she knew but couldn't quite place. This Stephen stopped coming to church and she made excuse after excuse for him. This Stephen drove her son out of the house and out of the country. Would Matthew really have left if he hadn't discovered his father was screwing the church organist? After resitting his A levels – for the second time – he was supposed to be going to university, not overseas. There had been other flirtations, of that Rain was certain, but whether or not they were full-blown affairs she was less sure. On

234

reflection she thought not. But Jane was different, pushier, more determined than many mistresses who put up with their lot, and it had caught Rain unawares. Had Rain fully understood Jane's fear and resolve – a middle-aged woman engaged in an affair with a married man, she had no security, no long term prospects – Rain would have fought for Stephen, put in the work earlier. But it was Jane who got there first. His children were grown-up, she'd argued, his wife had a career, a vocation, would always be looked after no matter what, and Rain loved another (God) more than she could ever love Stephen. He had to make a decision, she'd said, and he chose the woman who needed him most, he said.

As if confirming his reasoning, Rain had been so shocked, she'd not cried, or hurled abuse, or begged him to stay. He would leave on Sunday. A friend's flat would be tenant-free by the weekend. It would give them time.

Then, the accident. She hadn't even had a chance to tell Saffron. It was a truth she could bury.

It was dark when Rain woke. She rolled over to check the digital clock on the bedside table. An hour or so before dawn. Pulsing with an energy she'd not felt in months, Rain pushed herself out of bed and crossed to the fitted wardrobe. She flung open the double doors and reached in, tearing out Stephen's shirts and jackets with the ties draped round the coat hanger handles, tossing them onto the bed. Why hadn't she done this before? It was ridiculous to keep them. There were so many people, some of her parishioners, who would be grateful for clothing of such quality.

You always were vain, Stephen, like Ben, she thought, as she picked up a silk shirt, one Stephen kept for best. She caught a waft of his aftershave. How extraordinary that a scent should linger so long after someone had gone. She picked up another shirt and held it to her face. A different scent this time, but just as familiar. Hers. Jane's. Rage tore through her. Rain lunged at the pile of clothes and swept them onto the floor in one wrath-filled movement.

'But did you love her?' Rain screamed. 'Did you love her as much as me? As Saff?' She fell to her knees.

No, of course, you didn't love her as much as Saff. You couldn't have loved anyone more than you loved Saff. Might she have persuaded you to stay? You never gave us a chance. You stupid, stupid, selfish bastard.

She thumped the mattress.

You never gave us a chance. Because you went and died. And you denied me anger and rage and the need to hate you for what you'd done to me. For what you would do to Saffron, your precious Saffron.

'You've broken my heart, Stephen. Broken it.' Her voice rasped, cracked and hoarse from the force of her wrath.

'And you were wrong. WRONG. I didn't love our Lord more than I loved you. Impossible. I forgave you and treasured you, I knew your faults and I loved you. I would have done anything for you. ANYTHING. And now I cannot even hate you. I cannot shame you and make you feel guilty. I cannot punish you. I cannot play the wronged woman. You shit. You total and utter shit. Selfish to the bloody end. You might have even done it on purpose.' She fell to her knees near the head of the bed, flung the pillows across the room and continued to pound the mattress with her fists till she was breathless and could beat or shout no more.

'You can hate him, Mum. You must, for a time. Because you also loved him. Love him. You told me that. Can't have one without the other. You have every right to feel angry. Be angry. Rage and then you can repair.'

Rain lifted her head from the mattress and saw Saff standing in the doorway, crying. How long had she been there?

She stood as Saff crossed the room and they wrapped their arms around each other and there they remained, in a trusting, faithful embrace that seemed to last for ever.

Chapter Twenty-four

'I can smell summer on the breeze, I tell you, I can,' Eifion trilled from the balcony below. Joe smiled. It was true. The air felt drier, even on cloudy days, and the smell of the sea was less pronounced.

He dipped the brush into the tin, wiped off the excess paint and pulled the bristles up the posts. Painting was satisfying. The prep was dull but once the paint went on it was gratifying. An instant result. The hourly rate wasn't as high as for skilled work, like carpentry; Eifion had apologised when he first suggested the job to Joe, but it was work, and a lot of it.

'Cash in hand, if that's OK?' Eifion had said.

'Only way I like it,' Joe replied.

The grandest hotel in town, on the seafront, the one that seemed to emerge from the rock and sit on the shoulders of the pier entrance, needed tarting up for the season. The balcony balustrades were solid, but the paintwork was chipped and had faded from what might once have been sunshine yellow to a dingy magnolia.

After the balconies there were the windows to paint. Even with a large team the work would take weeks. Joe didn't hesitate. He wasn't bothered about the poor money – so long as he had enough to pay the rent, eat, and have some left over to spoil Saffron from time to time, he didn't care. He was grateful to Eifion who'd merely shrugged and said, 'One good turn.' The thought of moving on from Coed Mawr had filled Joe with dread and this was a reprieve of sorts. The only way he would leave now was if Simon called and told him he must.

Joe felt lighter than he'd felt in years and on the best days he even considered asking Simon to stop trailing Allegra. *Forgive those who trespass against us.* The desire for revenge no longer consumed him, days went by when he didn't think of it at all, but he hadn't told Saffron his history, and he needed to remain hidden until he was ready to tell her. For he would tell Saffron. He couldn't keep it from her; he didn't want to. It was a risk but one he had to take.

Warm, he stripped off his T-shirt before turning back to the railings. As he dipped his paintbrush into the pot again, he caught sight of a woman on the pier below. Tall and slim with light red hair, he couldn't quite make out her features from this height but she was waving at him. Confused, he considered peering over for a closer look, but Joe didn't relish looking that far down; his vertigo would surely get the better of him.

He didn't know anyone in the town other than Saffron, Rain, Ceri and Eifion. Tyson had moved on to another job for Derek and Joe couldn't say he was sorry. Joe was working on the top floor at the insistence of the hotel manager, a weasel-like young man with a superiority complex. 'Top to bottom. Only way to do it,' he'd said.

The woman waved again, furiously. As he looked a second time, he saw she bore a strong resemblance to Saffron. The form of her. He put his paintbrush down and leaned forward.

Whoa. The height made him dizzy, the familiar nausea rose.

'Joe! Joe! It's me. Can you take a break?'

The automatic doors swooshed open; a blast of warm, stale air assaulted his cheeks. There, in front of him, on the pier, was Saffron. She looked very, very different. Same black jeans, black T-shirt, and heavy black boots. Same fair skin and blue, blue eyes, but there was no thick, black eyeliner and smudgy, charcoal eyeshadow. Her eyes were enormous pools framed only by long, brown lashes. With less make-up and in broad daylight, he noticed, for the first time, just how many freckles were scattered over her nose and cheeks. Maybe they'd come out in the sun.

But it was her hair that altered her so dramatically. Loose and tumbling over her shoulders in soft waves, it was the most glorious golden-orange. Contrasting sharply with her familiar black attire, it shone in the sunlight like a halo. If you ignored the clothes, the Doc Martens, and pierced ears, she could have been an angel, or Botticelli's Venus, or a Pre-Raphaelite model. He was stunned. She remained still and flushed as he stared. As the colour bloomed on her cheeks, his insides churned. If he'd been blind-sided by her beauty when he first met her, it was nothing to his reaction now. She was achingly lovely, a creature from another world, incongruous on the grotty pier with the stink of chip fat and burnt sugar on the breeze.

He stepped towards her and picked up a lock of her hair with an index finger. 'It's not a wig then?' he said.

'Nope. Do you like it?' she said, straight-faced. She sounded nervous.

He nodded. 'Your natural colour?'

'Kind of. It's as close to my natural colour as synthetic dyes go. Close enough to allow my hair to grow out without looking like a two-tone monster.' She screwed up her nose.

'How close?' He coiled another lock round his finger. It felt soft and silky.

'Pretty close. Red is the hardest colour to mimic, especially what you'd call ginger as opposed to auburn. Impossible to get it bang on, according to the hairdresser.'

'Unique and difficult. Figures.' He smiled and she smiled back.

'So what do you think?'

'I love it.' He leant forward and kissed her, forgetting where he was, not caring.

They pulled apart when some smart Alec yelled at them to get a room. Saffron repeated her initial question. Could he take a break?

'Not really. The manager bloke, right slave driver. Bit of a control freak and he's enjoying the power. If he catches me now I'll be in trouble. Is it important?'

'It is, but I've another option. You free straight after work tonight?' she asked.

'Let me see. Need to consult my diary, what with my hectic social life.'

'Yeah, yeah, Billy no mates. You're free, right?'

He didn't even get a chance to nod before she continued, 'The decision about the pier ballroom is being made this afternoon in some council meeting or other. Mum, Mair Shawcroft and others involved in the campaign are organising a celebration/commiseration do in the church hall and there's a problem with the door again. I can ask Eifion but I guess he'll be in the same position as you?'

'He's working in the hut this afternoon, so he might have some flexibility. Fits the hotel job around the shop. Not sure how he persuaded bollock chops to go for that ... Natural charm, I suppose.' He glanced over his shoulder, looking out for the manager. He'd been away from his post for way too long already. But she did that to him, forced him to take risks. She'd be his undoing.

'He's got plenty of that. Look, I'll meet you here, yeah? Six o'clock. And I'm so glad you like it.' She pointed at her head and smiled, radiant.

'Why the change?' he asked. He'd read somewhere that when women changed their hair, the colour, had it cut, it commonly signified another, more significant, shift. Hair went from long to short after break-ups, dark to light with a new career.

She shrugged. 'The end of mourning. Or a different kind of mourning … This is the real me. Weird, huh?'

'Weird's OK by me. See you later.' He waved and she turned and walked off the pier. He noticed a quiver in her voice when she said a different kind of mourning. Something was troubling her, despite the smiles and sunny hair.

It had been such a relief to hear that Joe liked her hair, to see how much he liked it. The hairdresser's bill had been astronomical; Saffron could hardly believe it, never having had a professional dye before and rarely having stepped inside a salon full stop. It was eye-watering, and she would never have done it had Rain not offered to pay. It was kind of her mum, a way of making up for the cruel, ugly words. Saffron had bought flowers and prepared Rain's favourite supper: Thai green curry with tofu and scented rice. It hadn't been easy finding lemongrass or tofu in Upper Coed Mawr, but Saffron liked to shop local and retailers in the community loved her for it. In the end, the greengrocer had ordered it in specially, in return for the recipe. It was sweet of him. After all, they both knew he could have found a recipe online in seconds.

Though she hadn't originally dyed her hair dark for her mum – far from it; it had been all about her and her feelings – Saffron had been worried that a return to red would be too much of a reminder of her dad. She owed her locks to her father's genes and after her mum's revelation, Saffron wondered if it might be better to stay dark.

For Saffron, the news that her father wasn't the saint Rain had been making him out to be was hurtful, but not altogether shocking. After she'd put Rain to bed she'd admitted to herself that she'd known her father to be more than a flirt. She'd blocked all those memories. She wasn't so different to her mother after all. As a child she'd not understood why the sight of Daddy holding other women's waists as he led them into church made her feel peculiar, but it did. One Christmas, when she must have been ten or eleven, she'd noticed her father resting his large hand on a distant aunt's thigh as they sat in the living room playing charades. The aunt, a tall, pretty woman whose long, painted fingernails fascinated Saffron, had slowly and carefully removed Stephen's hand and placed it on his own thigh. A joke of some kind was shared – too grown up for Saffron to understand – and the adults continued with the game but, eyes watery, Rain had jumped up and hoofed it to the kitchen, claiming everyone's glasses needed refilling. Home during the long medical school holidays, Saffron had noticed how their lives had grown apart. Her dad liked to party, her mum didn't. But she also knew, or thought she knew, that he'd loved Rain.

Witnessing her mum's pain was torment. More distressing than she could have imagined, and when her own anger surfaced, she caught a glimpse, momentarily, of what Rain was going through. She hated him for being so … weak. It took a while to work out which quality of her father's caused him to choose the path hc did, but it was his weakness, his malleability. He did love Rain, but his mistress exerted more pressure so he bowed to her will. Rain was too nice. Always had been, probably always would be. It was her nature. And in this, Saffron and her mother differed.

I'm not a good person. I'm the sort who lies to people, pretends to mourn someone for almost two years, does nothing as their father lies dying.

Saffron loved her father deeply and in the end such love superseded all other emotion. She couldn't hate him for long. He wasn't perfect. So what? Who was? There were so many worse crimes and he wasn't here to defend himself. Rain's goodness drove her crazy too, at times; it must have been the same for him. And such goodness threw an unforgiving light on other's foibles. Everyone appeared tarnished next to such a gleam. Perhaps it was a relief to be with an individual as flawed and warty as himself. Who was she to judge?

Outside the entrance to the hotel, ten minutes early, Saffron shifted from foot to foot. She picked up a strand of hair and held it to the evening sun, enjoying the way the light bounced off it. She pulled it to her nose. It smelt of chemicals and perfume. She'd fretted Joe would no longer fancy her. There were people who loathed ginger hair and she had no way of knowing if Joe was one of them. Or how much her looks mattered to him. A lot, judging by the look in his eyes earlier. She smiled. A dandelion seed drifted by, catching on her top. She picked it off, feeling as light as the weeds littering the grass verge. Clocks, they're called dandelion clocks. At the thought of clocks her chest tightened. Time was running out. A decision regarding her future would have to be made, and soon.

Her mood shifted the instant she saw him emerging from the hotel. Tall and strong, even in silhouette he turned her insides liquid. Though he wore a T-shirt, the memory of his bare back lingered, the ripple of muscle as he'd bent to put his T-shirt on the floor, the wings of his scapulae, muscles like the shifting, solid plates of the earth. And the tattoo. Large, shaped like a crescent moon, it stretched from mid-back to the base of his neck. Rather than a singular image, it was a series of small ones: A colony of bats, volant. She hadn't been able to make out the detail.

He came towards her. Blood raced through her veins, setting her senses alight. After days in the sun, his tanned complexion highlighted those extraordinary eyes, the contrast between golden skin and his green eye marked; that with his hazel eye less so, though this in itself emphasised the difference between the two. He took her breath away. In one clean movement he swept off his cap and bent to kiss her. Before their lips met his phone rang.

'Shouldn't you get that?' she asked.

He shrugged, pulled his phone from his back pocket, read the screen and nodded. 'Give me a second, yeah?' he said into the phone. He looked back at her and mouthed, 'I'll be as quick as I can.' To her surprise he turned his back on her and whispered into the phone, moving away as he did so. Her interest wouldn't have been piqued if he'd spoken at normal volume, if he'd not turned around and walked off. She took a pace forward and strained to listen, fighting with the traffic chugging past. It was difficult to hear anything. She caught a name, Simon, she thought. She couldn't think of many boys names beginning with 'S' other than Stephen or Steve, and there was definitely no 'st' sound. She watched Joe, attempting to read his body language. He gave nothing away. He stuffed the mobile back into his pocket before turning back and throwing her a devastating grin.

She waited for him to explain but he didn't.

It's normal, isn't it, to explain what you've just spoken about, or to whom? People do it without thinking. 'Work,' a roll of the eyes, 'sorry about that.' 'It's my brother. Girl trouble.' Or is it only women who feel the need to constantly explain, justify their actions?

'Everything OK?' she said, after a pause, unable to quash her curiosity.

'Just great,' he said, smiling.

So that's that then. He's so secretive. Perhaps Mum's right: He's not to be trusted. She's only trying to protect me. She likes him, but she doesn't trust him. And if she doesn't ...

'You? You seemed troubled earlier.'

'Just worried about the outcome of the meeting. You know, to decide the fate of the ballroom.' She had no idea why she was lying, or where the anger that simmered within her had come from.

'I'm interested too. I've a fairly good idea which company would move the bats with care, for one thing. Any news?'

'Not that I'm aware of. Been at the shop all afternoon. We'll find out soon enough. C'mon.' She marched up the incline, trying to stamp out her disquiet, leaving him behind.

He caught up within seconds and grabbed hold of her arm, forcing her to stop. She spun to face him, fury rendering her silent for a moment. 'What's up? You arrange to meet me here, to talk, and then you go all silent on me,' he said.

'You never tell me anything,' she blurted. 'I know virtually nothing about you and you give nothing away. Your home reveals nothing other than a penchant for fantasy video games, history, and a total absence of interest in food preparation. You've never even shown me any of your art. You prefer beer to wine, you like dark chocolate and instant coffee, and you're more educated than your average carpenter, a boarding school boy no less. I'd also guess that you're from down south. And oh, you like bats. Bats!' She threw her arms in the air.

'That's unfair. I told you about Allegra.' He held on to her arm, refusing to let her go, pressing his fingers into her flesh. It didn't hurt but there was force.

'Only because you had to.' She poked his chest with her free hand, hard, nail first. 'I found the photo, remember? And while we're at it, I don't think for one minute that was the whole story either.'

He winced and loosened his hold, releasing her. 'Where's all this come from, Saffron? Why so angry? What have I done?' He sounded hurt and confused and surprised.

Where was this rage coming from? She felt herself crack, splintering.

Chapter Twenty-five

Joe understood what it was like to have your illusions shattered, to discover that the mirror you'd held in front of someone was distorted, like those in fairgrounds which made tall people short and thin people wide.

'It's horrible to realise someone you thought was honest, isn't. I get that. I really do,' he said, reaching out for her hand.

Horrible. Not the best description for feelings which rip you to shreds.

'My dad's not dishonest. Wasn't. He was weak. There are worse crimes.'

Instead of appeasing her, he'd made her angrier still. He wanted to kick himself. How could he possibly understand? Saffron's discovery of the truth about her parent's marriage was different to his discovery of the truth about his life. From what she'd said, she didn't idealise her father; she'd left that to Rain. Poor Rain. What an awful thing to have to go through. Her sense of bewilderment, grief, all shot to pieces. No wonder she was all over the place. She'd denied herself true grief, when she needed to grieve twice over. For her marriage, the man she'd known, and the man himself, the loss of the man as he was then.

Saffron raged on, stomping up the hill, 'And we'll never know if he really would have gone. I can't stop myself from believing that he'd have changed his mind, before or after. That he'd have come back to us, in the end. To Mum.' She stopped, lifted her hands in supplication. 'Me! Pinning everything on some vague hope. I don't do faith.' She walked on again, her sentences punctuated by huffs of exertion. 'But we never got the chance to find out. How can Mum believe in a God, a Jesus, who allows such totally shit things to happen to nice, decent people. People who do good and pray for world peace, the poor, the barmy, and every other bleeding heart that drops by. And bad people get away with all sorts. It's not fair. Not fair at all.' Quite breathless, she paused, hands resting on her thighs.

He stepped in front of her. 'No, it isn't. Sometimes, being crapped on isn't personal. It's indiscriminate. Like getting hit by pigeon,' he looked to the sky, 'or seagull shit. They're not aiming for you, they're just flying about. You happened to be underneath.' He reached for her hands again and this time, she let him hold them. He rubbed his thumbs across her palms. 'What happened to you and Rain wasn't fair, wasn't fair at all. You didn't do anything wrong.'

'Neither did you. She left you.'

He looked at the floor. It wasn't true that he'd done no wrong, but Saffron wasn't to know.

Tell her. Tell her. Now is the time.

He let go of her, took off his cap and ran fingers through his hair, stopping at the crown, holding onto a chunk of hair. He scratched. 'Saffron –'

The slap of liquid on concrete made both of them jump. 'Jesus Christ!' Joe shouted, as guano splashed from the pavement and onto their jeans.

Through groans of disgust, Saffron started to laugh, to howl. 'Oh my God. You couldn't make that up. The timing. It's like yoghurt. A pot full. I've never seen so much seagull shit in all my life.'

A middle-aged man, incongruous in the early evening sun in a cagoule and wellies, walked by. 'Now there's luck for you!'

'Lucky if you've got a tissue?' Saffron said, still

laughing.

'As it happens.' The man pulled out a packet of Kleenex. 'There's a storm on the way,' he added, nodding at the sky before continuing on his journey. It was cloudless as far as Joe could see.

They wiped themselves as clean as possible, Saffron alternately giggling and groaning. Perhaps there is such a thing as divine intervention, Joe thought, as Saffron linked her arm in his and urged them on to the meeting, her mood light once more, all thought of what he was about to say forgotten.

The church hall was rammed when they arrived. With young and old alike. Joe was impressed. Rain had done a good job of rallying the troops and Joe hoped supporters appreciated her efforts, unconventional though they might have been for the more senior members. Whether or not it would translate to increased engagement with church activities would remain to be seen. He hoped so. Rain needed a bit of luck right now.

Ceri pushed her way through the throng, three bottles of Pilsner in a vice-like grip. She passed Joe and Saffron a bottle each and swept her gaze round the room. 'Looks like the offer of free beer did the trick, eh?'

'The news?' Saffron said.

Ceri beamed. 'The best. Your mam's going to make an announcement soon. Dad's rushed off to buy fizz.'

Saffron raised her eyebrows and Ceri laughed. 'I know. Pushing the boat out, eh? Always took him for a mean old bastard, but he likes your mam.'

Joe glanced at Saffron who smiled and said, 'She likes him.' There was no malice or rancour and he felt an urge to whisper in her ear: I love you. Love you. Instead, he leant over and placed a kiss on her cheek.

The crackle of a microphone silenced most of the crowd. Rain appeared on the small stage and made a brief, impassioned thank you for the work everyone had done raising support in the town and putting pressure on the council. 'The pier ballroom will be restored to its former glory. It will be a focal point for the people of Coed Mawr to use and enjoy, and it will have the added benefit of attracting more visitors to our beautiful resort! Our prayers have been answered.' It was the only reference to faith and once again, Joe found himself admiring Rain's approach. Slowly, slowly, catch the monkey. Wasn't that the expression?

'Think this'll get more people in chapel?' he said to Saffron as the crowd clapped and cheered. The cheers more than likely the result of a few bottles of strong lager.

'Doubt it. But it doesn't matter. The goodwill of the town is enough, along with the recruitment of a couple of wealthy ex-members.' Saffron nodded at a well-turned out couple to the right of the stage. 'They fell out with the last pastor. Paid a large chunk of his stipend. They love Mum now, apparently. They run a development company, specialising in restoration. They're after the ballroom contract. Who'd have thought faith could be so fickle, huh?'

Joe nodded. 'Let's go. I'll make supper. You said you wanted to talk,' he said, desperate to have her to himself.

'What you got in?'

'Nothing,' he said, with an apologetic sigh.

'Co-op on the way up then.' She took his hand and led him out of the hall.

Unable to sleep for the second night in a row, Joe rose shortly before dawn. It was pointless lying in bed staring at the warped beams of his bedroom ceiling, and dawn was his favourite time of day. Bats were at their most social, so it was the best time to catch them. No one was around, unlike at dusk. He needed a distraction from his troubled thoughts. He couldn't take his mind off the conversation he'd had with Saffron; the conversation in which he had remained silent. In which he should have come clean.

She was considering applying to a hospital nearby to complete her training. Well, at least nearer than King's where she'd done the earlier years of her training. She had asked him what he thought, which meant, he presumed, that this change of plan was connected to him and their relationship. She'd not used that precise word, relationship – she'd fudged it in much the same way he would have done – but that's what she meant and that's what it was.

At first he'd excused it as a few dates, something to ease the loneliness and boredom of his existence. But it was so much more than that now; it had been almost from the start. He'd been in denial. He loved her. He wasn't infatuated, he wasn't obsessed; he was in love. Genuine, you-are-my-soulmate love. He knew this, but he hadn't told her. Initially, he'd kept schtum because he couldn't be one hundred per cent sure of his feelings. After all, he was one screwed-up bloke. But now he held his silence because he was frightened. Frightened she might not reciprocate his love, frightened of being let down again, frightened to trust.

She isn't Allegra. She is nothing like Allegra. She is everything Allegra isn't.

He padded downstairs and filled the kettle, shivering as he peered through the kitchen window at the garden. He waited for the water to boil. Mist rose from the dew-laden grass, the longer stalks bowing to the earth under the weight. After the torrent of rain the night before a beautiful day beckoned. The strange man in the wellies had been right, there'd been a terrific storm shortly before midnight. He'd recently got round to buying a kettle, finally, and it had boiled before he'd had the chance to tip coffee and sugar into his mug. He couldn't get used to the speed of electricity compared to the range.

Hugging the mug he wandered outside, bare feet

sinking into the peaty, sodden ground. What was he to do? To say? She mustn't apply to Bangor or Wrexham on his behalf; he might have to move on at a moment's notice. If she did, it must be for Rain, not him. But he couldn't explain this to her without revealing the truth and telling her might mean the end of everything.

But you have to tell her. Any love she may or may not feel for you will be based on a lie if you don't.

He gulped down the coffee and went inside for another cup, his bones aching from lack of sleep. After another drink, and a shower followed by tea and toast, it was barely six o'clock.

With hours to kill before he was due at the hotel, Joe did what he always did when troubled: he walked. As he spent so much time on the waterfront he chose to ramble up the hillside, sweeping behind the tall trees. Once out of the shade of the tree canopy, the soft ground became harder and rockier as he progressed upwards. It was such a glorious morning, for a time, he forgot about his dilemma and gave in to the sheer joy of being alive. At the peak of the rise, exhausted, he threw himself on the ground and stretched out, like a starfish, eyes closed. He toyed with the idea of falling asleep here on top of the mountain, but it was too breezy, too cool, he had too much on his mind. A wisp of dark smoke trailed across the sky. Who lit a fire in this weather, or burnt garden rubbish at this hour? He pushed himself into a sitting position, imagining himself gazing over the town spotting the home of the early-rising stoker. But there was no need to search. Granite-coloured smoke snaked from the sea into the clear blue sky, smudging it like charcoal. It came from the end of the pier. The ballroom was on fire and judging by the plumes of smoke, it wouldn't be long before flames lashed at its already delicate structure.

Joe's first thought wasn't the threat to a once exquisite art nouveau building, a building that was to be preserved and restored to its full glory, but which could only be restored if something, however frayed, existed. That was his second thought. His first was the threat the fire posed to the bats. The place where they were raising their young. It was their home.

He leapt to his feet, without taking his eyes off the pier. He couldn't believe it. How had the ballroom caught fire? He recalled the empty cans and cigarette butts he'd found on the dance floor when he'd tiptoed in with Saffron, Ceri and Eifion. But they'd not been added to, or removed, when he'd gone back to check on the bats, to follow his hunch that the ballroom was a maternity roost. The conditions were good: south-facing, warm, free from human interference and predators, plenty of nooks and crannies to settle in. The bats would have scattered at the first whiff of smoke, carrying their pups with them. But where would they go? It would leave them so vulnerable.

And the ballroom. The beautiful ballroom.

Call Eifion, he's close to the seafront. Eifion? The Fire Brigade, you bloody idiot! Call 999.

He slapped at his back pocket for his phone. Damn. He'd forgotten it. He never went anywhere without his phone. Sleep deprivation, it played havoc with everything. As he raced down the hillside, he cursed his forgetfulness, his rashness in deciding to go for a walk, before realising that if he'd not taken a stroll, he'd never have seen the smoke. By some miracle, for which he thanked the universe, he did not fall or even stumble as he flew back to the cottage. There in minutes, he dialled 999, followed by Eifion, who he roused from sleep.

Joe charged outside and jumped into the Land Rover, hoping it would start first time. It had been temperamental of late. As if understanding the importance of the mission the Landy fired immediately. 'Atta girl,' he roared, as he sped down the lane, sending flinty stones spinning into the air.

Joe was first on the pier. Without the whir of sirens, Joe didn't know the fire brigade had arrived until he felt heavy footsteps reverberating on the wooden planks behind him as he charged towards the ballroom. Without stopping, he turned around, only slowing his pace enough to ensure he didn't fall over. Firefighters waved and yelled at him to go no further. He saw the figures in full fire-fighting clobber. They stampeded towards him, some with hoses looped over their arms. There weren't enough of them, he was sure. Alarmed, the blood thundered in his head, blinding him. He turned back and charged onwards. The air thickened with fumes as he drew nearer to the ballroom.

Even with the best will in the world, plus strong thighs and healthy lungs, Joe ran out of steam. The firefighters might have been weighed down by their protective clothing, but they'd not walked up a hill and sprinted back down on less than two hours' sleep. Joe's legs buckled. Two of them were on him in seconds.

'Are you mad, man? You'll get yourself killed,' one screamed.

'Will your hoses reach? Are more coming?' Joe croaked. 'We can't let it be destroyed.'

Tapping into strength reserves he thought were depleted, he pushed them off and staggered on, the acrid smell of burning filling the air.

Chapter Twenty-six

Saffron had never seen the beach and promenade so crowded. A safe distance away, everyone faced the pier, hands peaked over foreheads. High-vis jackets lined the beach like beacons, police holding the throng back. Orange flames licked the ballroom roof and black smoke billowed upwards, poisoning the sky. Two RNLI boats rose and fell with the swell on the waves below the ballroom. Arcs of water from hoses on the beach pumped towards the heart of the blaze. In the middle of the pier were more firefighters, hoses stretched to breaking point, aimed at the ballroom.

Beside Saffron, Rain gasped and clamped a hand across her mouth. Saffron took hold of her mum's free hand. Rain whispered, choked, 'How could this have happened?'

Unable to say anything sensible, and not wanting to tell Rain of her suspicions given that it would mean explaining why she'd been trespassing on the pier, Saffron pulled her mother along the promenade. 'Let's get closer,' she said. Saffron remembered the signs of life on the dance floor and feared someone might have been caught unawares. It would have been easy for a tramp or homeless teenager to fall asleep with a cigarette between their fingers, smoke inhalation would prevent them from regaining consciousness. She'd dealt with that and minor burns before, but nothing too serious. Casualties here could be much, much worse. Her body on high alert, when she spotted the ambulance she knew she was ready to help and it felt good. So good.

She heard her name being called over the hubbub of the

small crowd hovering near the pier entrance.

'Saffron!' There it was again: a female voice, familiar. It could only be Ceri.

She pushed her way through the throng, dragging Rain behind her, until they neared the ambulance. A police officer stopped her going any further, though there was no sign of activity around the ambulance itself.

'Stay back now, Miss.'

She leant to one side, peering beyond the policeman. She couldn't see anyone. 'I'm a doctor,' she said. 'Almost a doctor. I might be able to help. Offer advice.'

'Almost?' the policeman said, eyebrows raised.

'Saffron.' Ceri appeared beside her. Her voice was high-pitched, quivering. 'I saw you down the prom. Thank Christ we Welsh are midgets and you're so bloody tall. We've been shouting for you. Knew you'd be down here somewhere and no chance of hearing your phone.'

'It vibrates.'

Ceri slapped her forehead. 'What a bloody idiot.'

'Why? Why were you calling me?' Saffron said.

'Joe's been hurt. He raised the alarm. First to see the fire. Bloody early it was, when he called. Thank God he did. Would be so much worse if he'd not been up –'

Saffron heard her mother gasp. She grasped Ceri by the shoulders, her fingers pushing into her friend's pliant flesh. She resisted the impulse to shake Ceri. 'Where is he? What happened? I have to see him.' She looked again towards the ambulance, nauseous, legs wobbly, heart pounding. She felt Rain's hand on her arm.

'He's gone to hospital in another ambulance. With Dad. Not serious, the paramedics reckon. More of a precaution really, they said. I wanted to go but they said only one. Never been in an ambulance. Been in a police car but never –'

'Ceri, shut up. Which hospital. Tell me.'

Not serious, she said, not serious.

258

Her mind played Ceri's words over and over in a loop. But what if Ceri was mistaken? Saffron didn't think she could bear it. Was this to be her punishment? To lose a man she really did love?

'County. Bloody hell, what a numpty. Fancy not telling you straight away,' Ceri said.

Rain spoke and Saffron jumped, she'd forgotten her mother was there. 'We'll get a cab. Did you bring your phone? I forgot mine in the rush.' Saffron pulled it out of her back pocket. 'Of course you did. Surgically attached, isn't it?' Rain continued with forced lightness as she took the phone from Saffron. 'Don't worry, Saffy. As Ceri said: a precaution.' Rain moved away, the phone at her ear. Saffron followed with Ceri in tow, still talking. She had no idea what Ceri was saying.

A&E was busy, people milling everywhere. Mothers with children, a workman cradling what looked like a broken arm, and a surprising number who appeared to be drunk. Rain was appalled; it was eight thirty on a weekday morning.

While Saffron and Ceri waited at reception, Rain scoured the room for seats. She felt somewhat dizzy. No breakfast, that would be it. And a terrible shock. Only days since their little victory and it seemed like all their efforts had been in vain. Eifion had sounded devastated when he'd called. He was apologetic for waking her but he felt that she would want to know as soon as possible. 'There may even be people who'd welcome your presence down there, Reverend. Who might need to pray,' he'd said, shyly. Despite the shock of the news, or perhaps because of it, she'd laughed, and said, 'I wouldn't bank on it. Perhaps only our developer friends,' before ending the call, throwing on some clothes, and going to wake Saffron.

She looked around the room for Eifion but there was no sign of him. Perhaps he was in with JJ? Wherever JJ was.

She sat on a free seat. Joe. She must call him Joe. She'd been misled all those months ago when Saff had said that everyone called him JJ. No one did. Mind you, few knew him by name or sight, full stop. Only Ceri, Eifion, that Tyson lad, and, of course, Saff. There must be others though, surely? At the hotel, a landlord, the congregation, and campaign crew? She'd misjudged him. What he'd done today was brave. Some might say a little foolish.

Bats! Who'd have thought he'd risk his life for a bunch of ugly mammals and an old pier?

As she thought on it, Rain warmed to Joe even more. Anyone who cared about those more vulnerable than themselves had to be nice. He was kind to animals. A good sign. He would be kind to Saff.

'This taken?'

Jolted from her thoughts, Rain glanced up. A young man, a little younger than JJ – Joe – hovered over her, pointing at the empty seat next to her.

She looked towards reception. Saffron and Ceri were still waiting to be seen and the desk was empty, staff too busy dealing with medical emergencies, she imagined.

'No. Do sit down.'

He plonked himself down and unhooked a bulky camera from around his neck with one hand. He nodded. 'Twisted my wrist and I'm left-handed. Typical, huh?'

Rain wanted to suggest that he make an appointment with his GP and stop clogging up casualty with non-emergencies but refrained. He might be a visitor, not registered with a doctor, though he looked familiar. She was unable to place him. She was intrigued by his camera and longed for a distraction from her rumbling belly. The WI shop didn't open till nine o'clock.

'I wouldn't have thought photography was a dangerous sport,' she said, smiling.

From the blank expression on his face he didn't get the joke.

Undeterred, she continued. 'Is it a hobby, or work?'

This question he could answer, it seemed, and his relief was palpable. 'Work. *The Herald*.'

There, she had him. He worked for the local newspaper. He'd taken her picture outside the church, not long after she'd first arrived in Coed Mawr and was trying to raise the profile of the chapel and the plight of its roof. He'd interviewed her too. Nice enough man, not the brightest but presumably that's why he remained in local news and hadn't hoofed it down to London and the nationals.

'You took my photo,' she said. 'The chapel in Upper Coed Mawr.'

'So I did.' He smiled, though his tone conveyed a distinct lack of genuine interest. 'What you in for?' he asked, when she didn't turn away.

Rain explained about JJ – Joe – and the race to the pier to stop the fire and save the bats and ballroom. In the telling of the tale, she got quite carried away and embellished a few of the facts, as far as she knew them. It was a great story and Joe was quite the hero, she realised. Why, without him raising the alarm, who knows what might have happened? People might have been killed (she wasn't sure how, but the reporter didn't challenge her and so she continued); the fire would certainly have taken a much stronger hold, and bats were a protected species, didn't he know?

The reporter nodded, enraptured, and it was only when he asked if he might record some of the facts that Rain's stomach churned from something other than hunger. Had she gone too far? She'd not lied. The bare bones were solid. She nodded back.

He took out his notebook and wrote down the details.

'And he's here, in the hospital, now?' he said, looping the camera strap back around his neck.

Rain nodded again, mute.

He stood and she heard him whisper, 'Fantastic,' before he offered his hand – the good one – and said, 'Thank you so much, Reverend. This is a story everyone should hear.'

She watched him approach reception as a member of staff returned. Bouldering his way through the queue he collared the woman, an administrator from the looks of her smart suit, and after a couple of seconds he trotted through a set of double doors with Saffron and Ceri scurrying after him. Rain pushed herself from her seat, stumbled between the tightly packed chairs, and hurried through the doors, ignoring the cries of the administrator. 'You must speak with reception before going anywhere, please!'

On the other side of the double doors Rain turned left where she found another, smaller reception. Again, unstaffed. What on earth was happening to the NHS? Beyond that was a corridor with individual cubicles, all closed off.

There came a shouting from the far end and the reporter burst through the curtain which offered patients a degree of privacy, clutching his camera in front of him. He raced down the corridor towards Rain with Ceri in pursuit. Faster than Ceri, he swept past Rain, who, in the confusion, blocked Ceri's path. The reporter disappeared back through the doors.

'Heavens. What was that all about?' Rain said.

'Bloody bastard!' Ceri yelled.

A nurse poked her head out from behind another curtain and scowled at them. 'I'll have you thrown out,' she said.

'I've got to go anyway,' Ceri said, to no one in particular. 'Duty calls. Kids are waiting for me. Good of them to give me a bit of slack.' She looked at Rain. 'Say good bye to Saff, will you? And Joe. Tell him if I see that slimy git, I'll punch his lights out as well as busting his camera.' And with that she too disappeared. The nurse popped her head out again and Rain squeaked, 'It wasn't me,' before turning to the small reception where a member of staff now sat staring at a PC.

'Can I help you?' the girl said, calmly.

She must see things like this all the time, thought Rain, before asking which cubicle Joe Jones was in and might she pop up to say hello? She already knew, but it seemed polite to ask.

Joe was sitting up in bed when Rain peered round the curtain. Saff sat on the edge of the bed. There were no medics around.

'I came to see how you were doing?' She felt like an intruder, and she was troubled by something as yet unidentified. A heavy feeling in her stomach had taken care of her appetite at least.

It was Saffron who answered. 'He was better before that reporter pitched up. What a rude bastard. Who does he think he is? Snapping away like that, without permission.' She turned to Joe. 'How did he know where you were?' She held onto Joe's hand. Rain envied him that. How lovely to have someone hold you in times of crises.

'Where's Eifion?' she asked.

'He left as soon as the nurse gave me the all-clear. Just waiting for official sign-off. Has to be a doc.' He smiled at Saff. 'Hotel manager's a pig and it's bad enough me not being there, let alone Eifion too.'

'How are you, JJ? Joe.'

'OK, thanks. I didn't get close enough to get hurt. Lungs are fine. Clothes stink.' He smiled and waved her in. 'They got it under control yet?'

Rain remained where she was. 'Getting there. We won't know the extent of the damage for a while. I'm so glad you're all right. Thank God.'

'That's what that reporter said.' Saffron turned to face Rain.

Fixing on Joe, Rain said, 'The reporter ... it might have been my fault ... I'm so sorry. He was here, in A&E, waiting to be seen, for a bad wrist,' she held up her left hand. 'We got talking ... I had no idea he'd come storming in after you.'

'Course you didn't. They might not even print it. Not much of a story really and Ceri might have blocked the shot anyway. She's fierce, that one,' Joe said.

'Oh, it is a story. I wonder how he took the shot. He had a sprained wrist, you know. I think you're a hero.'

'So do I,' echoed Saffron, and she leant forward and kissed him.

Rain slipped away without saying goodbye. Joe was fine and that was good. He was good. She hoped he would be good to her daughter.

Chapter Twenty-seven

It was bad. A photograph, blurred, but if you knew who you were looking for, unmistakable; a big bold title; a half page article including his name, his profession, the fact that he'd worked on the chapel roof, that he'd supported the campaign to save the pier ballroom (an exaggeration, in truth), that he wasn't a local, been in the area a year. Damn, damn, damn. Joe folded the newspaper and threw it onto the toilet floor. A colour photograph of the blazing ballroom stared back at him. At least the photograph of him wasn't on the front page.

He shuffled on the toilet seat lid, sat back, resting against the cistern, arms folded. So it had come to this: hiding away in a hotel toilet reading the Saturday edition of a regional newspaper. It was possible they wouldn't find it, that he would remain hidden, that he could stay here, stay with Saffron.

Saffron. His guts twisted at the thought of her, of leaving. What the hell was he going to do? He couldn't stay. He couldn't go.

You need to speak with Simon.

He lifted his backside from the seat and pulled his phone from his front pocket. It had been there too long; it was getting uncomfortable. He'd only moved it to sit down.

Sighing, he found Simon's contact and hit call.

'Yo. How goes it?' Simon sounded buoyant.

'Shite.' He could almost hear Simon deflating as he explained. 'Right, look, bro, here's what we do.' Joe didn't bother reminding Simon they weren't related in any way;

it seemed petty under the circumstances. 'Stay cool. Let me do the worrying. What's to say they'll have seen this rag? Her man's snooping in Ireland, yeah? Totally the wrong trail, man. Totally. Give me till Monday. Not so easy at the weekend.'

Joe wondered why, in a twenty-four-hour global society, it being a weekend made any difference to what Simon could and couldn't find out. 'You got a woman, right? With her now?' He heard an apologetic grunt. 'Simon, don't make me beg. Please. If you possibly can. Call me tonight?'

'Give me till six this evening, OK.'

'You're the best.'

'I know.'

Bang on time, Simon called. Joe was at the cottage, pacing up and down the tiny lounge. He'd been in for fifteen minutes and hadn't even made himself a drink. He wasn't sure he'd be able to swallow anything.

There was no need to panic, Simon said. Allegra's man was still sniffing around in Ireland, County Cork, and he showed no signs of moving back across the water.

But now Joe was troubled by something else. If the reporter was ambitious there could be more trouble ahead. Did he keep up with news outside of the county? The story had been pretty big at the time; it made the nationals for a day or two. With a little digging, he might connect the 'pier hero' with Marcus Whittaker. If this bloke was a good journalist, he'd smell a story. He'd wonder why Joe had been so reticent about having his picture taken, about appearing in the paper. He might go for the other story.

'Simon, there's something else,' he said.

The silence on the other end of the phone spoke volumes.

'You thinking what I'm thinking?' Joe said at last.

'Yup. You might get lucky with the Batman story, but

if he follows it up Allegra is sure to find you,' Simon said. All 'yos and bros' gone, he spoke in his clipped, public-school-educated accent. 'But right now I can't think of anything we can do. You're gonna have to sit tight.' Simon changed the subject. 'How damaged is the ballroom?'

'Difficult to be sure right now, but the fire service did an amazing job. I reckon it's salvageable.'

'Well, that's good news.'

'Sure is.'

Joe flopped onto the sofa after Simon rang off. Numb. He stared at the chimney breast, its bare brick, the charred logs sitting in the grate, there since April. Not so very long ago he'd thought he might use them again come the autumn. He'd allowed himself to imagine that Saffron might be here, with him, on an early October evening when the temperature grew sharp enough to light a fire. Perhaps she'd not long returned home after a day at the hospital. After a day working on a piece of art – a sculpture from wood or stone – or as a carpenter, he'd have cooked supper and opened a bottle of red, allowed the wine to breathe.

When she'd hinted she might apply nearby he'd told himself she mustn't on his behalf. Could he ask her to apply to London as she'd originally planned? Explain that he would come with her? He wasn't tied to Coed Mawr any more than she was. Less. Saffron had Rain. He would say an opportunity had come up: one he couldn't say no to; that he had to go immediately but he would write as soon as he'd settled. It would be all right.

It would mean abandoning plans for revenge. But in truth, what plans? He hadn't thought about getting even for so long now he barely knew if it was what he wanted after all. Coed Mawr had been a hiding place at first – a dim corner, somewhere no one would think to look. Somewhere to lick his wounds and rebuild his life. Plot retribution. Maybe. But he'd grown fond of the place; more than fond. And there was Saffron. Initially regarded as a distraction from all that felt rotten about his life, she'd shown him all that was good and beautiful and right. His heart hurt; it actually hurt.

The other option would be to come clean, as she'd done. Saffron might be OK with it; he dared to hope she would. But everyone else in Coed Mawr? Rain, Eifion, Ceri, the members of the church who waved if they saw him in the street? An ache at the base of his neck was growing more persistent, creeping over his skull. A killer headache was on its way and Saffron was due in less than an hour.

He pushed himself from the sofa and picked up the bag of groceries. He was going to make paella, the recipe scrawled on a piece of paper stuffed in his back pocket. It was the most adventurous dish Eifion cooked, he'd told Joe before dictating the ingredients and instructions, but it was straightforward. 'Minimum skill, maximum result,' he'd said confidently. 'I might take a pan of it over to the Rev next week. Food's a great comforter, you know.' Joe agreed, remembering the midnight snacks he and Simon shared in the dormitory. Biscuits and chocolate and crisps, all packed by Simon's mother, little understanding it was also food for Simon's tormentors. Plump and shy, Simon grew weightier and more and more unhappy till the day his parents realised what was going on and transferred him to another school. The day he left was the worst of Joe's young life, but they'd pledged to stay in touch and they had. Simon was a friend and Joe didn't have many of them.

'Gorgeous smell. What are you cooking?' Saffron said, as she plonked a kiss on Joe's cheek and bounced through the cottage door. She felt ridiculously happy.

'Paella,' Joe said, looking dazed but totally gorgeous.

There were times when she looked at him and thought she might evaporate with sheer lust. In the past, she'd heard other women use silly expressions like 'turning to jelly', but now she understood it was more stupid than she'd first thought. Jelly was way too solid. In Joe's presence, hell, even when she thought about him, she became liquid, like jelly before it sets. Formless, slipping about, ready to fill whatever shape she could find, whatever shape Joe desired.

'Yum. Not sure who to eat first. You or it. I'm famished.' She pushed up against him, sliding her arms round his waist, up under his T-shirt, enjoying the firm sensation of his chest against hers, running her fingers up his spine, skimming vertebrae protected by flesh damp with sweat. She rested her head on his shoulder and kissed his neck, round his ear and along his jawbone to his mouth. Stubble scratched against the delicate skin of her lips intensifying bolts of desire which shot from her mouth to the most secret part of her.

He took hold of her hands and prised her off him, kissing each palm, before looking at her and smiling. Below his eyes, she saw the purple blush of late nights and worry. 'You're cheerful,' he said. 'How so?'

'You're here. Unharmed. Fit.' She raised her brows salaciously. 'Very fit.'

He smiled.

'I'm here.' She brushed his cheek. 'The ballroom isn't damaged beyond repair. Official. And I've made a decision.' It was true. She could hardly believe it, but that morning she had woken with the certain knowledge she must stay near Coed Mawr. She would look for foundation jobs in North Wales' hospitals. One would have her, she was confident of that; her grades had been excellent. Rain needed her, but, more importantly, she wanted to stay. She couldn't leave. Not while Joe was here.

He was staring at her, and though she couldn't be sure

– she still found him impossible to read – she had a hunch he'd guessed. His eyes gave nothing away. 'I'm hoping you'll want to celebrate.'

Leaning forward, he kissed her forehead. 'I will.' But there was no joy in his tone and Saffron's legs felt distinctly boneless.

'You OK?' she whispered.

'Yeah. Got a bit of a headache, that's all. Nothing food, wine, beer, and you, can't cure.'

After supper they sat on the floor facing each other, leaning against the sofa, heads cradled in hands, legs curled, like a reflection of one another. Each cupped a glass in their free hand. The smoky tones of a dead blues singer poured from the tiny speaker plugged into Saffron's phone. Shadow divided Joe's handsome face, a shaft of light from the small window behind her illuminating his amber eye. There was an alien quality to him, other worldly and precious. She ached with love. She pulsed with the need to demonstrate that love; they'd done little more than kiss, explore the external landscape of one another's body. She'd done with waiting.

'It's so dark in here, even in summer. Doesn't it depress you?' she said.

He shrugged, indicating that it might.

'I need light. Space.'

He tugged at her black top and she laughed.

'Around me, not on me.' She took a sip of wine, her belly fluttering, even after the bowl of paella. 'So what do you think? I can't tell if you're pleased or not.'

'You're very, very lovely.'

'Loveable?' she said, a breath more than a word.

'Oh yeah,' he replied, almost as quiet.

She reached over and placed her glass on the coffee table. Then she took his glass of beer and placed it next to hers. She pushed him gently so that his back rested against the sofa and straddled his thighs. He went to speak and she put a finger over his mouth before pulling her T-shirt over her head and flinging it across the room. Conscious of her pale skin and the freckles splattered across her cleavage, she dipped her head. She couldn't watch him watching.

Head still bowed, she ran the flat of her hands over his stomach and across his pectoral muscles. She felt him tremble. He reached out and swept a hand across her chest, embracing her shoulder. Goosebumps studded her arms and she felt herself shudder, though she was not cold. He pulled her into him and before their lips met she whispered, 'I love you.'

Melded together, they lay on the floor, exhausted, exhilarated. Silent. There was no need for words; there were no words to describe how she felt.

Joc hadn't spelled out his feelings for her before the kiss, but he hadn't needed to. To Saffron, his actions spoke more than any words ever could. Afterwards, he cupped her face and rested his forehead against hers. They lay there for minutes. Sweat dried on their brows. She listened to the sound of their breathing slowing down, returning to the rhythm of everyday life, though her life, her existence, would never be the same again. It had shifted on its axis, permanently. She thought of her mother and marvelled at the progress she had made towards a kind of normality. Rain had lost the love of her life and she had carried on. Only her faith allowed her to. Right here, right now, Saffron couldn't imagine how that was possible. If anything happened to Joe, to them, she would surely die.

'Let me look at your tattoo,' she said at last, kissing his knuckles. She prised her hands free from his, and rolled him over. The bats were detailed, like drawings from a natural history book. She could make out the veins in the diaphanous sheath of flesh stretched over the bones of the wings, the small teeth of the bat that snarled as it swept towards Joe's neck.

'Did it hurt? she said.

'It was worth it.'

'They're extraordinary. Scary and ugly. And fascinating. They draw the eye.'

'They're beautiful. Bats don't deserve their bad reputation.'

Saffron couldn't argue with that. Instead she leaned in and kissed the angry bat, her hands clutching Joe's warm shoulders.

Chapter Twenty-eight

Joe imagined them welded together, the sweat on their foreheads drying like glue to bind them. He wanted to stay like this for as long as possible, delay the parting. He could not leave Coed Mawr; he could not.

He'd known it would be like this. He loved Saffron, and now they'd given that love physical expression there could be no return to a state of 'before'. It was why he'd resisted for so long. He'd been surprised by his own restraint. Jesus, he'd wanted her from the minute she'd kissed him so unexpectedly on the promenade on that cold spring night.

It had been such a long time since he'd been with a woman, he'd been nervous. But it was so natural, so right with Saffron, and it was better than with anyone, even Allegra. Sex with Allegra had often felt like a battle of wills, each of them fighting for dominance, control, desperate to ensure their own needs were met. They were selfish lovers, he realised. It hadn't been like that with Saffron, quite the reverse. Of course, there'd been clumsy, awkward moments: dealing with socks was never sexy, ditto condoms. They'd clashed teeth occasionally when kissing, Saffron's hair caught in his fingers, knotted round and round them, their sweat-sticky skin squelched as they rolled and moved apart. But they'd laughed and kissed and known that none of it mattered because lovemaking in real life was nothing like in the movies, even when it was very, very good.

'Stay the night?' he said, when she'd finished tracing her finger across the images on his back.

'Your sheets clean?'

He rolled over to face her and screwed up his nose. 'Think so.'

She laughed – he loved the sound of her laughing – and pushed herself into a sitting position, pulling her knees to her chest. 'Oh, Jesus, you should see these carpet burns.' She inspected her elbows and groaned again.

His knees and elbows were raw as well, though he'd escaped the ravages of stubble scratches on his cheeks. Her chin was pink too. 'Let me get some Germolene. I've got some in the kitchen.' He wandered to the door and turned. Her hair was ruffled and matted, her eye make-up smudged, her cheeks and neck flushed. She looked sluttish and sexy and he wondered if she'd ever looked as lovely. He didn't think so.

After he'd tended to her burns and she to his, they gathered their scattered clothes and climbed the narrow staircase to Joe's bedroom. Saffron texted Rain: *Don't expect me till morning Xxxx*. They fell into bed and made love again and again.

Joe stared at the ceiling, despairing, listening to the sound of Saffron's light breathing as she slept. Would he ever sleep again? After the exertions of the evening he'd hoped he would collapse from exhaustion. He was thirty, not nineteen, and couldn't remember the last time he'd made love more than twice on the same night. But his mind whirred non-stop, playing the same conversation over and over, ad infinitum.

He would stay in Coed Mawr. Sod it. Sod Allegra. He would tell Saffron the truth and be damned.

He would stay in Coed Mawr and keep quiet. It was possible Allegra wouldn't find him. The newspaper story had been overlooked. Saffron would finish her training locally. They would see each other on her days off, live happily ever after.

He would leave Coed Mawr and take Saffron with him. He'd make something up to explain. They would go to London or wherever and live happily ever after.

He would leave Coed Mawr. No. No. No.

He might have to. He rolled over and watched her. Beautiful, clever, good Saffron. He didn't deserve her.

In the morning, Joe felt sick with tiredness and he'd still not come to a decision. He watched her again, as he'd done most of the long, long night, the gentle rise and fall of her breasts, a strand of orange hair across her neck, the long, brown lashes resting on cheeks dusted with freckles. The sight of her made him melt. He ran an index finger under a lock of hair, sweeping it over her shoulder. She opened her eyes, dreamy and only semi-conscious.

'Hi,' he said.

'What time is it?' she croaked.

'Just before ten.'

With an alertness that took him by surprise, she leapt out of bed. 'I promised Mum I'd set up chapel for the eleven o'clock service. Mrs So-and-so is ill and she didn't want to call anyone else on a Saturday evening.'

She rummaged through the crumpled heap of clothes on the floor, retrieved her knickers, turned them inside out and yanked them on, before clambering into her jeans, hopping from foot to foot as she tugged them up her long, lean legs. He must have looked surprised because she added, 'I'm not staying. Just setting up. You around later?' She tied the belt of her jeans and scooped out hair caught beneath her T-shirt. It tumbled down her back, her titian waves highlighted against her dark top. He yearned to tug her back into bed, to lose himself, and all thought of what he should do, in her sweet flesh, in the ecstasy of lovemaking.

'Well?' She stared at him, eyebrows raised, crouched and tying her boot laces.

How long had he drifted off for? It could only be seconds, she was in a rush. He had to talk to her today, one way or another. 'Sure. Give me till mid-afternoon. Say three?'

Christ, he was a first-class procrastinator. Why not earlier? He had nothing important to do. He'd be unable to give a carving he was working on the focus it required. Instead, he'd probably fart around gaming.

'Great. Give me a chance to have lunch with Mum. Catch up. Far side of the beach if it's still bright? Tŷ Melyn if not? I fancy a Bakewell tart.' The guest house they'd retreated to after Saffron had told Joe about Ben and the crash and Stephen had become a haunt. It was always empty mid-afternoon and the landlady was friendly and welcoming. If she had no cakes they made do with tea and ginger nuts. 'My weakness,' she'd told them, patting her rounded stomach.

He followed Saffron downstairs, kissed her goodbye, and watched her belting towards the lane. She burst with energy, with the pure joy of being alive. He felt like a man in the dock, waiting for the judge to return.

Saffron bombed into the manse, splashed her face with water, and brushed her teeth before heading over to the chapel. Rain was checking the PowerPoint presentation as she dashed in.

'Sorry, sorry,' she said, flapping her hands and checking the table at the entrance for up to date newsletters and something to do other than look at her mum. 'I'll get the Bibles.'

'Don't panic. You're not late. How was your evening?' In her peripheral vision Saffron saw Rain look over from the iMac. She appeared calm, interested, without any trace of her usual desperation. Such eagerness to please had lessened considerably of late, Saffron noted, and the panic attacks and periods of fevered cleaning had almost disappeared. Her mum looked relaxed and pretty, her blonde curls bouncier than ever.

'Fine.' Saffron shuffled the papers on the table. It was stupid to be embarrassed.

'That all?'

'It was nice, thanks. Now, what do you want me to do once I've got the Bibles?'

Nice wasn't the right word. They both knew that. But Saffron didn't read romantic fiction, or watch romantic dramas. She didn't have the vocabulary to describe the evening, her feelings for Joe, and she wouldn't have shared them with her mum regardless. For the mechanics of the act, the chemical, hormonal and physical changes to her body she could have written an essay, but to put into words what occurred in her heart, in her soul? Impossible. She loved him; couldn't be without him; there was nothing more to say.

Once parishioners started filing into the chapel, Saffron made herself scarce. After a bath and change of clothes, she prepared a lunch of bread, cheese, and salad and then went back to the chapel to help clear up and prepare the space for the long evening service. She didn't wash her hair, not wanting to erase his scent, the musky, slightly vinegary smell of him. From time to time, she grabbed a handful of her hair and pulled it across her nose, inhaling him, as if to remind herself he existed, that he wasn't spectre or dream.

Rain had invited Mair Shawcroft and another elderly lady for lunch. Saffron beefed up the salad, adding more greens and herbs from the garden. She opened a packet of Brie and popped another baguette in the oven to warm it, and washed a punnet of strawberries before placing the fruit in a crystal bowl reserved for special occasions. She threw a linen cloth over the table, and enjoyed the vibrancy of the glistening greens and reds against the pure white fabric.

In the warm, golden light of the dining room, the women were relaxed and entertaining. Rain and her guests teased Saffron gently about her affair with the 'handsome carpenter', becoming whimsical as they reminisced about their own youthful flirtations and love affairs and, in Mair's case, somewhat more earthy undertakings. Rain stroked the tablecloth and told her guests that it was a wedding present from an elderly aunt, a gift Stephen hated using when the children were small. 'It'll be ruined! Peanut butter and Marmite stains!' In the end it was Stephen who'd stained it when he'd reached for the salt cellar one evening and knocked over a glass of Merlot.

'You'd never know,' Mair remarked, casting her eyes across the table.

'There!' Rain pointed and laughed. 'Just got to know where to look.'

Saffron noticed with pleasure that Rain spoke of Stephen with warmth and a realism that had been absent for so long. Rain was remembering the man she'd loved, the man who'd loved her. A breeze rippled through the windows, lifting the curtains into the dusty air, the diaphanous fabric reminiscent of a wedding veil. Saffron bit into another strawberry, the sweet juice pouring down her chin, and wished she'd opened a bottle of white wine. There was everything to celebrate and Rain would not have objected. The grandmother clock in the corner chimed the hour and Saffron decided to make her way down to the sea, to enjoy a walk along the promenade before meeting Joe on the sands.

As she ambled down the rise towards the promenade her heart sang. The pier was busy, even for a glorious Sunday afternoon. It was not yet half past the hour, plenty of time to kill. She waltzed past the doughnut stall, the man clutching a bunch of balloons and towards Eifion's rock hut. She could stop and say hello. Ceri might be around.

At the New Age hut, where a heavily tattooed woman sold tie-dyed scarves, skull rings, and Saffron's beloved patchouli oil, Saffron spotted Joe up ahead. She raised her hand and was about to call out when she realised he was talking with someone, a petite woman. He'd not seen Saffron. Who could the woman be? Joe knew so few people. Realisation seeped through her, like ink on blotting paper. It could be Allegra. The long, brown, wavy hair, bronzed limbs.

Saffron lowered her arm and snuck behind a rail of velvet dresses with lace-up fronts and black T-shirts decorated with Celtic knots and symbols. She shuffled the coat hangers, as if she was looking for something, but her eyes were fixed ahead. Too far to hear the conversation but close enough to witness its passionate intensity – all flailing arms, and then, my God, was that a kiss? Her spirits plummeted as her mind went into overdrive. Had Joe planned this meeting? He couldn't have; he'd asked to see her, Saffron. Why would he not say anything? But if it was meant to be a secret why meet in a public place? For sure, he couldn't have known she would be early, that she would wander on to the pier, but it was risky nevertheless. Her heart battered against her ribcage. This was bad. Something wasn't right. And if it wasn't Allegra, who was it?

A high-pitched screech lanced the clammy air, a baby's cry, and Saffron spun round, her back to Joe and the mysterious woman. Coed Mawr was a small place, she knew everyone he associated with and that wasn't many; a few churchgoers, Rain, Eifion, Ceri. Shaking, she fiddled with rings displayed on a table outside the hut, head bowed. Heavy footsteps pounded past and she sneaked a glance. Brown wavy locks swung across a slim back. Saffron turned back to look up the length of the pier. Joe had disappeared. But where to?

A split-second decision had to be made. Saffron dropped the opal ring she was clutching and raced towards the pier exit, her eyes fixed on the woman's back.

Chapter Twenty-nine

Saffron tailed the woman from the promenade to the shopping arcade, uncertainty about what she might say when she finally plucked up the courage to stop her, *if* she plucked up the courage to stop her, growing with every step. But she was increasingly sure it must be Allegra.

Hi, I'm Saffron. I'm Joe's girlfriend. What are you doing here? wouldn't cut it. It sounded so ... so ... lame. Who was to say Allegra hadn't swung by to collect some of her CDs or cutlery? Bollocks. Joe didn't have any CDs and little in the way of cutlery. Perhaps Allegra took the lot? Had they lived together? Joe had never said.

He's not said much, full stop.

Saffron was so busy running through imaginary conversations that she almost crashed into another shopper, the only person shielding her from the woman who must be Allegra. The shopper turned, clearly alarmed by Saffron's proximity, scowled but said nothing. Saffron heaved a sigh of relief. She did not want to draw attention to herself; she wasn't ready to confront this woman, this almost-certainly-Allegra who'd stopped in front of an electrical shop next door but one to Wynne's. She was checking her phone by the looks of things. With the shopper gone, the arcade was almost deserted and Saffron felt conspicuous. She dived into the entrance of Wynne's and peered in the window, pretending to inspect the miserable display; the dummy still minus a hand. The shop was dark, the owner resolutely resisting the push for Sunday opening.

'Saffron! Can't keep away, huh?'

It was Mrs Evans, the manager, brandishing a key. What was she doing here? Mrs Evans jerked her head at the window. 'You can help me spruce up this display if you like. I'll pay overtime.'

Panicking, Saffron bit her lip and shook her head. To her relief Mrs Evans merely laughed, turned the key, and pushed open the door. Her parting shot echoed round the arcade. 'Your loss, Saffron, love. See you tomorrow.'

Saffron turned away from Mrs Evans to find herself looking down into the face of the woman she was now one hundred per cent certain was Allegra. Eyes of different colours bored into her: one hazel, one green.

'So you're Saffron.' Allegra smiled, though only with her mouth; her eyes remained glassy. 'Marcus described you well.'

'Marcus?'

A genuine, if smug, smile spread across her face. My God, she was beautiful. Stunning. 'Ah, but of course. You know him as Joe, don't you?' She flicked a rogue strand of hair over her shoulder. It felt like a smack in the face to Saffron.

'We need to chat. There are things you need to know. Shall we go for a coffee? Can you recommend anywhere? I believe you're local,' Allegra said. And though her tone was kind, concerned, her eyes moved over Saffron like she was a piece of fluff to be removed from a jumper.

'I'm not sure we have anything to say to each other.' Saffron spoke in a manner she'd reserved for distressed patients, her attempt to match Allegra's composure. She was glad of her height, at least she could look down on this pint-sized beauty. In a perfect world she'd have walked away, head high, but she was unable to, trapped in the porch entrance of Wynne's. Her world had travelled a million miles from perfect in the past half an hour. Allegra was so close Saffron could smell the heady, expensive notes of her perfume.

Why, for fuck's sake, why, did I follow her instead of Joe. Marcus?

'You might not have anything to say to me, but I have plenty to say to you,' Allegra said.

Why is she being so horrible? She left him; she broke his heart.

Allegra smiled. She spoke again, even more softly this time, even kinder. 'There's so much you don't understand about Marcus. So much you deserve to know, so that you can understand.'

That Saffron knew little about Joe was true, but she did understand him. She did, didn't she?

Why did you lie to me, Joe? Who are you?

'I'd like to explain something about Marcus and me. Why we belong together.' Allegra touched Saffron's arm, pityingly. Instinctively, Saffron recoiled.

She wants him back.

Saffron could almost feel herself shrinking. She couldn't compete with this goddess. She was insignificant. Nothing. She didn't even know his real name.

Allegra turned and waved a slender arm in the direction of the arcade exit. 'I saw a café on the main drag. Didn't look too awful. We'll go there,' she said, confidently, walking away, clearly sure Saffron would follow.

And follow she did, her emotions veering from fury to devastation. Adrenaline pumped through her veins. But was she to fight or run? At school and university she'd always been contemptuous of those girls who fell out over men, fought for their attentions, but she wouldn't – couldn't – give up Joe without a battle. No way was she going to capitulate. Allegra's elegant dress rippled as she tottered off, the red silk shifting like sand in a desert storm.

Beware. This woman will be no pushover.

As they neared the café, Saffron nudged in front, determined to take back control. In her flat-soled boots, she walked faster than Allegra in her stupid little heels.

Saffron launched herself at the café door and stomped through without looking behind her, hoping the door would swing back just heavily enough to knock Allegra off balance.

The place was deserted bar a couple of bored-looking teenagers staring into empty glasses as if willing them to fill with vodka. Saffron scanned the room before deciding on a window seat. Sure, it could get embarrassing if people from the street saw them arguing, but it afforded a quick exit, should one be required. She snatched the menu from its stand, though she wanted nothing.

A waitress slouched over. 'Cappuccino. No chocolate,' Allegra said in cut glass tones. She sounded posher than ever in the dismal café.

'Semi or full?' the waitress sighed.

'Have you red top?' Allegra said.

But of course, this woman is taut and lean, no excess fat on her.

The waitress stared at Saffron.

'Just water, please. Tap'll do,' she mumbled.

She watched the waitress cross the room to the counter, her flip-flops slapping against dry, cracked heels.

She needs to treat that xerosis; some Aveeno cream at least.

Elbows on the table, Allegra rested her chin on her hands, and looked at Saffron. Her features were awash with pity and Saffron itched to wallop her. She'd not harboured such violent impulses towards anyone before. She sat on her hands to ensure she didn't.

'So … what has he told you?' Allegra began.

'About …?' Two could play at that game. No way was Saffron going to reveal what she knew first. She wondered if Joe had ever shown Allegra his art, and an unpleasant image of them disturbed her thoughts. She pushed it away.

'Me. Us. Him,' Allegra said, sounding weary, as if it was all a waste of her time.

'You …' Saffron shrugged in a not-a-lot-he's-forgotten-about-you manner. At least that's what she hoped the gesture conveyed. He hadn't told her much about Allegra, but she wasn't going to let on.

Allegra lifted her chin from her knuckles and tapped her chest with her thumbs. 'Let me guess … he's told you very little. Almost nothing. I'm the woman who left him, who broke his heart, and you think he's over me, that he's free?'

Saffron nodded. She couldn't help it.

Allegra continued. 'Did he tell you why I left him? That it wasn't by choice? That we were forced apart? That I've been waiting, longing, for the day we can be reunited? And that he has been too?'

'You're talking in riddles. I prefer plain speaking.' It was difficult to force the words out; Saffron's mouth was so dry. Where was the waitress with the water? It was the cappuccino that was taking ages. She could hear the spluttering and frothing of the coffee machine, though it sounded as if it were being made at the end of a long tunnel.

'Why do you think Marcus has been using an assumed name?'

Saffron remained silent, her heart thumping so violently she felt sure Allegra must hear it.

'He went to prison.'

Saffron shrugged. It wouldn't have been for a heinous crime, for something unforgiveable. Everyone makes mistakes.

'For me. He lied for me and went to prison for it. He took the rap for my crime. Can you imagine loving anyone enough to do that?'

The waitress appeared and placed the coffee in front of Allegra.

'Thank you, that's perfect.' She smiled at the woman, all charm.

Nonplussed, the waitress looked over at Saffron and said, 'I'll just get your water.' Saffron nodded, her insides trembling.

Please God, I hope she can't see me shaking.

Saffron wanted to shout at Allegra that it wasn't true, but it would have been impossible without a sip of water and anyway, she didn't know that it wasn't.

The revelation hovered between them. Allegra picked up two packets of sugar, tore them open, and poured the contents into her drink. She stirred slowly, the chinking of the spoon against the cup the only sound in the café.

Skimmed milk but sugar?

A whoosh from the tap and Saffron knew her water was on its way at last. She was grateful for the pause, it gave her a chance to think. To absorb what Allegra had told her, unpick it.

The water was lukewarm but Saffron didn't care. Her hand shook as she drank and she cursed her wayward, disobedient body. 'So why didn't he come and find you the moment he was out?'

It was Allegra's turn to shrug, dismissive. 'Because I've been in jail too. We were told to stay away from each other, but love is hard to stop, isn't it?'

'Quite the regular Bonnie and Clyde.' Saffron felt sick. She picked up her phone which she'd placed on the table beside her. She was late for her meeting with Joe. She had to know the truth. His truth.

She stood. 'Excuse me.'

Allegra gripped Saffron's wrist, nails digging into her flesh. 'He loves me. I'll get him back. You're nothing. Nothing at all.'

Saffron shook her arm free and staggered out of the café, pausing on the high street, blinded by the sun, its dazzling rays an insult to the darkness enveloping her.

The promenade was busy, that's why the arcade and the

café were so quiet. Everyone was out and about enjoying a beautiful day. Saffron ducked and darted between gaggles of teenagers, families with buggies and toddlers, and grannies ambling along, scanning the crowds for Joe. She'd never seen Coed Mawr so busy. Today of all days. It occurred to her that news of the ballroom fire must have drawn the tourists. How sad that people dashed to witness tragedy, to gaze on destruction and ugliness. Maybe they would notice Coed Mawr's shabby beauty too and come back.

'Sorry. So sorry.' She bumped into a solidly-built man.

Still reeling from the collision, her shoulder thumping – the force of the impact could have dislocated it – she spun to check the beach.

Her heart swelled. There he was, looking out towards the horizon, low-slung jeans, strong, broad shoulders, his long, smooth neck. She remembered how soft it felt when she kissed him there, the brush of hair at its apex, the tip of a bat's wing at its base. He turned, spotting her immediately amongst the hordes, as if his eyes were programmed to seek out her, and her alone. She stepped towards the promenade railing. He moved up the beach towards her. Her heart ebbed like the tide.

His face said it all. He knew she'd seen him with Allegra. She gripped the railing and leant forward, shouting, not caring that people might stare.

'What is your name?'

He came closer, so that he was standing on the beach below her, looking up, imploring. 'Does it matter?'

'It matters to me.'

He dropped his head, and held his forehead, the longer section of hair falling forward, obscuring his face. He could have been crying, or praying. Saffron pushed herself off the railings and raced to the steps and down onto the beach. She held him at the elbows, waiting for him to look at her. She became aware of a presence next to her. A flash of red. Allegra.

'Marcus?' Allegra said, reaching for him.

Saffron let go and screamed, 'Is it true?'

He looked up and nodded, his face awash with pain, remorse, regret? Saffron couldn't tell.

'I've been inside, yes.'

She screamed again, louder this time. She pointed at Allegra. 'Did you take the blame for her?'

He nodded again and Saffron gasped and clamped her hand across her mouth. Like a knife wound, she didn't feel any pain when the blade went in, when he admitted he'd been to jail. It was when it came out, with the second admission, that she howled and folded over, her chest on her knees, blood crashing round her brain like a tsunami, blinding her.

'I was in love. Thought I was in love,' he said.

Saffron stopped listening and held her breath. It had become clear.

This is my punishment: I am to lose my true love; he will be snatched away.

Light-headed, she stood upright and gasped for air, hyperventilating, tears spilling over her face. Joe reached for her and she pushed him away.

Saffron ran. The last thing she saw before she staggered off the beach was a slow smile of victory shadowing Allegra's beautiful face.

Chapter Thirty

It had been such a wonderful afternoon that Rain didn't think the evening service could top it. But to her surprise, it looked as if it might. The chapel was packed. The regulars were there, naturally, done up in their Sunday best. Some even wore hats, though Rain admitted this might have had more to do with the force of the sun's rays than the force of respect for God's house. Not that she bought into all that nonsense. Did anyone these days? Almost certainly not, though one or two of the most elderly parishioners commented how nice it was to see an effort being made to look smart for chapel, as they were wheeled through by carers disgruntled at having to attend. She nodded and smiled but neither agreed nor disagreed.

The chapel, with its thick walls, arched windows, and stubborn damp, was cool all year round and the heat of the early evening sun took Rain's breath away as she stepped outside the door to say goodbye to her flock. She removed her pink cardigan and tied it around her waist, enjoying the warmth on her bare arms. It was one of those moments when she felt the Lord's power and bounty at full throttle. It was perfect.

The last guest wobbled down the path and through the gate. Rain sighed, the moment gone. It would take only minutes to clear up and a long evening stretched ahead. She fancied sitting in the manse garden with a glass of icy, fizzy wine, a nice Cava. But she didn't know when Saffron would return – if she'd return for the night – and she couldn't drink a whole bottle by herself. She tipped her head to the sky. Candyfloss pink striped the blue. It was magical.

I will go for a walk. Why not?

'Hello there.'

Startled, she jumped. Eifion stood at the chapel gate. 'I hope you don't think me presumptuous, but I was wondering if you fancied a walk this evening? Lovely, isn't it? I closed the hut early. Didn't want to waste it. The evening, I mean. Ceri says it's no wonder I've got money troubles. Never make a businessman, me.'

'Small pleasures. They're what make life, not money and possessions.' She smiled. He looked good out of his overalls and ill-fitting jeans. He wore a pair of beige chinos and a short-sleeved, checked shirt. Rain found herself wondering what it would feel like to run her palm across the gentle curve of his belly, if he had a line of hair running from his navel, if his skin was smooth and soft to the touch.

A cough interrupted her thoughts. 'I'll be off then,' he said. 'Hope you didn't mind me asking.'

'Not at all.'

He turned to leave.

'I'd love to come.'

He swung back round, his face illuminated by an enormous grin, revealing those lovely teeth.

'Too beautiful to waste, as you said,' Rain continued. 'Give me a minute to lock up and grab my handbag.'

'Take as long as you wish. I'll be here,' he said.

Though it was after seven when they reached the promenade, it was still busy. 'I'd have to agree with Ceri, you'll never be the next Alan Sugar. You could be raking it in,' Rain said, pointing at the pier which thronged with people.

'I'd rather be here with you,' Eifion replied, turning to supposedly admire the skyline.

Rain caught the blush on his cheeks. To cover his

embarrassment, she ignored his comment and added, 'All come to check out the gory remains of the ballroom, no doubt.'

'They'll be disappointed. It's blocked off ages before the ballroom. The businesses further up the pier are rabid; they're losing money, all closed off like that. And there's no damage to their stalls. Safety issue, I suppose.'

'And here's you, shutting up shop of your own free will!' she laughed and he joined in.

'It's a bit bonkers down here for me. I'm not keen on the crowds. Shall we climb the rise and look from up above?'

'I'd like that very much.'

If Eifion had offered his hand, Rain would have taken it. But he didn't. Instead they weaved their way through the crowds separately, up towards the less well-known path to the top of the cliff. It was a steeper climb, but shorter and quieter, and as they were both good walkers they reached the summit in no time. Breathless and hot, Rain flopped on the grass and closed her eyes. Eifion sat beside her.

'Bit exhausting, isn't it? But worth it for the view.'

'Definitely.' She sat up to take it in.

'It's the thing I'd miss most if I had to leave, the view. The drama of it,' he said.

'You've lived here all your life?'

'Yes. Makes me sound very unadventurous, doesn't it? But I love it here. Don't want to leave. And it's not just the view; it's the people, the town, the pier, even the chapel, which, as you know, I hardly frequent. I'm like an old oak, roots so deep it'd kill me to move.'

Rain laughed. 'We can find adventure everywhere. Moving can be a form of running away.'

It was for me. But you can't run away from yourself.

'Have you found adventure here, in Coed Mawr?' he asked.

'I think so. I've found peace.' She looked into his eyes and held them there for what felt like an age. He broke the hold first.

'Are you hungry? It's getting late. We could have dinner.' He jumped to his feet.

'I ate a huge lunch …'

'Doesn't have to be much. Pizza, or we could share a bag of chips and sit on the bench by the toy train at the bottom of the rise.'

'Like teenagers?'

'If you like.'

'I like.' She held out her outstretched hand and he pulled her up from the grass with ease. His grip was firm, not bone-crushing, and his fingertips were calloused and rough. His was a secure hold.

They took the tourist train – the toy train as Eifion had called it – back down to town and bought a large fish and chips for one, and quibbled and laughed over how much vinegar to add. They agreed to go easy on the salt. Afterwards, they drifted through the windy streets, 'to walk off all that fat,' as Rain had put it. Outside Y Castell Eifion suggested a drink. Rain dithered. She wasn't sure she should be seen in a local boozer, older parishioners might not approve, and anyway she wanted to suggest a glass of wine in the garden of the manse. Would that seem forward? She didn't want to give Eifion the wrong impression. Whatever that was. She had no idea how to play this. She had met Stephen young; she'd been a faithful wife. And she wasn't even sure what 'this' was, if anything. Her head began to spin.

'I … I was wondering …' she began, but she was interrupted by a yell.

'Dad! Rain! Fucking hell, thank God, I've found you.' Ceri came running up the street, though it was more of a fast waddle. Her stride was severely restricted by her tight little skirt. Rain pushed unkind thoughts about pelmet skirts and weightier women from her mind. Ceri was a darling, if foul-mouthed.

Breathless, Ceri continued. 'Have you seen Saff?'

'She's out – with JJ. Joe,' said Rain.

Ceri leant against the stone wall which surrounded the pub garden. 'Oh Jesus, I'm knackered. Been everywhere. She's not with Joe. That's part of the problem.'

Confused, Rain could only shake her head.

'He's with some posh cow in a red dress. Saw them together, I did, down by the beach earlier. Went to introduce myself, as you do, and she said she was Joe's girlfriend. Except she didn't call him Joe. Right snotty bitch, she was. Looking down her nose. I wanted to lamp her.'

'Wouldn't have solved anything, love,' Eifion said.

'What did Joe say?' Rain heard the alarm in her voice. She'd always suspected something, hadn't she?

'He said it wasn't how it seemed – which makes it look worse not better, if you ask me – and would I go and find Saff. Tell her he'll explain everything after he's spoken to Allegra.'

'Allegra?' Both Rain and Eifion chimed in unison.

'I know. Bloody stupid name.' Ceri spat, pulling a cigarette from a packet retrieved from the waistband of her skirt.

'I wish you wouldn't smoke, Ceri, love.'

'It's the name of a Greek goddess,' Rain said, swatting a fly away.

'And an old car,' Eifion added.

'So what's happened?' Rain said.

'I have no idea. He was trying to shut the snotty mare up, but she was babbling on and on. He shouted again to find Saff and then he dragged her away. She was all over him like a rash. And if you ask me he's hiding something. I can't believe it, I can't. I thought he was decent, like, but it seems like he's been stringing Saff along.'

'He is a decent bloke, I'm sure of it,' Eifion said.

Rain stepped in front of Ceri. 'But you've not found Saff?'

'No. Been everywhere I have.'

'The manse?'

Ceri nodded and blew out a smoke ring. Rain was irritated by Ceri's apparent calm. Saffy would be so upset; beside herself. Smoke rings indeed.

'Nearly knocked the door in, I did,' Ceri said.

Rain turned to Eifion. She didn't need to say anything. He lifted his eyes and tipped his head in the direction of the manse. 'Another time. Go wait at home for Saffron; she'll need her mam. We'll keep looking round town, but I bet you she's home. Call me.' He gave her his number and she texted him hers immediately.

Rain hurried to Upper Coed Mawr and the manse.

The moment she pushed open the door, Rain knew Saff was home. The air carried a different scent when she was in; its mass was different too. Months ago the atmosphere in the house was heavy when Saff was about, of late it had been sweet and light. Now, it was oppressive again, as if a storm approached, though Rain had seen no such evidence in the evening sky. She glanced at the barometer. Stupid. It told her nothing.

Without understanding how, Rain knew that Saff had been home when Ceri called. She'd have heard the door – from what Ceri said she couldn't have missed it – but she'd have retreated into herself, like a tortoise. She'd done this since childhood, after every argument with Matthew or fall-out with her friends: tucked the soft part of herself away beneath a brittle exterior. As a child she'd sleep for hours and hours too – like hibernation.

Rain pushed the front door behind her, careful not to make much noise. She slipped off her sandals and crept across the tiled floor to the foot of the stairs. She lifted an ear. There, the faint sound of crying. Her heart clenched; her breathing became shallow. Saffron was hurting and that meant Rain was hurting. She tiptoed up the stairs, the wood of the banister cool against her sweating palms.

She knocked gently on the door before entering when she heard a muffled, 'Yeah?'

Saffron was sprawled on her bed, face down in a recovery position. Rain had no idea what to say. Running up the rise to the manse, all manner of thoughts had scooted through her head, good and evil. She'd ranged from 'he'll come to his senses', to 'you could be mistaken', to 'forget all about the bastard', to 'we'll cut his balls off'.

In the end, she sat at the bottom of the bed and stroked Saffy's nearest foot, running her thumb up her Achilles' heel, something Saff had found comforting, loved, from babyhood. Rain said nothing. She let her daughter weep, and watched her back, rise, fall, and shudder, until the sobbing finally abated. Saffron rolled onto her side and looked at Rain plaintively. She sat up and threw her arms about Rain, who stroked her beautiful, golden-red hair.

'My angel,' Rain said.

'Oh, Mum,' said Saff and the crying took hold once more.

Downstairs, Rain crashed and banged round the kitchen, furious. Saffron slept, exhausted. Unable to relax, to sit still even, Rain emptied the cupboards around the cooker. Why, they'd not been cleaned since they'd moved in and that was coming up to a year ago now. Out came the spice jars, bottles of oil, sauces, and gravy granules, leaving sticky rings on the white cupboard shelves. Rain scrubbed away, bleach fumes searing into her nostrils, burning into the flesh on her fingers. She'd not bothered with rubber gloves. Once the cupboards shone, she began to cook. Saff would be hungry when she woke. She must eat. Rain didn't want a return to the rake-thin Saff of a few months earlier.

She threw vegetables onto the chopping board and hacked away at them. She lobbed them into a pan and added stock from the fridge. She recalled a film she and Stephen had watched years ago, about a woman whose cooking contained her dominant emotion at the time of preparation. This would be hate and bewilderment stew. Could she even serve it up to Saff? She might not wake till morning anyway.

Rain stirred. She took slow, deep breaths, filling her lungs from her diaphragm. How she disliked being right, this time. She had thought him slippery early on. But he was worse than that.

A criminal and a cheat! Horrible.

She checked herself. When he first came into her home, she'd liked him. Joe, Marcus, whatever his name was – who was to say he wasn't lying to this Allegra woman? She harrumphed. Ceri was right; Allegra was a ridiculous name. But he was good-looking and well-spoken and utterly charming. Delighted to have young male company, she'd invited him in. For heaven's sake, she'd asked him to coffee mornings, encouraged him to do the work on the chapel roof. It was all her fault. Men, they were all bastards, they really were. But this. This surpassed everything. She looked at the ceiling and said, 'Sorry. Don't really mean it. Not all men.'

But this Joe might be. Saff said he'd gone to jail for this woman. What crime had he committed? It must have been serious to warrant a custodial sentence; prisons were jam-packed these days. Didn't you have to kill someone to get sent down? The man they knew as Joe Jones had lied to Saff, to everyone. He had broken her daughter's heart. He was a bastard.

'Sorry,' she said to the ceiling once more.

Chapter Thirty-one

Joe watched Allegra's orange VW beetle roaring down the dirt track from his cottage. Dust billowed in the air. He waited for it to settle, until tyre tracks were the only physical evidence that Allegra had dropped back into his life. If only the emotional and psychological fallout could settle as easily. Fat chance. He sighed and walked towards the Land Rover, heart increasingly heavy as the elation at getting rid of Allegra diffused.

He'd played it all wrong. He should have told Allegra to fuck off on the pier, to hell with the scene, he should have fled, gone to find Saffron immediately, explained everything, and then he wouldn't be in this mess. Why the hell hadn't he considered that she might come down into town early, as soon as lunch was over? After all, it was a beautiful day. He'd known that Allegra had got to her the minute Saffron looked over the promenade railings, even before Allegra appeared beside her like a spectre.

Joe had lied to Allegra when she'd turned up on the pier. He'd been caught off guard, but he wasn't entirely surprised. After all, he knew she was looking for him. It was one reason why he'd hidden away and he'd dreaded it, mostly because, until recently, he'd not been sure how he would react to seeing her, if he was truly over her. He'd not felt guilty about lying; it'd felt good. He'd wanted to slap her, not kiss her, when she stood on tiptoes, stroked his cheek and threw him that nauseating, lizard-like grin she thought was seductive. She'd tasted foul and it was hard to disguise his repulsion, but he was well-trained in duplicity. 'I've thought about you so much, Marcus, darling. I nearly died thinking you might never want to see me, that you wouldn't forgive me. I had no contact address after you were released. I thought you were dead.' She gasped, the corners of her eyes filled with tears, crocodile tears. She was an expert at crying; she would have made a good actress.

He nodded, and she continued, 'I can't believe you've holed yourself up here. Must have been hell.' She'd stroked his nose. 'You know, I have considered that you might have been hiding from me ...'

'Just biding my time. I knew where you were. You're out early.'

'I was sooo good in there. All for you,' Allegra said, in her baby voice. She had no idea how unsexy she sounded. He recalled the cuddly toys lined up on her bed when they first met. How had he ever fallen for this woman? Been so beguiled by her? He felt sick. Until that moment, he'd not fully appreciated just how over her he was. He didn't hate her; he pitied her, and she was utterly inconsequential to him, emotionally. Practically, she was a first-class pain in the arse.

Unbeknown to him, she'd been watching. She'd seen Saffron leaving the cottage that morning and put two and two together. It wouldn't have been hard. She trailed her to the manse. His gut twisted at the thought of Allegra spying on Saffron, dissecting her beauty, the way she moved, where she lived. How he wished Allegra'd presented herself to him at the cottage, as soon as Saffron had gone. It would have been so much easier. But no, she'd slipped away and reappeared at the worst possible time. Typical. He could have kicked himself for taking a walk on the pier before going to meet Saffron. He might have avoided Allegra had he gone straight to the beach.

Allegra had challenged him about the 'ginger woman' almost immediately. He'd presented the relationship as a friendship, unaware she'd seen Saffron leaving the cottage at first. Allegra had fired questions at him, machine-gun-style: what does she do for a living, is she clever, what is her name? He'd given as little as possible away, though a name had spilled out. 'Saffron. Unusual,' Allegra had sneered, as if only she had the right to a distinctive name. Desperate to get Allegra away from the seafront, he'd made up an excuse, said he had a business associate to meet, and would she meet him back at the cottage? Evidently, she'd not gone straight there.

Trouble. Allegra was a massive bundle of trouble, though trouble didn't really do the carnage she brought in her wake justice.

After Saffron had fled the beach, Joe had turned to Allegra, expecting her to challenge him for the lie he'd told on the pier. She didn't. Instead, she linked her arm in his and suggested they retreat to the cottage, 'to make up for lost time.' Stunned, he allowed himself to be steered up the steps to the promenade. There, they bumped into Ceri. Garnering his wits, Joe said as little as possible and virtually dragged Allegra to where she'd parked her car. Clearly, she thought him desperate to rip her clothes off. How wrong she was.

With every step, Joe's rage had built. But having to control what he said, how he behaved, was exhausting. The traffic was awful and by the time they reached the cottage Joe was in control of his emotions and longed only to be rid of Allegra as fast as possible. Out of the car, he steered her round the house, saying only, 'Garden.'

'Al fresco. How exciting,' she tittered, running her fingers along her collarbone. At the sight of the scrubby grass, she added, 'If a tad uncomfortable. There's no rug.'

She lunged towards him, lips puckered. He pushed her away, registering her disbelief. Was she really that deluded?

'Oh, baby, it's been so long.'

She was.

'Not long enough.' There was no emotion in his voice.

'Sorry?'

He watched her eyes, those mirror images of his own, pool with tears. He was almost surprised at how unmoved he was. His mind was full of Saffron, concern for her; he felt nothing for the woman before him. Not even hate. Now that did surprise him.

'What did you say to Saffron exactly?' he asked.

Allegra smiled through her tears. 'Only the truth, darling.' She tapped his chest, then her own, with an index finger. 'You, and me. You'd do anything for me. We're meant for each other.'

'Wrong and wrong. I lied to you. In the letters I wrote while I was inside, here, on the pier. I've dreamed of revenge, seeing you suffer.'

'You could never lie to me,' she whispered.

'I have.'

'I've suffered.' She fluttered her eyelashes and he resisted the temptation to laugh.

'I don't love you. It's easy to lie when there's no love, isn't it?'

Ignoring his pointed remark, she continued, 'You don't mean that. You'll always love me. You can't escape me. I see it in your eyes.' Her voice rose higher and higher. She reached for him again.

This time, he didn't step back. He leant forward, holding her gaze, hands gripped about her wrists, holding her at bay. 'I hate you.'

'You don't mean that. You've not learned how to forgive me yet, that's all.'

'Strike that. I feel nothing for you. Not a thing.'

Allegra's eyes darkened. 'You'll tire of her. She won't keep you for long.'

'I love her.'

'You need me.' A shriek more than a sentence. Her

300

arms began to thrash.

'No, I don't. I never did.' He released his grip and pushed her, without force, away.

'You can't do this!' she screamed.

'Hard to believe, isn't it? That someone – a man, *me* – can refuse to bend to your will, resist your charms.' He drew speech marks in the air on charms, aping one of her many irritating habits. The implication behind the gesture wasn't lost on her. 'You're so spoilt, so self-centred, so blind to the realities of love, to what it actually is, that you honestly thought you could do what you did to me and that I'd *still* love you. Incredible. Almost unbelievable. But I know you, and I believe that you could. You are so blind, and you have a lot to learn, if you even can. I'm not sure that you're capable of true love.' There was no cruelty in Joe's tone, which remained even, rational.

Allegra began to shake. Her mouth opened, as if to form words, but nothing came forth. She was quite, quite, shell-shocked.

'Now I want you to leave. I've wasted too much energy on you already.'

She slapped him, hard, across the face.

He didn't feel a thing. 'I'm done with you. Go,' he said.

It was as if the slap took the last remnants of her strength, her self-delusion, and she crumpled, crying properly now, honestly, heaving, grasping-for-air sobs, which shook her entire body. Snot poured from her nose, saliva from her mouth.

Perhaps prison has taught her something after all.

'You'll never be done with me,' she said.

You cannot touch me. Not now. Not ever.

He laughed. 'Oh, but I am. You are dead to me.'

She turned back. 'I'll ruin you,' she sobbed.

'Do your worst,' he said, knowing she couldn't. He followed at a distance as she stumbled back to her car, snivelling, and watched as she climbed in, to make sure she left. For good.

In the Land Rover, Joe rested his head on the steering wheel. He was certain Allegra would not contact him again. But that was the least of his problems: he might never win Saffron's trust; she might despise him for what he'd done, for keeping the truth from her. It might be all over. She might never believe that he'd intended to come clean, but he couldn't carry on without trying.

His body ached, a dull pain far inside him chipped away at his soul. He took a deep breath, turned the engine back on, and headed down in the direction of the manse. The brightness of the day had passed and a mist hovered in the dusky air. It was still and quiet, like a graveyard.

Be quick, be strong, go and find Saffron.

There were no lights on at the front of the manse, but Joe felt certain Rain was at home and Saffron with her. Where else could they be? He hammered on the door, over and over, unrelenting. No reply.

He crouched on his haunches, lifted up the letterbox, and hollered into the hallway. 'Saffronnnnn! Saffronnnnn!'

No reply.

He lurched down the path at the side of the house like a madman and launched himself at the gate. Scrabbling about on the smooth wood, he failed to gain purchase and slipped down. He stepped back up the path and ran at the gate, throwing himself up it like a soldier on an assault course. Result. He clambered over, ignoring a splinter of wood which sliced into his thumb pad like an arrowhead. Light spilled on the lawn, a shadow fluttered. Someone was home, or was it the tree rustling in the breeze?

He rapped on the back door. No answer. He clenched his fist and banged. Nothing. He pushed through a dense bed of hollyhocks, gladioli, and shrubs to the window and pressed his face against the glass. Rain stood in the kitchen, hands clenched in front at her waist, like a statue, staring at him, eyes wide, shocked or terrified, or both. Palms flat against the glass, he cried out, 'Let me see her. Talk to her. Please. For the love of God let me explain.'

Kindness surfaced in Rain's startled eyes. She edged towards the glass, and Joe thought he'd done enough. But she stopped, quite suddenly, raised a hand to her mouth, and shook her head. 'Go home, Joe. Go home,' she said. She turned and walked out of the kitchen.

Joe lay on the grass and stared at the darkening sky. Clouds like cathedrals loomed, it might rain. A bird swooped overhead and then another creature darted from the eaves, faster and smaller. A bat. There was a bat roosting in the manse, maybe more. He watched the pipistrelle dive and swoop, hunting. Devouring insects, fattening itself ready for the winter. Survival. It was all about survival. Then came another and another.

He considered waiting, there on the lawn, till dawn. He would be there when she rose, came downstairs to make her morning coffee, instant not real. No, it would be too spooky, too weird, too criminal. He was trespassing.

Getting over the gate was even harder the second time. His mind still tore from one idea to the next and back again, ad infinitum.

Back in the street, he determined on his first idea: Go to Eifion's. By now, he too would know what had happened. Explain to Eifion, if he could, and ask for his advice, his support, if Eifion was prepared to give it. Joe had no idea if he would. Joe checked his watch. It wasn't too late. He increased his pace; the sooner he got there the better.

Chapter Thirty-two

Joe had never been inside Eifion's house. He only knew where it was because he'd dropped him off one time after work. The house wasn't all Eifion's; he rented a flat on the first floor, he'd said. A three-storey Victorian affair, the house had been carved up sometime in the late 1980s. Cheaply done, it was a 'right state', Eifion had said as an excuse for not inviting Joe in for a cuppa.

Joe studied the intercom to the right of the double door. The name plates were empty, bar the middle bell. Illegible lettering bled onto a scrap of yellowed paper. Joe recalled Eifion complaining about the couple above who'd stripped their floorboards, 'strictly against the terms of the tenancy, I'll have you know,' and then proceeded to practise some form of Irish dancing up there at all times of the day and night. The middle bell must be Eifion's. Joe pressed it, hard, and held his breath.

'Hellooo,' came Eifion's sing-song voice.

Joe bent into the speaker. 'It's me: Joe. I need a friend.'

'Now is that Joe, as in Joe Jones, carpenter and all-round quiet but nice guy? Or is it Joe as in Marcus Whatshisname?'

'Eifion, I deserve your contempt and mistrust, but, please, can you give me a few minutes? I need someone to hear my side of it. To hear the truth.'

Silence. Seconds that felt like interminable minutes passed.

'Shouldn't that someone be Saffron?'

'I've tried. Rain won't let me near her.'

'Can you blame her?'

'No.'

About to admit defeat, Joe stepped back from the intercom. The door buzzed. Astonished, he pushed, not expecting it to move, but it swung open to reveal a wide hall and a mat littered with junk mail. The dull scent of mildew wafted towards him as he stepped forward and a light clicked on. A bare bulb exposed the shabby hall. Joe made his way up the wide staircase, the bannister sticky beneath his hold.

Eifion stood in a doorway on the landing. Backlit, his face in shadow, Joe couldn't read his expression. 'Come in,' he said, 'Excuse the mess. I wasn't expecting visitors.'

Joe followed him into a narrow kitchen, the sink full of dirty dishes. 'I can offer you tea, coffee, or a tin of cheap lager.'

A good sign. He didn't mean to throw Joe out immediately. 'A beer would be great. Thank you.'

Eifion reached into the fridge and handed over a can. It was icy cold and Joe held it to his brow before pulling the ring and taking a gulp. He hadn't realised how dehydrated he was.

'Shall we go through to the lounge,' Eifion said, gesturing for Joe to leave the kitchen. It would have been hard for him to pass without making physical contact. In the hall, Joe stepped back and allowed Eifion to take the lead.

The lounge was larger than Joe had expected, with a rounded bay and sash windows. A spindly cheese plant obscured the view to the street. Eifion gestured to a velour covered sofa and Joe sat down. Eifion remained standing which Joe found disconcerting and intimidating – it was a bit like being in the headmaster's office at school for a telling off.

No less than I deserve.

'Well, first off, I need to know what to call you. Ceri says this woman in red called you Marcus.'

Joe wiped his brow; he was still sweating. 'I'd like you to call me Joe, but as this is truth time ... yes, I was christened Marcus. It's what I was called until I left prison, came here.'

Eifion pulled up a wooden chair – a dining chair, though there was no table – and sat down. 'Joe it is then.' He leaned back and folded his arms.

Joe saw it as a 'Well?' gesture, but then Eifion nodded and smiled, encouraging.

Joe didn't know how to begin.

The very worst thing, tell him the worst thing first. It can only get better after that. No. From the beginning.

'It was in the papers, a couple of tabloids. Not front page, but still ...'

'Ceri thought it might. She did a bit of digging. On the internet. But it's not that easy without a surname. Anyhow, you can't believe everything you read in those things, can you?'

Joe shook his head, and continued, relieved. The papers had lost interest, quickly, partly thanks to Allegra's father's influence and partly because other, more scurrilous, stories came along. 'I was in love. Floored, crazy about her, absolutely and utterly crazy.'

'Sex must have been good,' Eifion said, and despite the seriousness of the occasion Joe laughed. 'Sorry. Don't mind an old cynic like me.'

'We'd been to a party, in the countryside. Big posh manor house place. I hated those kinds of affair, and the people who held them, on the whole. A legacy of the private school I was dumped at after my parents died, I suppose. But it was the world I knew, the world I'd grown up in mostly, and Allegra's family were wealthy and influential – her father's high up in the civil service, her mother was some kind of a lady, old money, you know – and this sort of thing came with the package of being Allegra's man.'

'We all had you down as quite posh, though not that posh. What did you do for a living, back then? I can't see that kind of woman being with a tradesman.' Eifion put on a posh voice when he said 'tradesman' and Joe found himself smiling again.

'I ran my own business. An internet network, connecting people in the property industry – developers, purchasers, buyers and sellers of large office buildings, that sort of thing. The great advantage, for me, of it being an online network was that I rarely had to deal with my client base face to face.'

'Doesn't sound like you liked it much.'

'I didn't. After school, I cruised. Bit of a slacker, unsure what I wanted to do. I love nature, and making stuff. I had a dream of creating art, sculpture, from natural materials. Inspired by Andy Goldsworthy, I guess, but I lacked confidence without formal training and I needed to earn some money. It's something I planned to pursue here. My family were comfortable, but the pot wasn't bottomless. A friend of mine, Simon, set the business up and persuaded mc to help him run it while I decided what to do with the rest of my life. He was my only friend, as I was to discover later. Still is. Told myself I'd do it for a few years. And then things spiralled out of control … The business really took off and I got sucked in'

'You went to a party …' Eifion brought Joe back to the main story.

'We'd had a run of these kinds of events; everyone seemed to be getting engaged and throwing extravagant, ostentatious parties, desperate to out-do each other. It sickened me most of the time. All the money that was spent – wasted – on ridiculous flower arrangements, table decorations, waiters dressed up like penguins, string quartets that no one listened to. Vast amounts of rare, exotic food and drink – most of which was disgusting. Quite often I'd look around these marquees, these halls, and yachts, and wonder if these people had any idea how the majority of the population lived. How far removed they were from most people's experiences, in this country, let alone the developing world.' Joe paused, sickened by the memory, aware how it must seem to Eifion. 'Look. Sorry, this all sounds like I'm trying to justify myself. Make myself out to be this great bloke, privileged and rich, but with a social conscience. I sound like a wanker.'

Eifion raised his eyebrows – Joe couldn't tell if he agreed with his analysis or not.

'After a stream of these parties, I'd had enough and I needed to have a drink to get through it. I only went because Allegra liked to have me there and I'd not mastered saying no to her. Usually, I did the driving. I hate taxis and I'm not a good passenger.' He shrugged, as if that were his worst fault.

If only.

'We agreed that we'd take her car and she would drive, just this once. It was a pretty standard, dreadful to my mind, affair, and drinking hadn't done much to make it any more bearable. When we left, I wasn't drunk. I'd had a few, but I wasn't drunk. It's important you know that.

'In the car, we started arguing. Nothing serious. Allegra liked a good argument, and I went along with it because the making-up was amazing –'

'So it was all about the sex,' Eifion said, though he wasn't smiling this time.

'No. It was more than that. It was for me. Anyway, it was late, dark, few lights in windy country lanes and villages. Allegra was distracted. We were coming through a tiny hamlet, right on the outskirts, on a bend, when we hit something. On the left side of the bonnet. A heavy, dull thud.' He felt nauseous at the memory. 'It felt solid, like a badger or possibly even a deer, though I'd not seen anything. The car swerved, Allegra lost control for a moment, and braked. But then she started the engine and pulled away. I screamed at her to stop; to go back. After a few minutes, she turned back. Roughly where we'd felt the impact, we stopped. She looked over her shoulders to the road, to the verge. I followed suit. We couldn't see anything. She said it was more than likely an animal and it had crawled away. I insisted we got out to look. It could have been alive, suffering. I had to know. Reluctantly, she opened the door and clambered out. It was at this point I became aware that she wasn't completely steady on her feet, but I dismissed the thought. She'd had a shock; we both had.

'It was very dark. There was a light, from a house perhaps, some distance away, but that was it. I used a torch app on my phone and shone it along the kerb, on the grass verge. And that's when I saw it, a shadowy lump by the hedge, up ahead.' Joe's head swam, he felt dizzy, sick, as if he were reliving the moment when he realised this was no deer. 'I staggered towards the shape, the horror of what Allegra had done increasing as I neared. I smelt him first. Shit and piss and poverty and pain. He wasn't dead; he moaned as I hovered over him, unsure whether or not to touch him, to move him, in case I made things worse. That's what they teach you, isn't it? In first aid?' He looked at Eifion, making eye contact for the first time since he'd began. 'I called to Allegra. It was a man, he wasn't dead. Would she call an ambulance while I offered comfort? She hissed at me to come over. Shocked, not thinking straight, I apologised to the man and walked the few paces back to where she stood, leaning on the bonnet of the car, smoking a cigarette.

"We can't," she said.

I shook my head, uncomprehending. "We have to. He could die; we have no idea how severe his injuries are," I replied.

"I've had a drink, maybe two," she said, and I knew then she'd had more, despite our agreement. "Not certain

I'd get through a breathalyser, darling." She stroked my cheek. "We could go. No one has seen us."

She must have seen the look of horror on my face because she added swiftly, "We'll call the emergency services and then scoot."

"But he's seen me, or heard me," I said.

"He'll never be able to identify you."

"The police will trace the call. We can't leave him alone. He must be scared shitless. What if he dies?" I was yelling now, terror and fear blending. That's when she started to cry. I wouldn't relent on this, no matter how much I loved her. I couldn't abandon a man, a man who might be dying. And it was our fault. She asked how much I'd had to drink and begged me to say I was driving. I'd had three, maybe four. But I'd eaten and I'm tall, well built – and I was bulkier then, all that rich food and booze – large body mass, easier to absorb alcohol. I wavered. I couldn't be certain I would pass a breathalyser either. Allegra was beside herself by this point, crying, begging me to do this for her, because I loved her, because I'd said I would do anything for her. Anything. She had more to lose than me. She was a lawyer. If convicted of driving under the influence, she might lose her job, her livelihood, her reputation. Her family would be destroyed. It was their reputation on the line too.' Joe hung his head.

'So, in a moment of weakness, you agreed.'

'I was weak where she was concerned. I hate myself for it.'

'You took the blame for some selfish, reckless, heartless bitch. Would she have done the same for you, I wonder?' Eifion's expression told Joe that he knew she would not. 'You did time. How long did you go down for? And was she waiting for you when you got out? No need to answer that. Of course, she wasn't. So what's she doing here now? Want you to take the wrap for another of her misdemeanours, eh?'

Joe finished his beer and crushed the can in his fist. 'Story's not over yet, Eifion. It gets worse.'

The colour drained from Eifion's face. 'The man you hit didn't survive?'

Chapter Thirty-three

Joe's throat constricted, rendering him speechless.

'You went down for manslaughter,' Eifion said.

Joe shook his head and found his voice again. 'No. The death was deemed accidental. It was dark, a country lane. The guy might have been drunk himself. That's what the coroner said. Still strikes me as unjust. I went down for perverting the course of justice.'

'Well, thank God, she came clean in the end. A redeeming feature, I suppose,' Eifion said, the shock of Joe's confession still visible in his demeanour. 'How long were you in jail?'

'Twelve months.'

Eifion blew out noisily. 'Phew. That's harsh.'

'Good behaviour got me an early release. The judge gave me three years; he wanted to make an example, he said. I was privileged, successful, intelligent. I had everything going for me and I'd abused it. I was a disgrace, he said, and stupid beyond belief. I don't disagree. The man who died, was killed, had nothing. A homeless former soldier who'd served his country with honour and dignity. He'd been discharged after an injury and had never quite found his feet in civilian life. It seems he was making his way back to a barn where he'd been sleeping for some nights. Whether or not he was drunk, wavering all over the place, I don't care. He should never have died and I feel partly responsible.'

'Forgive me for interrupting here, but while I can see where the judge was coming from, it wasn't you who actually killed the poor man. He was unnecessarily harsh.

Brutal.'

'I lied. Repeatedly. And the lie might have stuck had the police not been so sharp and had the witness not come forward.'

'Witness? You said it was deserted. It was the middle of the night.'

'That's what we thought. But there was a local, out walking his incontinent old dog. He saw us as we sped through the village. Allegra had swerved at one of those mini-roundabouts. The brakes made a terrible noise.' Joe shuddered. 'This man, the dog walker, didn't think too much of it at the time, until days later, when the story hit the local press. The police were organising a reconstruction and had asked for witnesses to come forward. He walked into the local police station and swore he'd seen a woman driving. That stretch of the road was well lit. And combined with the police suspicions ...'

Eifion went to speak, but Joe raised his hand. 'I know what you're going to say ... He didn't see the crash, collision, I hardly know what to call it, so how could he and the police know it was Allegra driving and not me? They couldn't be sure. But I later learned that one officer had noticed how near to the pedals the driver's seat was. We were so stupid we'd not even thought to move the seat back. Allegra's tiny. And she'd refused a breathalyser at the scene. She was arrested for refusing to co-operate at first. The police interviewed Allegra and me again. I stuck to the script, religiously. I couldn't bear the thought of her going to jail; I didn't think she'd survive in there.'

'But Allegra came clean?'

'Not for a long time. She made it so much worse for herself. And me. And then she said the idea had been mine. That I persuaded her to lie.'

Eifion bowed his head and shook it from side to side. 'What a complete cow.'

'I thought she'd told the truth for me, because she

couldn't bear me taking all the blame. Because she loved me,' Joe sighed at his stupidity, his naivety. 'But I later realised it was because the evidence was all pointing towards the truth. Months later, in court, I was hurt and angry, when she'd said it was my idea. My sense of fair play was rocked. But I still loved her, I made excuses for her, said it must have been fear that caused her to lie. It was a desperate need to hold on to the idea of love.'

'It's still a very harsh sentence. Not that I'm any kind of expert on the law or anything.'

Joe shrugged. Joe hadn't told Eifion the part of the story that had finally crushed him, destroyed his faith in humanity, which was only rebuilt during his stay in Coed Mawr, when he met Saffron and Rain and Ceri and Eifion and the good people of the community. 'I deserved it. What hurt was the way people reacted. One person in particular. Lots of people cut me off. I'd expected that. We thought the business might take a hit, but Simon worked very hard to minimise potential damage. But when a friend, my best friend, turned against me ... He's a barrister. I asked him to represent me. He refused, said it would be too hard, unethical. I understood that, felt it had been crazy to ask, but he represented Allegra ... I've known him since ... forever. He bad-mouthed me, painted a real bad picture. He said Allegra lied to protect me. She still went down for perverting the course of justice and death by careless driving, though thanks to him the sentence wasn't as severe as it could have been.

'Judge said her career was a mitigating factor. Mitigating! But this friend, he didn't visit me in jail, didn't reply to my letters. Nothing.' Joe felt like a self-pitying prick. But it had hurt.

Eifion stood. 'Another cheap lager? Wish I could offer you something stronger, but there you go.'

Joe thanked him, choked and relieved by Eifion's belief in him. Not once had he questioned or doubted what Joe had said.

Eifion returned and handed Joe a can. He sighed. 'This mate ...'

'Freddy.'

'He fancied Allegra, I suppose, wanted her for himself? Was jealous of you? Had you ever done anything to offend him, wronged him in some way?'

'Not that I'm aware of.' Joe paused. 'Simon says Freddy has always been jealous. All of us were at school together. Freddy bullied me when I first arrived at boarding school, made my life a misery. As new boy I was the centre of attention ...'

'And you're clever and good-looking and charming. Think I'd hate you too.'

Joe smiled despite himself. 'Maybe. I didn't feel any of those things at nine years old, but ... Anyway, the school arranged counselling and a form of restorative justice. Freddy and I became buddies, best buddies. At least that's how it seemed. Simon believes he never got over his hatred, he disguised it well, but it never went away.' He paused, took a slow draught of beer, then stared into the teardrop-shaped hole in the top.

'Something else?' Eifion sounded incredulous.

'Turns out Freddy and Allegra are connected. Distant cousins, on their fathers' side. I only found this out about a year ago.'

Eifion whistled. 'So much for ethics.'

'And they went out together as teenagers. I never knew.'

'Urgh.'

'Perhaps they'll end up together. They certainly deserve each other.'

'You know, Rain, the Rev, would disagree, but some people are just bastards, through and through.'

Joe laughed. It felt good to tell the truth. He was fed up of living a lie, of keeping a low profile, staying away from people, being so mistrustful. He smiled to himself. Not that he'd done such a great job of staying away from people, not since he'd met Saffron. She'd pulled him into the world, helped him trust again, discover the good in people. Rain would be proud.

Eifion shifted in his seat. 'There are a few things I don't understand. Why keep tabs on Allegra? Get over it. She's out of your life, why keep a constant reminder? And how in the hell did she ever think you might want her back? She seems absolutely bonkers to me. Isn't she afraid you'll punch her lights out?'

'I'd never hit a woman.'

Eifion guffawed. 'You know what I mean. *Metaphorically* speaking.'

'Allegra is deluded, but ...' Joe sighed. 'She wrote to me, when I was inside, trying to explain, begging forgiveness. If she'd had any idea how harsh the judge would be ... yackerty-schmackerty. Said she would come to me once she got out and I gave her the impression I'd be open to seeing her, having her back.'

Eifion looked unconvinced. He sat there, silent. Joe had no choice but to explain, be honest.

'And ... oh, man, this is difficult to say ... I wanted revenge. Ugly, but there it is. I spent my time inside perfecting my woodwork skills, getting an NVQ, and planning revenge. I had ideas but they were all flawed. I came out, got a new life, hid away here, and continued to plot. I kept tabs on Allegra so that she wouldn't find me before I'd got a water-tight plan. Simon helped. And then, I met you, and Rain, and ...'

'Saffron.'

Joe nodded slowly, his chest constricting, his throat closing. He paused. 'And everything seemed better somehow and revenge seemed futile, and pointless, and destructive. Sounds unbelievable but I figured I might even forgive her. And Freddy.'

'I believe you. I believe every word,' Eifion said. 'Now, what are you going to do about it?'

'Rain won't let me near her. I could write a letter.'

'Who's to say she'll read it. She might burn it, unopened.' Eifion stood up. 'Rain is a good woman. She'll let you see Saffron. You just have to be patient. Now go home and get some rest. You look like shit and we've work in the morning.'

'I'm worried about this reporter geezer. What if he runs an exposé on the "pier hero"? I don't want to make things any worse for Saff, or Rain.'

'Don't worry about that. I have friends at the paper. And you know what? I don't believe people here would judge anyway. There's this notion we're narrow-minded, small town folk, and it's absolute rubbish. You're well-liked, Joe.'

Joe stood and offered his hand. He was more grateful to Eifion than he could express. For lifting the burden of deceit from Joe's conscience, for listening and believing, and not judging.

Eifion took Joe's outstrctched hand, but instead of shaking it, to Joe's surprise he pulled him into an embrace, a very masculine, slightly awkward hug. He thumped Joe's back a couple of times.

Joe felt as if he had another friend for life. A true friend, like Simon.

Chapter Thirty-four

The back of Rain's neck stung from the force of the late afternoon sun's rays. She tore at the band which contained a knot of hair on top of her head. On her knees in the garden, she was weeding the bed in front of the window. As her curls tumbled around her neck, and face, she felt the phone in the pocket of her jeans vibrating. It was a text from Eifion. He began by asking after Saff and went on to say if Rain needed a distraction he'd very much like to go out walking with her again. The sunset was predicted to be spectacular that evening.

Rain dropped the trowel – it was too hot for such backbreaking work – and texted back immediately: *Sod the walk. How about a drink? We never did have one the last time we saw each other.*

His reply bounced back before Rain had clambered to her feet. He'd love one and where did she fancy? She suggested a glass of wine   or beer if he preferred – in the manse garden. That way she wouldn't risk meeting parishioners in a boozer and they could admire the sunset. The views from the garden were divine.

After a shower, Rain padded into the bedroom in her underwear and opened the wardrobe. Rows of bright, floral patterned dresses and skirts swished to and fro. She pulled out a fifties style dress in black with pink polka dots. It stood out from the rest but she hesitated. Was it too dressy, too flirty, too young? She turned to the mirror on the inside of the wardrobe door and held up the dress. It was slimming and funky, and it would be cool without the petticoats. She threw it on the bed and caught sight of her almost-naked body. Instinctively, she went to turn away but she stopped and forced herself to study the woman before her. How would a stranger view this body? A woman past her prime. Excess flesh on the waist and hips, dimples on the upper arms and thighs, silver lines like threads running down a spongy stomach, it was a body that had never seen the inside of a gym. But there were curves in the right places, it was well-proportioned, and the skin was peachy in tone and soft to the touch. The curly blonde mop could have belonged to a woman in her twenties, and blue eyes sparkled in a gentle, fresh-looking face, even without make-up.

You won a genetic lottery and time has been kind to you.

She dipped her chin, put her hands on her hips, her weight on one leg, and thrust out her breasts, in a pastiche of an underwear model in a cheap catalogue, before bursting out laughing.

God forgive you, Rain de Lacy! What are you thinking? Get your clothes on!

She returned the spotty frock to its hanger and dragged out one of her old favourites. Sitting in front of her dresser, she ran a wide-toothed comb through her still-damp hair and applied some mascara and red lipstick with care. She was about to leave when she spotted the fabric flower behind a ramshackle collection of creams and perfumes. Securing it with a clip, she pinned the poppy above her left ear before drifting downstairs to fill bowls with nibbles, which she would serve with the wine and beer chilling in the fridge.

'Is this OK for you?' Rain gestured to the open kitchen window, out of which music poured. Saff had said Rain would like the album. Rain didn't enjoy much of what Saff played – far too heavy for her more populist taste – but her daughter had been spot on with this band.

320

'They're brilliant, aren't they? What else do you like to listen to?' Eifion asked, sipping at the Kir Rain had presented him with on arrival.

'What do you think?' Rain said, sure he'd wrinkled his nose.

'It's sweet.'

'I could add more wine, sharpen it up for you?'

Eifion shook his head. 'It's fine, really. Good to try new things, push yourself out of your comfort zone. Wouldn't you agree?'

'My tastes are pretty eclectic. I still love all those Britpop bands from my twenties, though I didn't get to gigs or dances and clubs. Too busy with the kids. Bloody nuisances!'

'Nothing to stop you now, of course.'

'No.' Rain looked out over the garden, towards the west and the horizon. She couldn't actually see the horizon; she'd stretched the truth about that. Eifion was right. What was to stop her going to concerts and all sorts? Certainly, what was on offer here in Coed Mawr was more limited than London, but there was a cultural life, and she'd never taken advantage of all London had to offer anyway. She'd found the choice overwhelming, and Stephen didn't like crowds or dancing.

I'm still young. There's an undiscovered world out there.

She turned to Eifion. 'Do you like concerts? Discos?'

He smiled that lovely, warm smile of his and said, 'Yes, though I don't go much. Last time I went was with Ceri to see one of those bloody awful boy bands. Only one there over twenty-five. I felt like the oldest swinger in town.'

'How is Ceri? Still childminding?'

'OK. She's applied to go back to college, an access course, she called it. Says she wants to be a primary school teacher; she's loved working with those kids. Found her vocation, at last, and some ambition and drive. Got that from your Saff, I suspect.'

At the mention of Saffron, Rain's heart clenched. She took a gulp of Kir and shuddered as it hit the back of her throat. 'Saff's tougher than she looks. Medicine is so competitive.'

'How is she?'

Rain rocked her head from side to side, like a puppet. 'Oh, you know ...' She wondered how much Eifion knew. He worked with Joe; he must have seen him most days at the hotel, unless the contract had come to an end. It had been a week and a day since Joe'd come creeping round the manse garden in the dead of night, shouting for Saffron. He'd called and called her since. Rain had watched the missed call alerts piling up on Saffron's phone screen.

'He's a good man,' Eifion said suddenly, colour rising on his sunburnt cheeks. 'Sorry. I didn't come here to fight Joe's corner. He's more than capable of doing that himself.'

You are a good man, Rain thought. Loyal, sensitive, kind.

She felt slightly woozy; wine on an almost-empty stomach. The crisps and nuts and crudités had gone nowhere. 'I've not seen him since Sunday. He came here. Did you know that?'

'He must see her. To explain. He deserves that. It's killing him.'

'It's too late; she's down in London, looking for somewhere to stay, a job. She didn't even take her phone.' The Saffron-sized hole in Rain's life was larger than she could have imagined. It wasn't as if they had lived in each other's pockets. Days would go by without them seeing one another for more than a couple of minutes at a time, especially of late when Saffy was out such a lot. When they'd first arrived in Coed Mawr, Saffron holed herself up in her room, but lately she'd become immersed in the life of the town. And, of course, Joe. Marcus. 'She was going to apply at a hospital locally ... but not any more.'

Eifion sighed. 'Joe's not the only one who'll miss her.'

Rain couldn't pretend to understand her daughter's actions. Saffron was so black and white. To not even want to hear his side of the story. It was inconceivable. Everyone deserves a second chance. Rain thought about Stephen. The alacrity with which her pent-up rage had dissipated shocked Rain. She knew there might be, and she expected, further eruptions of anger, but the overriding emotion was a calm, deep sadness. They had been denied the chance to try and work things out. She accepted that might have been impossible but she had wanted to understand, to hear Stephen's story. She didn't want him cast in the role of heartless adulterer, her in the role of victim, abandoned wife. With some space between them, more time to talk, she might have understood. Why he did it. Where they went wrong. To understand is to forgive.

'Tell me Joe's story,' she said.

They sat talking until the bottle of wine was empty. After Eifion recounted Joe's story, Rain had wanted to say she would tell Saffron, explain it all, but she couldn't. It had to come from Joe.

'He'd have preferred Saffron to be the first to hear it. He only told me because I was there. He was desperate. Fit to burst. He's ashamed and regretful, but he doesn't want it to define him.'

'And he's laid aside all thoughts of revenge?' Rain said.

'I believe so.'

'Only the weak never forgive.'

'You're one of the strongest women I know.' He stood up. 'Right, I should leave you in peace. It's been a lovely evening, thank you.'

Rain thanked him, for coming, for sharing Joe's past, for not judging Saffron.

At the front door, he said, 'We should do this again sometime.'

Rain laughed, unsteady on her feet. 'Let's stick with a walk. Not sure my liver can take it.'

'Whichever,' he said, offering his hand.

She took it and placed her left hand over their interlocked fingers. 'We might even dance in the ballroom once it's restored. *If* it's restored. I so hope it is.'

'Me too. And if it is, who knows … I might hold you to that offer.' He paused. 'Was it an offer?'

'It was.'

She stood, leaned against the doorframe, and watched him weaving down the path and out on to the street. His movements were fluid and graceful. He waved before he disappeared from sight and she imagined him a good dancer.

'You'll lose your job if you disappear for days,' Eifion said.

Joe was pushing a lid back onto a tin of paint. 'Might be longer. Do I look like I care?'

Eifion smiled and stepped onto the balcony to help Joe clear his workspace. 'What if you bump into Freddy?'

It was Joe's turn to laugh. 'London's a big place, Eif. What are the chances? Anyway, it'll be all right even if I do. I'm OK with all that. This is going to sound funny, but there's good come out of Allegra showing up. It forced me to confront everything, and it's made me realise that I don't hate them, that I can really move on.' He sounded positive, more positive than he felt.

It wasn't that Joe didn't mean what he'd said, he did, but the sense of desperation he felt at the possibility of not finding Saff, or of finding her and being rejected, threatened to stymie him. He needed to act, and act fast, without thinking too much. He stepped out of his overalls, grabbed his phone and shook Eifion's hand.

'Will we see you again?' Eifion said.

Joe shrugged.

'There'll be the pier job at some point. I'll keep my ears open just in case, yes?'

Joe nodded. He didn't want to give voice to the possibility that he would come back, alone.

'We'll miss you,' Eifion said, as Joe stepped from the balcony into the hotel room.

Joe turned back to Eifion. 'I'll miss you too. I like it here. A lot. It feels like home. More than anywhere I've lived.'

'Good luck.'

'Let's hope the Landy's up to the journey.'

Joe checked his watch. It was still early; he could be in London by teatime. A surge of energy flooded his veins. Back to the cottage to gather the essentials and then he'd be off.

Chapter Thirty-five

Fumes caught in Saffron's throat and she choked as she stepped out onto the platform. She watched the train pull out of the station, disappear into the black hole of the tunnel, before lifting her head to sky and sucking clean air into her lungs.

Outside the station, she waited for a cab. An old woman wandered past. '*Noswaith dda*,' she said.

'*Noswaith dda*,' Saffron replied without thinking. She'd been away over five months, though it had seemed much, much longer.

She paid the driver at the bottom of the lane. She didn't care that it was almost dark, that her case was cumbersome, that the wheels would struggle on the rough, icy ground of the cottage path. She wanted to walk, to gather herself, to feel the familiar earth beneath her feet. She wanted to surprise him.

Even Rain didn't know Saffron was back. If she had she would have insisted on meeting Saff at the station, or coming to collect her, taking her home to the manse, feeding her, before allowing her some space. Rain wouldn't have been able to help herself. And Saff needed to see Joe, Marcus, before anyone.

It was icy and still; the darkening sky weighted with cloud. A bird, or rodent, scrabbled in the undergrowth, the sound broken only occasionally by the squall of a lone seagull. Toes already stinging, she turned on the torch on her phone, took hold of her case, and began to walk; the echo of her footsteps and the wheels navigating the stones magnified by the quiet.

There was no sign of life at the cottage, though Saffron had deliberately not pitched up till after four, when Joe commonly returned from work during the short winter days. She knocked at the front door a number of times before peering through the small, grimy window. She left her case by the door and crept round to the back, grateful for the lack of fencing or bordering of any kind. There were no lights on at the rear either. The skeletons of the trees loomed over the garden, branches bare and spiky, trunks strangled by ivy. Though Joe had never been big on gardening, preferring a natural look, it was clear nothing had been touched for months. The grass was dusted with frost, long, and hunched over on itself.

A half-finished sculpture glossy with moss stood near where they'd sat and watched the fire burn out. It was hard to tell what it would become.

Saffron pushed her face against the kitchen window and held up her phone. A cup and plate rested on the side, next to the range. A good sign. She knocked at the back door – from habit more than anything – before trying the latch. Joe rarely locked it. Only locals knew of the cottages and many assumed they were derelict. The door creaked open. A huff of stale air assaulted her. She called out his name; there came no reply. She stepped over the threshold and picked up the mug. Spores of mould covered the interior. He'd left in a hurry, it seemed. How long had he been gone?

She wandered through the cottage. Nothing had altered. Aside from the layer of dust, silence, and cold, it was exactly as she remembered it. His books on artists, bats, and Welsh history were stacked up neatly, next to a lean selection of games. Upstairs, the bed was unmade and an open drawer in the chest revealed that he'd not bothered to take all his clothes.

She would never find him. She wouldn't even know

where or how to begin looking. She didn't even know what he was calling himself these days.

Saffron slumped on the bed and cried.

In an attempt to compose herself before seeing Rain, rather than calling a cab, Saffron walked to the manse, dragging her case behind her. She could no longer feel the cold. She was almost at the manse when a scream forced her to look up from the ground. She wiped the end of her wet nose, and looked down the street. It was Ceri, jumping up and down, running on the spot, fists clenched. Before Saffron could acknowledge her with a wave, Ceri hurtled towards her, still screaming, and threw her arms about Saffron's neck, almost knocking her over.

'Oh my God, it's so good to see you! I thought I was seeing things. Only came up this part of town for that special chocolate shop. Mum's birthday and I figured I'd better get her something special as I'm not paying no rent. I'm a student now, at college. You're not the only one with a career, you bitch!'

'It's good to see you too.' And it was.

Ceri paused and held Saffron by the shoulders. 'You been crying, girl?'

Saffron nodded. 'I've been to the cottage.'

'He's gone. You both disappeared off the face of the earth. No one's seen or heard from him in months. Not even Dad. He called him a few times, left messages. Nothing. He went looking for you in London.'

'Shit.' Saffron felt as if her insides had been torn out. The air felt colder still, creeping into her veins, freezing the blood which ran through them. 'I've messed up, Ceri. I'm an expert at it. I should have heard him out, when I had the chance. I've missed him, this place, you, Mum, the people. Everything. But especially him. I thought I would get over him. Get on with my life. Get my career back on track. But I can't get him out of my head, and I can't help feeling that I got it wrong. It's been eating away at me. That he isn't the sort of bloke to string someone along. And as time's gone on this feeling that he was telling the truth has grown and grown.'

A woman with a buggy came to halt before them. They muttered apologies and stepped aside to let her pass.

'He loved you, Saff. That was, like, mega obvious. Dad's not telling me everything. Says it's none of my business – which drives me bananas because it is my business because you're my mate and I love you. Even if you did piss off without a word. Dad says you need to hear it first, which is total bollocks because he knows.'

Saffron almost leapt with joy. Hope. 'So your dad's in touch with Joe?'

'Not exactly.' Ceri pulled a face. 'Not at all. Hasn't heard a peep. But he says Joe's all right. And if Dad says he's all right, then he must be.'

'But he's not here. He's not here.' Saffron punched at her forehead and howled. She was too late. It was over.

'Only two days?' Rain tried to hide her disappointment. It was so wonderful to have Saff home, nothing was going to get in the way of her enjoyment. Nothing. They sat at the kitchen table, cradling steaming mugs of hot chocolate, a plate of biscuits between them.

'I'm sorry, Mum. It's a flying visit, but the job's unrelenting and I've not long started this one.' Saffron leaned across the table and squeezed Rain's hand.

'Still enjoying it, though?' Rain said.

'Sure am. It's hard work, but I knew that already, and doing Foundation 1 a second time means I have an advantage over many of the other students.' She laughed. 'It's amazing how quickly it all came back. It's what I was put on this earth to do.'

Was this small nod to Rain's faith deliberate? Rain neither knew nor cared. It was lovely that her daughter could acknowledge her beliefs, even if she couldn't share them.

It was clear Saff was content in her work, but Rain could see that she'd been crying. She was even paler than usual, her eyes were red, and it was more than the long hospital hours and interrupted sleep. Rain thought of Joe and then, in rapid succession, Eifion.

How he warmed her. God's love was wonderful and beautiful, but life was richer with Eifion around. For a while, it had been a bit odd going out with Eifion. He was such a different animal to Stephen. Perhaps this helped? Who knew, and it didn't matter. At first, they'd kept it ever so casual, but here they were, months later, and Rain's feelings ran deeper than friendship and she suspected Eifion felt the same. Like Jesus, she would always love Stephen – for the life they'd led together, the future they'd built, the children they'd raised, but she allowed herself to be angry with him too, to remember his weaknesses, as well as his strengths. He was only human, after all. And she no longer had any regrets.

'And what of friends? Have you met any others since starting at Wrexham?' Rain asked.

Saff snorted. 'Do you mean friends or boyfriends, Mum?'

'Oh, I know it's not possible to get over someone that quickly, I just meant …' What did she mean? She had no idea. Eifion had told her that Joe had gone to London to search for Saff, and Rain knew he would never find her. She wasn't there. She'd returned to her training here in Wales, but she'd sworn Rain to secrecy. No one else knew where she was.

Saffron smiled, a cheeky glint in her eye. 'What I'd like to know is how things are going for you?'

'Wonderful, wonderful. Church is hectic at the mo – of course – Christmas swiftly approaches and all that. Miss Shawcroft pops in regularly, Mr Roberts is still a pain in the arse –'

'Not that stuff. Eif?'

Rain felt herself blushing. 'It's good.'

'You really like him.'

'Is that OK?' Rain's chest tightened.

'Are you kidding? Of course it's OK. It's more than OK. At least one of us deserves happiness.'

'Is it too early for wine?'

Saffron glanced over at the clock. 'Nah.'

'We could have a glass while we dress the tree. And I know it's a bit early for decorations but I fancy some sparkle about the place!'

Chapter Thirty-six

Saffron half expected it to have snowed overnight. The floorboards were icy against her bare feet when she swung out of bed and yet the air felt a degree or two warmer than it had the night before. She flung open the window, shivered, and gazed over the fields, now empty of crops, the brown earth hardened in regular furrows. To her left was the chapel, the frost-shiny slates of the new roof caught her attention. For a moment, he was there, sitting on the ridge, as he'd been that day when they'd watched each other, spellbound. A gust of wind startled her and when she looked again, he was gone. A bird fluttered from the manse eaves to her right. Then another and another. Or was it a bird? It moved so quickly. She remembered Joe's words after the fire: 'The bats will take their young to a new home. A cave, a roof, a loft.' It wasn't fully light; a bronze sheen glazed the countryside. Even in her despair, she registered how beautiful it was. But the fields weren't what she'd yearned for. She'd hungered for the sea. And Joe.

The house was quiet; Rain still slept after an evening of wrestling the silver tree from the cellar, untangling fairy lights, and rethreading baubles. They'd talked and drank into the small hours. Saffron picked clothes from the case on the floor. In the bathroom she splashed her face and brushed her teeth. After a mug of instant coffee, she wrapped up and headed to the beach.

Too early for the shops to open, there were few people around. Saffron was grateful. She looked forward to seeing familiar faces, but right now she needed to be alone, with her thoughts and her memories. Litter skittered along the promenade in front of her – a polystyrene burger box and a couple of crisp packets – no doubt pulled from an overfull bin by an enterprising gull. The tide was in and there was no beach to amble along. She leant against the railings, gripped the cold metal, and watched sea foam blowing into the sky. To the east was the pier, the charred remains of the ballroom skeletal against the pink sky. It appeared ghostly but, like a phoenix, the ballroom would rise again. It would breathe with new life, be beautiful and enjoyed once more. Drawn to it, she headed east.

Everything was closed. Shutters blinded the little huts, the lights of the Wurlitzer and merry-go-round were dull, their carriages shrouded with plastic covers. It looked tawdry and shabby, its magic gone, like a theatre set without the lights and music and expectation of the crowd. Her footsteps echoed on the boards as she headed towards the ballroom. Looking at it now it was hard to believe it could be repaired. Yellow tape sectioned off the area, a loose end flapped in the breeze, slapping against the morning air. A bird – not a gull, too small – flew out of a window, and Saffron wondered if the bats had come back after all. If they'd found another roost, if the young had flown the maternal nest, had found their own place in which to hibernate for the harsh months ahead, if they were fit and strong enough to survive till the spring when they would re-emerge and thrive.

She lifted the tape and crouched. A moment's hesitation and then under she went. She crept towards the ballroom entrance, testing each board before she put her weight on it.

'Be careful. It's dangerous.'

She stopped, but couldn't turn round.

'It's ugly now, but with care it'll be beautiful.'

'It looks ruined.'

'Nothing's ever ruined.'

Slowly, she turned to face him. Joe. Marcus.

He appeared unchanged, the same beautiful, extraordinary eyes of different colours, the dark hair, weightier on top, the square shoulders and broad chest. The same gentle, open expression she remembered after they'd made love for the first time on the living room floor of the cottage. Gazing at him, wondering why he was here, thinking on what she had to say and knowing that he might reject her, that it might be the last time she looked upon his face, was almost more than she could bear.

What's in a name?

'Some things are worth risking everything for,' she said, sweeping a strand of hair from her face.

'Sometimes we get it wrong.' His lips were pale; she detected a tremble.

Does he mean me?

'I'm sorry, Saffron. You deserved better.'

'You deserved better too. Running away was pathetic.' She shrugged, though her voice shook. 'It's a habit, I'm afraid.' The wind threw her words out to sea. She went to repeat the words, shout them out. She shifted her weight from one foot to the other.

There was a creaking, a splintering, and a sensation of the ground moving beneath her, melting away and then, with one sharp jolt, disappearing altogether. Time did not slow down as everyone says it does, it happened in a blink. One moment she was standing, staring into the face of the man she loved more than anything else in the world, the next, the world was tumbling, her legs dangling beneath her, kicking against the empty air, arms above her head, shoulders almost wrenched from their sockets.

She clung on with her fingers. Knowing she should not, but unable to stop herself, she looked down. A swirling, shifting mass of grey water slapped up against the steel girders which bore the weight of the pier. The waves carried the shattered boards up and down on the swell. Sea spray hit her exposed ankles and cheeks like needles. She pressed her fingers harder, her fingernails digging into the wood, and tried to heave herself up. Her upper arm muscles trembled; she groaned with exertion. No good, she fell back down, elbows locking, her frozen, damp fingers losing purchase.

Is this it? Am I to fall into the angry, cold sea, be swallowed up with the weed and shingle and foam? Bounce off the iron girders, bones shattered? I want to live. Really live.

'Saffron!'

She felt a hand grip her wrist, firm. She looked up: Joe, crouching, his other arm outstretched. She felt the weakened boards groan under the pressure of the extra weight.

'Be careful,' she screamed. 'You can't save me if you fall in.'

'Grab hold,' he yelled.

Terrified if she did not, she would fall; terrified if she did, she might pull him into the water with her, she hesitated.

'Do it!' he screamed, his voice laced with authority.

She took hold of his hand and he hefted, pulling, pulling her upwards. As she emerged above the parapet of the pier floor, he let go of her wrist and wrapped his hand under her armpit, heaving, tugging, pulling her over the charred boards and into the safety of his embrace.

Kneeling, they held on to each other, tight, as if they might never let go, before eventually loosening their hold and peering over the edge to the raging waters below.

'Let's get off the pier. We'll be in so much trouble if anyone catches us,' he said, at last. He stood and offered his hand once more. Grateful, her strength vanished, she took it, allowing him to lead her across the damaged floor to safety.

Back on the safe section of the pier, he let go of her

hand and stopped.

'Thank you. For rescuing me, yet again,' she said, staring into his eyes, pressing her thumbs against the raw skin of her palms.

He loves me, doesn't he? He's risked so much. Right from the start, he jeopardised everything for me.

He smiled, soft lines fanning from eyes of green and brown. 'I've a feeling that will be the last time anyone rescues you. I think you're more than capable of saving yourself. You always have been; you've just not known it for a while.'

Huddled against each other, battened into their coats, they sat on the bench outside Eifion's rock shop, arms entwined, and Joe told her his story. She sat silent, shocked, and saddened by what he'd had to endure. She'd been angry with him for lying to her, thought he was crazy to lie to the police, especially for a woman like Allegra. But above all she admired him. For accepting responsibility and his punishment, for learning from the experience and trying to be a better man. For caring about old buildings and bats. For being kind to her mother and Eifion. For loving her, with all her faults. There was so much to say that Saffron didn't know where to begin, and she didn't know if any of it needing saying after all. She loved him. He loved her. Nothing was insurmountable. It felt so good to be honest; one hundred per cent honest with each other.

'Do I call you Joe or Marcus?'

'Joe. Always Joe. Marcus was another person.'

'How did you know I was here?' Saffron said.

'Eifion texted me. He'd called many times before, but I'd not returned any of them. I didn't want to be reminded of Coed Mawr, you …'

Ceri. She'd told her dad that Saffron was back. Joe must have driven through the night.

337

'What about your career? Medicine?' said Joe. 'Isn't that in London?'

'I've been here ...' She saw the confusion in his eyes. 'Near here. I figured if you did look for me, you'd start in London, so I ... You're good at hiding, you know all the tricks. I took a foundation post in Wrexham, it was easy to switch. I'm going to specialise in health care for the elderly. And once I've completed my foundation years, I'll stay somewhere close – there are loads of places.' She glanced over to the seafront, the candy-coloured guest houses, care homes, and hotels framing the bay. She thought of Mair and Rain's motley crew of chapelgoers. 'I love it here and there are plenty of old folk. The young all leave.'

He cupped his hand at the back of her neck and drew her to him. Words blew against her lips, filling her lungs, her heart, a kiss of life. 'Grow old, here, with me?'

'Sure.' She smiled and gazed towards the ballroom, the easterly wind unable to cool the warmth within her. She imagined exhibitions and events, Joe's art, music, choirs, and dancers bathed in a golden light from coloured glass panels in the domed roof, sunlight reflected off the myriad mirrors adorning the walls. 'But let's do a lot of living first.'

Hands linked, they ran down the deserted pier towards the light of the town.

To find out more about Laura, book club information,
events, and future novels, visit:

www.laura-wilkinson.co.uk

Twitter: **@ScorpioScribble**
www.facebook.com/laurawilkinsonwriter
Instagram: **Laura_Wilkinsonwriter**
Pinterest: **laura1765**

For more information about **Laura Wilkinson**
and other **Accent Press** titles
please visit

www.accentpress.co.uk